THE SPAGHETTI SET

Family Served Italian Style

A Novel about
Two Italian-American Families

Rose Marie Boyd

authorHOUSE®

AuthorHouse™
1663 Liberty Drive
Bloomington, IN 47403
www.authorhouse.com
Phone: 1-800-839-8640

First published by AuthorHouse   04/26/2011

ISBN: 978-1-4567-4983-5 (sc)
ISBN: 978-1-4567-4984-2 (e)

Printed in the United States of America

This book is dedicated to All my family.

Acknowledgements

Proud of my Italian heritage, I drew upon it for inspiration in writing this fiction. My mother, Emilia Tammaro, immigrated to America from Italy, as did her father and many of her seventeen siblings. My father, Othello Maisto, born of Italian immigrants, grew up in the United States with ten brothers and sisters. Over the years, I heard numerous anecdotes regarding these relatives, their triumphs and their tribulations. With the memory of those tales as kindling, my imagination ignited and motivated me to contrive events and characters described in this book.

Although the novel's setting simulates the Italian-American neighborhood where I grew up and a few of the circumstances in the storyline mimic those of real life, the characters in this book do not depict actual people. Nor are the experiences they encounter in the chapters historically factual. I concocted the scenarios plus the characters' virtues, idiosyncrasies, and flaws. I apologize if there are any incidental inaccuracies of Italian language, grammar or culture.

An Italian language class at Yavapai College and a laughter-filled trip to Italy, both taken with my dear friend Carol Bettino, were catalysts in jumpstarting this novel. I am grateful to her and all my friends, family and fellow book-group members who read the various drafts of my manuscript and provided much-needed feedback and encouragement. I especially want to express my utmost appreciation to Dorci Leara for all the time and effort she expended in scrutinizing my chapters. I found her perseverance in providing constructive criticism and intuitive tips to improve my writing style invaluable. I also thank Nancy Whitney-Reiter for editing my Italian grammar. Finally, I acknowledge my husband Carl's patience while I spent countless hours at my computer.

Chapter One

"*Dio santo*, I can't take this much more!" The skirt of her sundress flapping in the June gusts, the Italian took flight across the weaving deck and skidded to a halt at the ship's side rail. She grabbed hold of its top wrung, hoisted herself up and leaned forward, parallel to the water. Dampened by the exertion, her hair clung to her scalp, the curls a tangle of seaweed.

Another passenger spotted the human gangplank and cried out. "Teresa Camara!" He dashed up to her and, snatching her by the waist, yanked her back to safety. "*Sei pazza?* I ought to have you committed!" He carted the brunette a distance from the rail and then dropped her to the deck, close to a full bucket of water.

Unable to hold back for another second, Teresa vomited into the pail, its overflow splashing her sandals. "Antonio, you idiot!" She swiped her mouth on the back of her forearm. "Why can't you leave me alone?"

"A brother tries to rescue his crazy sister and what does he get? Nothing but *ingratitudine*."

"Want me to be grateful? Help me wipe my shoes." Her face buried in her hands, she sulked as Antonio whipped out a handkerchief and patted her sandals dry.

Oblivious to the drama, the veteran freighter steamed ahead across the chop of the Atlantic at a steady speed of 11 knots. Instead of the wartime supplies it once transported for the Allied forces, it carried 9,000 tons of commercial cargo along with fifty passengers, Teresa the queasiest of the lot. The days at sea had taken their toll on her stomach and her nerves.

"I never expected it to be this bad," Teresa moaned. "How much longer before we get there?"

"Just two more days to go." Her brother placed a palm on her bare shoulder, his calluses rough but comforting. "Compared to all the years it took for Papà to arrange this trip, what's another 48 hours?" When the freighter lolled to the stern, Antonio maneuvered his hand to the small of her back. "America's waiting. Are you ready to . . . ?" The roar of the engine drowned out the end of his sentence.

Teresa shouted back, "*Sì . . . sono più di pronta* . . . more than ready to get off this ship!" Fists clenched, she pounded her foot against the floorboards. "*Mattina e sera*, night and day, I've paced these ugly decks, too nauseous to relax for a second." Aware that the sway of the boat hadn't bothered her brother in the least, she narrowed her eyes and studied the casualness of his stance. *Why me?*

"I can't even hold onto a meal for more that a few seconds before, presto, I'm ready to feed the fish." Absorbed in her own self-pity, she didn't notice the stowaway meowing nearby or the remains of a mouse the seasick cat had regurgitated.

"*Povera ragazza* . . . poor, poor girl." Antonio pacified.

When a woman who was almost as green around the gills as Teresa dragged by nibbling on a soda cracker, Antonio stopped her. "Excuse me, *signora*. Have any crackers to spare for my sister?" With a nod of compassion, the woman handed him a few and then hobbled towards the aft of the ship. "Here, Teresa, eat these and, for God's sake, stay away from the rail!"

"No, *grazie*." Teresa pushed his arm away, knocking one of the crackers out of his hand. "Can't even stomach *them* anymore." Catching sight of a handsome deckhand nearby, she lowered her voice to a whisper. "They give me gas."

"I'll say." Antonio pressed his mouth against the back of his forearm and trumpeted a discordant melody, a parody of serious flatulence. Hearing it, the sailor turned around and grimaced at Teresa and then hurried away, his nose lifted in disgust.

"He actually thought it was me!" She smacked her brother's arm. "With you around to embarrass me every chance you get, I'm doomed to be single."

"Oh, who am I kidding?" With exaggerated drama, she extended the fingers of both hands down the front of her frame. "Look at me, a skeleton compared to the other women on the ship." She poked the back of one fist against her hip and thrust out her buttocks. "Tell me. How am I supposed to catch a decent man?"

His hair blown back by a strong breeze, Antonio patted Teresa's rear end. "Don't sprain any muscles over it. There'll be plenty to eat in America." She smacked his hand away and, when another passing sailor leered at her small but firm rump, Antonio's grin mutated into a scowl. "If Papà doesn't fatten you up, I will."

Teresa's expression soured at the thought of her father. Although the image of the man was vague in her mind, she hadn't forgotten the sternness of his voice when he had announced his imminent departure. She was nine years old the day her father sailed from Sicily with two of her brothers and left her mother stranded in their hometown of Trapani with the youngest two of five children.

"How could Papà abandon us the way he did?"

"What're you talking about?" Antonio rolled his eyes. "He left to start a better life for us in America, not to abandon anyone."

Sure he did. Dried by the wind, Teresa's locks now swung free with skepticism. "He should've taken all of us with him in the first place."

Antonio clicked his tongue in annoyance. "How many times do I have to tell you? Papà was flat broke at the time."

As if he cared . . . he hardly bothered to write. "Poor Mamma," Teresa's throat constricted. "Don't know how many times I caught her crying after Papà shipped out."

"Crying?"

"*Sì.* Once, when I asked her why, she whispered more to herself than to me, '*Tuo padre*, he made his promises but who knows who's keeping him warm in America.'"

"You're making that up."

"No, *è vero*. At the time, I was too young to imagine what she meant. But, now, an awful bedroom scene comes to mind." Teresa grimaced at the vision of her father, his arms and legs entangled with those of a stranger.

Antonio suppressed a smile. "Shame on you."

"I remember her words, '*Non vedrò mai la terra promessa.*'"

Teresa's mother had convinced herself that her husband would never arrange for her to join him in America, the promised land. Four years after her husband left them, their mother's prediction that God would claim her first came to pass. She literally died of a broken heart, a congenital coronary condition.

Teresa sniffled. "We were . . . *così giovani* . . . too young to realize how awful Papà treated Mamma." Refusing to add fuel to Teresa's fire of indignation, Antonio shook his head in denial.

Barely teenagers at the time of their mother's death, they had also been too young to fend for themselves. So, until he could arrange for their immigration to America, their father enlisted the help of their eldest sibling, a married sister who lived in the city of Palermo.

"Just be thankful for Nina." He contemplated why she had agreed to house them, sardines packed tight in the tin can of a small apartment.

Before he had a chance, Teresa blurted what Antonio was thinking, "Papà never sent her the money he promised her, did he?"

"He probably forgot," said Antonio, still feeling obliged to defend his father.

Antonio can be so naïve. Teresa propped a hand on her hip. "Well, at least we earned our keep."

Nina had used the situation to her advantage. In compensation for the expense of two extra mouths to feed, she insisted that Teresa tend to her young children and Antonio stock shelves in her husband's food market.

"I'm not sorry." Antonio flexed his biceps. "The hard work helped me build these muscles. But you? What did you do besides play with the **bambini** or fool with Nina's old sewing machine?" With a finger held up to his lips, he tilted his head to the side and lifted his eyes to ponder the answer. "Hmm, let me see." He looked back at Teresa and snickered. "Oh, yes. You stuffed your face."

Antonio's ill-advised attempt to lighten the mood unsuccessful, Teresa's cheeks flushed purple with anger. *The nerve of him! I sewed the children's clothes at a fraction of the cost that they charged at the **negozi**.* She flipped up a hand. "It wasn't all fun and games!" Considering the ramifications of all the food she gorged out of boredom, Teresa added, " Besides, if I hadn't gained weight then, I'd be invisible by now."

"Invisible?" He looked her up and down. "Not quite. But I must admit losing all that baby fat does agree with you."

Unappreciative of the backhanded compliment, Teresa pouted. "Thanks."

"Hey cheer up! You seemed so happy the day we found out we were headed for America."

Teresa lifted her nose. "**Sì, contenta**. I was thrilled that Papà *finally* made the arrangements." She placed the back of one hand against her forehead and, knees bent, feigned a faint. "But nearly collapsed once I caught sight of this . . ." she pointed to a smokestack, "this deathtrap. I never thought we'd make it this far."

"Come on, Teresa, you're so dramatic. It's not that bad."

"That's your opinion!" Teresa gave Antonio her back then spun around not two seconds later. "The very day we sailed off, I promised myself that I'd do all I could to help the relatives we left behind." Teresa raised a fist in the air. "And I will! I swear it."

"I'm sure you will, Teresa." Antonio smiled. "You're very determined when you want to be."

Teresa expelled a forced breath, along with some of the bitterness toward her father. "Antonio, will you be able to pick out Papà in a crowd? After all these years, I'm not sure I'd recognize him . . . even if he spat in my face."

"Now why would he spit in your face, Teresa?" Antonio laughed.

"Well, we'll be a burden until we can earn a living for ourselves. And what if he has lady friends . . . **amanti**? We may get in the way."

"You must be joking! **È vecchio**. Papà's over fifty by now, too old to fool around with women." Antonio chuckled. "**Sono sicuro il suo uccello non vola**. At his age, I'm sure his bird can't even lift its head out of its nest."

"What's that supposed to mean?" Teresa suppressed a giggle. *Let Antonio wonder if I understand.* She figured her brother would be furious if he knew how many advances she'd dodged in the last year alone.

Antonio sobered. "Never you mind."

Another wave knocked against the side of the freighter. "Think Papà will try to push me around like he used to when I was a boy?" Antonio paused and mustered some bravado. "He better not try or I'll lift him up by his suspenders . . . toss him across the room."

"Sure . . . sure. You say that now. *Vedremo come sei coraggioso.* Let's see how brave you are after he knocks you off your feet." Teresa laughed out loud, baring two black keys that blighted the ivory of her smile. When she realized she'd exposed a flaw, one that might hamper a future objective, she quickly covered her mouth. Frowning, she dreaded the possibility that, even in America, she might not be able to afford to have her cavities filled. *How can I attract a rich **Americano** like this?*

As the ship seesawed once more, the stowaway cat crawled behind the water bucket, curling into a queasy ball of fur.

Oblivious to anyone's distress but her own, Teresa paled and clutched her belly. "Oh no, not again!" She turned away from her brother but, before she could make it back to the bucket, released a mouthful of stomach acid, barely missing the feet of a passing deckhand. His face twitching with annoyance, the sailor ran off to fetch a mop.

***Brava**, Teresa, good way to scare off another man!"*

Chapter Two

A young man, whose legs stretched long and lanky, slipped out of the front seat of a 1939 LaSalle, slammed the Buick's door and leaned against its dented frame. Arms folded tight under the gray of the New Jersey sky, he propped a heel on the running board. *Of all people, why'd I let Iggy convince me to chip in and buy this wreck?* His foot dropped to the ground. *Ought to have my head examined.* Spinning on the soles of his loafers, he tapped an impatient rhythm on the roof of the jalopy as he stared at the entrance of the Motor Vehicle Building. *How much longer?* The time necessary to register a vehicle was more than he expected.

He glared at the yellow paint lining the curb where the auto was parked in a tow away zone. *Damn Iggy! Took off with the keys.* Worried that he'd be the one to get the ticket if a cop stopped, he began to pace back and forth in the brisk breeze. *Sure cool for June.* Despite the wind, a fly successfully circled his thick head of brown hair, skied three inches down the length of his nose and ricocheted off its tip to land on the sleeve of his varsity sweater. Smelling salami and provolone, the insect tried to dive into his pocket. Finally realizing what the bug was after, the fellow swatted at the pest but, refusing to leave, it circled his head several times before it took off in search of another target. *I wish Mamma would ask before she sticks food in my pockets.* His stomach growling, he retrieved the sandwich, removed its wrapper and devoured it in two bites. Instead of satiating him, the appetizer-sized **panino** left him craving even more food. Crumpling the waxed paper, he tossed it into a nearby trashcan and then resumed his vigil by the car.

An army jeep, whose headlights and grillwork sneered at the LaSalle's lackluster finish, halted parallel to the jalopy and the soldier behind the wheel called out to him, "Hey, Mack Matteo . . . long time no see."

Mack squinted, recognizing the bully that had tortured him for four years at Benton High School. *Just my luck.* "Is that you Freddie Brutto? What brings *you* here? I thought your family moved out of this town."

"Did," Freddie verified. "Just passin' tru on my way back ta da base. Re-enlisted."

Incredulous, Mack pulled in his chin. "No kidding?"

"Yeah, well somebody has ta keep an eye on all dem damn Nazis." Freddie pushed his army cap further back on the crown of his head. "What about yer puny ass, Mack? Where'd dey station it durin' da war?"

Though wanting to give a nasty comeback, Mack hesitated. "Well, I . . . uh . . . never made it into the service. Graduated from Boston University, though. Earned a degree in accounting." He hoped Freddie didn't question the reason for his military exemption. *Hate to lie but...* Mack refused to admit, to this high school adversary of all people, that his epileptic condition was what kept him out of the war. Fortunately, Freddie didn't ask for he was distracted by Mack's varsity sweater.

Acting shocked, Freddie pointed a finger at Mack. "Skinny Matteo made letters? Don't tell me college can turn a bookworm inta a jock."

"No," Mack hated to admit. "Worked part-time as the P.E. Department's statistical analyst."

"Sound's excitin'," Freddie spoofed.

"Saved enough to buy this car." Mack smacked the hood of the LaSalle.

"A real beauty!" Freddie mocked. "What ya gonna do wit dat degree now, Mister Accountant?"

"The family business . . . just started at the bakery. I'm supervising the storefront for now." Mack was expected to eventually assume management of its finances, but he didn't want to boast anymore than he already had.

Freddie wrinkled his nose. "Now tell me, Mack. Did all da Matteos skip out on der patriotic duty?"

Mack clicked his tongue in annoyance. "No, Freddie. For your information, all my brothers enlisted." His voice dropped an octave. "Romi was killed in action."

"Humph." Freddie pressed on, "So what happen ta da udder two?"

"What's it to you?" Mack spat back.

"Canna guy ask?" Freddie blinked his eyes with innocent curiosity.

Resenting Freddie's nosiness, Mack expelled an exasperated breath. "Well, if you must know, Frank came home with a purple heart for a leg injury and, after my dad died, he took over as general manager of the bakery." Mack failed to mention that, a few months later, Frank eloped with Geneva Tazzoni, his high school sweetheart. "But Iggy served until the war ended." Frank had been furious that Iggy had toured all of Northern Italy with his war bride instead of rushing home to help him with the business. "Enough information for you, Freddie?"

Freddie ignored Mack's sarcasm. "Lucky guys . . . got handed a business on a silver platter. Well, gotta go. Too bad der's no time ta buy ya a beer. I'm due back at base in a hour. Shippin' out tomorrow." Freddie drove off with a wave and a beep.

Thank God! Too soon if I never lay eyes on him again. Mack shoved his hands into his pockets and kicked a stone across the sidewalk. *Lucky all right.* He had always dreamed he'd work for a large public accounting firm and rack up enough experience to start his own one day. But since the bakery's funds financed his degree, his mother had insisted that it was his turn to lift some of the load off his brothers' shoulders. Now he was saddled with the bakery too . . . at least until he paid back the tuition . . . not quite what he'd planned.

To start out, Frank had asked Mack to check the bakery's financial records, to become familiar with the accounting operations and evaluate how smoothly they were running. Complying with the request, Mack had looked over the bakery books first chance he got. *What a shambles!*

When the bakery's longstanding accounting clerk, an Italian hired by their father decades earlier, died several months back, Frank had been frantic for a replacement. Taking advantage of the situation,

Iggy recommended a Hungarian bookkeeper, a man who wasn't as experienced as Iggy claimed, nor as respectable, but who was willing to do whatever Iggy requested of him. Desperate and overwhelmed by management of the baking and storefront operations, Frank dispensed with the usual background check and hired the Hungarian.

After spending some time sifting through the sloppy ledgers, Mack had his suspicions that Frank would regret his decision to rely on Iggy's recommendation for he'd already found several obvious errors. Mack didn't look forward to straightening out the mess. *It'll take me forever.*

Mack turned toward the Motor Vehicle Building and glanced up at the sturdy figure of a man who jogged down its steps, his hair slick but for the haughty swell in the front. Midpoint on the stairs, the fellow paused, adjusted his crotch and hiked his trousers higher above his waistline then boosted the collar of his jacket up against his muscular neck. With shoulders squared, he continued down to the bottom. Mack grimaced. *Iggy even dresses like a thug.* As his brother approached, Mack ran a hand over his own more conservative haircut while he evaluated Iggy's rugged features. *What do women find so appealing about him?*

Iggy smacked his hands together. "It's official. Car's registered in my name."

"What do you mean: *your* name? The car belongs to both of us. If anything, it's more mine than yours," Mack complained. "I put up the bulk of the money."

"Form called for the owner to sign it. What else did ja want me to do? You weren't there." Iggy held up a palm. "No difference anyway. We both know who owns the car." He turned his face to the left to conceal a smirk. "Sides, I'm the one served with the best mechanics in the army, not you." Iggy ran a hand along the body of the LaSalle, circled to its driver's side and kicked one of the wheels. "You ain't got no knack for fixin' it, do you?

"Well, no." Mack shrugged. "But I get priority use of the car. That was the deal. Right?"

"Sure. Take it easy," Iggy scoffed. "You don't wanna get too cranked up or you'll fall down in one of your ugly-ass fits." He flipped his wrist in an effeminate mock and raised the pitch of his voice, "If Motor Vehicles gets wind of your *delicate condition,* they'll rip that driver's license outta your back pocket, roll it up and . . . ," he switched to a deeper and ominous tone, "shove it up your tight ass."

Color rose up Mack's neck as he clenched his fists. *Just like Iggy to hit a guy below the belt.* Iggy was well aware that, for years, Mack's seizures had been controlled by medication.

Iggy snickered until his stomach growled. "Hey, I'm starved."

"Then let's go right home or we'll be late for dinner again."

Licking his lips, Iggy rubbed his abdomen. "Boy, I'd love to sink my teeth into a juicy-ass steak tonight." He shifted his stance and, with arms folded tight, brooded. "But no doubt Mamma cooked up a meatless dish like she does every stinkin' Friday. If not, she'd hop a boat to Rome and confess the mortal sin right to the damn Pope." Before Mack had a chance to make his way over to the driver's side, Iggy slipped behind the wheel and revved the engine. "Get in. Hope Frank doesn't spend the whole fuckin' meal talkin' business."

Flipping up his hands in defeat, Mack sulked back to the passenger-side door and grudgingly slid into the sedan. As he slammed the door shut, Iggy zipped the jalopy out of the parking space and floored the gas pedal.

Mack cringed at the deafening grind of the engine and pressed a hand against the dashboard. "Slow down, Iggy!"

"What a pussy-assed chicken!" Iggy threw back his head and laughed. "No wonder the army didn't want you."

Chapter Three

As the freighter approached the harbor late in the afternoon of June 20th, Teresa stared wide-eyed at the New York City skyline in the distance. Unlike the war-torn cityscapes of Italy, all the buildings were intact. "Antonio, *guardi!* No sign of bombings here." She then spotted the Statue of Liberty. "Ah, a torch greets us. A good omen, no?"

Shielding his eyes from the sun, Antonio inspected the statue and broke out in a smug smile. "Uncanny, the lady holding it looks a lot like you, Teresa. Wonder if her *culo* is as tight, or her lips as loose."

Distracting her from her brother's sarcasm, the ship's self-appointed mascot rubbed it's fur against Teresa's leg. While she bent down to pet the gray tabby that she had befriended during the last two days of her voyage, the ship sent up a swirl of steam from its smokestack and blasted its horn to the cheers of the weary passengers. Startled by the noise, the cat darted under Teresa's skirt. The closer the vessel got to the pier, the closer the tabby clung to her legs. As Teresa peered over the bottom rung of the ship's railing, more freighters came into view along with the score of longshoremen whose muscles bulged in their efforts to strip them of their cargo

Still annoyed that her father had arranged such poor traveling accommodations for them, Teresa stood up and bellyached into Antonio's ear, "Finally we arrive . . . two stowaway rats on a dirty cargo ship . . . six years late and worse for the wear." As if the tabby understood Teresa's aversion to rodents, the fur on its arched back stood straight up.

Frowning, Antonio held an index finger against his lips. "**Stai zitta.** Stop whining and be happy we're here now."

Teresa ignored her brother's reprimand and, with her palms clasped tight, shook her hands in Antonio's face. "If only Papà hadn't postponed our trip so many times. While we waited, I begged God ten times a day for him to send for us . . . **più presto possible** . . . the sooner the beter."

"It wasn't his fault the war broke out and . . ."

"**Sì**, the war . . . another good excuse for Papà." Teresa's shoulders sagged. *It made us enemies to the **Americani**.* Rubbing its fur against her leg, the tabby tried to comfort her.

Although U.S. citizenship had protected her father and brothers from the restrictions and internments suffered by thousands of Italian immigrants branded "enemy aliens," World War II brought a halt to Teresa and Antonio's immigration.

"Stop the complaints, Teresa. Nina and her husband did fine by us under the circumstances."

Teresa sneered. "You think so, do you?" Despite the fact that Nina had promised to enroll Teresa in school, she never got around to it. "It's her fault I'm so stupid."

"You can't blame Nina." Antonio chuckled. "You were born that way."

As if Antonio was the one who called her stupid in the first place, Teresa kicked him in the shin. "If I'm so stupid, why did Nina always ask for my advice about running the business?" Noting Teresa's agitation, the cat hissed at Antonio.

"**Beh!** Tell your cat to keep away or I'll throw him overboard."

"Don't you dare!" Teresa objected. "You're despicable. First you insult my intelligence then you threaten to kill a poor, little cat."

"I was only joking."

"Then take back what you said about my being too stupid to give Nina advice."

"**Mannaggia!** Don't be so damn sensitive. Besides, Nina had no one else to ask. When Mario and I left to fight, our poor sister was forced to run the business single-handed."

"Single-handed?" Teresa baulked. After Mario had shipped out with his fleet and Antonio was inducted into Mussolini's army, Teresa pitched in to take up the slack.

"**Va bene**, so you helped a little."

"A little?" Teresa waved a finger in her brother's face. "You know I worked my knuckles to the bone until the market was bombed." Once food became scarce, Teresa and Nina scrounged day by day to find food for the children, often with nothing in their own bellies except a crust of bread and some water. "We went to sleep hungry during the rest of that god-awful war."

Antonio smirked, "A good way to lose baby fat."

"It is not funny, Antonio."

Defending Teresa, the cat tried to claw at her brother's trousers but, before Antonio could retaliate, Teresa picked up the tabby. She held it protectively in her arms, reminiscing about how helpless she'd felt during the war. As the American planes dropped bombs over their heads, Teresa had huddled petrified with Nina and her children in foul shelters, weeping over relatives that perished in the destruction.

"I was so miserable during the war . . . terrified." When the cat spotted one of the ships rats, it darted out of Teresa's arms, scratching her in the process. Rubbing her arm, she stared at her brother and waited for his acknowledgment of her suffering, present and past.

"I know, I know, Teresa." Antonio frowned. "I'm sorry. I wish I'd been there to protect you, but I was forced to fight. It wasn't easy for me either."

"Antonio, I don't blame you." *To think, two of my brothers fought for America . . . and Antonio almost died for Italy.* Teresa clenched her fists. "It was that Fascist pig Mussolini's fault for siding with Hitler. I'm glad they hung the devil upside down, dead for all to see. They should have sliced off his testicles too." The freighter's engines rumbled in agreement.

"Such harsh words." Antonio pulled in his chin with mock disbelief. "Bitterness doesn't agree with you, Teresa." When she stuck out her tongue at him, he laughed. "See how it spoils your pretty face." He recoiled in self-defense, in time to evade the smack Teresa attempted to lay on his arm. "It's over now; let's get on with our lives."

"*Va bene*," Teresa acquiesced and gestured toward the pockets of people that waited along the dock. "How will we know which is our family? How will we recognize them?" In the last eight years, Teresa and Antonio hadn't exchanged pictures with any of their American relatives, not even their father. "If they aren't here, what'll we do then?"

"Don't strain your *cervello*. Save that little brain of yours for more important things." Antonio laughed. "Like how you'll learn to cook a decent meal."

"*Che dici?* Was it my fault Nina kicked me out of the kitchen after I burned one lousy loaf of bread?" *She was so darn fussy about her precious bakeware. Besides, there was no decent food to cook after the war began*. Teresa considered the ramifications of her lack of culinary skill. "How am I supposed to attract a decent *Americano* if I don't know how to cook?"

"Turn off your tongue and use your brain."

"Look who's talking," Teresa shot back as she jerked up her palm, "the boy with no experience with women and no education. What about your **cervello**? How will *your* brain figure out how to earn a living or attract a respectable woman?" When her brother cringed, Teresa halted the counterblows. *Men can be so sensitive*. "Sorry, Antonio. Let's call a truce. No more bickering today. **D'accordo?**" Antonio's pathetic nod encouraged her to pacify him further. "You'll do fine in America. **Sono sicura.**" Teresa pinched his cheek. "What woman has the strength to resist your handsome face or your sense of humor?"

Antonio pushed her hand away. "**Basta!** Enough fooling around! Are you sure we didn't leave anything in the cabin?"

"**Sì**, Antonio. What was there to leave?" She pointed to the two valises by their feet. "We brought so little with us." Teresa looked down at the dress she wore and fingered the seams she'd taken in by hand. "Do you think these tucks will hold? I hope they don't split apart. I'd be so embarrassed."

"I'm sure they'll be fine. You're such a good seamstress, Teresa."

I want to make a good first impression on Papà and our brothers. Teresa looked off into the distance. "Some day I'll own my own sewing machine." *Make myself beautiful clothes.*

Antonio patted her arm. "Sooner than later, I'm sure."

Subsequent to the captain's orders to drop anchor and lower the plank, Teresa and Antonio walked arm-in-arm down the ship's ramp shoved between the other passengers, all anxious to set foot on solid ground. After they passed through U.S. Customs where the tabby was confiscated from her suitcase, a tearful Teresa gripped Antonio's arm. "I wanted to keep him."

"Don't worry. You'll find another pet in America."

"It won't be the same."

"Come on, let's go find Papà."

After a few minutes of scrutinizing the crowd, Teresa pointed towards a group of people surrounding a huge welcome sign, ***ANTONIO E TERESA, BENVENUTI.*** "Look, Antonio." The acid in her stomach churned. "I expected Papà, maybe our brothers and their wives. But who are all the others?" Antonio shrugged.

Once they approached the group and were attacked with hugs, kisses and hails of welcome, Teresa and Antonio were inundated with introductions to unfamiliar relatives. While Teresa's head spun in confusion, a rather diminutive gentleman with white sideburns and a salt and pepper mustache advanced from the back of the crowd, his arms opened wide.

The man, dressed in a double-breasted grey suit and a black fedora with a feather inserted into the grosgrain band, directed his tear-filled eyes into those of Teresa's and Antonio's. "***Finalmente siamo insieme***. At last reunited!"

Teresa watched her brother rush toward the man. Antonio grasped the man's shoulders and stooped to give him a peck on each cheek. "Papà, good to see you again."

So, this midget is our father? Signore Arturo Camara? Teresa assessed the small man. *Not what I expected . . . much, much shorter and way, way older.* She felt no inkling of emotion toward him. As far as she was concerned, the man was practically a stranger.

Signore Camara turned toward Teresa and gestured for her to approach him. "***Bambina mia***, my youngest and most beautiful daughter*, **per favore vieni qui a Papà***. Come on, hug me and give me a kiss."

I am his youngest daughter. But his most beautiful? **Beh!** *How would he know? He hasn't seen Nina in years.* With hesitance, Teresa limply embraced her father but held back when it came to a kiss. She wondered if his request for affection was sincere.

Ignoring her lack of enthusiasm, Signore Camara squeezed her arms while he kissed each of her cheeks with gusto. Before he released Teresa, he shouted over his shoulder to the crowd, "***Andiamo a celebrare!*** Let's go home to Benton. We'll celebrate with food and wine."

Teresa looked back once more toward the ship they'd debarked. Though she was glad to be rid of the seasickness, she already missed the tabby.

Chapter Four

Iggy breezed the sedan onto a driveway on Steward Street and screeched to a halt adjacent to a white masonry structure with a classic federal roofline. The three-tiered detached dwelling stood conspicuous and more opulent in the neighborhood of mainly two-story row homes. Although the front of the building was stoic in its flatness, its architect had expanded the interior space of each level by incorporating bay windows on both sides. At the rear of the house, a detached garage consumed the majority of yard space.

Mack stepped out of the LaSalle carrying a vase of flowers in his left hand and stared at the jalopy's dull finish. *What can we do to spruce it up?* "Iggy, don't you think a good coat of wax might make this baby shine." Attracted by the mums, an industrious bee circled the vase, eager for their pollen.

"Sure," Iggy responded with haughty nonchalance. "Anytime you want to wax it, let me know and the car's yours for the day."

Mack sneered at Iggy. *Will he ever bother to work on the car as we agreed?*

After Iggy wrenched the vase from Mack's hand, he headed toward the front of the house. "These flowers ought to stifle Anna." Even though he considered it a man's right to do whatever he wanted to his wife, he figured the insincere token of affection would appease her and get Anna off his back. She'd been infuriated with him when he returned home after midnight the previous evening. When the bee landed on Iggy's forearm, he whacked it dead without a second thought, "Damn pest!"

Following behind Iggy, Mack scowled. *Would've served the hypocrite right to get stung!* He was angry because Iggy had parked in front of the flower shop and refused to drive home until Mack went inside and purchased some flowers for Anna. *What in God's name did Iggy do to her this time?* They climbed the front porch, entered a foyer that flaunted a vaulted ceiling and wide staircase, and then passed under a threshold into the living room where, across from the dormant fireplace and baby grand, a phonograph operated in full swing. The player's speakers belted out an operatic aria from Verdi's **Otello**, its volume in competition with the animated dialogue that emanated from the dining room, a bilingual blend of Italian and English. At their approach, the seven individuals gathered around the long mahogany table halted their conversations.

"Ah! Iago and Macbetto." The woman's heavy Italian accent attested to her heritage. "**Dove siete stati?**" She adjusted her gray bun. "Why you late? You no wear watch?"

Mack approached the woman, stooped down and kissed each of her cheeks. "Sorry, Mamma. Iggy insisted we stop for flowers."

"Where's Anna?" Iggy demanded.

Signora Matteo huffed. "Iago, you wife, she no come down from bedroom all day. What her **problema**? Anna, she no help me do nothing." She headed to the kitchen to retrieve a serving utensil.

Iggy followed his mother. "Come on, Mamma. How many times do I hafta tell you? Anna's allergic to the stuff in detergent and polish. Don't be so hard on her." Iggy had concocted the excuse since he didn't want his wife to do any housekeeping. He preferred her to be well-rested for other more important marital responsibilities, ones that took place in the bedroom later in the evening. Amenable to this arrangement, Anna refused to succumb to her mother-in-law's annoying pressure.

Signora Matteo didn't buy Iggy's persistent lie, nor did she intend to abandon her goal to have Iggy's wife share in the housekeeping. But, without directly contradicting her son's excuse for Anna's laziness, she presented a strong point of contention. "*Beh!* She no can use broom or dry dish? To fold *pantaloni* . . . press shirt is no so *difficile.*" Still disgruntled, she reached into a kitchen drawer, retrieved the appropriate utensil and waved it in Iggy's face. "Is time to eat." Iggy at her heals, she returned to her chair in the dining room.

"I'll go get Anna." Irritated that his meal would be delayed, Iggy marched toward the staircase, grumbling over his shoulder, "Start without us."

Meanwhile, Mack took a seat next to a petite olive-skinned gal who appeared a tad younger than he. "Hey, Juliet. How's my favorite sister?"

Her loose chestnut waves bouncing, Juliet shook her head in disapproval. "Why do you let Iggy lead you around by the nose, Mack?"

Ignoring the criticism, Mack directed his chin toward a hefty guy who dominated the opposite end of the table across from Signora Matteo and raised a hand. "Hey, Frank." Without lifting his wrist from the table, Frank returned the greeting with a casual wave of his fingers. Mack smiled at the celery stalk of a lady seated at Frank's right. "How're you doing, Geneva."

Geneva patted the chignon at the nape of her neck. "Fine . . . and you?"

"Not bad." Mack's smile faded when he glanced at the stiff-lipped prude directly across the table from Juliet. *Patricia looks a lot older than twenty-five.* "Hi, Patricia." He nodded at the earthy-looking man to her left. "Jake."

Perched at the edge of a chair, Patricia squawked at Mack, "You held us up for fifteen minutes. The food is already starting to get cold. You know Mamma won't say grace until everyone expected arrives home. Have a little consideration, why don't you? This is the third time this week that we've had to wait."

Mack winced. "Sorry." *Why should I apologize? Iggy's the one to blame, not me.*

Patricia pointed her beak at Jake. "Say something, don't just sit there." His ruddy complexion coarsened by the most pronounced five o'clock shadow in the room, Jake hunkered lower in his seat instead.

Once Signora Matteo dished out servings of lasagna in proportion to the size of each person at the table, she folded her hands. In cue, the remaining family members all bowed their heads as she recited a short grace in Italian followed by a spirited gesture to begin the meal. "***Mangia, mangia! Buon' appetito.***"

In unison, the family replied, "***Buon' appetito!***" The room quieted down and they began their dinner.

A few minutes into the meal, glass crashed against the floor above them and they all stopped eating to glance up. When the sounds of a tussle ensued, highlighted by Iggy's gruff bark, heavy footsteps and a muffled screech, Signora Matteo frowned in indignation while, unfazed, the others returned their attention to their plates.

* * *

Upstairs, Iggy kicked pieces of the shattered vase aside with his foot. "Damn it! Why'd you go and do that?"

Iggy's shapely wife Anna leered at him with vengeful eyes. Not long after she'd arrived in America, she realized she'd been duped. What she had considered a clever move, exchanging the poverty of Naples for the affluence of America, wasn't worth the aggravation she endured as wife to an unloving and disrespectful man. The life of an underpaid Neapolitan barmaid didn't seem quite as wretched now as it had when she first met Iggy, a sex-starved American soldier.

Bitter as usual, she wanted to chastise him not only for his recent bad behavior, but for all her disappointment. She yelled at him in Italian, "***Dio Christo!*** Do you think a mere vase of flowers is enough to make up for the way you treat me? Last night you came home with the smell of another woman on your clothes; the night before, too drunk to know my name. If you want to make up to me, bring me something I can use, like jewelry. You steal enough money. Why not spend some of it on me?"

"You're nuts. I don't take anything that isn't mine."

"Oh no? What about the bankbook you hide in the back of your closet. I may not read English, but I can add numbers. The ones in your bankbook add up to more than you've earned."

"Shut up!" Iggy's face turned beet red with anger. "Someone might hear you."

"So it's true! You are a thief." She flopped down on the bed, crossed her legs and thought for a moment. "Your secret's safe as long as there's something in it for me."

Iggy gritted his teeth. "Just what do you want?"

"What you promised . . . a life of leisure. Make your mother, that gray-haired **strega,** leave me alone. The witch is still pestering me to do housework and . . ."

"Leave my mother out of this!"

When Iggy stomped closer and grabbed her by the hair, Anna shrieked, "You're just like her, bossy and mean."

Iggy tugged harder. "If you know what's good for you, you'll never disrespect my mother again. And if I was you, I'd forget all about that bankbook. It has nothin' to do with you."

Anna pulled away from him. "I won't mention it again as long as I get a spending allowance from now on."

In a frustrated rage, Iggy shoved her against the wall.

* * *

Once the upstairs commotion ended, Frank swiveled toward his brother-in-law. "Jake, how's the job hunt goin'? Land anythin' permanent yet?"

"Nah, only odd jobs here 'n dere." The defeated expression on Jake's face revealed his discouragement. Steady work had been tough to find since he'd been discharged from the navy. "Not much call for ammunition handlin'."

"Well, before Iggy comes down, I wanted to ask you if you're interested in workin' with us at the bakery. We need a responsible guy to speed up deliveries. Iggy has a hard time keepin' on top of things, messes up orders. I'll pay you a decent salary. Since you're part of the family now, I might even cut you a share of the business someday. It's hard work. What do you think? Can you put up with my obnoxious brother? As long as you let Iggy think he's in charge, he might cooperate."

"Sure, I can do dat. Right up my alley. Why dis is great! When can I start?" Jake squeezed Patricia's hand.

"If tomorrow's not too soon, we'll see you at 6 a.m."

"See who at six?" Iggy dragged his voluptuous wife into the room, her flushed face tilted downward. He pushed her toward the seat next to Mack's, then yanked out the last chair and plopped down with a thud.

Though the other women at the table eyed Anna's low neckline with disapproval, Mack smiled at her. "Anna, you look nice tonight." Unresponsive, she sat down.

Frank averted his eyes from Anna's breasts and looked at Iggy. "Jake's joinin' us in the business. He'll be workin' with you in deliveries startin' tomorrow. Show him the ropes."

"Yeah . . . sure. Thanks for consultin' me," Iggy replied with sarcasm. "Who gives you the damn right to make decisions behind my back?" He pounded the table. "I own an equal share of the bakery."

Everyone looked down at their plates except Frank, whose face turned blood-red, and Signora Matteo who wrung her hands. "Iago . . . Franco, please . . . you Papà, he no talk ***affari di*** business at table. Why you do?"

After Iggy helped himself to a plateful of lasagna, he confronted Jake with an authoritative air. "Report to me tomorrow and I'll have you sweep out the trucks."

Jake glanced at Frank who shrugged back an implied *I warned you.*

Mack eyed the three men and settled his gaze on the top of Jake's head as his brother-in-law dove into his plate. *Wonder if Jake realizes how devious Iggy is. If he doesn't, it won't take long for him to find out.*

While everyone else settled down to their meals, Signora Matteo tilted an ear toward the parlor and sighed in appreciation of the soprano's talent. With a saddened expression, she faced Juliet. "***Tuo padre*** . . . he loved ***l'opera.***"

Juliet placed her hand on top of her mother's. "Yes, Papà certainly was fond of opera."

In fact, her father had been so enchanted by Verdi's operatic compositions that Signore Matteo disregarded the possible repercussions to his offspring when he decided to name several of his children after the composer's operatic characters. Embarrassed by the mockery, her brother Romeo was the first to switch to an alternate name, Romi. Juliet, baptized Giulietta, along with her other siblings soon followed suit and chose nicknames, or Americanized versions of their birth names. Juliet recalled one of the times her mother complained about it, not long after her husband's death. "Why you no respect ***la memoria di*** Papà? ***Americani*** names . . . ***ma perché?***"

Prepared for a defense, Juliet answered, "We were born *here* in America, not Italy."

Hunched low in her seat, her curly mane draped over half her face, Anna scattered her food with her fork. She raised her head to reveal features unremarkable except for the intense gray eyes that glared at her husband. In strained Italian, barely loud enough for Mack to hear, she fumed at Iggy, "***Non sei rispettoso.*** Do you feel free to push me because I'm at your mercy here, far from my ***famiglia?***" Iggy's lack of response incited Anna to grip her fork tighter. A hateful sneer directed at Iggy, she seethed once again over all the false promises he had made her. "Lies . . . lies. ***Sei un bugiardo.*** If you gave me the money, I'd return to ***Italia*** tomorrow just to be free of you, you nasty liar."

Mack shook his head. *Even his own wife thinks he's awful.*

Juliet and Patricia stood to serve the next course that sat on a buffet table positioned against a far wall. Juliet fluttered her lashes. "A fellow flirted with me at the office this week."

Patricia pursed her lips at her sister's whispered revelation. "Is he Italian?"

"Well, maybe on his mother's side."

"You know, Juliet, Mamma and the boys will never approve of him if he isn't."

Juliet clenched her fist. "Too bad!" Since few single men had survived the war, she refused to let anyone hamper such a rare chance at romance. "A girl *has* to broaden her idea of what's suitable nowadays."

Patricia held up an index finger. "You better watch out or Iggy might make mincemeat out of the guy."

"He'll never find out. Will he?"

Patricia pressed her lips together and ran her index finger and thumb across them. "My lips are sealed." She hesitated a moment before she spoke up again, "I knew Frank would come through for Jake. This new income will help us save for..." The second Juliet turned back to the buffet table, Patricia fingered her stomach. "I won't wait much longer to break the news. I'll be the center of attention. Geneva will be so jealous."

Juliet swung around. "What news? Tell me. I don't keep any secrets from you, do I?"

Patricia smiled. "You'll find out soon enough . . . soon enough."

In the meantime, Geneva concentrated on the protruded veins at her husband's temples, contemplating how Iggy always managed to annoy him, almost to the point of explosion. With a specific motive in mind, she whispered into Frank's ear, "A soothing back rub later, how's that sound?"

Frank smiled. "Just what the doctor ordered." He squeezed Geneva's leg under the table. "What would I do without you?"

Geneva eyed Frank's dish with a frown. "Honey, you don't have to eat everything your mother heaps on your plate. If you eat lighter and exercise more, maybe we might be luckier at you know what."

"What are you talkin' about?"

"You know, Frank." Geneva moved his hand to her stomach. "You know."

"Oh that . . . it'll happen soon enough. Stop pesterin' me about it, Gen. Don't I have enough pressure with the business and dealin' with . . ." he tilted his head toward Iggy, "him?"

Geneva shoved his hand away, "Sorry, Frank, I didn't mean to *pressure* you."

"Oh, come on, Gen, let's not argue at the table. Let's talk about this later."

"Fine, Frank. It's so like you to evade the issue."

Mack squirmed in his seat. *Sure seems like there's a lot of tension in this room. I can distract them all.* "Hey, everybody, guess what?" Once he had everyone's attention, Mack announced, "Iggy and I bought a car. It's a LaSalle sedan. Anyone want a ride after dinner?"

Iggy stood up. "Yeah, *my* car's a gem. I'll give you all a ride later."

Mack gritted his teeth. "Our car, Iggy, *Our* car!"

Iggy dismissed Mack with a flip of his hand. "Yeah, whatever."

Chapter Five

After the awful meals she'd been unable to stomach on the freighter, Teresa found herself powerless to resist the scrumptious feast her sisters-in-law Virginia and Natalia prepared for their welcome celebration and, consequently, overindulged on the delicacies. Finished with a helping of antipasto, she loaded her plate with a generous sample of each of her favorite dishes: dumpling-like potato **gnocchi** served in a fresh basil tomato sauce, veal **scallopini** and eggplant **parmigiana**. For desert, Teresa chose two mini **sfogliatelle**, seashell-shaped pastries made with a flaky crust layered over a not-too-sweet ricotta and candied-fruit filling.

Her stomach more than satiated, Teresa glanced around the room at her newfound relatives, practical strangers that had welcomed her and Antonio so warmly. *Family . . . feels good to be a part of this one.* Having spent the better part of the afternoon getting acquainted and making small talk with them, she decided she'd learn more about their true natures if she observed them from a distance, watching how they interacted with each other.

In one corner of the room, arms flailing, her two oldest brothers debated in heated Italian over matters concerning their grocery store. Paulo, a handsome cross between Antonio and Teresa, tried to convince his brother Tommaso, a chubbier version of his father, that they should expand their business. "If we don't grow, the bigger stores will steal our customers."

"No! Specialty products, individual attention . . . that's what our customers want. Cater to their needs and they'll keep coming back. You'll see."

Infuriated by his older brother's stubbornness, Paulo stalked off. He approached his wife Virginia, a chic lady in her late twenties. "Tommaso has his head buried in the dark ages! How will we ever get ahead?"

Virginia, having overheard the dispute, hugged her husband and patted his back. "If you're patient, he will come around. You'll see." She glanced at Tommaso's wife, a dowdy woman in her early thirties as she gathered dirty dishes. "Now, if Natalia was smarter, she'd charm him into an expansion. But you know she has as much charm as an ox."

Paulo grinned. "Don't be catty, **cara mia**."

Teresa then focused her attention on a penny card game in which Antonio and the remaining family members were boisterously engaged. When it was her father's turn to deal, he rolled up his shirtsleeves and, picking up the 40-card deck of Italian playing cards, shuffled them. "I say we switch to **Scopa** and play for higher stakes." Contrary to the other players' agreement, one cousin scowled at the notion. Signore Camara scoffed at him, "Don't be cheap, Nardo. Put up your nickels." Not interested in gambling, Teresa wandered over to a sofa in Tommaso's adjoining parlor and sat down, content to enjoy the comfort of its cushions while she inspected the rest of the room's furnishings. *I wonder if Papà's **casa** is as nice as this one.*

* * *

Waking at daybreak, Teresa sat up with a yawn and examined the small bedroom in the dim morning light. In front of one wall covered in a muted pink and green floral pattern, a distressed wooden rocker held court, while on the opposite wall a vanity mirror topped an antique bureau. "**Che fortuna!** My own bedroom!" *Like a princess.* She patted the twin mattress and sighed gratefully, "Ah." *No more tilting back and forth all night.* Sliding out from under the sheet, she switched on the overhead fixture and startled a spider. In a Tarzan-like maneuver, the long-legged creature swung down from the ceiling on a silk vine and, skirting her feet, disappeared into the thick jungle of dust under the bed.

Teresa glanced at the bureau. *Natalia said she collected some second-hand clothes for me.* So exhausted the evening before, she hadn't bothered to check, but a good night's sleep had revived her curiosity. Her face lit up in anticipation, Teresa tiptoed over to the dresser and opened each drawer to inspect its contents. "**Non ci credo!**" She pulled out dresses, blouses and skirts in various sizes and colors. *Never expected this much.* Some of the clothes looked like they'd hardly been worn. *Can't wait to alter them to fit me.* She held one dress in front of her and twirled around in a circle.

Amid the jumble, Teresa located a wraparound robe that she slipped into before she tidied the room and then exited into a corridor. Two other doors lined the narrow hallway. She entered through the first and found herself in a cramped bathroom that contained a toilet, a claw-foot tub and a pedestal sink. She spun in a circle. *What . . . no bidet? Hah!* She'd expected America to be more advanced than Italy. Making quick use of the facilities, she approached the last room ahead of the stairs.

Teresa stepped beyond the doorway to discover an unadorned room with a double bed next to a tall armoire. *Poor Antonio . . . such tight quarters with Papà.* She wrinkled her nose. *His snores are atrocious from a distance. Up close they must be unbearable.*

A rumpled coverlet lay at the foot of the mattress. *Guess I'm expected to make their bed.* She reluctantly reached for it and, as she bent down, the juices in her stomach churned. "Ugh, **troppo da mangiare** . . . much too much to eat last night."

"Today, I pay the price," she complained out loud. Teresa considered her gastric discomfort undue punishment, especially since she'd regarded the food as a tasty reward for enduring the long and arduous trip to America. *So unfair.*

The bed made, Teresa backed into a window. Through its panes, she surveyed a side alley and grimaced at the rusty chain-link fence which separated her father's property from his neighbor's. She approached another window on the far wall and spotted a lone fig tree planted in the middle of a garden. *Fresh tomatoes and figs? Love them!* Her belly protested with a growl.

At the top of the staircase, Teresa grasped the banister with one hand as she descended the steep staircase and clutched her midsection with her other. She crept through the parlor where slatted shutters provided privacy from the street. A dusty-rose sofa and armchair dominated one end of the narrow room while a reproduction Victorian dining table and sideboard occupied the other.

After Signore Camara's gruff voice emanated from the next room, Teresa tiptoed toward it and poked her nose into the small kitchen where her father sat across from Antonio. Unmindful of her presence, Signore Camara pounded the Formica-topped table, rattling the basket of fruit and newspaper sitting on top of it. "Look me in the eye, Antonio!" As if oblivious to the tension in his father's growl, Teresa's brother gazed out the side window noncommittally.

Why's Papà so agitated with Antonio? Teresa shrugged. *Better him than me.* From the archway, she perused the kitchen and flinched at the sudden hum of the electric refrigerator. *What's that noise?* At the far end of the room, Teresa spotted a gas stove and, frowning at its thick iron grates, hoped her father didn't expect her to cook. If he did, he'd be in for a rude awakening. Her attention diverted back to her father, whose neck by that time had flushed purplish-red. *My, my, still has a short fuse.*

Furious that his son favored the idea of employment with his brothers in their produce store rather than work with him at the tool factory, Signore Carmara pounded the table a second time. "***Hai una testa dura!*** Tell me, why must you be so stubborn, Antonio?" When his son still failed to respond, Signore Camara rose from the chair and aimed his snarl closer to Antonio's face. "***Stupido***, you can earn much more money at the factory than as grocery clerk?" He flopped back down and crossed his arms.

Maybe I can distract Papà. With a weak smile, Teresa entered the room. "***Buon giorno***. I hope you both slept well."

Although her father ignored her, Antonio mumbled an offhanded "***Buon giorno***," but quickly refocused his eyes on Signore Camara. "Papà, Tommaso promised me a decent salary since I already have market experience; and Paulo said I'd get a discount on fruits and vegetables. What's more, working there will give me a chance to get to know them better." Antonio raised a hand for emphasis. "Someday, I want to open my own market. What better way to learn how business operates in America?"

"I give up! Be a fool if you like. But remember, you'll pay the same room and board no matter what!" Signore Camara stood up and bumped into Teresa. "***Dov' è la nostra colazione?*** Our breakfast has been delayed long enough. What're you waiting for, an invitation to start cooking?"

Teresa shrugged her shoulders and held out her palms in a futile gesture. "I don't see an icebox. ***Che cucino?*** The eggs . . . where?"

Signore Camara grabbed her by the wrist and led her to the refrigerator. He pulled open the door and introduced her to the bounty of its lighted interior, the shelves loaded with eggs, butter, milk, various vegetables and a slab of ***capicolla***, a spicy lunchmeat made from pork shoulder. He gestured for her to take her pick of its contents. "***Subito! Tengo fame***. Antonio must be starving too."

Although her stomach flip-flopped at the sight of the food, Teresa selected the butter with one hand and two eggs with the other. Her hands full, she glanced at the stove and bit her lip in consternation.

"What are you, helpless?" Her father grabbed a few more eggs and the ***capicola***, let out an exasperated sigh, and led her to the gas range. He opened the oven door loaded with a supply of pots and pans and demonstrated how to light the burner with a match, then, leaving her to her own devices, shared sections of the Italian newspaper with Antonio.

Teresa fumbled at the stove and, despite her desperate efforts, fried the **capicola** well beyond recognition and over-scrambled the eggs so that the **frittata** ended up resembling moldy cottage cheese rather than a pork omelet. She cringed as she presented the catastrophe to her father and brother. "**La colazione è pronta.** Time to eat."

With his expression leery, Antonio helped himself to a tiny portion of Teresa's **frittata**. However, her father refused to sample the slop. Instead, he threw the platter into the sink, shattering it in the process, and then stomped from the room shouting over his shoulder, "**Meglio che t'impari a cucinare o tutti moriremo di fame!**"

Antonio smirked as he rose from his chair, "Don't worry, Teresa. Papà exaggerates. You'll learn to cook way before we starve." He gave his sister an affectionate pat on the shoulder, picked up an apple from the basket on the table and followed his father from the room. "Papà, another reason I don't want to work in the factory . . ."

Teresa sneered at her father's back. *Who cooked the old goat's meals before me?* Her stomach flip-flopped once more but she waited until Signore Camara and Antonio were out of earshot then, in grateful relief, released a ripple of gas, "Bbbrrrrp."

Chapter Six

On the morning of July 10th in the office above Matteo's Bakery, Mack perched on the edge of a chair and leaned his elbow on the desk. "Well, Frank, I've checked out some of the numbers." Mack had studied the accounting records for a few hours every evening since he'd started working at the bakery.

Anxious to find out if his suspicions had any validity, Frank looked over Mack's shoulder. "Uncover anything fishy? Fill me in quick before the bookkeeper shows up."

Mack tapped a pencil on the blotter. "Looks like some sales receipts were never recorded, or possibly posted to the wrong accounts. In at least one quarter, taxes went unpaid."

"Any penalties involved?"

Mack spun around. "I'll check into it."

"Is this Hungarian crooked or just plain incompetent?" What Frank really wanted to know was if Iggy deliberately recommended someone willing to steal for him.

Since the day Frank had been foolish enough to take Iggy's recommendation to hire the non-Italian, Frank had been too busy with the day-to-day operations of the bakery's ovens and storefront to pay much attention to the books. That is, until Iggy slipped and said something that aroused Frank's misgivings about Harry's allegiance.

In order to accost Iggy and his probable lackey with accusations, Frank needed solid proof of any thievery. Although Frank hadn't yet taken Mack into his confidence, he believed his college-educated brother was clever enough to uncover solid evidence Iggy couldn't refute, if it in fact existed.

"Can't say just yet. The books are in such a muddle, it's hard to tell." Mack didn't want to make any accusations of purposeful wrongdoings until he was positive.

"But are we in the red?"

"Patience, Frank. Audits take time." Noting the cross look on his brother's face, Mack wanted to reassure him. "Meanwhile, I'll keep a closer eye on Harry."

Unable to hold in his annoyance, Frank shook his index finger. "Anythin' underhanded goin' on, you can bet Iggy has somethin' to do with it." He felt Iggy was at the root of most of his problems. "Ever since he came home from the war, there's been nothin' but trouble." His grimace deepening, he began to hobble around the room.

"Leg bothering you, Frank?"

"Obvious, huh? Acts up whenever I get agitated and, with Iggy around, I can't ever relax, not even for a minute."

"I'm not surprised," Mack commiserated.

Frank jerked his chin upward. "You don't know the half of it." The tension in his shoulders tight, he pounded a fist into the opposite palm. "The shit I've had to put up with!"

"Feel free to unload, Frank. I'm on your side. What's Iggy done?"

"All sorts of crap." Pacing around, Frank elaborated in a gruff voice, "For instance, a couple months back, he bragged about how much he saved us on truck maintenance. Insisted I give him a bonus. Not even a week later, a slew of our trucks failed inspection. The drivers had to scramble with less than half the fleet. They almost didn't finish deliveries. Wanna know why so many of the trucks failed?"

"I can imagine."

"Iggy bribed a Motor Vehicle Inspector to pass the trucks, no matter what. When the guy got fired, Iggy's scheme caved."

"So what'd you do?"

"I flipped out and took away Iggy's control of the fleet. That is, until Mamma insisted I give him another chance."

"What else's Iggy done?"

"Give you another example of his infuriatin' gall. Six months ago, asked him to handle the employee Christmas party. The idiot went overboard and ordered a filet mignon dinner, with an open bar to boot . . . way above budget. But that was the least of the problems. About eight of the drivers got downright drunk and all hell broke loose, trashed the place. Restaurant insisted we pay for the damages."

"Iggy cover it?"

"No, are you kiddin'? He used brash tactics, if you know what I mean. Convinced the guilty drivers to pay up, or else." Frank let out an exasperated breath. "Somehow, he always gets away with everythin'."

"Know what you mean. Guess what he managed to do to me?"

"What?"

"The sneak registered the car we bought *together* in his name alone, even though *I* put up most of the money."

"Yeah, sounds like somethin' he'd do. Well, anyway, keep me posted on the audit." Frank limped out of the office.

Not even five minutes later, a puny man with a pointy nose carried a steaming mug into the room. He grunted at Mack, "Mornin'."

"Morning, Harry." Mack followed the bookkeeper on his way to his desk. "Can we go over ledger postings?"

Harry halted midway and stretched on tiptoe to pull on the ceiling fan's chain. "Yeah, okay," he reluctantly agreed. "But lemme finish my coffee."

As the blades began to whirl, Mack got a whiff of the man's unwashed armpits, the acrid smell blending with the aroma of his coffee. *Ugh!* Shuddering, Mack pulled back in disgust, his nose twitching at a stench worse than decomposing vermin.

"While you're waitin', open the window," Harry suggested. "Damn stuffy in here."

I'll say! "More than happy to." Mack hurried toward the window. "Don't know why I still get confused between debits and credits." *Got Harry convinced I'm not too bright. He'll never suspect I'm wise to him.*

Mack flung open the window and cleansed his nostrils with the fresh morning air. "Ah!" Lingering there against the sill, he wondered if Harry was indeed Iggy's current accomplice in crime, and whether or not his devious brother had originally maneuvered Harry into the bookkeeper position with the express intention of siphoning off company funds. *If Iggy's to blame, do I have the nerve to rat him out? Makes my blood curdle to imagine his reaction if I did. Who knows what he'd do to me?* He pictured Iggy seizing him in a headlock and hammering away at his skull. *But Frank's counting on me.*

As he weighed the dilemma of courage versus cowardice, Mack glanced down from the window and spotted Teresa Camara crossing to the opposite side of Whitman Street. Magnified by the sun, the copper highlights in her hair swayed counter to the swing of her hips and, when she turned her head, her bronze eyes sparkled over defined cheekbones and a delicate nose. Mack gasped. *What a beauty! Never saw her in the neighborhood before. Wonder who she is.*

Teresa waved on the tall dark-haired young man behind her. "Antonio, **sbrigati!** Hurry up or we'll both be late."

Mack frowned. *Hope he's not her fellow.*

When the bookkeeper hit the total button on the adding machine, Mack refocused on him. "Harry, another thing. Accounts receivable and payable . . . tell me again, how do we transfer from one to the other?"

Chapter Seven

On a sultry Sunday in July, a month after they anchored in America, Teresa meandered down the street arm-in-arm with Antonio.

"**Quest'è l'ultima volta**, Teresa. This is the last time I'll walk you to church. Sunday's my only day to sleep in and I've been late to work one too many times on Saturday. You can manage these four blocks to St. Christopher's on your own."

Teresa shook her head. "What will Papà say?" Her father refused to let her go anywhere but to work without an escort. The relaxed stroll to church on Saturdays and Sundays was her best opportunity to casually observe people in the neighborhood.

Antonio threw up a hand. "Papà will never know. He's still snoring right now."

"If he throws a temper tantrum, I'll tell him it was your idea." Teresa sighed, let go of Antonio's arm and mumbled, "I'd better not forget to say another prayer of thanks for Virginia's help."

"Why, what did Paulo's wife do for you?"

"Oh, she just gave me some advice," Teresa answered reluctantly.

"Advice about what?" Antonio fished.

"Well, if you must know, after Papà's steady harassment, I was embarrassed but desperate. I begged her to teach me how to cook a few simple dishes."

"No exaggeration, Teresa. Your cooking was awful. I'll have to thank Virginia myself."

Teresa smacked his arm. "**Che dici?** It wasn't that bad."

"That's what you think." Antonio clasped his hands together and chuckled. "Please, I beg you. Ask her for a few more lessons. Papà and I need a little variety."

"You do, do you? How will I find the time? I work too you know."

They walked a half block in silence before Antonio spoke up again. "Papà complained to me yesterday."

"About what, my cooking? Thought you said it improved."

"No, not that. He moaned that you don't pay your share of the expenses."

"*È così ingrato!*" Teresa clenched her fists. "Papà doesn't appreciate any of my efforts. Not only do I give him all my salary, I keep house and cook at the end of a long workday." She let out an exasperated breath. *And to think, if not for Tommaso's wife, I'd still be unemployed.* Natalia had taken it upon herself to find Teresa a job at the dress factory, within a week of her arrival no less.

"Teresa, *devi dirmi la verità* . . . nothing but the truth. Do you take any cash from your pay envelope before you give it to Papà?"

Teresa's spine stiffened. "What makes you ask that?"

"Well, I noticed you don't cover your mouth when you smile anymore. If you handed all the money to Papà, how did you pay for those fillings?"

"*Va bene,*" Teresa admitted, a flush rising to her face. "I confess. I did take out a little. But I'm sure God forgives me. I found an inexpensive dentist to fill my front cavities. Used some of the money to make an initial payment. He agreed to wait for the rest." Anxious to improve her smile so she'd be able to attract a respectable American man, Teresa had begged her sister-in-law Natalia to introduce her to a local dentist who understood Italian. On her second Saturday in America, Teresa had charmed the old Italian-American into agreeing to fill her front cavities on the spot at quite a reduced rate. Her improved smile was dazzling.

"What's more, I put aside a bit to send to Nina's children. Hope Papà doesn't discover the bundle I hid in my dresser. You won't tell him now, will you, Antonio?"

"Not if you promise to introduce me to a pretty girl . . . *una bella signorina che parla Inglese.*"

"Why one that speaks English and where would *I* find one?"

"At the dress factory, of course. I need someone to teach me the language." Antonio had found that many of the grocery store's customers didn't speak Italian. He needed to learn English and thought an attractive native might make the experience more pleasant.

"Sorry, most of the workers at the factory are immigrants like us and I'm the only single one. Not speaking English hasn't been a problem for me so far, but my sewing speed . . . that's another story. Piecework, I hate it! How will I ever earn a higher salary if I can't sew fast enough? Maybe if I say a prayer, Papà won't need to complain next time I hand him three-quarters of my pay." Teresa huffed. "When I'm married to a rich **Americano**, I won't have to stress over money."

"How do you expect to meet such a prince if you don't speak English, Teresa? Besides, Papà watches over you like a hawk."

"**Lo so,**" Teresa acknowledged. "He scowls at any man who looks in my direction."

Both times that a relative had introduced Teresa to an eligible immigrant at a family gathering, her father stared the fellow down until he got discouraged and walked away. Though Teresa lacked interest in either of these men, she resented her father's possessiveness.

"Papà prefers to keep me as his **schiava**, a slave to his commands." Teresa sulked at the thought of the household chores that needed to be completed before she returned to work on Monday, dreading most the endless cobwebs that some industrious spider wove faster than she could remove them.

Antonio smirked. "How can you think that of your own father?"

"**Non è difficile**. Actually, it's very easy." Teresa paused and reconsidered her father's attitude toward suitors. "Maybe Papà's doing me a favor by scaring off immigrants. Like I said, I'm determined to find myself an **Americano**."

Teresa sighed again as she pulled out a lace handkerchief from her purse and patted her neck. "If only Papà showed a little appreciation now and again, it might make the wait for my **Americano** a little easier."

"Do you expect to meet this American in a church of all places?"

"I'll let you in on a little secret, Antonio." Teresa giggled. "I'm not as religious as you might think. Mass on Saturday and Sunday gives me an excuse to give the few **Americani** along the way a glimpse of the new Italian import."

"Are you shameless, sister?" Antonio snickered. "Besides, where will that get you, Teresa, without a proper introduction?"

"Never know when I might get that opportunity."

"Wishful thinking!" A few yards from the church steps, Antonio halted. "I'll be back in an hour. Next week you're on your own." He headed toward the closest coffee shop.

Distracted by a crowd of woman gathered at the top of the stairs, Teresa collided with an inattentive young man who happened by, Mack Matteo. Startled out of his daydream, Mack attempted to balance the two of them by grasping her arms. "Excuse me, Miss." Their gazes interlocked for an awkward moment.

Pulling away, Teresa excused herself, "***Scusami***," and scurried up the steps. She smiled when she realized the young man spoke English with no Italian accent. *Why he's my first real **Americano**!* She'd forgotten about the old dentist. At the top of the stairs, she stopped and took another peek at the fellow over her shoulder. *Hmm, polite, attractive and as tall as Antonio. I like that. Wish I knew someone to introduce us.*

Mack stood there mesmerized before he looked down and noticed that the young beauty had dropped her handkerchief. He picked it up and called out, "***Signorina***," but by that time Teresa was already inside the church. Mack walked away and, with the hanky held up to his nose, sniffed a trace of her perfume. *She's the girl I've seen from the office window.*

Chapter Eight

Early Monday morning, Mack held Teresa's hanky up to his nose and sniffed her fragrance as he stared out the office window. *If only . . .*

"Hey, Mack," Frank snapped his fingers. "Ready for our meetin'?"

Mack stuffed the handkerchief into his pocket and shook his head as if to clear it, but the vision of the Italian goddess refused to fade away. "Ever see a woman so beautiful that you can't get her out of your mind?"

"Yeah, Greta Garbo. Wasn't for the pinup poster you sent me, don't think I would've made it home from the war with all my marbles."

"No, I don't mean a fantasy. I mean I real live girl, flesh and blood, right here in Benton, New Jersey."

"Found someone, did ja? Italian?" When Mack nodded, Frank mussed the top of Mack's hair. "Good. Mom'll approve. Gonna bring her home to meet us?"

"Well, you see, I only ran into her, literally I mean, by accident yesterday in front of St. Christopher's." Mack's eyes glazed over. "She said, '***Scusami***,' then ran up the church stairs before I had a chance to talk to her. I've no idea who she is or where she lives. If I bump into her again, maybe I can introduce myself."

Frank laughed. "Look at you. You're smitten. But no decent immigrant will pay you any mind if you approach her on your own. You need a proper introduction to an Italian girl."

"I know you're right, but a fellow can dream, can't he?" Mack glanced out the open window. *Hope she isn't already engaged or, worse yet, married.*

Frank waved a hand in front of Mack's face. "Wake up. Time for business."

Mack checked his wristwatch. "Sure, sit down, Frank. Some serious matters to discuss before Harry shows up."

His war wound throbbing, Frank lowered himself onto a chair. "Okay, make it quick. There's work I need to supervise downstairs. Two of the bakers are out sick."

"You'll agree it's worth your time once I show you what I uncovered in the audit." After Mack breezed through the evidence of underhanded financial manipulations that diverted funds on numerous occasions during the last half of the fiscal year, Frank requested further clarification.

The more substantiation Mack presented, the tighter Frank's jaw clenched and the heavier his breathing became. "What's the bottom line here? How much was swindled?"

Mack swallowed hard. *Hope Frank has a strong heart.* "About three thousand. Not only that, we'll owe a couple hundred in tax penalties." Mack eyed the veins that protruded at his brother's temples. "Frank, notice the dates. It all happened after you hired Harry. Prior records seem to be in order."

"So, Harry *is* a shifty crook?"

"Definitely. He's the one who juggled the numbers. But," Mack hesitated, "I'm sure he has an accomplice."

Frank narrowed his eyes as he envisioned his sinister brother Iggy shaking hands with Harry. "What makes you say that?"

"Well," Mack leaned forward, "I caught Harry whispering on the phone more than once about bank deposits. It must've been . . ." He caught himself and finished without mentioning Iggy's name, " . . . his partner."

"And who do you think that might be, Mack?" Frank responded in a tense voice, knowing full well what answer he expected.

Mack pulled back. "I'm just an accountant, Frank, not a psychic." *Even though we both know Iggy's probably involved, we can't outright accuse him without solid proof, can we?* Perspiration beaded on Mack's forehead.

Frank squeezed his chin. "Before I fire his ass, I'll confront Harry. If he doesn't agree to give back every stinkin' penny, I'll threaten him.

"With what?"

"An embezzlement charge."

"You'd call the cops?"

"Only if I have to. It'd be bad for business." Knowing how squeamish some of the bakery's customers were about the police, Frank preferred not to get the authorities involved. "Do you think the weasel will cooperate?

"If you fire Harry, he might refuse to tell us who his accomplice is. Give me a chance to keep closer tabs on him. Maybe next time I eavesdrop on one of Harry's phone conversations, he'll slip up and call his partner by name." As the sweat dripped down the side of Mack's face, he reached into his pocket.

"All right." Frank stood up. "But only if you're sure you can keep him from stealing anythin' else."

"He won't have another chance to finagle the books. Not with me looking over his shoulder." Mack turned away from Frank and grimaced. *Or will he?* When he retrieved Teresa's hanky, a vial of pills crashed to the floor, opening on impact.

Frank stared wide-eyed at the large capsules that scattered every which way, mimicking Mexican jumping beans, ones filled with manic moth larvae. "Whoa! What are those--horse pills?

Mack wiped the perspiration from his face. "No, but they sure are hard to swallow." He stooped down, gathered up the pills and inserted them back into the vial. "Doc Piccolo upped the strength of my medication."

"Why's that?" Frank asked, the concern apparent in his voice. "You haven't had any more seizures lately, have you?"

"Not since the porch incident." Mack stood up, frowning at the memory. Three years ago, he had convulsed on the side porch of the house. His head striking against the concrete resulted in a minor concussion. "But after I told Doc Piccolo about the leg twitches and the weird odors . . ."

"Twitches . . . weird odors?" Frank wrinkled his nose.

"Yeah, I've had several episodes. First my leg twitches then I smell something I can't quite identify. Doc Piccolo called the twitches 'petite mal tremors' and said they weren't unusual before a grand mal seizure. He didn't want me to risk another convulsion so he increased the strength of my medication."

"Well, I guess it's better to be safe than sorry," Frank conceded.

Mack dreaded the prospect of another seizure. "Loss of control in public . . ." he shuddered. "It sure puts a crimp in my social life."

"It can't happen with the stronger medicine. Right?" Frank patted his shoulder.

"The threat's always there at the back of my mind," Mack lamented.

"Dwellin' on it won't do any good, Mack."

"How can I forget? Iggy jumps at every chance to remind me. That is, when he's not rubbing his veteran status in my face. It wasn't my fault the Army rejected my enlistment application." *Can't help it if I've got a condition.*

"Be grateful they did."

"Easy for you to say," Mack griped.

"I know it's no picnic," Frank commiserated as he massaged his sore limb. "But neither is my bum leg. At least the exemption gave you a chance to get your degree."

"Yeah, but the guilt still gnaws at me when I hear war stories. And, when Iggy broadcasts the fact that I didn't serve to anyone within earshot, it makes me blazing mad."

"Our brother fires me up too. Matter of fact, I think he takes pleasure in annoyin' all of us."

"Mamma must've been possessed by the devil when she delivered that Satan."

"How much you think an exorcism costs?" Frank scoffed.

"Hey, maybe we can just *kick* the hell out of him," Mack snickered.

"I'm game, little brother, if you are," Frank smirked.

"Or," Mack held up a finger, "we could return him to hell for a refund."

Frank laughed out loud. "An even better idea!" As he stood up, his expression sobered again. "Thanks for uncoverin' the fraud, Mack." He flashed two taut fingers at his brother. "Give you two weeks tops to get some solid evidence we can use against Harry's so-called accomplice. Agreed?"

"Agreed." As Frank limped toward the exit, Mack again wiped his forehead. *Hope I don't let Frank down. Damn Iggy! He deserves to get caught.*

After a glimpse at his watch, Mack retrieved two pills from the vial then downed them with a drink from the water cooler. He crumpled the paper cup and tossed it into the trashcan. *About time I faced my condition like a man. I refuse to let it hold me back anymore. No more excuses. I'm going to find myself a woman.*

Approaching the window, Mack spotted Teresa on her way to work. *Exquisite! Can she be the right one for me? Somebody who'll accept me, epilepsy and all?* Mack expelled a forced breath. *Must be a way I can meet her. But how?*

Chapter Nine

Halfway through the mass at St. Christopher's the next Saturday, Teresa disregarded the Latin litany and instead surveyed the old women in attendance, whispering under her breath, "***Sembrano prugne seche***." *So wrinkled they can definitely pass for dried-up* *prunes. Where are all their daughters and sons? At home still asleep?* Although Catholics were required to attend mass on Sundays, Teresa also opted to attend mass each Saturday for an additional hour reprieve from the drudgery of household chores. Besides, the walk to and from the church gave her another opportunity to scout the neighborhood.

Adjusting her sunbonnet, she twisted her neck to the far left and spotted a female with a much smoother complexion. *Ah, finally someone closer to my age. I like her stylish* **cappello**. Below the feathered hat that Teresa so admired, the full-bosomed brunette donned a tailored dress with a buttoned bodice, the neckline cut low enough to expose more than a fair share of cleavage. Teresa wondered how the priest would react when this temptress knelt before him to receive Holy Communion. *He's human for heaven's sake.*

Teresa caught the young woman's eye and they exchanged smiles. *Hmm, think I've spotted her here before. She might dress to the hilt, but she always looks lost, lonesome like me. Maybe she needs a friend too.* Teresa bit her lip to keep from laughing at the notion that only old hags and eager fools, ones praying for true love, attended Saturday morning mass. *Guess no one warned her. If she's out to meet a man here, she must be sorely disappointed.*

Teresa sighed. *Would love to share my dreams with another female.* The women at the factory where she worked were all quite satisfied to brag about their children and cooking skills and talked of nothing more. Stubborn, they refused to listen with an open mind to her ideas and hopes for the future. Teresa resented one woman in particular who had laughed out loud at the mention of her aspirations in marriage, claiming she would need a gilded cage to catch a rich **Americano**. Teresa lifted her chin. *Humph, I won't let the mockery discourage me.*

Eager for some fresh air and sunshine, Teresa hurried out the door at the end of the mass and skipped down the church steps. She halted at the bottom and spun around when the busty fashion plate tapped her on the shoulder. "**Scusame**, **signorina**. Care for some company on your way home?"

Delighted, Teresa flashed her dentist's handiwork, "**Sì**. Why not?" She held out a hand and introduced herself. "**Mi chiamo** Teresa Camara. I'm a new to this country."

Anna returned the smile and shook Teresa's hand. "Pleased to meet you, Teresa. **Mi chiamo** Anna Matteo."

As they headed homeward, Teresa inquired with a casual air of curiosity, "How long have you lived here in America, Anna?"

"*Poco tempo*. I arrived with my husband over a year ago, though it seems more like a century. I met him after the war when he was still stationed with the *Americani* in Naples, my hometown." Wishing she hadn't enlisted her brother's aid in devising a plan to entrap the young American soldier into marriage, Anna sighed regretfully.

Unlike Teresa, Anna chose not to comply with all the Catholic Church's strict directives. "My husband insists we sleep late on Sundays. So I come to church on Saturdays and pray for a chance to see the Mediterranean again." Wondering if she'd be welcomed home, Anna mentally shuddered at the image of her father's horror-stricken face. After her brother had informed him that a soldier sneaked into Anna's bedroom, the old man had burst into her room to find her and the American making love on the floor. Since Iggy had violated his *virgin* daughter, Anna's father insisted Iggy marry her. Her mother had been mortified.

Unfortunately, the siblings' plan had backfired. Not only was Anna disgraced in her parent's eyes, she was stuck with a stingy chauvinist for a husband. Until she recently discovered Iggy's illicit bank account, he had refused to provide her with an allowance, a discretionary fund she might tap in order to compensate her brother for his help in ensnaring Iggy. Now that she was receiving hush money from Iggy, she decided not to use any of it to repay her brother. Instead, she was spending it to complete a new wardrobe for herself.

"And you, Teresa, from where in *Italia* do you come?"

"I was born in Trapani, a port town on the west coast of Sicily. But, when my mother died, my brother and I moved to Palermo. We lived there with our sister's family until our father arranged for us to join him here in America a little over two months ago. We would have arrived years ago if not for the miserable war." Teresa cringed at the memory. "Weren't the bombs terrifying? And the shelters dreadful?" She remembered feeling like a mouse in a dark hole, huddled in fear of hungry cats.

"*Sì*, know what you mean. Dank and dreary. When I met my husband, he swept me off my feet with promises of a pampered life in America." Anna grimaced. "He never warned me that my mother-in-law would expect me to slave around the house, especially in the kitchen. My husband, like a typical man I presume, well . . . uh . . . his high expectations revolve around another room. I won't mention which one."

Wide-eyed, Teresa pursed her lips. *Does she mean what I think she means?*

They walked in silence for a minute before Teresa spoke up. "Your dress and hat, so *elegante*."

Grinning impishly, Anna looked down at her latest outfit, the first of many she'd acquired with Iggy's dirty money. "My husband insists I buy the best."

"Someday, I want to run a boutique, a place where I can sell my own original designs."

"Such high ambitions, Teresa," Anna adjusted her hat. "Me? I'm content to lounge and eat *cioccolate* all day." Her lips twitched as she contemplated a box of bittersweet chocolates that she'd considered insufficient retribution for one of Iggy's marital infractions. "Though my *suocera* pesters me, I've no intention of lifting a finger to help her." She pointed up the street. "That big house belongs to her, my bossy mother-in-law, not me. My mother never expected me to cook or clean *her* house. She did it without any help, as well she should've."

Teresa cringed at Anna's insolence. "You're lucky your mother's still alive." She sighed sadly. "Mine died long ago, when I was a little girl. I still miss her."

"I don't miss mine in the least." Anna grimaced. "She always favored my brother Angelo. But I do admit, I'd rather have her around than my mother-in-law. Life would be much nicer if the pushy witch wouldn't hassle me."

Shocked by Anna's brazen disrespect, but incited nonetheless, Teresa relayed what she considered an even worse scenario. "Think your situation is bad? When I served the first meal I cooked for Papà, the man threw the full dish in the sink, and shattered it into tiny pieces. You've no idea what I put up with. It doesn't matter that I hold down a full time job. My father expects me to do all the housework. What's worse . . . he's suspicious of any man that lays his eyes on me. I can't wait to get married to escape him."

Anna laughed. "*Povera ragazza!* Your father . . . my mother-in-law . . . maybe if we put our heads together, we can figure out a way to deal with the tyrants." Anna stopped in front of the largest and most impressive house on Steward Street. "This is where I live with my husband's *famiglia*."

"Such a magnificent home!" Teresa exclaimed. "Compared to my father's humble shack, it's a palace. What's your husband do?"

"Oh, he works with his brothers in the family business," Anna threw up a hand, "nothing impressive. And your fiancé, in what line of work is he?"

Teresa blushed. "Oh, I'm not engaged *yet*, but I plan to meet a handsome *Americano* any day now."

Anna's eyes lit up. "I've a great idea! I'll introduce you to my husband's unmarried brother. Iago and Macbetto bought a new car. If you'd consider going a week from Sunday, I'll ask them to take us for a ride to the State Park." She didn't notice the look of consternation on Teresa's face since she was busy wondering what bedroom treat she might offer Iggy in order to persuade him to go on an outing with his brother and a blind date. Various scenarios played out in her head as they continued to walk.

In the meantime, Teresa contemplated a possible friendship with this young woman. On the one hand, she found Anna's sharp tongue with its disrespectful edge disturbing, especially considering the fact that she openly criticized her elders in front of a stranger. On the other, Teresa appreciated Anna's sympathy in regards to her own difficult situation with her father. Moreover, Anna's offer to introduce Teresa to her brother-in-law seemed too good to pass up and the opportunity to ride in a new car tempting. *Might be fun.*

"*Sì,* if Papà doesn't object, I'll go with you," Teresa eventually agreed. She bit her lip for she had only seven days to persuade *il Duce* that it was acceptable for her to go. *Which one's the brother, Iago or Macbetto? Both have strange names.*

"*Bene,* see you next Saturday at church. We can finalize plans on our walk home." Anna climbed the stairs to the front door and waved. "*Arrivederci.*"

"*Arrivederci,* Anna," Teresa returned the goodbye with a smile and whispered to herself as she walked off, "*Finalmente!*" *Though it's long overdue, I'll get to meet an eligible **Americano**. Hope he's handsome.*"

Anna . . . what was her last name again? "*Mamma mia,* I've forgotten already!" Teresa peeked over her shoulder at the Matteos' house one last time. *Well, this Anna certainly found a rich Americano in her soldier husband. Great improvement over the ruins of Naples. Wonder what kind of business they own.*

At the third intersection, Teresa made a left onto Whitman Street. As she passed Matteo's Bakery, she glanced into its storefront window and noticed a tall young man behind the register. She averted her eyes in a flash. "*Dio santo!*" *The **Americano** I bumped into last Sunday. I'm so embarrassed. He must think I'm a clumsy ox.* Teresa again peered into the window and, after Mack's eyes lit up in recognition, she dashed away. *I'd forgotten how attractive he is. Too bad he's a common store clerk.* She quickened her step. *I'd better hurry home before Papà wakes up.*

* * *

With a smile on her face, Anna turned the doorknob. *At last, another clever Italian woman, someone I can stomach. If we become friends, life here in America might become more tolerable.* She pushed opened the front door and entered the vestibule. *If I ever told Teresa about some of Iago's expectations, how would she react? I wonder. Can she handle this kind of information? Unmarried woman can be so sensitive about personal matters.* She shrugged her shoulders.

Anna removed her hat and glanced into the mirror above the polished credenza. *Teresa's far prettier. Am I stupid to mix with such a beautiful woman? Perhaps I'll look plain in comparison.* She turned to the side and eyed her bustline. *Can a good figure make up for an ordinary face?* Anna sucked in her breath and pushed her breasts forward so that the decorative buttons on the bodice of her dress stood stiffly at attention, like Swiss guards protecting pontifical treasures. *Maybe.*

Hmm . . . do I tell Teresa about Macbetto's medical condition? No, she might reject him outright and then my plans for an outing will go up in smoke. I'll keep it to myself for the time being. What would Macbetto like me to do? On second thought, she brushed off all concern for her sickly brother-in-law's preference. *Who cares what he wants?*

* * *

Coated with the stench of cigars and whiskey, Iggy staggered into the bedroom late that night, stripped and leered at his sleeping wife. Under the spell of a dream, Anna squirmed and, sighing, raised her pelvis as she enjoyed a sensuous moan. When Iggy grabbed her by the hair, she awakened and shrieked at him, "*No!* **Che fai?** Leave me alone, you brute!"

"Shut up! You'll wake the others." Iggy pushed up her negligee and straddled her. "Dream about me, do you?"

"That'd be a nightmare." She wriggled her body in an attempt to free herself of him. However, the more Anna resisted him, the firmer his thighs gripped. She retaliated with sarcasm, "So **romantico!**"

"Come on, give in. You're my wife. It's your duty." When Anna stopped struggling, Iggy thrust his hips forward. "Uh, take that!"

I can play rough too. Anna dug her nails into Iggy's back and, despite her initial resistance, closed her eyes and, using her imagination to conjure a more appealing partner, gave in to her sex drive. But all too soon, Iggy relieved himself with a grunt and rolled over.

"**Mannaggia!**" Anna seethed. "Can't you ever last long enough to satisfy me?" She punched both fists into the mattress and glared at Iggy's snoring figure. "Damn you, you arrogant lush!"

Chapter Ten

At the dinner table the following Wednesday evening, Signora Matteo made sure everyone's wine glass was full to the brim, then, taking her seat, rushed through grace and, before anyone had a chance to pick up a fork, beamed at Patricia. "***Ho il piacere***. I most happy to say…"

"Mamma, please! Let Jake tell them." Patricia turned to her husband. "Jake?"

Signora Matteo crossed her arms over her bosom and pouted at having one of the few benefits of being the matron of the family so abruptly confiscated. Obviously, she didn't understand why Patricia had bothered to share the privileged information without expecting her to be the first to divulge it to the family. She was positive that if Signore Matteo had still been alive, he'd be announcing the milestone.

The family's attention diverted to him, Jake hesitated then sat up straighter. "Dere's sometin' Patricia tinks I oughta tell ya."

Patricia glared at him. "Jake, don't you *want* them to know?"

"Sure," Jake squirmed, "but why make such a big deal 'bout it?"

"Aren't you *proud*?" Patricia prodded.

Jake lifted his shoulders. "I guess."

Iggy banged the table with his fist. "Enough hemmin' and hawin'! Spit it out, why don't you? I'm hungry."

An indignant glance directed at Iggy, Jake stood hoisting Patricia along with him and possessively wrapped an arm around her waist. "Okay, here goes." He patted her abdomen. "Patricia's expectin'. Baby's due end a year."

Proud to be part of this growing Italian clan, Mack raised his wine glass. "***Buona fortuna! Alla Famiglia!***"

Everyone else, bar Geneva, picked up a goblet and parroted Mack's good luck wish and hail to the family. However, before anyone took a swig of Chianti, Geneva shot up from her chair. Unable to swallow her distress, she scrambled from the room, saliva dribbling from the side of her mouth.

Frank put down his glass and, at a fast limp, scurried behind his wife as she raced across the parlor, through the vestibule and up the stairs. He didn't catch up to her until she leaned over the banister at the first landing. Wheezing, Frank draped his arm across her shoulders. "It . . . it's okay, honey. We . . . we have plenty of time." Geneva buried her face in his chest, his flaccid muscles cushioning her sorrow.

Once her sobs simmered down to a whimper, Frank lifted her chin. "Come on, Gen, go wash your face. You'll feel better. Then we can go downstairs and congratulate Patricia and Jake."

* * *

Back at the table, while Mack sprinkled parmesan cheese onto his spaghetti, Juliet picked up the serving platter of meatballs and sausage and walked around to the other side of the table. "Here you go, Patricia, take some protein." As her sister helped herself from the platter, Juliet expressed pity for her sister-in-law, "Poor Geneva, she so wanted to be the first. She must be devastated."

"How can you excuse Geneva's awful behavior?" Patricia grumbled. "Where's my support?"

Juliet rolled her eyes. "Oh, you're right . . . as usual. Sorry." She cleared her throat. "I am so happy for you and Jake."

Patricia held up her chin and, rubbing her stomach, retorted in an arrogant tone, "Well thanks, Juliet. Maybe we'll consider asking you to baby-sit sometime." She picked up her fork and spitefully raised the volume of her banter, "By the way, what happened with the young Casanova at your office? Did he ask you out yet?"

"Keep your voice down, please." Juliet glanced sideways at Signora Matteo, busy bombarding Anna with pointers on housekeeping. "Well, if you must know," she whispered. "He asked me to go to a picnic with him this Sunday afternoon. Please don't tell Mamma. I don't want to get her in a tizzy. I won't even mention anything about him unless it gets serious between us. Why stir up the pot? I'll pretend to go out with the girls." Patricia shook her head in disapproval.

Meanwhile, Anna placated Signora Matteo with apathetic nods. At the first opportunity, she shifted toward Mack and grasped his arm. "Macbetto, **richiedo un favore**," she mumbled under her breath. "Please. It's only a small favor. I have a friend. She's new to this country and desperate for some male companionship. I promised to introduce her to a handsome **Americano** and you're the only eligible bachelor I know. A ride to the state park would be a nice first date. If you say yes, Iago might agree to chaperone. Otherwise, I'll spend another dreary Sunday alone while my husband cavorts about town."

Mack put down his fork and wiped his mouth with a napkin. "Sorry, already made plans to stay in and catch up on my reading." *If Anna's friend is desperate for a date, there must be something wrong with her.* He bit his bottom lip when his sister-in-law let out a pathetic sigh. *But look at Anna. Poor girl, Iggy never takes her anywhere.* "Oh, okay, I'll go."

Anna patted Mack's hand. "*Grazie tanto*. You won't regret it."

As Mack grimaced, Anna twisted toward her husband. "Iago, **mio amore**," she whispered into his ear. "I've arranged for your brother to meet my new friend Teresa. He's begged for us to come along on a ride next Sunday afternoon. You know how shy he is. He'll need you to keep the conversation flowing. Won't you agree to go? If you do, I promise you won't be disappointed in the bedroom tonight."

Iggy laughed behind his hand. "Mack has a date? What kind of broad would agree to go out with an epileptic? She must be ugly as sin. If nothin' else, it oughta be good for a laugh. Why not? *Sì, sarà un buon scherzo.* Sides, a little variety in the sack's long overdue. I've just the right thing in mind."

"*Grazie.* You'll be happy you agreed, Iago."

Iggy refilled Anna's goblet and shoved it into her hand. "*Beve,* drink it all up. Couple glasses of Chianti will work like magic to get you in the mood."

Anna smiled at Iggy, then turned away with a scowl and downed the liquid all in one gulp. *Sì, I can use some magic . . . magia nera . . . black magic to change Iago into someone più simpatico. Hmm, someone nicer, like the handsome postman.* Her facial expression softening, she lowered her head and licked her lips, nonchalantly running a hand along her cleavage. *Next time he delivers the mail, I'll stoop low enough to give him a generous view. Who knows? May lead to something. Iago's game of infidelity wouldn't bother me in the least if I had another man to satisfy me.*

When Signora Matteo and Juliet left the room to retrieve another course from the kitchen, Iggy angled his chin toward Patricia. "Well, Sis, one of you gals has to be the first to spit out a baby. Thank God it's you and not Anna. I don't think I wanna deal with a pukin' wife and smelly diapers just yet."

Anna fingered her waistline. "Why a woman would want to ruin her figure is beyond me." Taking her marital frustrations out on her pregnant sister-in-law, she looked coldly at Patricia and flipped up a hand. "*Però* . . . if she didn't have a figure to ruin, I guess it wouldn't matter."

Unprepared for the icy words that struck with Titanic audacity, Patricia's jaw sunk towards the floor. Recovering from the shock, she exclaimed, "What nerve!"

Although Iggy enjoyed ribbing Patricia with his negative view of pregnancy and impending parenthood, Anna's comments caused him to wonder why his wife still hadn't conceived. *We've been married for over a year. God knows I've screwed her enough times.* Never doubting his own power of procreation, he questioned Anna's. *Is there somthin' wrong with her?* He never imagined that she'd feign severe menstrual cramps during her most fertile times of the month in order to practice the rhythm method of birth control. Despite its high failure rate for most Catholics who used this technique, Anna had been successful so far. Annoyed at the prospect of someone else's child underfoot, Iggy wrinkled his nose in distaste. "Kids, they're nothin' but a pain in the ass!"

While Patricia brushed off Iggy with a disgusted wave of her hand, Jake snarled at him through gritted teeth, "Tanks for puttin' such a positive light on it."

Mack jerked his thumb toward Iggy. "Leave it to him to be pessimistic."

"Can't any of you take a little humor?" Iggy held up both palms and lifted his shoulders. "What'm I supposed to do? Tell him how wonderful it'll be around here with a screamin' brat?"

Mack tipped his wine glass toward Jake. "I'm sure you'll make a great father."

Jake shrugged his shoulders. "Hope so."

When Frank and Geneva walked back into the room and approached the table, Frank coughed into his hand. "Jake, we want to congratulate you and Patricia. Your baby will be a welcome addition to our family."

Still red-eyed, Geneva stood mute until Frank nudged her. "Yes, can't wait to cuddle your baby." They both sat down.

The corners of Patricia's lips angled up in a haughty grin as Jake replied, "Tanks. Dem words mean a lot ta Patricia."

Iggy threw up a hand. "What a bunch of sentimental crap."

A few minutes later, Signora Matteo and Juliet returned with platters of stuffed eggplant and garlic zucchini. As everyone else delved into their meals, Iggy caught Jake's undivided attention. "You might need a few extra bucks now that Patricia's got a bun in her oven," he murmured behind a hand. "See me after dinner and I'll let you in on a good deal." Iggy emphasized the value of his proposal with in a sharp wink.

Chapter Eleven

"But, Papà," Teresa pleaded on Thursday evening as Antonio lounged on the sofa a few feet away, "it will only be for a few hours. I've told you that a respectable couple will chaperon us."

Teresa shifted from foot to foot. *Five days in a row I've tried to convince this stubborn man. What else will it take? Will it make any difference if I mention their family's business? Beg on my knees or kiss Papà's feet? Only two more days before I run into Anna again.* "**Sono sposati**. They've been married for over a year."

Signore Camara stood with arms folded tight across his chest. "The answer is still no. I forbid you to mix with strangers." He stomped his foot. "***No! Assolutamente, no! Basta discorso.***"

"***Perché no?*** Is it because you think I'll neglect the housework?"

A flush rose up Signore Camara's neck. "That has nothing to do with it."

"Don't you want me to marry someday?"

"Well, someday of course, but you're young. When the time's right, I'll find the perfect man for you," Signore Camara vowed. "It's my duty to protect you. If I don't, who will?"

"I will, Papà." Antonio stood up. "I'll go with them and ward off any trouble."

Signore Camara snarled at his son. However, with no excuses left to thwart the encounter, he gave in with an emphatic lift of his index finger. "***Va bene,*** in that case, I'll allow it." He turned his back toward his children and blinked his eyes with a nervous twitch. "We'll see how this ***mascalzone*** behaves." Signore Camara spun around and poked a finger against Antonio's breastbone. "Stay between them at all times," he ordered through gritted teeth. "If this rascal says or does anything improper, use whatever force is necessary to dismantle his face. "***Capisci?***"

"Of course, Papà, I understand . . . whatever you say." Antonio revolved full circle to face Teresa and lifted his brow to boast his successful intervention.

"I'll keep my distance from him, Papà. ***Prometto,***" Teresa promised. *I can't believe it. The grouch actually agreed!* On the way to the stairs, she nodded acknowledgement at Antonio. "The old fool," she whispered. "He thinks the world revolves around him."

While Teresa raced up the steps, Signore Camara raised his palm up and twisted his wrist in frustrated dismissal and then glared at Antonio. "Son, your sister's honor is in your hands. Do not fail me!"

"Absolutely not, Papà." Antonio backed away from his father.

Signore Camara slunk up to the front window and stared out with his face crumpled in a grimace. After a few minutes, he grumbled to himself as he rotated on his heels. "If she finds a husband, who will . . . ?" and flinched when he bumped into Antonio who had moved up on him. This time the flush rose up into his face. "What're you looking at?" He pushed his son out of his way and headed for the kitchen.

Antonio followed behind him. "Papà, have I told you of the girl I've run into at Tommaso's house?" Although Signore Camara shook his head without bothering to face him, his son persisted, "Papà, listen to me. The first time I met Mina, she mentioned that her father owns the grocery store, the one five blocks from here. She claimed he plans to gift the store as a wedding present to her and the man she marries."

"So? Good for her." Signore Camara entered the kitchen with Antonio at his heels.

"The last time I saw her, she told me her father was looking for a storefront manager. When I showed some interest, she invited me to meet him the very next day. Signore DiSalva made me an offer, one that's hard to refuse."

Signore Camara halted in his tracks and confronted Antonio again. "Is that so? ***Dimmi di questa proposta***. What did he offer you?"

"Well, Signore DiSalva wants me to run the day-to-day operations of the storefront with his daughter's help while he tends to the butchering. He offered double my current salary." Antonio approached his father and placed his hand on Signore Camara's shoulder. "What do you think, Papà? Shall I accept the position? Do you think Tommaso and Paulo'll be offended?"

"Your brothers got along fine without you before you came to America. I, that is, *you* can use the extra money, what with the cost of living in this expensive country. ***Sì, accetta l'offerta***. Don't be an idiot. Accept the job with a kiss on each of Signore DiSalva's cheeks." Signore Camara banged his right fist into his left palm. "You can tell your brothers that I approve."

Antonio swiped his forehead with the back of his arm. "There's only one snag," he sighed. "His terms of employment."

"What terms?" Signore asked offhandedly.

"Well, if I understood correctly, he expects me to date his daughter."

Signore Camara pulled in his chin. "You call that a snag? I call it opportunity!"

Antonio picked up an apple from the basket on the kitchen table and juggled it between his hands. "Well, you see, she's not that pretty. As a matter of fact, Mina's quite homely. The idea of dating her doesn't thrill me."

"There must be something good about her," Signore Camara prodded.

"Mina . . . hmm. Let me think." Antonio muttered more to himself than to his father as he took a bite of the apple, "She's pleasant enough I guess." He paused to chew. "Healthy. Has good teeth and a nice body . . . big breasts." He swallowed. "She's an American citizen with a high school education. Offered to teach me English and interpret until I learn." He burrowed deeper into the apple.

"Sounds like a decent girl to me," Signore Camara encouraged. "Besides, how can you refuse the possibility of owning a store at such a young age?"

With his cheeks bulging, Antonio mulled over the idea as he tilted his head from side to side. "Perhaps you're right," he garbled. "But her looks . . ."

"Ha! Don't tell me you consider **bellezza** important?" Signore Camara mocked. He grabbed a banana from the basket and turned to exit the room. "Beauty, it doesn't last. Believe me, I know."

His mouth half full, Antonio spoke to his father's retreating figure, "I hear you, Papà, but I don't think I can wake up to that face every morning."

Signore Camara brushed off his son's concerns with a twist of his wrist. "You'd get used to it."

Choking at the thought, Antonio spit out what was left in his mouth and wiped his lips on the back of his hand. "I can always quit," he mumbled into his wrist. "Can't I?"

* * *

Meanwhile, alone in her room, Teresa twirled around. *Un Americano . . . finalmente!*

What do I wear? Teresa leafed through the dresser drawers. *What kind of clothes will the Americano like? A neckline cut low like Anna's?* She looked down at her small breasts and wrinkled her nose. *No, I have no cleavage. Besides, I want to look respectable, don't I?*

She pulled out a huge pinstriped dress from the dresser. *I'll take it apart. Use the material and redesign it into something stylish. Hope Virginia will let me use her sewing machine again. Three days left. I have to hurry.*

As she busied herself with the task of undoing the seams, Teresa's mind wandered. *Wonder what Anna's brother-in-law looks like.* She pictured the young man behind the register of Matteo's Bakery. *Will he be as good-looking or as tall?* Teresa shook her head. *What difference does it make? Money can make up for anything, can't it?*

Chapter Twelve

The next Sunday after mass, Geneva perched at the edge of a leather ottoman and beamed at Frank who fingered the ivory of the baby grand, swaying his shoulders in sync with Beethoven's Symphony No. 5. As the melody filled the parlor and traveled throughout the rest of the house, Signora Matteo entered the room, dishtowel in hand, and parked herself in an armchair.

Her two daughters traipsed in behind her and leaned against the far wall. "Tell me why Papà never bothered to set up piano lessons for us," Juliet whined sarcastically out of the side of her mouth.

"For the same reason he never gave us a share of the bakery," Patricia grumbled under her breath. "We're girls."

"He always favored the boys." Juliet folded her arms and sulked. "So unfair."

"Who said life was fair?" Patricia extended a hand toward Frank. "Take him for example. All that talent."

"Yes, what a waste," Juliet agreed.

Frank had rejected the Juilliard scholarship Geneva's father had arranged for him when he returned maimed from the war. Instead, Frank had postponed the pursuit of his musical aspirations to comply with his ailing father's request that he supervise the bakery. It was supposed to be a temporary position until Romi returned from the battlefront, for Romi was the son Signore Matteo had groomed for eventual management of the business.

"To think, Frank could've been a concert pianist by now," Juliet lamented.

Again, Patricia presented the reality of the situation, "Come on, what was Frank supposed to do? Somebody had to take over the bakery."

Though many women assumed traditionally masculine roles during the war, Signore Matteo had never wanted his wife or daughters to involve themselves in his business which employed a slew of sweaty old men. Adamant that a woman's place was in the home, he refused to give them permission to enter the bakery, except on escorted tours. As he saw it, Frank was the only family member available to take over supervision of the bakery after he fell ill with a severe heart condition. Both Romi and Iggy were still fighting overseas and Mack was way too young at the time. So, from his sickbed, Signore Matteo had regrettably asked Frank to delay his plans to attend Julliard.

Signore Matteo prepared for his imminent demise by willing the house on Steward Street to his wife and leaving an equal share of the bakery on Whitman St. to each of his sons, with the stipulation that a portion of the profits be used to maintain their mother's household. He assumed that both his daughters would eventually marry and be supported by their husbands. Therefore, he did not provide for them in the will. He also specified that sufficient money be set aside for Mack to finish college. He didn't believe his epileptic son capable of physical labor and an accountant in the family would ultimately come in handy.

Without putting it in writing, Signore Matteo had anticipated that both Iggy and Mack would eventually contribute their proprietary efforts to the business because, in the long run, it would be to their benefit. He mistakenly assumed that the severity of war would mature and sober Iggy into a man ready to face the drudgery of hard work.

An optimistic man, Signore Matteo never foresaw the friction that the strategy of his will would create between his surviving sons. Nor did he expect his daughters to resent being excluded from his limited fortune.

Feeling obliged, Frank complied with his ailing father's wishes and became temporary manager of the bakery. However, much to his and Geneva's chagrin, Frank was never able to hand over the keys to his brother Romi. For soon after his father passed away, Romi died in the bloody battle of Normandy. And when Iggy finally came home from Europe, it became obvious to Frank that his least favorite brother didn't possess the ability or integrity to run a profitable and legitimate business. Before long, Frank resigned himself to his fate and, thereafter, only staged intimate piano recitals as an enjoyable escape from the drudgery of everyday life.

"Poor, poor Frank," Juliet sighed. In a signal to her daughters to be quiet, Signora Matteo held a finger to her lips. Taking the reprimand lightly, Juliet murmured her next comment from behind a hand, "You have to give Geneva credit for loyalty." Even though her sister-in-law's dreams for Frank had evaporated, Geneva married him anyway.

Frank finished the symphony. While he bowed to the enthusiastic applause of his private audience, Iggy stomped into the parlor, clad in a bathrobe and slippers. When Frank raised his head, Iggy flicked his arm in the air. "Can't a guy get some peace and quiet around here? It's Sunday mornin' for Christ's sake, my only day to sleep in!" Iggy plopped down on the couch with his legs spread wide enough to reveal his lack of undergarments.

As Geneva, Patricia and Julia averted their eyes in unison, Frank tried to grab his brother by the throat, but their mother shoved between them and thwarted his attack. Frank stumbled backwards while Signora Matteo swatted Iggy with the dishtowel. "Iago, go put on *pantaloni!*"

Iggy stood up and swaggered toward the vestibule wearing a haughty expression. "What's the matter, Frank? Afraid your wife might see what a real man looks like?"

Her face wrinkled in distress, Geneva scurried up behind her husband and gripped his arm in an attempt to stop his lunge. "Don't.

He's not worth it, Frank. Just ignore him. Please!" His jaw clenched and his eyes locked on Iggy's back, Frank froze a moment then relaxed his shoulders, exhaling the fury from his nose.

As Iggy drew near the staircase, Mack descended the steps and noticed his brother's scowl. "Hey, Iggy, what's up?"

With brute force, Iggy shoved Mack against the wall and pounded his way up the staircase. "If you wake a tiger, he attacks!"

"Hey, I don't know what's bothering you, but don't take it out on me," Mack shouted at Iggy's back, then straightened his clothes and strode into the parlor. "Why's everyone look so angry? What happened in here?"

"Don't ask," Frank snarled with a tight jaw.

Signora Matteo approached Mack and squeezed his hand. "Macco, *vuoi qualcosa da mangiare?* You want eat? I cook for you, no?"

Mack winced. *Whenever she calls me Macco in front of the others, it makes me feel so immature.* Although Signora Matteo detested her adult children's use of nicknames, she reserved the right to use her affectionate pet name for her youngest son whom she still privately perceived as her sick little boy. To his mortification, she doted on him at every opportunity. "Not now, Mamma, I'm not hungry, but thanks anyway."

Patricia headed toward the kitchen. "Espresso anyone?"

"No, thanks." Geneva shook her head and, leaving by way of the vestibule, called over her shoulder, "Coming upstairs, Frank?"

"In a few minutes, Gen." Frank trudged back to his instrument and, taking his frustration out on the sheet music, crumpled the pages and stuffed them into the piano bench, slamming the lid closed.

Anxious to be on her way, Juliet approached the coat closet and, with a sideways glare, dared Patricia to reveal her true destination. "I'm going to Maria Conte's house . . . a cookout. Don't expect me home for supper. Okay, Mamma?"

"*Va bene*, for me you say '**Ciao**' to Signora Conte." Signora Matteo performed an about face and followed her eldest daughter. "Patrizia, espresso *disturba il bambino*. Tea more good for baby, no?"

Mack glanced over his shoulder for any sign of Iggy prior to addressing Frank, "Let's go for a ride. I need to tell you about a new glitch in the situation with the bookkeeper." He gestured toward the side door in the dining room.

"Yeah sure, I need to get outta here." Frank flung up his arms with exasperation. "What else's wrong now? Every time I turn around there's some other problem." He let out a forced breath. "I thought Geneva and I might have a peaceful Sunday for once. Fat chance with Iggy around." He followed Mack out the door, limped toward the LaSalle and jerked open the passenger door. Frank grabbed hold of the car's frame and hoisted himself into the LaSalle, the seat springs squeaking their protest.

Once Mack entered the jalopy and started it up, he grimaced at the gas gage. "Look at that, Frank. Less than a quarter tank. I filled it up two days ago and used the car one time since." He banged a clenched fist onto the steering wheel.

"Is Iggy takin' advantage of you?"

"In a big way," Mack fumed. "If he wasn't my brother, I'd . . ." When Frank slammed the car door shut, Mack flinched. "Take it easy, Frank. This wreck's on its last legs as it is."

"Sorry, Mack. Iggy's got me all riled up again. You won't believe what our disgustin' brother did in front of the girls." Although Frank knew Iggy would've gotten the better of him, he ranted anyway, "If Geneva hadn't stopped me, brother or not, I'd have smashed in his face."

"What'd he do this time?" Mack grilled.

"I don't wanna talk about it." Frank rubbed his bum leg.

Mack stepped on the gas pedal, the grind of the engine a low-pitched lament. "Iggy didn't even make one promised repair on the car."

"You didn't really expect *him* to fix it, did ja?" Frank questioned in disbelief.

"That was the deal we made. I'd put up the bulk of the money. He'd recondition the engine and hammer out the dents in the body."

Frank shook his head. "Mack, Iggy has no mechanical skill."

"What do you mean?" Mack snapped. "He told me he was assigned to the army's Vehicle Maintenance Division."

"That was the division all right but he was a cook, not a mechanic. Boy, did he dupe you." Frank smacked his lap and howled until tears rolled from his eyes.

Not amused in the least, Mack bit his lip and flared his nostrils. "Iggy always tests my patience to the limit."

"Iggy tries everyone's patience." Frank rolled down the window. "So, tell me. What's up with the bookkeeper? Did Harry drop any clues to his accomplice?"

"No, sorry to say." Mack steered the car forward, turned right at the end of the driveway onto Steward Street then glanced at Frank. "He called in sick on Wednesday and Thursday. Remember?"

Frank scratched his arm. "Yeah, what of it?"

"Well, since Harry didn't show up on Friday either, I decided to investigate." Mack stopped his narration to make a left turn at the first intersection.

"Investigate what?" Frank sat up straighter.

"His whereabouts. I dialed the number on his employment application. Wasn't I surprised when a lady answered and said no such person lived there? Frank, I said his name twice to make sure she heard me right. She still insisted she didn't know Harry. I checked on another form he filled out and, wouldn't you know it, Harry gave the same number there."

"It's possible he put down the wrong number once." Frank narrowed his eyes, "But twice?"

"Let me finish. I took a ride to the address on Harry's application. It turned out to be a liquor store with no apartment above it. I went inside and asked for him by name. The owner said he never heard of him. Now what do you make of that, Frank?"

"I think we've been hoodwinked." Frank gritted his teeth and pounded the seat on either side of him. "Time to confront Harry's accomplice."

Mack lifted his shoulders. "Who?"

"You know who," Frank squawked. "Iggy!"

"Without Harry to finger him, we've got no proof Iggy's in cahoots with him. Iggy will deny he's involved, Frank. He'll play innocent as he laughs behind our backs. Let's hope, when Harry comes in on Monday, we can get him to confess."

"That's *if* Harry comes in." Frank flipped up a hand. "Damn! I should've confronted him last week. Now, if he never comes back, we'll have to eat the loss and keep a close eye on Iggy. I'll change the lock on the office door. Nobody will have the key except the two of us. If Iggy complains, it's too damn bad. Now that you're an accountant, there's no need to hire another bookkeeper. Right?"

"No need at all." Mack tapped the steering wheel. "You never know, Frank, Harry just might show up on Monday."

"Sure . . . sure." Frank looked off into the distance. "If Iggy does one more thing today, I think I'll . . ." He bit his lip. "Wait a minute. Aren't you goin' out with Iggy this afternoon?"

Mack winced. "Yeah, thanks for the reminder. I tried hard to forget. We're supposed to take a ride to the state park with Anna and one of her friends." Mack's shoulders sagged as if the notion weighed them down. *Wish I didn't promise to go along.*

"I can't believe you agreed to a *blind* date, let alone one with Iggy involved."

"What was I supposed to do? Anna practically begged me," Mack lamented. "Do you think Iggy put her up to it?"

With a pat on Mack's arm, Frank offered a bit of sarcastic sympathy, "Good luck, brother, you'll need it."

"You can say that again," Mack groaned.

Frank grinned and repeated, "Good luck, brother, you'll need it." Chuckling, he added some sarcastic advice, "Watch out, Mack. Iggy might try to take off into the woods with your date." Within seconds his mood sobered. "I bet Anna never knew what she bargained for when she hitched a ride to America with that bastard."

Chapter Thirteen

Twenty minutes later, when Mack and Frank returned to the house via the side entry, Iggy slipped out the front vestibule and commandeered the LaSalle. He glanced down at the gas gage. *Just enough to get where I wanna go.* He sped through the neighborhood and, reaching an alley where a posted sign pointed the way to the *Italian-American Men's Club,* he screeched to a halt and backed into a space in front of a fire hydrant.

Exiting the car, Iggy encountered a stray dog, one with a matted collar of white fur in an otherwise tan coat. "Go pee someplace else, you scroungy mutt!" He kicked the mongrel with such force that the poor animal flew across the pavement and landed hard on his right side, his front leg twisted under him. The stray growled a feeble protest. "Arggg! Arggg!"

As the injured dog hobbled away, Iggy entered the alley and sauntered toward the facility's main entrance. Blazing down, the sun illuminated the narrow passage and heated his back. Halfway there he hesitated and tilted his head to the side. Feet shuffled behind him. He spun around and, eyes shielded from the glare, squinted at a silhouette. "Who goes there?"

As the shadow approached closer and transformed into the Hungarian bookkeeper, Iggy wrinkled his nose and expelled a disgusted grunt. Dressed in rumpled clothes which hung loose from his puny frame, Harry reeked of a combination of cigarettes, alcohol and perspiration.

Harry sneered up at Iggy. "That younger brother of yours' been breathin' down my neck. Mack's on to me, I tell you. He's been playin' dumb but, come to find out, he's a fuckin' college graduate. Why didn't you warn me?" He leaned in closer to Iggy. "If I had any clue, I woulda skipped out long before now. I ain't goin' back." He thrust out a palm. "Give me the grand you owe me, thirty percent of the take."

"You little punk!" Iggy jabbed Harry in the chest. "You don't deserve it, not one filthy penny." Iggy had deceived Frank regarding Harry's stellar references only because the Hungarian had assured him that he knew an undetectable way to shift money from the bakery's business account to Iggy's private bank account. "You swore my brothers would never figure it out." Iggy flexed his muscles and lifted his arms in an offensive posture. "Get outta here, you worthless piece of shit, before I beat the crap out of you."

Harry staggered backwards. "I may look like a pushover to you, but I swear you'll regret this. No one reneges on me! From now on, you better watch your back."

Iggy stepped forward, grabbed Harry by the collar with one hand and lifted him off his feet. "This is just a taste of what you'll swallow if I get wind your ugly mug's within a hundred miles of me or the bakery." He gritted his teeth and rammed his free fist into Harry's abdomen. When Iggy let go of his shirt, Harry crumbled to the ground.

With an arm clutching his stomach, Harry scrambled to his feet and dashed away. At the end of the alley, he peered over his shoulder. "Watch your back, Iggy . . . your back."

As Harry disappeared into the neighborhood, Iggy lifted his hand and twisted it in a dismissive gesture. *Ha, like he's any threat to me. Why'd I ever trust a twerp like him in the first place? Frank ever accuses me of bein' Harry's accomplice, I'll outright deny it, hand on the bible if need be. I'm a pretty good actor . . . Hollywood's loss. Sides, without Harry to spill the beans, he's got no shred of proof. That little runt won't dare show up again, not if he knows what's good for him.*

"Damn!" Iggy stomped down a foot in frustration. *Had plans to party with that money.* He pictured himself stepping out of a limousine followed by several beautiful women. *What the heck. I'll come up with another scheme. More ways than one to fatten my wallet with the bakery's lettuce.*

Ain't Frank lucky I'm part of the fuckin' family? Imagining the angry look on his brother's face when he found out about the diverted funds, Iggy smiled. *I love messin' with him.* He laughed his way down the alley. *Not my fault the devil parks his ass on my shoulder.* Stopping at the steps of the men's club, Iggy contemplated the benefit of blood ties. *Seems no matter what I do, my stupid family puts up with me. Humph! Guess blood is thicker than water.*

* * *

Four and a half beers later, Iggy leaned his elbow against the counter of the club's bar and gazed sullenly around the room, sulking over why his schemes usually failed in the end. Eventually, he caught the bartender's eye in the mirror and slurred, "Hey, Vince, I'm a smart guy, ain't I?"

Vince spun around. "If you say so, Ig." Rag in hand, he approached Iggy and wiped the counter around his glass.

Iggy picked up his beer. "I oughta' be rich by now, what with all the people I've screwed out of a few bucks over the years. But somehow the money melts in my hands." If he didn't squander it on rounds for his **paesani,** Iggy usually gambled it away at the track or shoved it down some hooker's bra when his wife refused to cooperate with his idea of a good time. Since Anna had stiffed him for some hush money, even his bankbook balance had dwindled. He thought he should invest what was left of the embezzled funds in something solid. *But what?* "What's a guy like me supposed to do?"

Vince shrugged. "I donno. Ever hear what they say about a fool and his money?"

Iggy stood up. "You callin' me a fool, Vince?"

Vince backed up. "Nah, Iggy, you're one of the smartest con men I know."

Iggy plopped back down on the barstool. "Glad you see it my way. Didn't wanna smash your ugly mug and get my hands all dirty." He sipped his beer. "You know, I'm not one to give up. I've already set the wheels in motion for my next stab at a fortune."

"Oh, is that so?"

Iggy swallowed a mouthful of beer. "You know what I mean, my new numbers gig."

"Right." Vince stifled a laugh. "That oughta make you stinkin' rich."

"It sure as hell better. I need out of that damn bread factory. The work sucks. Not that I plan to give up any of the profits mindja. Papà left us all an equal share of the business." Iggy stared Vince in the eye. "His Last Will and Testament didn't say nothin' about how much sweat I hafta pour into it, did it?"

"Why're you askin' me? I'm a bartender, not your lawyer."

"I've gotta recruit me a few more runners. That's what I need to do. I already drafted my stupid brother-in-law." Iggy looked down and noticed the time on his watch. "Damn. I'm supposed to pick up the wife in five minutes. The woman nagged me into a trip to the state park. I'll never hear the end of it if I don't show face."

Vince smirked. "Ain't that sweet?"

Iggy grimaced. "Maybe the chick she arranged for my little brother will be prettier than the wife. You know, Anna's not the best-lookin' broad in town."

"I didn't say that but, tell me again, why'd you marry her, Ig?"

"None of your damn business!" *If I wasn't such a horny soldier . . .* He cringed at the memory of the first time he met Anna's shotgun-toting father. *Almost shit myself when he barged in on us.*

Vince pointed to Iggy's wristwatch. "Better hurry, time to meet the wife."

Iggy downed the last of his beer and threw a couple of dollars on the counter before he staggered toward the door. "See ya later, Vince." He headed back to the LaSalle, started it up and sped down the road.

Halfway home, he slammed on the brake. *What am I rushin' for? Nobody's goin' anywhere without the car.* He parked the LaSalle, sprawled out in the back seat and took a sobering catnap.

Chapter Fourteen

At 1:20 p.m., Iggy reversed the LaSalle into the driveway and turned off the motor. Pushing the sheers aside, Anna peeked out the dining room window and grumbled, "*Finally!*" **Finalmente, Iago è qui**. *Late's better than never. If I don't complain, maybe he'll behave himself today.* Dressed in a tight shift, high-heeled sandals and a pastel sunhat that softened her angular features, Anna puckered in front of the mirror above the sideboard and re-applied some lipstick.

Mack clenched his fists. *Inconsiderate bastard! If not for the anxious look on Anna's face, I'd have bowed out of this blind date about twenty minutes ago.*

Once Iggy leaned on the horn, Anna picked up her purse and turned toward the door. Mack grabbed her hand and stopped her. "**Lo facciamo aspettare**. I refuse to rush. It's Iggy's turn to wait." Mack adjusted his tie and eyed his sister-in-law in the mirror. "You look nice today, Anna. That hat suits you." He hooked his thumbs into his vest pockets. "Did you remember to bring some bread for the ducks?" Anna held up her purse and reached for the doorknob, but Mack scooted in front of her and blocked her path. "Are you sure you turned off the lights upstairs? Why don't you go check?"

"**No, andiamo!**" Anna shrieked. She fretted that Teresa's father would change his mind and not allow his daughter to go with them. Then her plans for an escape from the usual boring Sunday afternoon might go up in smoke. "We're already late. We need to leave now."

Mack stood his ground and refused to budge. "No, Iggy needs a taste of his own medicine."

"Move out of my way!" she shouted. "My friend is waiting."

Unable to bear Anna's defiant stare for very long, Mack expelled a forced breath and opened the door for her. "Go ahead if you insist."

Anna rushed down the side porch steps and slipped into the front passenger seat of the car. "Iago, where were you? I was worried." *Worried that you wouldn't show up, you thoughtless oaf.* Iggy shrugged.

Mack counted to one hundred before he exited the house and ambled slowly to the jalopy's back door. In retaliation for his brother's delay tactics, Iggy shifted the gears into neutral and released the brake pedal as Mack reached for the door so that the car and door handle coasted forward out of Mack's reach.

Huffing in annoyance, Mack waited until the car came to a complete halt before he cautiously grabbed hold of the handle and opened the door. With a chuckle, Iggy again released the brake pedal the moment his brother stepped into the vehicle, causing Mack to clunk his head on the door frame. "Hey, knock it off!"

Iggy turned to his wife. "Did ja say somethin', Anna?"

Eyes narrowed, Mack fumed. *Look at him, so full of himself. I'll ignore him.* He folded his arms across his chest and, though he seethed inside, he bit his tongue and remained speechless while Iggy mutely picked at his nails. Anna glanced from brother to brother with an exasperated look on her face.

Under the pressure of Anna's frustration, Mack was first to break the silence, "Come on, Iggy. Let's go."

Iggy snickered, "What took you so long to get out here? It's not polite to make a guy wait." He started the engine and shifted gears, jerking the car forward. "Anna, you look decent today," he said in offhanded Italian. "What happened?" He gawked down at her cleavage.

Anna twisted her chin to the right with a dismissive snap then rotated toward Mack. "My friend's name is Teresa Camara. She came to this country a few months ago and lives with her father, a friendly old man." Knowing full well that Signore Camara was as cantankerous as they come, Anna suppressed a smile. *Hah, can't wait till Macbetto meets him.* Reluctant to play up her friend's pretty features, Anna decided to promote her personality instead. "Teresa's a nice girl . . . good sense of humor. But, like me, she hasn't learned the English language yet. That's not a problem, is it?"

"*È nessun problema.* No problem at all." *Nice . . . sense of humor? Hmm, does that mean she's ugly?* Mack envisioned a battleaxe with acne. *Oh well, I don't have to marry the girl.*

Iggy interjected in English, "Come on, Mack, be honest. You'll check out her *ass,* not her accent." He poked his wife's chest. "Maybe you'll get lucky and she'll have big knockers like Anna's." Though she didn't comprehend the English words, she imagined they were derogatory and quickly pushed his hand away.

Mack smacked Iggy's head. "Please! A little respect for your wife."

"Aw," Iggy protested. "She don't understand English."

* * *

While Iggy and his brother continued to argue in English, Anna ignored them and contemplated. *Macbetto is the least annoying in his famiglia.* Still, he's a Matteo and today he'll pay a small price for what I've had to endure in that stuffy household. ***Beh! Mi devo vendicare****.* Anna curled her lips in a wicked grin. *Revenge is sweet.*

This sense of vindication evoked a sinister glimmer in Anna's eyes. *Wasn't it mean not to tell Macbetto about Signore Camara's strictness? Or Antonio's offer to chaperon?* Though she stifled a giggle, the corners of her lips lifted higher. *Will he squirm under the old grump's inspection? Or clam up under her brother's watchful eye?* She swallowed a malicious laugh. *Hee-hee, can't wait to see the sick boy's reaction.*

Anna experienced no guilt whatsoever for misleading Mack, especially since she didn't think he would suffer for very long. *I'm sure Teresa's good looks will more than make up for it all.*

* * *

After a stop at the gas station, where Iggy conveniently fled to the rest room, leaving Mack to pay for the fuel, Iggy sped to Chambers Street. "***Ecco, e questa!***" Anna squealed. "Stop right here. This is her house." Iggy slammed on the brake in front of an unremarkable brick townhouse, the number "116" pasted on its mailbox.

Mack wrung his hands. *When I told my last date about my epilepsy, she refused to go out with me again. I ought to just give up on women.* He sat up straighter and reprimanded himself. *Enough! I made a resolution to face things like a man. Today's a good day to start.* "Anna, I'll go to the door and introduce myself if you don't mind."

"Go right ahead." Anna restrained a laugh. "Remember, her name is Teresa Camara."

Mack climbed the Camara's front stoop where he tapped on the door and waited. No one answered. After he looked over his shoulder at Anna who coerced him with a repeated flip of her hand, he knocked again somewhat harder.

The door cracked open and an older gentleman peered out. *Guess this is Teresa's father.* "**Buon giorno, Signore Camara. Mi chiamo Macbetto Matteo.**" Mack's lip twitched as he continued in Italian, "I'm here to take out your daughter." He gestured toward the LaSalle. "My sister-in-law and brother are waiting in the car." Signore Camara didn't bother to respond to Anna's friendly wave. "Sorry we're a bit late," Mack apologized." He paused to give Signore Camara a chance to answer, but the man remained mute. "We're going to take a ride to the state park." Mack shuffled his feet. "It's beautiful this time of year."

Closemouthed, Teresa' father yanked the door open wider and examined her suitor from head to toe, ignoring the extended hand he offered. After a few nerve-wracking seconds, Signore Camara stepped back to allow Mack just enough room to squeeze by and motioned for him to enter. "*Va bene, entra.*"

Mack stole into the small parlor where a much younger male sat on the sofa. *He looks familiar.*

Antonio rose from the couch to stand eye-to-eye with Mack and offered his hand. "*Ciao*, I'm Teresa's brother. *Mi chiamo* Antonio."

Mack gripped Antonio's hand and gave it a firm shake. *Anna didn't mention a brother. Hmm.* "Glad to meet you Antonio. *Mi chiamo* Macbetto Matteo. My friends call me Mack." The tension in Mack's shoulder's relaxed a bit.

"Teresa, *il giovanotto* is here!" Antonio shouted up the stairs. "Your date . . . he finally showed up."

Soft footsteps descended the stairs and, with each step downward, a bit more of Mack's blind date appeared, beginning with two sleek ankles followed by firm calves, a stylish pin-striped dress pinched close to a trim waistline, perky breasts and a slender neck surrounded by flowing hair. Finally, the floppy brim of her sun bonnet made its debut, unfortunately concealing her facial features. Although the body of this angel was heavenly, Mack held his breath, worried that her face would be disappointing in comparison.

Mack let out a gasp when she raised her head. *Oh, my God, it's her!* His heart pounded hard against his ribcage and a layer of perspiration formed on his lip. *Will she remember me?*

The instant Teresa's eyes connected with Mack's her mouth fell open and her face lit up in recognition. Overcome by his tender gaze, she offered him a coy smile.

Antonio spoke up, "Teresa, this is . . ."

"Macbetto Matteo," Mack finished.

Teresa approached Mack and held out her hand. "Nice to meet you, Macbetto."

I always hated my name but, from her lips, it sounds magnificent. Mack took her hand and squeezed it between his. "The pleasure's mine, Teresa Camara." A blush rose to her cheeks.

At Signore Camara's disgruntled cough, Mack let go of her hand. "***Scusami***, I didn't mean to be rude."

Antonio offered a break in the awkward silence that followed, "***Andiamo***, let's go. The others are waiting."

Mack glanced at Antonio, paused and then raised his brows in question at Teresa.

"***Mi dispiace***." Teresa twisted her hands together. "Sorry to say, Papa refused to let me go out with you until my brother agreed to chaperon. I hope it's not a problem."

Comprehension lit up in Mack's eyes. *Antonio . . . he was the guy with Teresa the first time I laid eyes on her.* His dream-girl was now a reality but so was her brother.

"Don't worry, Teresa. There's plenty of room in the car." Mack placed his right hand at the small of her back to guide her out the door.

His head trembling in agitation, Signore Camara barked at his son, "Antonio!"

Once Antonio stepped between Teresa and Mack, he led her outside while Mack turned to close the door and offered Signore Camara a nervous grin in farewell. Teresa's father narrowed his eyes and lifted a tight fist. "Keep your hands off my daughter! ***Capisci?***"

Mack nodded rigidly as he pulled the door shut. *Dirty trick Anna pulled on me. Friendly my ass! Wasn't prepared to deal with such an irritable old fart. Never expected her brother to come along either . . . like I'm so bad Teresa needs a third guardian angel.* As he walked down the front stoop, he tried to brush off Anna's deception. *I won't let it ruin my mood.* He was eager to spend time getting to know Teresa.

As the trio approached the LaSalle, Mack rushed ahead and opened the car door for Teresa. *Glad I waxed this baby. Look at her shine!* He ushered Teresa into the car, shut the door and scurried to the other side followed by Antonio.

Before Mack had a chance to slide in next to Teresa, Antonio shoved him aside and squeezed into the middle. He ducked his head, glanced toward the Camara house where Signore Camara stood guard at the window and acknowledged his father with a nod and a wink.

His face screwed up in frustration, Mack boosted himself in next to Antonio who was muttering something private into his sister's ear. *So this is the game plan.* Mack took the opportunity to lean forward and whisper sarcastically to Anna, "**Grazie**. Thanks for the warning." Anna smiled mischievously.

After having observed the parody of musical chairs in the rear view mirror, Iggy jibed in English, "I see you're on a *real* double date, Mack. Which one will you kiss goodnight?" He pumped the gas pedal several times and re-started the engine.

Antonio looked at Mack with a quizzical expression. "**Che ha detto?** I don't understand English very well. Please translate."

Mack glared at Iggy. "My brother wants to know if you're comfortable." Antonio nodded in response.

Over the groan of the engine, Mack made formal introductions, "**Antonio, questo è mio fratello** Iago **e sua moglie** Anna. Iago, this is Antonio and his sister Teresa."

Antonio smiled. "Anna and Iago, nice to meet you." Anna twisted toward Antonio and, fluttering her lashes at him, sat up straighter to accentuate her bustline. With his lips appreciatively pursed, Antonio nodded and Anna beamed at the implied compliment. Disrupting what he considered normal behavior between a man and a woman, Iggy leaned over the seat, acknowledged Antonio with a lift of his chin and offered Teresa his hand.

Teresa reciprocated with a demure smile. "**Iago, piacere di conoscerti.**"

Iggy licked his lips and grasped Teresa's hand tighter. "The *thrill's all* mine, **Signorina**!"

Anna smacked Iggy's arm. "Iago, behave yourself!" Determined not to let him spoil her chance at a good time, she forced a laugh. "Don't mind him Teresa. He won't bite."

Teresa grinned, "I should hope not."

Mack gave Iggy the evil eye and then proceeded in Italian, "Sorry if our car's uncomfortable. We just bought this jalopy and didn't get around to fixing it quite yet." *Hope the tape holds down the springs under Teresa's rear end.* "Antonio, be careful you don't step through that loose floorboard under your feet. The last person that fell through wound up flat as a **frittella**." The comic image of her brother leveled into a pancake prompted Teresa to giggle. However, Mack's attempt at humor escaped Antonio, for he was staring out the window, preoccupied with his own thoughts.

Navigating the LaSalle, Iggy ogled Teresa in the rear view mirror while she engaged in small talk with Anna. Trying to ignore his brother's audacity, Mack made an effort to chat with Antonio. "Did you land a job in Benton yet?"

"**Sì**," Antonio responded in the affirmative, providing no further details.

"Do you own a car?" Mack asked, challenged to keep up the conversation.

Antonio shook his head as he stared straight ahead. "**No**."

Mack tried again, "Is it hard for you to get around town without one?"

"**Sì**." Antonio nodded offhandedly.

"If you're ever strapped for transportation, I'd be happy to give you a lift," Mack suggested.

"It's not necessary, **grazie**." Antonio twisted his focus from window to window in an obvious attempt to determine where they were.

Mack folded his arms tight across his chest. *This is useless. I'll just shut up.*

Antonio tapped Iggy's shoulder. "**Qui. Lasciami qui**. Let me off at this intersection." After Iggy screeched the car to a halt, Antonio leaned forward. "Iago, pick me up at this corner in four hours. **Va bene?**"

Iggy saluted Antonio in the affirmative. "**No problema**. I like a man who knows exactly what he wants."

Teresa seized Antonio's hand. "What will Papa say?"

Antonio shook his head. "**Niente**. If you don't tell him, neither will I." He climbed over Teresa and exited the vehicle then waved a farewell as he started down the street with a confident swagger.

"I can go faster now that the car is a little lighter," Iggy quipped in English as he stepped on the gas pedal and made a sharp turn around the corner. The car tilted and Teresa knocked into Mack. "You can thank me later, brother."

Steadying Teresa, Mack's hand lingered on her shoulder a moment too long. Teresa glanced down at his fingers, then redirected her focus into his eyes and dazzled him with a smile. His stomach churning, Mack snatched his hand away and offered Teresa a tentative grin in return.

Anna interrupted their mute exchange, "Teresa, why don't you tell Macbetto and Iago about your trip from Italy to America?"

"**Mamma mia**, that awful crossing, **un viaggio dall'inferno!** Iago and Macbetto, I'll tell you my surprise when, instead of an ocean liner, my father booked the devil's own freighter. It was *sooo* bad . . ." Teresa took a deep breath for dramatic effect. "After two days, I threatened to jump overboard and swim to America rather than be tortured by the engines' awful racket." She crossed her hands over her chest and shook her head for emphasis. "Honestly, the ship's constant sway made me so sick. The same school of fish stalked the trail of my vomit, **una striscia lunga,** from one end of the ocean to the other." Teresa held up an index finger. "And, as if that wasn't bad enough, I swear they recruited the one-eyed captain from a pirate ship. If not guzzling whiskey on deck, he was sleeping it off in his quarters. The grungy deckhands were forced to steer the boat three quarters of the way across the Atlantic."

Mack snickered and Iggy laughed out loud.

"Go on." Feeling completely lighthearted for the first time since arriving in America, Anna bounced in her seat. "Tell them about Antonio's hassle with the sailors."

"Poor Antonio," Teresa cupped both of her palms, "his hands were full in his attempts to keep the pretty boys at bay." She leaned forward and turned to make eye contact with Mack. "At one point, he threatened an overconfident one with the loss of his manhood if he goosed him one more time."

Iggy glanced in the rearview mirror in time to witness Mack's face turning a shade of crimson and, thoroughly amused by his brother's embarrassment, chuckled so hard he almost lost control of the car. "Teresa, you do have a way with words." He patted Anna's hand and whispered, "I like your friend. She's cute." Anna looked warily at her husband and wondered just how cute he thought she was.

With casual camaraderie, Teresa grasped Mack's hand and giggled, "Macbetto, relax. **Scherzavo**. It was only a joke."

With an awkward twist of his mouth, Mack grinned back at her. "I knew that."

* * *

Arriving at the park a half-hour later, Iggy tugged Anna out of the car, "Come on. Let's take a walk."

"**Sì**." Anna held up her handbag. "I brought some bread to feed the fish and ducks. Let's go to the lake."

With his rear to the car, Iggy grabbed at his crotch and whispered to Anna, "No, Butch here needs some attention first." He fingered her cleavage. "You've got me all heated up." In reality, it was Teresa's fresh looks and personality that had excited him. "Once he settles down, then we can check out the scenery."

In a more positive frame of mind since her earlier flirtation with Antonio, Anna decided to interpret Iggy's vulgar request as a compliment and, therefore, willingly acquiesced. "**Va bene**, over there behind that thick clump of bushes." Husband and wife concealed themselves in the brush and left Teresa and Mack to fend for themselves.

Once appeased, Iggy buckled up and, with uncharacteristic affection, grasped Anna by the hand and guided her on a stroll through the park, following not far behind Mack and Teresa, pointing out woodland creatures he spotted here and there. "Check out them two squirrels up in that tree, Anna. I think they're doin' it right there on that branch." With his arm across her shoulder, he then led her down the path to the lake. "Maybe we can catch some ducks humpin' in the water."

Anna laughed. "Oh, Iago, you have a one-track mind."

Iggy spotted Teresa in the distance. "Who can help it with such a sexy broad nearby?" Anna smiled thinking Iggy meant her.

On the way to the lake, he gave her an occasional pat on the derriere, like he used to when they were touring Italy on their extended honeymoon. Determined to make the best of the day, Anna squeezed his arm in return. By the time they were halfway to the water's edge, she was fresh with new enthusiasm and hugged him. When she felt his manhood stiffen, she tried to reciprocate with a kiss.

Looking over his wife's shoulder at Teresa in the distance, Iggy resisted. "Later, Anna. I can wait till tonight. Come on, let's keep walkin'. There's so much to see." He dragged Anna to a spot where he could get a better view of his brother's date.

Surprised at his willingness to hold off but, nonetheless, interpreting it as a change for the better, Anna wondered if Iggy's considerate affection would last beyond the day's excursion. *Who knows? Time will tell.*

Meanwhile, on Mack and Teresa's private trek from the car to the park's center, Mack focused his undivided attention on Teresa and, shortly, her continued animation became contagious. He loosened his tie and told humorous stories of his college days and strange experiences with ornery customers at the bakery. "One lady insisted that she gave me a dollar instead of a nickel. After I let her look in the cash register, she accused me of black magic and bopped me over the head with a loaf of bread."

Teresa smacked Mack's arm, "**Non è vero.** You made up that story."

Mack held up his right hand and laughed, "No, Teresa. As God is my witness, I swear it's true."

Before long, Mack steered Teresa to the lake's edge, rolled up his pant legs and slipped out of his loafers and socks. "Come on, Teresa, let's wet our feet and cool off." When she sat on the ground, he cupped her ankles one at a time and helped her out of her sandals. "Have you been to the Jersey shore yet? There's nothing like the ocean under the moonlit sky on a summer's night." He took her by the hand and led her to the water's edge. "I can picture you on the beach . . . your bare toes in the sand . . . your hair blowing in the wind."

While Mack submerged himself ankle-deep in the cold water, Teresa stuck a toe in but pulled it out in a flash. "I'd love to see the ocean again as long as my feet stay on steady ground. I refuse to get seasick again." Teresa picked up her sandals and ran through the grass along the edge of the lake. Mack waded out of the water, grabbed his shoes and socks, and chased behind her. He caught up to her at the other side of the lake and dropped to the ground next to Teresa, his chest heaving with exhaustion.

Mack took Teresa's hands in his and gazed wistfully into her eyes. "Teresa? Teresa, I think I . . ."

"**Sì**, Macbetto," Teresa sighed.

"Teresa, I'd like it if . . . I mean if you'd like . . ." Mack hesitated.

At that moment, their chaperons approached and Anna tapped Teresa's shoulder. "Sorry, but it's time to go. If we don't leave soon, your brother will be left stranded on the corner."

Teresa inhaled a deep breath and answered Anna although her eyes never left Mack's, "Of course, **andiamo**." Teresa giggled. "God forbid Antonio waits too long on that sizzling sidewalk. He'd shrivel up like a piece of fried bacon." While Teresa buckled her sandals, Mack rolled down his pant legs, stuffed his socks into his pocket and slipped his bare feet into his loafers.

On the way back to the car, Mack stopped Teresa. "Would it be okay if I called on you again?"

Teresa looked down at the ground. "I think that might be nice." When Mack lifted her chin and searched her eyes for reassurance, she beamed. "**Sì**, I'd like to spend more time with you but," her smile faded, "first you'll need to get my father's approval."

Chapter Fifteen

After Iggy circled back to the same spot where he had dropped off Antonio, Teresa grasped Mack's hand and scrutinized the neighborhood. "I hope he shows up soon." At her brother's eventual appearance, she leaned out the window and confronted Antonio, "**Finalmente!** You . . . you had me worried."

"What's all the fuss? I'm barely a minute late." Antonio entered the LaSalle, squeezing in between Mack and Teresa. "For my father's benefit."

Mack nodded acquiescence as he scooted to the far side of the car. *I can play along.* Once they arrived in front of the Camara residence, he leaned forward. "May I escort you to the door, Teresa?"

Antonio squelched the idea with an upward jerk of his hand. "**No, non ti sforzare**. It'd be much better if you didn't. Let's not test my father's patience." He tapped Iggy's shoulder. "Thanks for the ride, Iago. **Arrivederci, tutti.**" While Antonio reached in front of Teresa and opened the car door, she glanced at Mack and shrugged an apology, then exited the car followed by her brother.

Anna twisted in her seat, "Teresa, I'll see you next Saturday at church." She batted her lashes one last time at Antonio. "**Ciao, bello.**"

Iggy waved a farewell. "It was fun today. Let's do this again sometime, Teresa. I'm sure Mack won't object. See you around town, Antonio."

As Antonio grabbed her elbow and led her to the front stoop, Teresa called out over her shoulder, "**Sì**, let's. **Arrivederci.**"

I hope she really means it. Mack stuck his head out the car's open window. "**Arrivederci**, Teresa! I'll be in touch." Before he pulled back into the jalopy, the droppings of a cardinal flying overhead landed in his hair.

The lucky omen went unnoticed by Mack for his attention was riveted on Teresa, but Iggy refused to pass up the opportunity to rub it in. "I knew my college-educated brother was full of crap." Laughing, he spewed a bit of sarcastic advice, "Oughta try Brylcreem, Mack. A little dab'll do ya. Work's hellava lot better than bird-shit!"

Teresa didn't respond to Mack's farewell or notice Iggy's snide remarks, for her mind focused elsewhere as Antonio opened the front door. "Antonio, do you think Papà will give me a hard time about my date with Macbetto?"

"**Sì, certamente**, it's in his nature." Antonio gestured for Teresa to enter first.

Teresa stepped over the threshold into the parlor. "But I had such a good time. If he got to know Macbetto, I think Papà would learn to like him and let me go out with him again. He's such a nice fellow." Teresa bit her lip as she removed her hat. "Do you think Papà stewed all day?"

Antonio trailed in behind her. "Depends on whether or not he found something to amuse himself."

"By the way, Antonio, where'd you go today? I'm sure you didn't come home."

"Home?" Antonio shook his head. "No, I'm not that stupid. I went to Mina's instead, a spur-of-the-moment English lesson. Better than listening to Papà moan all afternoon." On cue, the sounds of Signore Camara's groans and the creak of a metal bed frame leaked through the upstairs floorboards. Antonio pursed his lips. "Hmm, Papà napping? Unusual, don't you think?"

Teresa flinched at what sounded like the pound of her father's headboard against an upstairs wall. "A nightmare? Or maybe he's dreaming of new ways to spoil my social life."

"Huh . . . huh . . . huh." Their father's repeated grunts resounded like an underpowered engine trying to make it up a steep hill, that is, until a high-pitched voice floated down the stairs.

"*O, Arturo, dami di più*. Please give me more!"

Chugging away, Signora Camara picked up speed. "Huh-a-huh-a. Huh-a-huh-a. Huh! Huh!"

"*Sì..sì*," the female encouraged. "Don't stop now!"

With a puzzled expression, Teresa blurted, "What's going on?"

Antonio scoffed, "Come on, Teresa, guess."

"Oh, my God!" Teresa muffled a giggle then sputtered, "And he's worried about my virtue!"

Antonio chuckled. "Whatever made me think the old man didn't dabble anymore?"

"Antonio, please, you'll burst my appendix," Teresa tittered.

After Antonio threw himself down onto the sofa and chortled into a cushion, he lifted his face toward Teresa and predicted, "If he's still virile enough, there'll be little *bambini* crawling around before we know it."

Teresa gasped, "God forbid!" At that point, their father's bed banged into the wall even harder and his impassioned yowl resonated down the stairs followed by several loud pants. "If Papà keeps that up much longer, his lungs may collapse."

Antonio held up both hands in resistance. "Don't expect me to resuscitate him. Not with that moustache." Amused by his own humor, Antonio expelled a howl of laughter and pounded his foot against the hardwood floor so that, in no time at all, the moans halted. Antonio and Teresa stared expectantly at the ceiling. A hush permeated the house for an uncomfortable minute before muted voices filtered down from the second floor followed by the hesitant shuffle of feet.

Upstairs, Signore Camara slipped into his trousers. The scowl on his face barely hinted at the exasperation he felt over his children spoiling another one of his trysts. The prior Friday night, he was forced to cancel a rendezvous to accommodate Antonio's change in social plans. Two weeks earlier, one of his precious sick days had been squandered. As luck would have it, Teresa came home that very day with menstrual cramps, forcing him to push his lover out the back door. With a precious bottle of wine and his efforts at verbal foreplay wasted that afternoon, he'd been so upset that, in the heat of his anger, he almost regretted welcoming his two youngest children to his household.

While his full-figured lover scrambled for her clothes, Signore Camara approached the banister. Leaning over it, he bellowed down to the first floor, "Teresa . . . Antonio, why are you home so soon?"

"Papà, it's been over four hours," Antonio hollered up the staircase. "How long did you expect us to be gone?"

Signore Camara hemmed. "I lost track of time." He paused again then ordered, "Both of you, wait for me in the kitchen. I'll be down in a few minutes."

Giddy, Teresa led the way to the kitchen where a half-empty bottle of Marsala wine and two dirty goblets, one lipstick-stained, perched at the edge of the table. "I need a drink. How about you, Antonio?"

"Good idea," Antonio snickered. "A glass of wine ought to wipe this ridiculous picture of Papà out of mind."

A few minutes later, a disheveled Signore Camara tiptoed halfway down the stairs and leaned over the banister. Once he determined the coast in the parlor was clear, he signaled up the staircase where his woman waited, her hair tousled and blouse askew. After the brunette crept down the steps and slipped into her shoes, Signore Camara ushered her out the front door with a pat on her fanny and whispered, "**Cara mia**, I promise I'll find a way to lure them out for good so we can make love anytime we want, day or night. But, Concetta, you must be patient while I figure out the details."

Signore Camara shut the door and pondered his current frustrating situation, grounds for a dramatic change of attitude regarding Teresa's and Antonio's taking up residence in his house. He realized his strategy to increase his coffers had boomeranged. His children's pay envelopes contained much less than the room and board he had anticipated. Another thing that irritated him was the total lack of privacy. Not only did he have to share a bed with his son, and the bathroom with a daughter who left her scanty lingerie out to dry, he was reprimanded when he felt the need to belch or pass gas. Gone were the days when he could take pleasure in the healthy necessity of physical release.

In retrospect, Signora Camara realized that his life had been quite satisfactory before his children's arrival. Though Teresa was indeed a better homemaker, Concetta had provided some light housekeeping, an occasional meal and, most importantly, had been a willing and steady partner in his bedroom. Now, the woman was adamant that she would not return to his house until he could assure her total privacy. No, the little financial profit he enjoyed from Teresa's and Antonio's arrival was not worth the many inconveniences. But, now that they were here, he couldn't very well send them back.

Signore Camara tucked his undershirt into his pants and pulled his suspenders up over his shoulders before he entered the kitchen in his bare feet and unzipped trousers. When Signore Camara approached the kitchen table with his family jewels exposed to the air, Antonio promptly blocked Teresa's view so she wouldn't take notice and signaled his father to zip up. Embarrassed, Signore Camara turned his back to secure his fly and spun around red-faced. "My children, I've had some time to think today." Teresa pressed her lips tight and Antonio stifled a smirk.

Signore Camara held up an index finger. "Maybe I've been a little too stubborn on the subject of courtship. You, Teresa, seem ready to find a man to marry. I need to put my personal feelings aside and allow it to happen." He approached his daughter and placed a hand on her shoulder. "That young man, Macbetto, he looked respectable. Does he have a job? Can he support a family?"

"Oh yes, Papà. His family owns the **panetteria** on Whitman Street. He's even educated. In fact, he has a diploma from the **università**," Teresa boasted.

Impressed, Signore Camara nodded. "You don't say?" The notion that there might be some benefit to an affiliation with a prosperous family entered his mind. How he might profit he wasn't quite sure. However, if there was a way, he wouldn't hesitate to take advantage of it. "Let's invite him over next Sunday so I can get to know him better and decide if he's a suitable match for you." He switched his focus to Antonio who had also aligned himself with a well-to-do family. "And you, son, bring around the grocer's daughter."

"If you insist, Papà," Antonio yielded reluctantly.

"We can all get together over dinner." Signore Camara gestured palm-up toward his daughter. "Teresa can cook one of her scrumptious meals."

Shocked at the compliment, Teresa sucked in her breath. "Why, of course, Papà, whatever you think best."

Satisfied that he had taken the first step on his journey back to an independent and comfortable lifestyle, Signore Camara sauntered out of the kitchen.

When Teresa glanced wide-eyed at her brother, Antonio held up his wine glass in response. "Lucky timing for us, wouldn't you say? It gave Papà a reason to mellow out."

"Certainly did." Teresa tapped her glass lightly against Antonio's and downed the rest of her wine. "Well, we now know how Papà amuses himself while we're out."

Antonio puckered his lips and squinted at the ceiling. "I wonder how often he gets to rise to the occasion."

Teresa smacked his arm. "Antonio, really!"

Chapter Sixteen

At 5:45 a.m. the next morning, Iggy dragged himself toward the dining room as he tied the belt of his robe tighter. *Maybe that's what they mean when they say marriage is all about give and take.* He rubbed his eyes. *For a few lousy compliments yesterday, Anna let it all hang out last night. No hassle.* He pursed his lips and nodded. *Hmm, not such a bad deal.*

After he got a glimpse of Jake's rear end departing via the side door, Iggy followed the strong aroma of coffee into the kitchen. There he found Frank seated at the butcher-block table, stuffing his disgruntled face with a donut. The dark circles under Frank's eyes attested to his sleep deprivation.

Grabbing a mug from the cupboard, Iggy taunted, "You look awful, Frank. What did Geneva do, keep you up trying to make a baby?"

Frank clenched his fists and glared at Iggy's back. "No, for your information, I had to handle the nightshift another stinkin' time. God forbid you pitch in when the head baker calls in sick."

Iggy proceeded to the cast-iron stove where steam still drifted up from the coffee pot that Jake had left half-full. "Maybe we oughta call you Head Asshole instead of General Manager, huh, Frank?

Frank swallowed hard to keep his cool. "Iggy, I need to ask you somethin'."

"Later, I'm not even awake yet." Iggy picked up the coffee pot.

"No, now!"

Iggy didn't bother to face Frank but instead poured himself a full cup and took a slow sip before he answered, "Sure, why not? Monday mornin's always suck with Jake hasslin' me over every stupid thing. You might as well be a thorn in my side too." *Too early for this shit.*

"Listen here, smart mouth," Frank barked. "Didn't you swear that Harry came highly recommended?"

Cup in hand, Iggy spun around with an innocent look on his face. "He did by a friend of a friend of a friend."

"Some friends!" Too angry to consider the consequences, Frank jumped the gun. "That shifty asshole stole us blind from the start. He fixed the bakery's books and pocketed $3,000."

Iggy lifted his mug. "Didn't you check Harry's references, Frank? Ain't that what you're supposed to do?"

Frank cringed. By opening his mouth too soon, he realized he had spoiled what little chance there might have been of catching Harry red-handed. Seething at his own stupidity, Frank felt the veins bulge at his temples. Nonetheless, he continued to let off steam. "Damn crook! If I ever corner the bastard, I'll squeeze a confession out of him. Make him tell me if he had an accomplice . . . an inside partner . . . a shyster who signed him up for the sting. I'll force them both to give back every stinkin' penny."

"An inside man?" Not worried in the least, for he was sure Harry had skipped town by then and wouldn't be around to finger him, Iggy couldn't resist needling his brother. "Humph, can't imagine who that might be." Knowing full well that Frank would never turn him into the police, thus exposing their family to criminal scandal, he was sure he'd come out of the larceny unscathed. "Who do you suspect, Frank?"

"Never you mind," Frank growled. "It's confidential."

"Well then, if you can't trust me with your *top secret* information, I guess there's nothin' I can do." Iggy smacked his hands this way and that as if to disengage himself from the problem. "How will *you* cover the shortfall?"

Frank hung his head in defeat. "We'll have to swallow the loss." He sat up straighter and snarled, "But from now on, Mack's in charge of all the accountin'. He'll report directly to me. I ordered him to keep the upstairs office locked. *Capisci?*"

Incited by his brother's audacity, Iggy stomped over to Frank's chair and wielded his free arm in the air as he towered over his brother's head. "Yeah, I understand." He poked a finger into Frank's chest. "You think you're the lead in the show around here. Well, Mr. Top Banana, that's a lotta crap! Do we need to read Papa's will again, Frank? It's right there in the strongbox." Iggy jabbed Frank's shoulder. "And, aside from that, who gave you the right to tell Jake you plan to cut him a share of the business? I'd never agree to that and you damn well know it!"

A deep flush rising up his neck, Frank attempted to stand but Iggy held his brother down with a firm grip on his shoulders. Furious, Frank sneered up at him instead. "Who ran the bakery while you traipsed across Europe and Mack hit the books? Nobody else helped me call the shots after Papà died. My decisions kept the business goin' then and they will now!"

Iggy backed off. "Well excuse me for defendin' my country to the bitter end, not like some disabled cowards I know." Leaning forward again, he narrowed his eyes and spat into Frank's face, "If you haven't noticed, mister, I'm back in the picture. So, from now on, you'd better include me in all decisions, especially the ones affectin' my profits. You hear me?"

Frank gritted his teeth. "Yeah, I hear you."

Iggy downed a gulp of coffee and then waved his mug toward Frank. "And furthermore, Buster, I insist on a longer vacation. Two weeks is nowhere near enough time to make up for all my fuckin' efforts!" Cup in hand, Iggy stormed from the room.

Frank pounded the table and shouted after him. "Damn you, Iggy! One of these days, I'll wring your thick neck." He shoved the rest of the donut into his mouth before he exited the kitchen and hobbled out the side door, slamming it shut behind him.

* * *

At work that same day, Signore Camara asked around the tool factory to find out if anyone was familiar with Matteo's Bakery. Several coworkers indicated that they were loyal customers. One man, a foreman and friend of the Matteo family, was more than willing to sing the praises of its young owners. "Ever since my **paesano** Signore Matteo died, his sons have run the bakery with a competence that would've made their old man proud. In fact, they've even improved the business. The bread's crispier and the service is much friendlier nowadays. I see nothing but prosperity in store for the three Matteo boys."

"You don't say. I'll have to try their bread myself." The idea of adding another successful business to his family's résumé appealed to Signore Camara. His two eldest sons owned their grocery store outright. Antonio, if he played his cards right, was in a position to eventually take over another. Signore Camara decided that it might be wise to encourage a relationship between his daughter and the Matteo boy, a successful business owner. One never knew when such an affiliation might come in handy . . . free bread was the least he could expect.

He was about to ask more about the Matteos when the foreman was approached by an employee with a technical matter. "Excuse me. I'm a busy man. I can't waste anymore time on idle chatter." Disappointed at the brevity of their encounter, Signore Camara was determined to find out more about the family from some other source. Since his eldest son had connections in the business community, he thought that perhaps Tommaso was familiar with the Matteos. He intended to ask him first chance he got.

* * *

After working a couple hours of overtime, Signore Camara headed home, making a detour so that he might pass in front of Matteo's Bakery to get a firsthand look at the establishment. He approached its storefront, which at that late hour posted a "CLOSED" sign on its door, and glanced into the main window to focus on Mack Matteo. The younger man was in the process of emptying the register of the day's proceeds. Signore Camara's eyes opened wider when he caught sight of the large amount of money Mack wrapped for bank deposit. When Mack looked up and noticed there was someone at the window, Signore Camara slipped away, further convinced that Mack might make a fine son-in-law.

Chapter Seventeen

Teresa primped in front of the dresser mirror Saturday morning, singing an off-key version of *"O Sole Mio."* In order to avoid the auditory torture, a cardinal nesting close to Teresa's window, the same bird that had sullied Mack's hair the previous Sunday, abandoned her eggs, heedless of the possible impact on their incubation.

Finished with the first chorus, Teresa pondered Anna's willingness to stop by the bakery for a few minutes on their way home from church that morning. *I want to see Macbetto. It's been six whole days.* She checked her change-purse and was satisfied she had enough to purchase a loaf of bread.

Determined to improve her appearance, Teresa picked up a roll of toilet paper from the dresser, ripped off a generous amount and stuffed a portion down each cup of her bra, manipulating the fill until the lumps were smooth and pushed tight against the dress. *There, now I won't look too flat next to Anna.* She ran a hand down her hip and inspected the dowdy housedress she'd transformed into a classy shift. *Hmm, not bad if I say so myself.* "*Se Dio vuole* . . ." *Sì, if God wants, one of these days I'll use my design skills to earn a wad of money.*

While Teresa practiced different versions of a flirtatious smile in the mirror, she noted how the red of her lipstick accentuated the whiteness of her teeth and the Mediterranean tone of her skin. *The dentist . . . truly a wise investment. Maybe I'll pay him off by the time I'm a grandmother.*

Teresa then slipped into a pair of open-toed shoes, wrapped their straps around her ankles and buckled them tight. *The thrift store, what a God-send. Without it, who could afford accessories?* Having negotiated a small spending allowance with her father, she'd been surprised at how far she was able to stretch it at the secondhand shop. She picked up a scalloped hat from the dresser, placed it at the back of her head and draped its netting forward over the top half of her face. "*No c'è male.*" *No, not bad at all.*

After she gathered her purse and rosary beads, Teresa tiptoed down the staircase. *Don't want to wake Papà.* A stair squeaked. *If I do, the grump will growl at me.* She hurried down the rest of the way, but, before Teresa headed out the door, she approached the sideboard where a slender vase displayed a long-stemmed rose. Sniffing the aroma of the red blossom, she once again read the attached note with breathy ardor, "*Una cosa per ricordarme, Macbetto.*" Teresa sighed at the memory of finding it on the front porch. *Ah, my heart skipped a beat. How could Macbetto ever think I'd forget him?*

When Teresa stepped outside the door and turned to lock it, a baritone voice projected behind her, "*Buon giorno, Teresa. È possibile che t'accompango in chiesa?*"

Teresa spun around with a smile. "*Buon giorno, Macbetto. Sì,* I'd love your company on my way to church, but I thought you worked the storefront on Saturdays?"

"I took a break to come see you. By the way, did you find the rose I left on your porch?"

As Teresa bounced down the steps, the load in her bra shifted enough to expose a chunk of tissue. She clamped one hand to her chest and pointed the other toward a maple tree across the road. "Macbetto, look . . . a cardinal!"

"Where?" Mack rotated on his heels and scrutinized the tree.

While the search for the bird occupied Mack, Teresa grabbed hold of both clumps of toilet paper and shoved them into her purse, getting rid of the evidence. *Phew! Thank God he didn't notice.* "Oh, never mind. It flew away." Teresa grabbed Mack's hand. "*Il fiore è bellissimo.* The rose, it's absolutely lovely. Nice of you to think of me."

Mack stared into her eyes. "Teresa, I haven't stopped thinking of you since we were last together."

"Same here." Teresa fluttered her lashes.

Teresa grasped the arm Mack offered and, as they headed down Chambers Street toward the church, she glanced back at the house. *Glad I didn't wake up the grizzly.*

To break the silence, Mack struggled for something to say. "Your dress is *bello*, Teresa. You look lovely in it. It fits you perfectly."

"*Grazie.*" Teresa held out its skirt. "Can you believe I designed and sewed it myself?" *He doesn't need to know the fabric came from hand-me-downs.* "Someday I'll come up with my own line of women's fashion for retail sale. But I'll need to get a sewing machine first. I can't expect to use my sister-in-law's machine for business purposes, now can I?" Teresa pouted. "Too bad I won't be able to earn enough to buy one anytime soon."

Mack halted. "Why not?"

Teresa wrinkled her nose and urged him forward. "Ha, at the rate I sew? I don't make anywhere near enough money. That dungeon of a factory values speed instead of skill. Piecework, I hate it! It was meant for mindless idiots, not an artist like me. But, since I have to earn my keep, I'm forced to serve my sentence in that dreary prison." *Please spring me free, Macbetto!*

With an emphatic finger held up, Teresa chattered on, "One day I'll buy the best material available to sew original and stylish designs. So many ideas float around in my head. But for now . . ." She raised and lowered her shoulders.

"I really get a kick out of you, Teresa, the way you tell a story." He paused to consider the whole picture. "Beauty, good sense of humor and a creative mind to top it all off . . . what a fantastic combination." He wrapped an arm around her shoulder. "You're one of a kind, Teresa, like no other girl I've ever met. I'm impressed that you want to start your own business someday. With your design skills and determination, I've no doubt you'll succeed." Flattered, Teresa smiled up at him.

A half block later, Mack shared his own aspirations, "You know, I have plans for the future myself. Even though I'm obligated to work in the family business until I repay my college tuition, I intend to become a CPA." When Teresa looked at him with a puzzled expression, he explained, "That's a certified public accountant. If I pass the test, I can start my own accounting firm one of these days. I can't foresee myself working with my brothers for the long term. There're too many hands in the pot, if you know what I mean. Instead, they can be my first paying customers."

"*Veramente?* How ambitious, Macbetto. Ambition is like the tide; it pulls me toward a man." Teresa snuggled closer to Mack.

A few steps from the church, Mack stopped in his track and faced Teresa. "I'd like to, I mean, may I take you out on a date again? How does a ride to the beach this Sunday sound?"

Teresa pulled in her chin. "*Domani?*"

"Yes, tomorrow. I'll ask Iggy and Anna to join us again, even Antonio, anything to make it more acceptable to your father." When Teresa didn't respond, Mack spurted, "I'm sorry about the short notice. I meant to ask you earlier in the week, but since you don't own a phone . . ."

"Macbetto, it sounds like fun. But, as I told you last Saturday, you need to convince Papà first." Teresa cleared her throat. "Actually, my father suggested you come for dinner." She ignored Mack's skeptical expression. "Are you available tomorrow afternoon?"

"Are you sure your father wants *me* to visit tomorrow?" Mack ran a finger along his collar. "I can always come another time, Teresa. Really, I can accommodate whatever your father . . ."

"Relax, Macbetto. Papà's bark is stronger than his bite. I'm sure he'll mellow once he gets to know what a nice person you are." *God, forgive me if I lie.*

Mack hesitated before he agreed, "Well, okay, if you think it's a good idea. What time should I show up? I'll bring the wine. Red or white?"

Since she didn't know what she intended to prepare for dinner, Teresa ignored the reference to the type of wine. "Come at 2:00 p.m.? I'll cook an early supper."

Mack nodded. "Fine, 2:00 it is."

Teresa rewarded Mack with a smile. "I look forward to tomorrow, Macbetto."

Mack winked and patted his chest as he stopped in front of St. Christopher's. "***Il mio cuore batte per te***. I'll count my heartbeats until we're together again."

Teresa laughed as she made her way up the church steps. "I'm sure you will, Macbetto." She approached her new friend. "Hi, Anna."

Anna smiled, "***Ciao***, Teresa," and then called out to Mack, "***Pari contento. Sì***, you look like a happy, lovesick fool."

Red-faced but cheerful, Mack waved a goodbye, "***Arrivederci!***" Heading toward the bakery with a playful skip in his step, he belted the first verse of "***O Sole Mio***" in a baritone rendition that rivaled Enrico Caruso's:

> ♫***Che bella cosa na jurnata 'e sole,***
> ***N'aria serena doppo na tempesta!***
> ***Pe' ll'aria fresca pare gia' na festa***
> ***Che bella cosa na jurnata 'e sole.***♫

A block away from the church, he hesitated before starting the second chorus. *What have I gotten myself into? Teresa's father, how can I win over the old grouch?*

* * *

Later that afternoon, Signore Camara entered his sons' grocery store and approached his eldest, a younger and portlier version of himself. "Tommaso, **dimi.** What do you know of the Matteos, the family that owns the bakery on Whitman Street?"

"**Perché?** Why do you care about them?" Tommaso picked up a burlap sack.

"Well, your sister met one of the brothers." Signore Camara held up an index finger. "I thought I should find out if his family is respectable."

"As far as I know, they are." Tommaso tore open the burlap with his bare hands.

Signore Camara shifted his chin forward. "How much money do they have?"

Tommaso shrugged as he dumped red apples from the sack into a bin. "I guess they must be well off. They live in a huge house, the biggest one in the neighborhood."

"Really?" Signore Camara's face took on a devious expression. "This fellow might be a good catch for your sister. I'll see what I can do to make sure he doesn't get away."

"Papà, money doesn't always buy happiness. Let Teresa take her time and get to know the man before . . ."

Disgruntled, Signore Camara cut him off. "Time? Who has time?" He grabbed two of the apples and marched out of the store without offering to pay for them.

Chapter Eighteen

Later that Saturday night, on his way home from a lucrative poker session, Iggy strutted down Steward Street reeking of cheap whiskey and stale cigars. He patted his pocket and grinned with satisfaction. *Not a bad take.*

When sensual moans emanated from a Packard sedan parked under a streetlamp, Iggy stopped to peer into its opened window and snickered at the couple necking in the backseat. *Guess I'm not the only lucky schmuck tonight. No doubt he'll get into that hottie's panties before long.* He licked his lips as the bulge in his groin extended. *Wait till I get home, Anna won't know what hit her.*

When the brunette came up for air, Iggy retreated into the shadows, his crotch deflating at the sight of her. *Holy shit, it's Juliet!* He continued to scrutinize the situation from behind the lamppost as his sister's redheaded companion moved into the light. *With an Irishman for Christ's sake! What the hell's she doin' with the likes of him?*

"Hey, get over here." The redhead drew Juliet into his arms. "We're not finished."

Juliet resisted, "I can't, Devin. I've got to get home. It's already past eleven. I'll have to sneak back in as it is."

"Aw, come on, no fair. We can't stop now. Ya can't turn me on and off like a light switch, ya know." Devin nuzzled her neck. "Don't ya love me anymore?"

"You-you know I do but I-I can't," Juliet stammered as she shied away.

Devin refused to let go. "What are ya, a tease?"

"I said no, Devin," Juliet insisted and pushed him off.

Shoulders squared for battle, Iggy sprung forward and jerked open the rear door of the sedan. "Get outta the car, Juliet!"

"No!" Juliet protested without any hint of gratitude. "Leave us alone and mind your own business. I'll take care of myself."

"Like hell you will!" Iggy snatched Juliet from Devin's grip and tugged her out of the Packard. "GO ON HOME . . . NOW!" He then reached in and yanked Devin by the collar. "You fuckin' leprechaun, think you can mess with an Italian broad and get away with it?"

"Hey, whata' ya doin'?" Devin shouted as Iggy dragged him out of the car. "Who the hell are ya?"

Mortified, Juliet pounded Iggy's back and screeched, "Stop it! Stop it!" She stumbled to the concrete when Iggy pushed her away with his free hand.

Vicious as a pit bull, Iggy punched Devin between his green eyes, then jabbed a hook into his gut. "For messin' with my sister. I better not see your carrot top anywhere near her again. *Capisci?*" After Devin slumped down and fell to his knees, Iggy kicked him in the groin. "That'll teach you a lesson. Get your ass outta this neighborhood before I tear you limb from limb." With a smug demeanor, Iggy slapped his hands together, this way and that.

Juliet latched onto her brother's arm, "Iggy, you hurt him!"

When she tried to get around him, Iggy foiled her attempt. "Oh no, you don't! I'm takin' you home!" Hoisting her up, he slung her over his shoulder and schlepped her toward the Matteo residence a half block away.

Juliet kicked and screamed. "Let go of me, you brute! I love him!"

"Shut up. Whata' you know about love?" A sympathetic bystander, the stray dog Iggy had abused the previous Sunday, grabbed hold of Iggy's pant leg in defense of Juliet. Nearly loosing his grip on his sister, Iggy tried to shake off the white-collared dog, but the mongrel wouldn't let go until they reached the Matteo residence. Finally exhausted, the heroic mutt limped away growling, a shred of Iggy's cuff the only souvenir of his courage.

When Iggy dragged her into the house via the side door, Juliet implored, "Please, I beg you. Let me go back to him. Devin's hurt."

"So what, let him suffer." Blocking her escape, Iggy sneered, "He deserved worse for gropin' you like you're some cheap **puttana**. Stay clear of that Irish letch."

"I'm nobody's whore and Devin's no letch. We've been together for a whole month already. He said he loves me." She pounded her brother's chest. "You had no right to get involved! You ... you **rompipalle**, you've totally ruined my life."

Iggy grabbed her by the wrists. "Ballbuster? Whoa! Raunchy talk for an uppity chick like you, ain't it, Juliet? Sides, I did what any decent brother woulda done. Go find yourself an Italian asshole like Patricia did." When he let go of her, Juliet dashed toward the vestibule. Overtaking her, Iggy pushed her up the staircase. "Go to bed before you wake up one of the holy rollers. You don't want none of them findin' out what you were up to with that Irish scumbag, do you?"

Juliet bit her fist and slumped up the stairs, gulping deep breaths. When she got halfway to the top, she spun around. "You'll be sorry, Iggy! One of these days, when you least expect, I'll ..." At the top of the stairs, she broke down in tears and, as Iggy forewarned, smashed into one of the other women of the household, namely Patricia. "Move out of my way!" Juliet scurried off to her bedroom.

Having heard the heated dialogue between her brother and sister, Patricia stared wide-eyed at Juliet's back. Though she was annoyed at Iggy's disrespect for both her husband and her faith, she was more that shocked at Juliet's alleged indecent behavior. Making the sign of the cross, Patricia prayed silently for her sister's soul.

Chapter Nineteen

The next morning, Signora Matteo knocked on Juliet's door. "Giulietta, is time for church. **Sei pronta?**"

Juliet's sniffled behind her locked door. "No, Mamma, leave without me."

Signora Matteo jiggled the knob. "What wrong, Giulietta? You are sick?"

"No, I'm just not going today. Please leave me alone," Juliet whimpered.

Signora Matteo crept away whispering to herself, "***Povera ragazza***, why poor girl cry. She no talk to me no more. ***Madre di Dio, che posso fare?*** What a mother can do?" Her face creased with concern, she descended the stairs toward Patricia and Geneva who waited in the vestibule. "Giullietta, she no feel good today. We go." She walked out the door.

Glancing up the staircase, Patricia muttered to Geneva, "Last night on my way to the bathroom for the umpteenth time, I overheard Iggy and Juliet arguing over her boyfriend."

Geneva adjusted her straw hat. "I didn't know she had a new boyfriend."

"Juliet told me all about him, but," Patricia looked over her shoulder, "for obvious reasons, insisted on keeping it a secret from the rest of the family."

"What do you mean?" Geneva moved closer to Patricia. "Why all the secrecy?

"The fellow's Irish," Patricia explained. "When Iggy caught them together last night, he pounded the daylights out of the redhead. I tried to warn Juliet to stick to her own kind, but she wouldn't listen to me."

"An Irishman?" Geneva covered her mouth. "My, my."

"I'm sure he'll steer clear of Juliet from now on. Iggy made sure of that. Not that I agree with his tactics, mind you." In front of the vestibule mirror, Patricia draped a mantilla over her head. "By the way, Geneva, Jake surprised me with real estate papers. Can you believe it? He bought a house for us."

Geneva pulled in her chin. "What? How did he afford one? Did he get a G.I. loan? Frank refuses to apply for one. He doesn't trust the government."

Patricia reached into her purse and retrieved a tube of lipstick. "No, I suggested it but Jake squirreled enough away to buy a rundown house. Bought it for cash at a sheriff's sale." She puckered her lips and applied some color, fire-engine red. The shade did nothing for her face except accentuate an inflamed pimple, one that had spontaneously erupted that morning and now engulfed her chin. Hoping no one would notice it, she reeled out a tissue and dabbed at the festering pus before she faced Geneva. "He's going to renovate it for us. Should be as good as new by the time the baby's born."

Too shocked to swallow, Geneva sputtered, "That's impossible . . . what with the room and board your mother charges." Enough spittle sprayed through her lips to dampen Patricia's blazon smugness. "No way he could have saved that much so soon. Frank and I have been scrimping for months now and we're nowhere ready to buy a house, no matter how shoddy."

Indignant, Patricia wiped the moisture from her face. "You're just drooling with envy. Jake wouldn't lie to me." She turned away from her sister-in-law, smoldering as she mumbled under her breath, "If he did . . ."

Signora Matteo poked her head into the vestibule. "Patrizia . . . Geneva, ***andiamo!*** We go now. Is sin to be late ***per la messa.***"

* * *

From the third floor landing, Jake peered over the banister and, watching Patricia exit the house behind Geneva, assumed that Juliet and Signora Matteo had already left. When Mack and Frank finally made their way down to the first floor, he expelled a sigh of relief. Convinced that the coast was clear, that no eavesdropper was within earshot, he descended the staircase to the second story. Passing Juliet's bedroom, he approached Iggy's door and knocked firmly.

"Buzz off . . . we're sleepin'!" Iggy growled as his wife rolled over, but Jake pounded harder. "Who's there and whata' you want?"

"Iggy, I gotta talk ta ya while da girls are at church," Jake whined. "It's important!" Although what he wanted to discuss was highly confidential, he didn't worry about Anna since she understood very little, if any, English.

Meanwhile, distracted by the commotion in the hallway, Juliet wiped her eyes dry and got up from her bed. She approached her locked door and, stooping down, leaned an ear close to the keyhole. In that position, she clearly overheard the men's voices.

Iggy cracked open his door. "This better be good."

Jake cringed. "Listen, I gotta stop runnin' for ya. Patricia's suspicious." When Iggy rolled his eyes in disbelief, Jake continued, "Really, Patricia's badgerin' me about where I got da money. She'll take a conniption fit if she learns da troot. I can't work for ya no more."

"You that spineless you'd let a *woman* control you?" Iggy scoffed as he stepped out into the hallway in his bathrobe, closing the door behind him. He secured the sash of his robe tight around his waist. "No, sir! A deal's a deal. I own you till you pay back all you owe me."

The day the loan officer at the bank told Jake that the dilapidated house was insufficient collateral for a construction loan, Jake was devastated. Intending to live up to his idea of a responsible husband and father, he grew desperate. After exhausting all other possibilities,

Jake eventually approached Iggy for a loan. He was prepared to pay double the interest that the bank offered on a passbook. With that as incentive, he expected his brother-in-law would gladly provide the cash he needed for tools and materials.

But Iggy had been unwilling to lend out the money he had so stealthily embezzled for just a promissory note. No, in order to persuade Iggy, Jake was forced to provide additional incentive. The one enticement that appealed to Iggy was Jake's offer to act as a lackey, handling Iggy's less desirable duties at the bakery until the loan was repaid. But, in the end, what really cinched the deal was Jake's agreement to run collections for Iggy's numbers operation as well.

Regretting that he had indentured himself to his unscrupulous brother-in-law, Jake looked Iggy in the eye. "Whata' ya gonna do, take me ta court? As long as I make regular payments, ya ain't got a case. Ya can't sue a guy ta keep up sometin' dat's crooked in da first place."

Iggy flexed his biceps. "Better ways to force a guy to play ball."

Hoping to discourage Iggy from using brute force, Jake expanded his chest. "For yer information, I won more den one boxin' match in my time." He failed to mention that, out of the ten lightweight boxing competitions held aboard ship during his stint in the navy, he had lost eight, one in a knock-out.

In mock defense, Iggy held up his hands, palms forward. "Oh, me and Joe Louis is scared!" Then poking Jake in the chest, he lowered his voice several octaves, "Listen here, Mr. Boxin' Champion, if you don't do everythin' you promised, I'll let Patricia in on your dark, dirty secrets. Whata' you think of that, Buster?" He shoved his face closer to Jake's. "Huh?"

After Jake muttered something indecipherable under his breath, Iggy shoved him aside and stomped down the stairs, through the vestibule and into the parlor. "A man can't even sleep in on a goddam Sunday!"

Dreading the self-righteous fury Patricia would lash out on him if she found out about his entanglements with Iggy, Jake marched down the stairs and grumbled out the front door, "Da rotten bastard! Somebody oughta knock da shit out of dat stinkin' blackmailer."

Meanwhile, Mack sauntered out of the dining room. "Hey, Iggy, how're you doing on this bright and beautiful morning?"

"Cut the crap. We all know you're actin' like a happy asshole cause you think you're in love. Just remember a hot chick like Teresa's gonna have a lotta horny men after her ass. Don't be surprised if she picks some other dick over a sick boy like you." Iggy pushed Mack out of his way and tromped toward the kitchen.

Mack scowled at his brother's back. *Had every intention of being upfront with Teresa till Iggy opened his big fat mouth. But is he right?* He worried that his medical condition was too big a problem for Teresa to overlook. *Will she think I'm not worth the hassle?* He advanced a few steps and, deciding he didn't have to spoil his chances by mentioning the epilepsy right away, the tight muscles in his shoulders relaxed. *I'll tell her if and when it gets serious between us.*

Chapter Twenty

Since Iggy had once again confiscated the LaSalle out from under his brother's nose, Mack traipsed on foot toward the Camara residence at 1:45 p.m. that afternoon. Teresa had never answered him regarding the color of wine to bring, so he had decided to play it safe and offer two bottles. He carried the white under one arm and the red under the other. *Maybe I ought to skip the wine today. Doc Piccolo warned me.*

Upon increasing the dosage of his seizure medication, Mack's doctor had advised that he should refrain from alcohol, but failed to explain why. He didn't tell him that the medication had a tendency to heighten alcohol's intoxicating effect. Mack tripped on a crack in the sidewalk. *But I drank the toast to Patricia's pregnancy with no problem, didn't I?* He didn't want to seem ungracious if offered a drink, nor did he want to explain that he was on medication. *Teresa's father might ask questions.*

A half block from his destination on Chambers Street, Mack began to have qualms. *How can a beautiful girl like Teresa take an average nobody like me serious? Iggy's right, I'm a fool!* Although disturbed at the possibility, he continued on his trek. A few feet away from the Camara residence, he sighted a red cardinal, the one that had defecated on his head the previous week. Intrigued by the bird, Mack came to a complete halt.

The cardinal, attracted by the sun's reflection in Mack's penny loafer, landed by his feet and pecked at the coin. Surprised at the bird's boldness, Mack reconsidered his own apprehensions, and, in an effort to increase his personal confidence, addressed the cardinal with bravado, "I'm tall, clean-cut if not handsome, a partner in a successful business and well-educated to boot. What more could a girl ask for?" The bird whistled his encouragement then flew off. Invigorated, Mack climbed up the Camara's front stoop, and juggling the bottles into the crook of his left elbow, knocked on their door.

His attitude toward his daughter's suitor drastically changed, Signore Camara opened the door and greeted Mack with a welcoming smile, "***Benvenuto alla nostra casa***." With his chin lowered in surprise, Mack extended his right hand in greeting. Stronger than he appeared, Teresa's father grasped it tight and yanked him into the house and, without allowing Mack a chance to regain his balance, reached up and patted his shoulder so hard it almost knocked the bottles from his arm. "So glad you were able to come, Macbetto."

His composure recovered within seconds, Mack gingerly offered Signore Camara the two bottles. "***Grazie***. Kind of you to invite me."

"Come in. Make yourself at home." Signore Camara perused the wine labels and, nodding his apparent approval, carried the bottles to the dining table.

"***Ciao***, Macbetto," Antonio called from the couch where he lounged next to a rather prim young lady with features chiseled in stone and an ample bosom that pressed tight against her bodice.

When Mack approached the duo, Antonio stood to shake Mack's hand and offered an introduction, "***Quest'è la mia amica***, Mina DiSalva. My friend and I work together in her father's grocery store. Mina, this is Macbetto Matteo."

"Friend?" Mina griped as she confronted Teresa's brother. "I thought we were *more* than just friends." Antonio shrugged noncommittally.

Turning her back on Antonio, Mina acknowledged Mack with a strained smile. "Aren't you one of the Matteo brothers who own the bakery on Whitman Street? We stock their bread in my father's store."

What's up between these two? "That's right. I'm one of the partners," Mack confirmed. "What business does your father own, Mina?"

"Alfonso's Market on Elm Street." Mina's face remained taut.

Mack slipped one hand into his pocket. "Your father's one of our best customers." *I had to say something. Didn't I?*

Annoyed that Teresa's brother didn't take their relationship seriously, Mina narrowed her eyes at him. "Antonio's our new storefront manager *for now*. My father intends to promote him to general manager *if* and *when* he lives up to our expectations." She folded her arms tight. "Remember, Antonio?"

Antonio twisted his lips at the insinuation and Mack squirmed in discomfort. *Is that a bone Mina held out to Antonio? He can't be that desperate, can he?* Mack pulled a handkerchief from his pocket and wiped his forehead before he spun toward Signore Camara. "Humid today. Wouldn't surprise me if it rained."

Signore Camara responded in a chummy tone, "Better for my garden. The day the plants ripen, I'll have Teresa make us some pasta with fresh tomatoes and basil." After he kissed the gathered fingertips of his one hand, he cast them up and out with a flip of his wrist. "***Delizioso!*** She's become quite a cook, you know."

"I don't doubt it, Signore Camara." Mack shifted his weight from foot to foot. *What do I say next? Where's Teresa? Ah, here she comes.*

An apron tied around her waist, Teresa came out of the kitchen and directed a magnetic smile at Mack. "***Ciao***, Macbetto." She approached Mack and, with her back to her father, squeezed Mack's hand tenderly and whispered, "I'm so happy to see you."

Before Mack had a chance to answer, Signora Camara stepped between them and pinched Teresa's elbow. "Stop wasting time." He had his agenda and didn't want his daughter in the way to spoil his plans. "Macbetto must be starving. I know I am."

"Don't worry, Papà. Dinner'll be ready in a few minutes." Exasperated by her father's rudeness, she turned to Mina. "Come on. Keep me company while I finish up in the kitchen. The men can amuse themselves." Subsequent to a disgruntled glance at Antonio, Mina marched behind Teresa into the kitchen.

As Mack watched Teresa and Mina disappear from view, Signore Camara sauntered to the sideboard by the dining table and, returning with a tray, placed it on the coffee table. "Macbetto, how about a small aperitif?"

Mack nodded. "***Sì, certamente.***"

Once Teresa's father filled three shot glasses with dry vermouth, Antonio passed one to Mack and lifted another for himself. Signore Camara held up the third glass and toasted, "***Salute.***"

Mack reciprocated, "To your health, gentleman," then followed Antonio's lead and downed the vermouth. The moment Mack lowered his glass Signore Camara refilled it and handed it back to Mack. After Teresa's father signaled encouragement with a wave of his fingers, Mack swallowed the contents of the second glass all in one gulp. To Mack's chagrin, Signore Camara continued to replenish his glass each time he finished so that, in a matter of minutes, Mack guzzled five servings of vermouth. When Mack swayed on his feet, Antonio guided their glassy-eyed guest to the couch. As Mack plopped down with a thud, Antonio followed his father to the sideboard and whispered, "Papà, what're you trying to do to the fellow? Drown him?"

Signore Camara pushed Antonio out of his way and placed the tray down on the sideboard. "***Beve come un pesce.*** It's not my fault he drinks like a fish desperate for water."

Antonio shook his head as he followed his father back to the sitting area. While his son remained standing, Signore Camara plunked down on Mack's right and fired a litany of intimidation into the younger man's face, "What are your intentions in regards to my daughter? Hope you don't plan to take advantage of Teresa's innocence. I expect only serious suitors to court her. Are you prepared to offer my daughter permanent security?" Shocked by his father's audacity, Teresa's brother grabbed hold of his arm, but Signore stomped hard on Antonio's foot. The pain enough to distract him from Mack's dilemma, Antonio grabbed hold of his injured foot and hopped away on the other.

With eyes almost crossed, Mack attempted to focus on the older man's lips. *What'd he say?* Despite his failure to grasp the significance of Signore Camara's last question, Mack wobbled his head in agreement. "**Certamente, Signore**, certainly."

"**Bene!**" Signore Camara turned to Antonio with a smug expression. "A man who knows what he wants. He'll make a fine husband for Teresa. Let's celebrate." His son powerless to stop him, he hollered out, "Teresa, Teresa, **vieni qui. Subito!** Please join us right now!"

Teresa entered the parlor as she wiped her hands on her apron. "**Che vuoi**, Papà? Why all the commotion? What're you so excited about?"

As Mina trailed into the room behind Teresa, Signore Camara gestured toward Mack. "Teresa, Macbetto has asked for your hand in marriage and I accepted his offer." With jovial enthusiasm, he thumped Mack's shoulder as Mina performed an about-face and slunk back to the kitchen.

Teresa, on the other hand, remained glued to the spot and, dropping her jaw in shock, she glanced helplessly at Antonio who lifted his shoulders in sympathy. "I tried to stop him, but . . ."

Signore Camara pushed Antonio aside and shoved Teresa down next to Mack who, oblivious to the import of the announcement, grinned like a halfwit. Exuding the aroma of vermouth, Mack garbled a greeting, "Nice of you to visit me, Teresa. When'd you get here?" He wrapped his arm around her shoulder and leaned his weight against her.

Grimacing, Teresa nudged Mack with an elbow. "Are you all right, Macbetto? How much did you drink?" *I can't believe this!* Deeming Mack a sensible fellow, not one accustomed to rash decisions or alcoholic excess, she assumed her father had forced the proposal from Mack after plowing him with vermouth. *I'm so embarrassed.* As Teresa expelled a forced breath, Mack toppled forward and heaved the contents of his stomach onto the lap of her apron, the vomit splashing back against his face and shirt.

Teresa extended her arms toward her brother. "Antonio, please do something!"

Antonio ran to the kitchen where he found Mina sobbing into her hands. "What's the matter with you?"

Mina lifted her face, her makeup running down it in hideous streaks. "Your sister's engaged. What about us?"

Antonio tapped his forehead with the palm of his hand. "***Mannaggia!***" He reared away from Mina. "I can't talk now. Macbetto got sick and I need to help Teresa. I'll be back in a few minutes." He grabbed a dishtowel and bolted out of the kitchen.

"Don't bother. I'm leaving!" Mina shrieked after him. Exiting by means of the rear door, she made her way to the street via the side alley.

While Teresa cleaned up the mess, she squabbled with Antonio over how to deal with Mack's current predicament. In her current state of agitation, she mistakenly believed her brother was also culpable in her father's scheme, at least by not doing enough to stop him.

In the meantime, Signore Camara sashayed to the front window with the corners of his lips twitching upward. He braced a thumb under each of his suspenders and mumbled, "One down, one to go."

Chapter Twenty-One

Once Antonio escorted Mack back to the Matteo residence, he returned home to a shrill confrontation. Not brave enough to take her wrath out on her father, the true target of her anger, Teresa shouted at Antonio, "***Stupido***, how could you do this to me?"

"Who me? What did I do?" Antonio defended.

"It's what you didn't do." Teresa stomped down her foot. "Why didn't you stop ***nostro padre maligno . . .*** stop the evil man from tricking Macbetto? I wanted to impress him with my cooking skills. Instead you let Papà pour endless aperitifs down the poor boy's throat. How many, Antonio?" Teresa threw up her arms in frustration. "Oh, what does it matter? He ended up too drunk to notice whether I fed him caviar or cow manure and obviously too dazed to realize Papà conned him into an engagement." Teresa charged at Antonio and pounded his chest. "You let our father make a fool out of Macbetto and of me!"

Antonio grabbed her by the wrists and held her at bay. "Have mercy! I wasn't the one who forced the vermouth on him." Antonio looked down at his sore foot. "Besides, I have proof that I tried to stop Papà. My swollen foot must be black and blue by now."

"If Macbetto thinks that I was in on the plot, he'll never want to see me again!" Teresa countered with vehemence as she tried unsuccessfully to kick Antonio in the shin.

"How can you say that?" Antonio laughed, trying to lighten the mood by shedding a humorous light on the situation. "You'll be together on your wedding day, won't you?"

Teresa pushed herself free from Antonio's loosened grip and sulked up the steps. "There'll be no wedding now, or ever, thanks to you and Papà." She snubbed her father when she passed him in the upstairs hallway and charged into her room, slamming the door behind her.

Signore Camara descended halfway down the staircase and, with an upwardly extended thumb, gestured toward the top of the stairs. "Antonio, what's wrong with your sister? She looks as if the Germans invaded America. Teresa ought to be ecstatic, no?"

"Papà, please. Do you really think that was a serious proposal of marriage? Macbetto had no clue what you were asking him. You don't have the nerve to hold him to it, do you?"

"*Certamente!* Most definitely!" Signore Camara squawked as he banged his right fist into his left hand and lumbered his way to the bottom. "A proposal is a proposal. Your sister's at the ripe age for childbearing and, since the man is well-established with a business, Macbetto will make a good husband for her. I'll hold him to his promise!"

"But, what if Macbetto has a problem?" Antonio figured if he exaggerated a possible defect, his father might reconsider his ridiculous stand.

"*Che problema?*"

"*Con la bottiglia.*" In a pantomime of a drunk with a bottle, Antonio extended a thumb from his fist and lifted it to up to his mouth while he wobbled his head. "What if he has alcoholic tendencies? If you'd reconsider, it'll give us more time to find out."

Signore Camara held up his forefinger and, with an emphatic twist of his wrist, contradicted, "What are you talking about? He didn't drink *that* much."

"Papà, I had to drag him home. Don't you consider that *too* much?"

"He probably thought he'd insult me if he refused the vermouth I kept pouring for him," Signore Camara contended.

"Aha! So it was your plan to get him drunk and force a proposal from him." Antonio insisted.

Signore Camara shook his head from side to side. "No, no, not at all. I just *asked* for his intentions. No one *forced* him to offer Teresa his hand in marriage. Now that he's made the proposal, there *will* be a wedding. I'll see to it!" Signore Camara spun around and marched into the kitchen.

Antonio sighed as he shrugged in defeat.

* * *

Drenched in the throes of a nightmare, one in which a mustached midget stomped over Mack and buried him in a tub of grapes, Teresa sprung upright at 2:00 a.m. and swiped her forehead. "***Mamma mia!***" *What a weird dream.* She expelled a sigh of exasperation. *No worse than what happened here this very afternoon.*

Dwelling on her bad luck, Teresa wiped a tear from her cheek and prayed, "***Dio, aiutami.***" *Mamma, please ask God to help me.*

Teresa reconsidered the situation with restrained optimism. *Maybe there's some chance Macbetto will give me the benefit of the doubt. What do I say to him if I ever get to see him again?*

Chapter Twenty-Two

His clothes encrusted with the residue of his own vomit, Mack curled on top of his bedspread the next morning and grimaced at the clank of a car door someone slammed outside, just below his window. His eyes still closed, he pressed a palm tight against each one of his throbbing temples. *Ugh, feels like my head's about to explode. How much did I drink?* He jolted when the outline of an aperitif glass emerged on the screen of his heavy lids and winced as it multiplied. *At least two shots, maybe three, or was it four?* The dead weight of apprehension sunk in the pit of his stomach.

Mack pried open his eyes and looked at the clock. *I feel like crap. Wish I had more time to recuperate.* Straining, he pushed himself up into a sitting position and stripped off his shirt. *Wait a minute. It's Monday, my scheduled day off.* He flopped back down and expelled a lungful of air. *Thank God.*

Did I take my medication last night? Mack lifted his hips and shoved both hands down into his pants pockets, but his fingers came up empty. *Where's my vial?* Twisting this way and that, he hunted around the mattress for the container to no avail, then sat up and pivoted at the waist in an attempt to scrutinize the rest of the room.

Flinching at each of a series of persistent knocks at his door, Mack abandoned his search and croaked a response to the blasted jackhammer, "Who's there?"

"Macco!" Signora Matteo screeched, the din piercing Mack's ear canals, his eardrums pulsating at the volume. "***Vieni a mangiare.*** You want I cook some eggs."

Mack stood up on unsteady legs and squelched his impulse to gag. "No thanks, Mamma. I don't want any breakfast. I'm not hungry."

"**Dottore** Piccolo, he say no skip meals," Signora Matteo nagged.

"I'll be down in a little while." Mack struggled out of his pants and, retrieving his shirt, dumped them both into his hamper. He yanked off the bedspread, slipped under the sheet and quickly passed out.

A few hours later, Signora Matteo jiggled the doorknob, nudging Mack out of a daze. With shrill authority, she insisted he wake up before she left for the market, "Macco, **svegliati!** I need buy food. I go soon. **Prima che vado**, you want I make for you **un panino**, **salame con** provolone?"

"Don't bother, Mamma. I can fix my own salami sandwich." Signora Matteo released the doorknob with a huff. While the thump of her heavy footsteps tapered off down the hallway, Mack fluffed his pillow and leaned back against it. His fingers intertwined at the nape of his neck, he closed his eyes and sighed. *Yesterday . . . ugh! Barely can remember what happened after I drank the vermouth.*

Fading in and out of his thoughts, sketchy scenes of the previous day's visit confused him. In one, Signore Camara flashed a smile and elatedly smacked Mack's spine. *What'd I say to make him so happy?* Mack's lashes fluttered and the image of Teresa's horrified expression loomed vivid. Mack shuddered. *Oh no, did I convulse in front of her?* When the vision mutated into Antonio's distraught face, Mack gritted his teeth and cringed at the disturbing memory it elicited. *No, but I was downright drunk when her brother dragged me home and dumped me on the front porch.* "How humiliating."

His eyes sprung open and, shaking his head at his own stupidity, Mack pounded his fists into the mattress. "I'm such an idiot!" *Why didn't I turn down the refills after the first aperitif. I swear I'll never repeat that mistake again.* He bit his lip. *Will Teresa ever forgive me?* He bolted up in a panic. *Will she even want anything more to do with me?*

Suddenly, with an abrupt jerk of his chin, Mack raised his nose and sniffed the air. "What's that smell?" *Like vanilla . . . but not quite.* Clouded by his hangover, Mack didn't quite make the connection between the unexplained odor and what was about to happen to him. The doctor's forewarning never entered his mind.

A tremor in Mack's left leg shook the bed and, without even a chance for him to comprehend this second implication, his whole body began to shudder. His head twitched and each of his limbs jerked in different directions while his respiration assumed an irregular pattern. Within seconds, he lost both consciousness and control of his bladder and, when the convulsions of his grand mal seizure subsided, his body went limp against the mattress.

Mack wallowed in his own disarray for several hours until he sensed the dampness and frowned. *A seizure? How many pills did I skip? Well, at least I'm in my own bed, no one to gawk at me.* Getting up, Mack stripped the sheets and stumbled to the bathroom.

* * *

Much later that evening, revived and relaxing in his easy chair, Mack buried his nose in a civil war saga. Another historical buff, his best friend Joe, had recommended the novel to him the last time they'd attended a soccer match together. He flipped a page and looked up when a heavy stomp halted outside his door. The knob wobbled and Iggy's bark penetrated the locked obstruction, "Open the damn door!"

"What do you want?" Mack snapped as he jumped up and turned the key that vibrated with Iggy's enthusiasm.

"I wanna congratulate you!"

"For what, Iggy? What are you talking about?"

The door unlocked, Iggy swung it open, almost bowling Mack over. "I ran into Antonio on my way home and he told me what happened yesterday . . . the good news."

"What good news? You been drinking again?"

"Look who's talkin'. I saw you slip in, drunk as a skunk, yesterday afternoon." Iggy grinned from ear to ear.

Of all eyewitnesses, why Iggy? Mack shoulders drooped. "Never again."

"Better not or Teresa'll give you what for." Iggy poked Mack's chest. "Never dreamed a doll like her would hitch up with a pussy like you. So when're you two gonna tie the knot? If you make it worth my while, I'll be your best man." Iggy raised the pitch of his voice to a shrill whine, "Or will you ask her brother just to please your sweetheart?"

Mack's jaw went slack. *No way! I didn't. Or did I?*

Chapter Twenty-Three

Thursday after work, four days after Mack's fiasco at the Camara residence, Iggy perched on the edge of a barstool and puffed solemnly on a stogie. Wrenching the cigar from his mouth, he downed the rest of the ale in his mug then hoisted it toward the bartender. "Hey, Vince, fill'er up"

Vince slid a fresh mug of beer along the counter, "There you go, Ig," and studied Iggy's expression. "So what's wrong now?"

"What're you talkin' about?" Iggy asked in a defensive tone.

"You got that look in your eyes, like somethin's weighin' you down. What's it this time?"

Iggy rubbed his chin, the stubble of his beard so thick he hardly touched skin. "Obvious, huh?"

Vince shrugged and proceeded to wipe the counter. "In this business, readin' faces comes second nature. You know, us bartenders can pick up on things the average Joe misses."

Iggy curled his lips with skepticism. "So what're you, a psychic now?"

"Nah," Vince negated. "But it's like my bar's one of them there confessionals. Guys'll let all sorts of stuff slip out." He held up a hand in defense of his position. "Mindja, I never force it out of 'em. Just rolls off their ugly tongues between the beers and the shots."

"Must admit, when I leave here, I do feel kinda' better. Not sure whether it's the booze or your half-ass advice."

Reminiscent of an old English bulldog, Iggy jowls sagged pathetically. "Tell you the truth, Vince, this bad luck I been havin' in my numbers gig is eatin' at my guts right about now. Had a good run the whole month of July, but swallowed me some steep losses in the last two weeks. Sides that, my one runner's givin' me a hard time about drummin' up new customers. You'd think he'd help me out." His expression distorted into one of a rabid pit bull. "That thankless ass owes me big time!"

"Oh yeah?"

"Yeah! I lent him the last of my change to fix up that dump he bought for my sister."

"I can see why you might be ticked."

"You know, the odds oughta' be in the bookie's favor. But somehow more than one creep's had a lucky streak lately." Iggy ran a nervous hand through his hair. "If I keep holdin' off, I'll be tagged as a deadbeat for not payin' up. I need some cash . . . fast!"

"Can always ask your brother Frank for it?" Vince suggested.

Iggy snarled at the notion, "I'd rather cut off my balls."

"Well, if you're desperate, you can catch a loan from Bruno Catorno," Vince advocated. "Should be in any minute now."

Iggy pulled in his chin. "A loan shark, what're you nuts?"

"Hey, it's up to you." Vince held up a palm. "But what other choice do you have? If you admit to the guys another one of your schemes caved, there'll be hell to pay."

"Maybe you're right. Let me see. A bridge loan for . . ." Iggy looked up at the ceiling as if calculating how much to borrow and whispered to himself, "Nine hundred to cover my losses . . . another five for whatever comes up."

"Whoa! You owe the guys that much? What if your bad luck doesn't let up?"

"Mind your own business, Vince."

"Humph!" Vince replied indignantly and turned away. A few minutes later, the bartender gestured toward the tavern's entrance. "Hey, Iggy, here's Al Capone now."

Iggy twisted around and spied a stocky fellow entering the bar with two **protettori**. The man, dressed in a pin-striped suit with the jacket draped over his shoulders and a fedora tilted low on the forehead, walked to the back of the room and sat down at one of the tables. He removed his hat and handed it to the taller of his bodyguards. Accepting the hat, the muscular thug stood against the wall directly behind him, positioned so he could easily defend his boss at a moment's notice. His shorter partner stood guard at the entrance.

Vince rushed over with a beer and placed it in front of the loan shark, "Here you go, Bruno, something cold to cool you off." He scooted back behind the bar.

Iggy approached Bruno with a wide grin. "*Ciao, paesano. Come va?* How's business these days?" When Bruno sneered in response, Iggy pulled a pungent stogie from his breast pocket and held it under Bruno's nose, a brilliant incentive to gain the favor of a shady character. "Cigar? Rolled it myself."

Sniffing the stogie, Bruno snatched it from Iggy's hand. Then, in a raspy voice, the no-nonsense businessman demanded to know what Iggy wanted from him, "*Che vuoi da me?*"

"A small loan."

"How much you want?"

"Fourteen hundred to hold me over for a couple of weeks. You know I'm good for the money, what with the bakery and all." Iggy shuffled his feet nervously. "Can you help me out, Bruno?"

Bruno scanned Iggy up and down then nodded. "*Va bene.*" He reached into the inside pocket of his suit jacket and withdrew a large roll of cash. "You know my terms?"

After Iggy gave him two thumbs up, Bruno counted out fourteen $100 bills, handed them to Iggy and confirmed his policy, "Double back or I break your back. *Capisci?* One month tops."

"Gotcha, no problem." Iggy's stomach growled and beads of perspiration gathered on his forehead. "*Grazie*, Bruno." He saluted the loan shark then spun around and gestured at Vince as he bolted toward the door. "Put Bruno's beer on my tab."

Outside, Iggy squinted toward the street where a small figure lurked at the far end of the narrow alley but when Iggy stepped forward and called out, "Get over here, you little shit," the shadowy form dashed away. Iggy threw up a clenched fist and shouted out, "Damn sneak! Go ahead, pick my pocket. See what it gets you." *Seems to be a pint-sized punk hiding around every corner these days.* "Humph!" *Let one of them try to rip me off.* Iggy scrunched his face and gritted his teeth. *He'd be one sorry ass!*

Chapter Twenty-Four

Early Friday morning, five days after Signore Camara coerced him into an inebriated proposal, Mack paced back and forth under the shade of the largest maple tree on Chambers Street, directly across from the Camara residence. It had taken him that long to build up the nerve to approach Teresa with an apology. He glanced nervously at his watch. *Hope she didn't already leave for work.* Rubbing his sweaty hands on his slacks, he fretted that his request for forgiveness might be too late.

Mack squinted toward Teresa's house when its front door jiggled open then slipped behind the tree as Antonio exited the residence, followed by his father not even ten seconds later.

Signore Camara called out to his son, "**Aspetta!** Wait for me, Antonio. I'll walk with you."

Once their footsteps faded into the distance, Mack poked his head out from behind the tree and seesawed on his course of action. *Should I knock on the door? No, I'll wait.* A scruffy tan mutt, one he had never seen before, appeared out of nowhere, providing him with a reassuring nudge. Bending at the knees, he ruffled the matted white fur of the dog's collar. "Thanks, buddy. I need all the encouragement I can get." Whimpering acknowledgment, the dog licked Mack's hand and then limped toward a nearby fire hydrant where a red cardinal roosted. Reinforcing the canine's support of the insecure fellow with a nod and a tweet, the bird then flew away.

Alone again, but a little less antsy, Mack waited until the Camaras' front door rattled open once more. *Thank God, she's still here.* He dashed across the street and reached the stoop as Teresa pulled the key from the lock. Mack gulped a deep breath. "Teresa, I have to talk to you."

Teresa spun around and peered into his eyes. Detecting no sign of animosity, she scrambled down the stairs, clutched one of Mack's hands, and rushed into an apology, "**Mio padre, mi dispiace come** *si è comportato*. It was disgraceful how bad my father treated you. Please don't hold it against me."

Realizing Teresa had shifted the blame, Mack dropped his jaw in surprise. "What?"

"My father, he didn't handle himself very well under the . . . the . . ." Teresa grasped for the right word, "the circumstances."

Feeling obliged to assume responsibility for his own behavior, Mack grasped Teresa's other hand. "No, I'm the one who's at fault. I shouldn't have drunk so much vermouth. If I wasn't so eager to please your father, I wouldn't have behaved like such a fool. If you'll give me another chance, trust me, it won't ever happen again. I promise." He released his grip on Teresa's hands. "But your father must be furious with me. He probably thinks I have a lot of gall suggesting marriage when we hardly know each other. Will he forbid me to see you again?"

"Oh no, quite the contrary, I'm embarrassed to say. My father's thrilled." Teresa wrung her hands. "He insists we're officially engaged. Don't you realize Papà tricked you into that drunken proposal?"

"He tricked me?"

"Sì." Teresa hung her head in shame. "He planned the whole thing . . . without my knowledge of course. I'd never expect you to stick to the engagement, but my father's another matter. He's stubborn. He'll hold you to it."

Her shoulders drooping, Teresa acknowledged defeat, "I'll understand if you never want to see me again, Macbetto. Who could blame you? I'd be very disappointed," her voice quivered, "but I realize how awkward it would be for you."

The prospect of losing the love of his life devastated Mack, so much so that he was willing to take desperate measures. "Teresa, I'd rather die than never see you again." He seized her hands and squeezed them between his. "I'd do whatever your father wants just to be with you. I'd roll down Niagara Falls in a barrel if he insisted. Please give me another chance!" Afraid that, intimidated by his fervor, she might refuse him, Mack forced himself to calm down, to speak in a less frantic tone. "We can consider it a conditional engagement."

As Teresa sucked in her breath at the unexpected turn of events, Mack stared at the ground and continued, "If, at any time, you decide I'm not the man for you, I promise I'll walk away, no strings attached." He lifted his chin. "I'd be on cloud nine if you said 'yes' right this very instant. But take whatever time you need to think about it, Teresa."

Averting her eyes to the billowy sky beyond Mack's shoulder, Teresa contemplated what her deceased mother's advice would've been. *Would Mamma have approved of such an arrangement?*

Since she had no way of knowing, she weighed her options independently as she lowered her eyes and studied her feet. *Why let this* **Americano** *slip through my fingers? It's like a fantasy come true.* She tried to figure out if she had any true feelings for Mack. *My heart skips a beat whenever he looks into my eyes. Does this mean I love him? Is it too soon to know?* Teresa bit her lip. *He says I can always call it off if I decide he's not right for me. Would I be stupid to refuse his offer? Even if it doesn't work out in the end, what harm can it do?*

Teresa raised her head and gazed into Mack eyes. "Macbetto, I don't need anymore time to think. No, I've made up my mind."

As Teresa paused, Mack braced himself. *I can handle rejection like a man.*

"I am attracted to you, Macbetto, and I think you are a terrific man but . . ." Mack held his breath as Teresa finished. "I'll only accept your idea under one condition: that you ignore any pressure you feel from my father."

Did I hear right? Is it possible? Was that a 'yes'? Mack gasped. *Oh my God, I think it was!* He embraced Teresa and whispered into her ear, "You've made me the happiest man alive. I promise I'll do everything possible to make it work. You'll be glad you agreed."

"To a trial engagement, right?" Teresa prodded.

"Whatever we call it." Mack lowered his arms. "I believe I do love you, Teresa."

"And I think I have feelings for you too." When Mack closed his eyes and dove in for a kiss, Teresa backed up a step. "Macbetto, I have to go now."

"Sorry." Mack straightened up and pouted. "I wanted to seal our arrangement with a kiss."

"They'll be plenty of time for that soon enough," Teresa insisted. "If I don't hurry now, I'll be late for work."

"Oh, okay." Wiping the disappointment from his face, Mack switched gears. "My LaSalle's parked around the corner. I'll drive you if you want."

"I'd love it!" Teresa pressed her lips together as she speculated. *What will all those skeptical women at the factory think now? Will they eat their words when they see me show up with an* **Americano***?*

Mack led Teresa to the LaSalle. *Now's the time to bring up the issue of my medical condition, isn't it? No, not yet. Let the engagement sink in first. Besides, I need to come up with a simple way to tell her. No sense shocking or confusing her.*

Chapter Twenty-Five

As the light of a nearby streetlamp streamed through their bedroom window later that same Saturday night, Iggy enticed his wife with slow tantalizing strokes. "Anna, not bad, huh?"

After having finished off a bottle of wine, neither partner was in any distress, be it from lack of intoxicating affection or from sober aversion. They were both ripe for sexual adventure. It mattered not that they lacked the amorous feelings that predisposed a lover to gratify his mate.

Surprised but nevertheless delighted by the positive change in Iggy's bedside manner, Anna closed her eyes and groaned with unadulterated pleasure, "*Sì, sì.* Don't stop." *Can't believe this. He's actually trying to please me.* As Iggy transported her to a hotter and spicier dimension, a cool breeze blew through the screen and further tickled her nerve endings. "Aaaaah!"

Watching dispassionately as Anna sizzled under his experimental touch, Iggy speculated. *Hmm, what if I . . .* When Anna expelled another sensual moan in response, Iggy grinned. *Who knew I'd be this good at . . . what's this called . . . oh, yeah, foreplay. Hah, maybe I oughta write one of those how-to sex manuals for the poor schmucks who don't gotta clue how to getta chick hot and sweaty. It'd be a best seller. I'd make a killin'. Sides, this messin' with Anna's good practice for when I shack up with a classy broad.*

Okay, enough is enough. My turn now. Iggy mounted Anna and, grabbing her two wrists, pinned them over her head as he had his way with her. Not minding in the least, Anna lifted her thighs to press against his and they rumbaed to and fro, their only music the rhythm of their spastic sighs.

In a pipe dream, Iggy envisioned his brother's fiancé while Anna's imagination placed her under the handsome postman she'd been trying to seduce. Despite being miles apart in spirit, husband and wife panted in unison, their flesh united as one. Iggy grunted and Anna arched her spine, gasping for breath.

While they continued to fancy themselves with partners other than their spouses, their blended perspiration glistened. But, before Anna approached the brink of ecstasy, Iggy jolted with unrestrained excitement, his apparition's name exploding from his lips, "Te-re-sa!"

Heedless of his wife's feelings, Iggy reverted to his usual post-coital behavior by nodding off.

Livid, Anna dismissed her own fantasy man and went rigid beneath Iggy. **Che sfrontatezza!** *How dare Iago think of Teresa as he makes love to me!* After several of her unsuccessful attempts to push him off, Iggy rolled over onto his side and ejected a god-awful snore. Feeling no guilt for having used her own imagination to conjure a more alluring lover, Anna seethed. *Knew it was too good to be true.*

Anna kicked her bare foot into his groin. "So I'm not pretty enough for you, huh, Iago?" While Iggy recoiled in his sleep, she poked a finger into his chest. "The floozy flirted with you behind my back, didn't she?"

Eyes narrowed and lips twisted in resentment, Anna bolted upright and folded her arms tight across her chest. "And I thought Teresa was my friend. Should've known better than to trust a Sicilian."

Chapter Twenty-Six

Mack picked Teresa up at 10:45 the next morning and drove the few blocks to St. Christopher's, arriving in plenty of time for the eleven o'clock Sunday mass. Together they entered the church and passed through its vestibule with Teresa's head held high and Mack's hand at the small of her back.

"Where do you want to sit, Teresa?" Mack muttered out of the side of his mouth.

"At the front if you don't mind," Teresa whispered back.

Along the way down the aisle, the click of Teresa's heels and swish of her refashioned skirt attracted the attention of more than a few pair of eyes. *Ah, so this is the mass more of the younger women attend. Don't they know it's impolite to stare? Guess I can't blame them.* She glanced up at her escort and smiled. *Macbetto does look **sofisticato** in a suit and tie.* At Mack's gesture toward the third row, Teresa entered in front of him.

Although she paid lip service with rote Latin responses to the priest's cues throughout the opening prayers, Teresa's thoughts wandered toward her impending introduction to Mack's mother later that afternoon. *I'm so nervous. What will she think of me?* She wondered if Signora Matteo would consider a factory worker a poor match for her college-educated son.

Teresa stiffened her spine. **Basta!** *Enough self-contempt, I'm not that pathetic. I know how to keep a neat, clean house, don't I? And* *what about my cooking? It's not that bad anymore.* She bit her lip. *What else I can brag about?* With a shrug of defeat, Teresa struggled to return her attention to the priest's invocations and mumbled additional Latin phrases where appropriate.

When the usher passed the collection basket down the aisle, she lifted her eyebrows at the fifty cents Mack deposited, much more than the three nickels she held ready to drop into it. Afterwards, while Mack belted the lyrics with relish, Teresa lip-sung the offertory hymn under the choir's camouflage. *Don't need to advertise that I can't carry a tune.*

As the mass proceeded, Teresa fantasized. *Ah, someday I might float down this very aisle in a white gown. That's if Dio finds it in his mercy to give me what I've always wanted. But what if Macbetto changes his mind?* She grimaced at the mental image of herself abandoned at the altar, the ridicule of eye witnesses. *No, not the way he looks at me. I don't think that can happen to me. Or can it?*

The usher drew Teresa's attention when he stood alongside the aisle and signaled their turn for the Eucharist. Mack exited the aisle and, allowing Teresa to precede him, followed her to the altar. Side-by-side, they knelt at the communion railing and, at the priest's imminent approach, stuck out their tongues for the Holy Communion wafer. Upon their return to their pew, Teresa bowed her head and prayed, veiled behind the privacy of her cupped hands. **Grazie, Dio**. *Thank you for plopping this wonderful **Americano** down at my doorstep. Oh, one more thing, please I beg you, make his mother like me.* She closed the prayer with the sign of the cross. Looking at one of the altars burning candles, she addressed her perpetually accessible guardian angel. *Mamma, do you think Macbetto and I are made for each other?* She accepted the flicker of the candle as a sign of her mother's approval.

In the meantime, behind the privacy of his own hands, Mack's prayers wavered between gratitude, supplication and barter. *God, thanks for saving Teresa for me. The wait was well worth it.* Mack winced. *Hey, by the way, if you don't mind, can you give me the courage to tell her about you know what? Please help me to convince Teresa that I can provide a respectable life for her, despite any drawbacks.* He squeezed his hands tighter against his face. *If you do, I swear I'll do my best to make Teresa happy and secure.* By the end of mass, Mack convinced himself that he'd keep no secrets from Teresa. *I'll tell her about my problem, soon, someday very soon.*

* * *

Outside in the church parking lot, Mack fidgeted in the driver's seat of the LaSalle and fingered the breast pocket of his suit jacket. *I want to give it to her before she meets the rest of the family. Hope she likes the setting.* Although he had realized the cost of the diamond would put a huge dent in his wallet, he couldn't resist buying it for Teresa when he spotted it in the downtown jeweler's window. *Thank goodness Mr. Weinstein agreed to a payment plan.*

Now how do I give it to her? What do I say? It's not very romantic to hand it over right here in the car, is it? Wait a minute, I have an idea.

In the passenger seat beside him, Teresa wrung her hands. "Macbetto, **sono preoccupata**. I'm worried about your mother. How will she react to me?"

"She'll welcome you with open arms," Mack reassured. "Listen, if I survived that ordeal with your father, you'll have no problem with Mamma." He switched to a grave tone and waved an index finger at her, "Don't make the same mistake I did. Whatever you do, don't drink too much."

Teresa went rigid with insult until she noticed the sparkle of amusement in Mack's eyes and giggled a response, "I'll drink a quarter of what you guzzled at my house, two gallons to start."

Mack chuckled and patted her hand. "What a sense of humor." With the tension in both their faces dissipated, Mack started the engine and made a left at the corner.

"**Perché vai in questa direzione**, Macbetto? Isn't your house in the opposite direction?"

"There's someplace I want to take you before we join my family, Teresa. It's one of my favorite spots in the neighborhood. Hope you like it as much I do. It's just down the road here a ways." Not even five minutes later, Mack parked the car beneath an oak tree near the entrance to a park.

"Come on, let's take a little walk." Mack opened his door.

Teresa smiled in agreement. "**Sì, andiamo**. It's a beautiful day."

Mack helped Teresa from the car and led her down a gravel path toward a gazebo where two cardinals nesting in its eaves serenaded each other, the male bird the same cardinal that had helped boost Mack's ego the day he met Teresa's father.

Mack turned toward Teresa, "What do you think?"

"**È così bello**. It's so quaint and romantic. Is this where you take all your lady friends?" Teresa teased.

"No, Teresa, just the ones that take my breath away."

Teresa fluttered her lashes. "And you're sharing it with me?"

Mack grasped Teresa's left elbow and guided her up the stairs of the gazebo then gestured for her to sit on the bench located at its center. Once she sat down and looked up at Mack, he descended to his right knee and cleared his throat.

While Teresa's mouth froze open and Mack's forehead dripped with perspiration, he addressed her in a strained voice, "Teresa, I've known you for barely two weeks. But in that short amount of time, I've fallen deeply in love with you. I hope that someday you'll feel the same about me." He paused for a few seconds unsure of himself, but at the male cardinal's whistle of encouragement, Mack continued, "We've both agreed to a trial engagement. Right?"

When Teresa nodded, Mack relaxed his shoulders and articulated the rest of his thoughts with ease, "If it's destined, we'll end up in the happiest marriage. How can we miss, with your wit and my laughter?" Mack reached into his inside pocket, pulled out a blue velvet box and opened it to reveal the diamond ring. Although he offered it to Teresa under the shade of the gazebo, it glistened nonetheless. "I bought this ring for you because I'm committed to our future together." He took hold of her left hand and stared into Teresa's eyes. "Teresa, will you please wear it?"

Teresa swallowed hard. "Why, Macbetto, you've taken me by surprise. **Mamma mia,** this ring is . . . is more than I ever expected. What can I say?"

"Say 'yes' and I'll see that you won't regret it," Mack implored.

"Are you sure? You don't know me *that* well. The ring, if it doesn't work out between us, what then?"

"I trust you, Teresa. I know you'd do the right thing." He slipped the diamond onto her finger.

"Well, in that case, of course, **sì.**" As Teresa stretched out her hand, the diamond sparkled back the prospect of happiness and security. "It's so **magnifico!**" She lowered her eyes and blushed. "I guess this means we're officially engaged."

Mack buoyed himself up and pulled Teresa along with him then enfolded her in a tight embrace before he pulled back and lifted her chin. They see-sawed their heads back and forth for a few awkward moments then sealed their pact with a tender kiss.

Lost in a romantic trance, Teresa relished the tingle that ran through her body while Mack's heart raced hard enough to send a flush to his face. In their state of euphoria, neither felt the presence of two young boys, their heads pressed between the railings of the gazebo. The youngsters ogled the lovers who dove in for another kiss and, after a few moments, chanted in unison, "He kissed her! He kissed her! K-I-S-S-I-

N-G! First comes love! Then comes marriage! Then here she comes with a baby carriage!" The boys roughhoused in a fit of hysterical laughter.

Startled by the interruption, the cardinals flew away and the engaged couple parted to stare at the boys dashing off through the bushes.

"*Che hanno detto?* Please translate their mischief for me." Teresa laughed as she looked from the bushes to Mack's expression which reflected his discomfort at the intrusion. "Macbetto, you look mortified. What did they say? It wasn't that bad, was it?" Without waiting for an answer, she raced down the stairs of the gazebo and ran along the path toward the car.

With a glance over her shoulder, Teresa taunted Mack who leaned on the gazebo railing, "*Prendimi se puoi.*"

In response to the challenge to catch her if he could, Mack sprinted behind Teresa and overtook her before she reached the car. He pinched her waist between his hands and spun her around. "*Ti amo,* Teresa," Mack whispered into her ear as he lowered her feet to the ground. "Do you think you can find a way to love me back?"

"Try and stop me." Teresa melted into Mack's arms as he gave her one last, passionate kiss.

Chapter Twenty-Seven

"*Quest'è la nostra casa.*" Mack held the front door open and ushered Teresa into the foyer. "Enter the insane asylum where the Matteos and our in-laws spin in circles. But beware! You enter at your own risk."

Oblivious to Mack's attempt at humor, Teresa sucked in her breath while she gawked at the chandelier and the crown molding. "*Meraviglioso!*" She followed Mack into the parlor where her attention drifted from the marble fireplace to the room's furnishings. "Do you play the piano, Macbetto?"

"I did when I was younger, but it's really my brother's thing. Frank's the one with the raw talent."

Teresa tiptoed over the Persian rug. "Macbetto, *la tua casa è elegante.* Compared to our house, it's like a mansion."

"It can be your home too, Teresa," Mack enticed as boisterous voices surfaced from the next room. "Come this way." He led her forward and, reaching the dining room entrance, loudly cleared his throat, "Ahem!" Conversation halted and eight heads turned in unison.

In English, Iggy broke the silence, "Look whose here, just when I figured Teresa must've dumped him."

Signora Matteo shook a tense forefinger at Iggy. "*Iago, non scherzare!*" Her wrinkles softening, she approached Teresa. After she introduced herself as Mack's mother, she welcomed Teresa into their home, "*Benvenuto alla nostra casa.*"

Teresa offered a timid smile. "*Grazie,* Signora Matteo."

Pleased that Mack had finally brought home a girlfriend, Signora Matteo elatedly squeezed the hand Teresa extended and, pulling her closer, brushed a kiss against each of her cheeks. She'd been worried that her shyest son might never find a woman. Still grinning, she stepped back to examine Teresa's frail frame, evaluating it the way she might a turkey for Thanksgiving dinner. "*Bella,* young and fresh, but too skinny." She pinched Teresa's cheek. "No you worry, Macbetto. I feed Teresa good food. I put meat on bones, *perfetta* for you in one month."

Mack clicked his tongue. "Mamma, don't be ridiculous. She's perfect now."

By the time a soft blush rose up Teresa's neck, Mack announced her status to the family with a lift of her diamond-studded hand, "Hey, everybody, good news. Teresa's agreed to marry me. We're officially engaged." As the information registered differently on each of their faces, Mack discouraged any response by quickly escorting Teresa toward Iggy and his wife. "Teresa, you already know Iago and Anna."

"*Sì, certo.*" Comforted by the two familiar faces, Teresa flashed a smile. "*Ciao*, Anna." She patted Iggy's shoulder and laughed. "Iago, we must stop meeting like this."

When Iggy ogled Teresa with a dreamy expression, his wife kicked him under the table and then trained an icy stare at Teresa. Mack ignored his brother's insolence, but Teresa flinched at Anna's negative reaction. *Il malocchio? Why the evil eye? For heaven's sake, I was joking. I thought she liked my sense of humor.*

However, before Teresa could further contemplate Anna's strange behavior, Mack guided her around the table and introduced the others. "This is my brother Franco, or Frank in English. He's the manager of the bakery and, as the oldest male, the *capo* of the family. Frank . . . Teresa."

"*Benvenuto,* Teresa. This is my wife Geneva. If you're new to the area, she can fill you in on all the best places to shop. She's an expert at it. Ask my wallet."

Laughing, Geneva slapped her husband's arm. "Oh, Frank, please!" She then addressed Teresa, "Did you notice the piano in the other room?" At Teresa's nod, Geneva bragged, "Frank's fantastic. I insist he play for you sometime."

With a restrained smile, Frank hesitantly agreed, "One of these days."

"I'd love that, Franco."

Mack urged Teresa forward. "This is my sister Patricia." At Signora Matteo's scowl, Mack corrected, "Baptized Patrizia . . . and her husband Jake, or shall I say Jacamo."

"Nice to meet you both."

"Patricia and Jake are expecting a baby," Mack disclosed. "What's the due date, Patricia?"

"December 28th. Jake and I can't wait. You know, Teresa, it will be Mamma's first grandchild." Patricia poked Jake's arm. "Honey, tell Teresa how hard the baby kicked last night."

"Kicked? I dint feel nuttin'. Must a been gas." But, when Patricia glared at Jake for providing the offensive response, he tried to compensate. "My wife's gonna make a great mudder. She's been studyin' dat book by Dr. Spook, inside 'n out."

"Spock . . . not Spook!" Patricia barked before she returned her attention to Teresa. "Dr. Benjamin Spock, the latest authority on childcare. If you're interested, I'll fill you in on the best methods of breastfeeding, Teresa."

"Patricia, please! Don't embarrass us." Mack guided his fiancé away. "Let's move on, Teresa." He stopped next to his younger sister's chair. "This is Juliet, or Giulietta as Mamma prefers to call this **bambina** of the family."

"Baby, huh?" Juliet rolled her eyes. "I'm barely 14 months younger."

"Sorry, no offense intended," Mack placated as Teresa stifled a smirk. "You might want to get together with Juliet for a film sometime. She's up on all the current Italian movie stars."

Pacified, Juliet addressed Teresa, "Have you seen the latest Anna Magnani movie? If not, we can go next week. It's playing downtown at the Grand with English subtitles." Not giving Teresa a chance to respond, she grabbed her hand and inspected the diamond. "Your ring's absolutely gorgeous!"

"**Grazie.** Macbetto has excellent taste."

"I'll say." With her heartbreak still fresh, Juliet sighed. "I want to hear all about the proposal, all the romantic details."

Anxious for an excuse to dodge the subject, Mack glanced at Signora Matteo, her hands poised for prayer. "Later. Mamma's ready to say grace. Let's sit down, Teresa." Mack held out a chair for Teresa and, once she was settled, sat down beside her.

Bowing her head, Signora Matteo led the prayer and immediately followed up with animated hand gestures, encouraging all to begin their meal, *"Mangia. Mangia. Buon' appetito."* Without hesitation, the family dug into several courses served end-to-end: soup, salad, *fettuccini al fredo*, and veal with peppers.

Noticing that Frank had not helped himself to any bread, Signora Matteo passed down the basket, urging him to take some, "Franco, *prenditi un poco pane*."

Once Geneva poked Frank in the ribs, he refused the offer, *"No grazie*, Mamma. There's enough on my plate." Then, at his wife's whispered encouragement, Frank reluctantly put down his fork and stood. "Come on, everybody. Let's drink a toast to Mack and his beautiful fiancé. Teresa . . . Mack, please stand."

Mack helped Teresa to her feet and put his arm around her shoulder. All the others, except Anna, raised their wine glasses as Frank gestured toward Mack and Teresa. *"Buona fortuna!* Good luck in your life together. Hope you're blessed with health, happiness and a houseful of . . ." He stopped short when he glanced at Geneva's pitiful expression. He didn't want to upset his so-far infertile wife by another mention of children. " . . . of good Italian food. Welcome to the family, Teresa." Anna again refrained when the family hailed, *"Buona fortuna! Alla Famiglia!"*

With few chances to take a bite, and despite the fact that her belly grumbled softly in protest, Teresa provided polite answers to an exhaustive litany of questions thrown at her in her native tongue.

Frank sipped his wine. "What town you from, Teresa?"

"Trapani, on the west coast of *Sicilia*. But my brother and I moved to Palermo to live with my sister during the war."

Patricia leaned forward. "How long've you been in this country?"

Teresa held up two fingers. "A couple of months."

Geneva's eyes opened wider and, unable to swallow her surprise, sputtered into her hand, "Two months? Is that all?" Picking up her napkin, she wiped the spittle from her palm.

By clearing her throat, Signora Matteo gained Teresa's attention. "You go to church? *Chiesa cattolica*?"

"Sì, **certo.** Saturday and Sunday at St. Christopher's." At the older woman's nod of approval, Teresa added, "That's where I met Anna." Unaware that she'd won no points by her affiliation with Signora Matteo's least favorite daughter-in-law, Teresa unsuccessfully tried to catch Anna's eye. "Just when I needed a friend most, Anna came to the rescue."

Jake garbled with his mouth full, "What's yer fadder do for a livin'?"

"Mio padre?" Teresa twisted her hands in her lap. "He works at the tool factory."

Annoyed at her husband's bad manners, Patricia swallowed hard. "What about you? Are you employed, Teresa?"

"*Sì.*" Teresa expelled a nervous titter. "There's no free ride at my father's house. I sew at the dress factory."

At a lull in the conversation, Juliet's eyes lit up with curiosity. "How long did you know Mack before he proposed to you, Teresa?"

Upon Teresa's hesitation, Mack reluctantly stretched the truth, "Enough time."

Skeptical, Geneva drilled, "Don't you think an engagement's a bit hasty, Teresa?"

"Well . . ." Teresa hemmed. "I don't know what's normal in America."

Uncomfortable with the line of questioning himself, Mack took a cue from the strained look on Teresa's face and interrupted the inquisition in English, "Come on, please give Teresa a chance to breathe. Stop the third degree. She'll be here all afternoon. So, please give her a break." He patted Teresa's hand and encouraged her in Italian, "*Mangi qualcosa*. Taste the veal and peppers. They're delicious."

Despite the fierce daggers Anna's eyes wielded at her husband, Iggy continued to devote his undivided attention to his brother's fiancé throughout the meal. Feigning the need to stretch, he stood up and approached Teresa from behind. "Can we get together again sometime?" Iggy squeezed her shoulder and finished with a chortle, "I'll invite Mack, but only if you insist."

Teresa responded with a cautious giggle then started to peck at her meal. However, before long, the ladies of the house, bar Anna, stood up and began to clear the table. "Can I help in the kitchen," Teresa offered.

Mack whispered into her ear, "You're our guest today. Let's go into the parlor and relax before desert." He pulled out Teresa's chair and led the way. With Anna in tow, Iggy traipsed close behind them, while the other two men involved in a business discussion brought up the rear.

Vying for Teresa's attention, Iggy made small talk while Anna, her arms tightly crossed in front of her, remained silent. Wondering why his sister-in-law was pouting, Mack leaned back and observed the innocent interaction between Teresa and Iggy. *Hmm, is Anna jealous? Does she know something I don't know?* He shook his head ever so slightly. *Nah!*

In the dinning room, Signora Matteo picked up Teresa's almost full plate. "I see why girl so skinny. *Mangia poco*. She eat like bird on diet." Once the ladies prepared the coffee for brewing and laid out desert dishes, they joined the others in the sitting room.

After a few awkward moments of silence, Iggy sprung up, approached Teresa and grasped her hand. "Hey, Teresa, tell some of the funny stories about your trip on the freighter. They were a riot." Anna directed a disgusted look in his direction.

"Well, if anyone's interested," Teresa surveyed the others.

"Yes, tell us," Juliet and Geneva encouraged in unison.

While Teresa retold the animated tales with gross exaggerations of the perils of the seas, Mack glanced at his brother Iggy and gave him a grateful nod. Iggy waved off the gratitude.

With everyone else captivated, Anna feigned boredom even though she fumed inside. *Look how Teresa throws herself at my husband . . . and Iago, the insensitive pig, has the nerve to dote on the tramp right in front of me.*

Caught up in Teresa's wit, Iggy and the others related tales of Mack in his youth and even Signora Matteo let down her guard referring to Mack by her pet name for him. "When Macco small boy, he want **una bambola**. Signore Matteo he no like son hold doll. He buy beads for Macco to count. How you say?"

"An abacus," Patricia provided.

"**Sì**, he give Macco beads and look my son now . . . he count so high." To Mack's chagrin, Iggy mocked him with a sputtering laugh.

The instant Teresa spied an old sewing machine tucked way in a corner of the parlor, she asked Signora Matteo, "Do you sew, Signora?"

"One time I sew. **Adesso è difficile.**" Signora Matteo massaged her knotted knuckles to emphasize how difficult it had become. "This hands no work no more." She explained that she'd tried to encourage her daughters' interests, but neither wanted to learn.

"Someday I'm going to buy a sewing machine." Teresa rubbed the tips of a thumb and index finger lightly against each other. "But you know how costly they are. If I can ever save enough, God willing, I plan to open my own dress shop."

"**Veramente?**" Signora Matteo reached for her watch, dangling from a gold chain around her neck and asked a rhetorical question, "You marry Macco, you stay home, no?" She examined the face of the dial and announced, "Is time for **caffè e dolce**. You like **tiramisu**, Teresa?"

Without giving their guest a chance to answer, Iggy jumped up. "I sure as hell do! Wait till you taste it, Teresa. **Delizioso!**" He twisted the tip of his index finger against his cheek, emphasizing just how delicious a dessert.

They all retreated to the dining room. Teresa, no longer the target of a firing squad, chirped along, contributing to the lighthearted conversation as she indulged in the **tiramisu**, thoroughly enjoying the liquor-soaked layers of sponge cake, creamy **mascarpone** cheese and chocolate. As she took a sip of coffee, Teresa eyed the one individual that hadn't thawed all afternoon. *Why has Anna been in such a bad mood? I'll find out first chance I get.*

Chapter Twenty-Eight

Listening to Frank Sinatra croon from the phonograph, the ladies of the Matteo household relaxed in the parlor later that afternoon. While Signora Matteo and Patricia sat side-by-side on the sofa in the center of the room, Juliet and Geneva faced each other at a game table to the far left of them. To their right, Anna sprawled on a chaise lounge in front of the dormant fireplace. Her face buried in an Italian gossip magazine, the busty Italian swayed to the music.

Juliet sipped her iced tea then picked up a deck of cards and flashed them at Geneva. "Gin rummy as usual?"

Geneva nodded then snarled towards Anna. "Look at her now. I guess her menstrual cramps weren't that bad. As usual, they lasted just long enough to get out of doing the dishes."

"Or anything else around the house." Juliet directed a disapproving glance at her mother. "Mamma stopped insisting she help."

"I guess she finally decided it wasn't worth the hassle."

"It's just not fair." Juliet bristled with annoyance. "Who gave Anna the idea she's a privileged guest?"

"Your brother Iggy, who else?" Geneva scoffed. "Probably a ploy to get her to marry him."

"Any other reason to marry such an insensitive jerk?"

"A ticket to America? Money?" Geneva fanned herself and swallowed a sip of her iced tea before she changed the subject. "So, Juliet, tell me. What do you think of Mack's fiancé?"

"I loved Teresa's sense of humor. Mack's lucky to find such a fun girl. Can't wait to get together with her again."

"Hmm, how long have Mack and Teresa known each other, a couple of weeks?" Geneva placed down her glass. "That's awful fast for an engagement."

"Ah, if it's true love, why wait? Besides, Mamma doesn't seem to object. Why do you, Geneva?"

"I don't object. I just wondered. What's the rush?" Unable to think of a good reason for the couple's haste except one, Geneva blurted, "Maybe she told him she's pregnant."

"What?" Juliet asked incredulously. "Mack's would never . . ."

"But Teresa might have considered it a good way to trap him."

"Don't be ridiculous. Why she's so pretty, she must have swept Mack right off his feet."

Still not convinced, Geneva quietly conceded as she picked up each card Juliet dealt to her. The remainder of the deck stacked facedown on the table, Juliet scraped up her hand, fanning the seven cards in a semicircle. "You're first."

Geneva scrutinized her cards and fastidiously reorganized them from lowest to highest. "I hope Mack told Teresa about you know what."

"Do you mean what I think you mean?" Juliet preferred not mention Mack's problem by name, for the word "epilepsy" made his condition seem even more ominous that it actually was. "Knowing Mack, he spilled the beans the moment they met." Juliet rearranged her hand by suit. "It's your turn."

"Don't rush me." Geneva picked up the five of clubs from the top of the deck and contemplated her strategy before she discarded a deuce of spades face-up on the table. "I'll give Teresa credit for guts. Or, maybe she doesn't understand what happens during a seizure."

Juliet cringed in response. Wiping the disturbing image from her mind, she lifted a king of hearts and added it to her hand then, without delay, discarded an ace of clubs. "Hey, by the way, where'd the guys go?"

Geneva grimaced. "Over to the club, where else?"

"Sometimes I wish I was one of them," Juliet whined. "They always have somewhere to go, no matter what day it is."

"Not that it's the best place for anyone to hang out. If they accepted Iggy, the members can't all be respectable."

Juliet leaned forward. "Think my brothers can make it through a game of bocce ball without a fight? There's been so much friction between Frank and Iggy lately."

"What do you mean *lately*? They've never gotten along." Geneva scooped up the ace Juliet had discarded. "Do you know what Iggy did this time?"

"Other than put a squash on my love life?" Juliet pouted.

Geneva lowered her voice, "Well, do you remember the bookkeeper Iggy introduced to Frank, the puny one Frank hired six months ago?"

"Yes. What about him?" Juliet held her breath until Geneva proceeded to fill her in on the sordid details.

Meanwhile, Signora Matteo crocheted ten lengthy rows of yellow yarn before she held up her progress to Patricia for inspection. "*Ti piace questo colore?*"

"Yes, Mamma, that color's perfect, whether the baby's a boy or a girl." Patricia returned her attention to the book propped in her lap as she conspicuously rubbed her abdomen. "What do you think of the name Luigi if it's a boy? It's Jake's father's name."

Signora Matteo released her grip on her project and massaged her knuckles as she asked if the baby would be the first grandchild in Jake's family, "*Sarà il primo nipote nella famiglia di Jacamo?*"

"The first?" Patricia flipped a page. "Why yes. What of it?"

"Then *il bambino* must take name of *nonno*. Is tradition," Signora Matteo asserted with a lift of her chin.

"We can always call him Luigino or Gino for short." When Signora Matteo wrinkled her nose, Patricia offered another prospect, "Maybe we'll have a girl and name her Angelina after you."

Signora Matteo smiled and patted Patricia's hand in agreement. "*Sì, sì*, I like *quest'idea*."

Patricia glanced over her shoulder at the other women before she grilled her mother in a subdue volume, "So, Mamma, what's your impression of Teresa?"

"*Bella*. Eyes . . . skin, nice." Signora Matteo nodded. "Make for Macbetto fine *bambini*."

"That's not what I meant." Patricia closed the book. "Do you think she can handle Mack's illness? I asked him if he told her. He said that he hadn't found the right moment yet."

"Teresa . . . she no need to know," replied Signora Matteo in a haughty tone. "*La medicina*, big pills, they make sickness go way."

"What if he forgets to take his medicine again and convulses in a seizure? Teresa ought to know what she's up against," Patricia insisted. "It's scary the first time. How will she manage?"

"We no make girl sorry. *Basta*, no more to say!" Signora Matteo folded her arms tight across her chest.

"Come on, Mamma. Don't be so stubborn."

"*Sono securo* Macbetto tell Teresa soon," countered Signora Matteo with certainty, dismissing the matter with a flip of her hand.

Jolting, Patricia switched the focus of the conversation, "Mamma, the baby's kicking." She pressed a palm against her navel. "Quick! Put your hand here."

Although Anna had not comprehended the full context of the mother-daughter exchange a few feet away, her back stiffened when she heard Teresa's name mentioned. Slapping the magazine onto her lap, she fumed. *No Matteo has ever given me a fraction of the attention they paid to that tramp today.* Brewing ever since Iggy had blurted

Teresa's name in their bed, Anna's cauldron of jealousy boiled over. *So the **puttana** thinks she can bat her lashes at my husband. We'll see how long Teresa hangs around here once I tell her about . . .*

Back at the card table, Juliet moaned in a hushed tone, "And now Devin won't have anything more to do with me. He ignores me at the office. I hate Iggy! He's messed up my best chance at romance, totally ruined my life."

"He puts a strain on mine too, Juliet," Geneva griped. "Who do you think has to calm Frank down after Iggy gets him all riled up?" Disgruntled, she smacked down the three of spades with more force than was necessary. "I wish we could move out of here." Oozing with bitterness, she snapped her head in Patricia's direction. "Jake bought *her* a house at a sheriff sale. I have no idea how *he* came up with the money so soon."

Through parted fingers, Juliet whispered, "I think he's involved in some scheme with Iggy. I caught the tail end of an argument between them." Juliet picked up another playing card. "Jake wants out but Iggy threatened to tell Patricia. It must be something underhanded. You know how Iggy is."

"I sure do," Geneva ranted. "As long as there's a profit in it for him, he doesn't care what law he breaks or who he hurts."

Juliet sat up straighter. "Speaking of Iggy, did you notice the way he drooled over Teresa?"

"Yes! At least Frank's smart enough not to stare at a girl right in front of me." Geneva poked an index finger into her chin and glared at Anna, "I'd say our sister-in-law's way to America cost her much more than she bargained for."

Juliet let out a forced breath. "Sometimes I wish Iggy would vanish from the face of the earth."

"I'll drink to that." Geneva held up her iced tea but, before she took a sip, she muttered her own addendum, "And may his wife disappear along with him."

Chapter Twenty-Nine

Whistling *Happy Birthday*, Iggy sauntered into the foyer late in the afternoon, on the day after Teresa's introduction to Mack's family. Convinced the odds would turn back in his favor, he felt confident he'd be able to reimburse the loan shark by the deadline, one month from the day he borrowed the money. *Bruno's trigger-happy goons won't have any excuse to come after me.* From the waistband of his pants, he pulled out and unbuttoned a short sleeved khaki shirt, the bakery's logo embroidered on its pocket.

I think I'll take me a shower . . . even shave. Wanna look spiffy tonight for my birthday. Hearing the water pipes rattling overhead, he glared up at the ceiling. *Who's hoggin' the bathroom?*

Distracted by his stomach's hungry growl, Iggy licked his lips, envisioning a birthday feast prepared by his mother, one which included his favorite, homemade **gnocchi**. His tongue salivated at the prospect of curling around one of the small, hand-rolled potato and semolina-flour dumplings coated in a spicy tomato sauce. *Mmm . . . I can't wait!* But when he inhaled a nose-full of air, he realized there were no delectable smells coming from the kitchen. *What's up with that?*

Footsteps on the stairway diverted Iggy's attention. Raising his head, he caught sight of Geneva, purse in hand, followed by Signora Matteo and Patricia, all dressed in their Sunday finest. Geneva looked over her shoulder. "Let's go. We don't want to get stuck at the table with Mrs. Castagna. She'll talk our ear off about all her ailments."

"No, we wait for Giulietta," Signora Matteo insisted.

Patricia stopped halfway down the steps. "I talked to Juliet this morning, Mamma. She said she'll meet us there."

Iggy confronted them at the bottom of the staircase and blocked their path, "Where're you dames think you're goin'?"

Geneva gave Iggy an icy stare. "Move out of the way, Iggy. We're already late."

"Tell me about it," he barked, expecting them to be repentant for delaying his birthday feast.

"We're going to The Altar Rosary Society's annual dinner at St. Christopher's. If we don't hurry . . ."

"What about my dinner?" Iggy protested.

With a devious smile on her face, Signora Matteo poked her head over Geneva's shoulder. "Iago, you wife . . . she cook **la pasta.**" When Iggy's lips twitched in annoyance, she taunted him even further, "What is **problema,** to cook **ragù** make her sick too?"

Geneva pushed Iggy aside and headed for the front door which she held open for her mother-in-law. "Let's go, Mamma."

Patricia pulled up the rear. "If you get desperate, Iggy, there're plenty of leftovers in the icebox. Oh, by the way, Frank, Mack and Jake signed up for a Rotary dinner tonight. You and Anna are on your own."

Iggy tightened his fists. "Where *is* my wife?"

"Anna? Soaking in a bubble bath, where else?" Patricia griped and slammed the door shut behind her.

"Leftovers? Tonight of all nights?" Iggy sulked over to the credenza, disappointed that no one had wished him a 'Happy Birthday' that day. *Not even Mamma.*

Shoulders slumped, Iggy flipped through the envelopes piled on top, next to a bulky manila-wrapped box and found none addressed to him. *Not one stinkin' birthday card. Wait a minute, what's this?* He turned over the lightweight box that held no evidence of any postage or postmark and inspected the label: "To: Iggy Matteo." *Huh?* He scratched his head, wondering how it had been delivered.

Thinking perhaps it was a birthday present dropped off by a secret admirer, Iggy grinned. *I can think of a few broads that fit the bill.* When he picked up the box and shook it, he heard nothing rattle inside. *Do I have the balls to open it in front of Anna? Nah, she'll take a hissy fit if it's a pair of red-hot panties.* He let out a hardy chuckle and tore into the package.

Iggy inspected the contents. The only thing visible was a manila envelope taped to the inside of the box. With disappointment written all over his face, he pulled it out. *Somebody's idea of a joke? Probably a stupid birthday card. Hey, maybe there's cash inside.* He tore into the envelope and pulled out a thick sheet of white paper, unfolded it and stared at it in disbelief. *What the hell? What kind of sick bastard has the nerve to send me this? On my birthday of all days! What's he, too chicken to stand up to me face-to-face?*

Iggy examined the letters which made up the words of a note, each in a different print style and color that appeared to be cut out from various magazine advertisements and pasted onto the page, some at odd angles, to form an unsavory message:

DEATH UNTO IGGY

Some psycho sure wasted a lot of time and effort to come up with this half-ass threat. Dubious that he had ever stepped on anybody's toes hard enough for a person to threaten his life, Iggy scratch his head. *Or did I?*

He shoved the note into his pocket, bolted up the stairs, and entered his and Anna's bedroom. Opening a drawer, Iggy pulled out a sheet of his wife's writing paper and her favorite pen. *Who, sides family, did I tick off lately?* He started to scribble down one name after another and, in a matter of minutes, filled both sides of a sheet. *Phew! This is*

useless. How the hell am I supposed to narrow it down to one asshole?
He crinkled the list and discarded it in the trash.

Though he'd never admit, even to himself, that he was somewhat intimidated by the threat, Iggy decided that the situation called for defensive measures. Adrenaline pumping through his veins, he jumped up and ruffled through the socks in the top drawer of his nightstand until his hand came upon the cold metal of a pistol. He pulled it out and, after releasing the safety catch, rotated the cylinder to inspect the chamber, verifying that each slot contained a bullet. *Knew it'd come in handy one of these days.* Shoulders squared, Iggy shoved the handgun into the waistband of his slacks and covered it over with his shirt. *Now let's see the coward try to mess with me.*

Chapter Thirty

As Teresa exited the kitchen Saturday morning and entered the parlor, Antonio slumped down the stairs grinding a fist into one of his eye sockets. "Aren't you going to mass?"

"**Sì**, and why are you up so early?" Teresa adjusted her bra strap. "I thought you took the day off."

"I woke up from an awful **sogno**." Antonio yawned. "In the dream, Mina and her father chased me, pinned me down and tortured me."

Teresa laughed. "What brought on such a nightmare?"

Antonio gripped his fists. "**Troppa tensione**."

"What kind of tension, work related?"

"Sort of," Antonio grimaced. "Both Mina and her father are pressuring me."

"About what?"

"A marriage proposal," Antonio reluctantly revealed. "I'm no where ready for a permanent commitment. Besides, I don't think Mina's the one for me."

"So tell me," Teresa giggled, "did Signore DiSalva threatened you with one of his butcher knives?"

"No, but he might as well have."

"What do mean?"

Antonio took a deep breath. "He told me to go look for another job."

"Why?"

"I already told you."

"Told me what?"

"That I won't commit to Mina."

With a baffled expression, Teresa demanded an explanation, "What's one thing have to do with the other?"

"Well, because Signore DiSalva hired me with the understanding that . . ." Antonio hesitated.

"*Sputa la risposta!* Antonio, what understanding? Out with it!"

Antonio held up his hand in annoyance. "Let me finish, Teresa! The truth is, he promised to give me a raise if I courted Mina. Now that he pays me a higher salary, a ring's expected next. They're both furious since I refuse to talk about it."

"Aha! *Now* I understand why Mina gave me the cold shoulder yesterday." Teresa plopped down on the couch. "*Così stupido!* How could you be so stupid?"

Antonio shrugged. "At the time, his offer seemed too good."

"Well, obviously, it's not that good. You don't want to get stuck with someone you don't love."

"Papà said I shouldn't pass it up. That I'd get used to her."

"You'd listen to him? The man who only brought us here to see what he could squeeze out of us?"

"Now that you put it that way . . ."

"Have you been doing a good job at the store?"

"Signore DiSalva's made no complaints in that department. The profits have gone up since I started and, on my day off, the customers ask for me by name."

"Then, I don't think he'll fire you. But you will have to be upfront with both of them."

"That's easier said than done. Mina won't take no for an answer. Believe me, I've tried."

"Try harder!" Teresa considered what role she could play in the matter. "Do you want me to talk to Mina about it?"

"No! Stay out of it," Antonio insisted. "I'll handle it my own way."

Frustrated at her brother's pigheadedness, Teresa criticized, "How you let it get this far is beyond me."

"Hey, look who's talking." Antonio shook an accusative finger in Teresa's face. "The woman engaged to a practical stranger."

Teresa smacked his hand away. "Macco's no stranger. In the last couple of weeks we've become very close."

"Who's Macco? Don't tell me you're engaged to *two* men?"

"Don't be an idiot, Antonio. Macco is what I call Macbetto. The nickname rolls easier off my tongue."

Antonio shook his head. "Not even engaged a week and you're changing his name already."

"Macco doesn't seem to mind. Besides, the ladies at the factory think it sounds masculine." Teresa held up her diamond-studded hand. "Naturally, once they spotted my ring, the lot of them turned green with envy."

Antonio scoffed. "***Sei pieno di te stesso.***"

"How dare you call me arrogant!" Teresa proudly centered the gem on her finger. "I'm just happy an educated and prosperous man asked me to marry him."

"Well, tell your *rich* fiancé it's not polite to drop by uninvited. Twice this week, he showed up at dinnertime. With his appetite, second helpings were out of the question," Antonio bellyached. "Papà and I need more to eat, not less."

"Papà didn't complain."

"Not in front of you and your ***fidanzato***. No, he snarled and took it out on me after you left the room."

Teresa threw up a hand. "Well, from now on, I'll just cook more food."

"And suppose he doesn't show up? What then, Teresa?"

"I can pack the leftovers for your lunches, Antonio."

"In that case, tell your Macco he's welcome any time. His company does have some advantages." Antonio headed toward the kitchen. "With a stranger around, Papà somehow manages to control his anger," he tweaked his nostrils, "and his gas."

Teresa wrinkled her nose. "Thank God!" When she spotted a black and white composition pad sitting next to her purse on the end table, she addressed her brother's back, "Antonio, did I mention I signed up for an evening class?"

"No. What kind of class?"

"To learn English?"

"Where?"

"At the local high school . . . Tuesday nights."

Antonio spun around. "I didn't know that they offered one. Who told you about it?"

"Carmela Compagna, the new hire at the factory who sits at the machine next to mine." Teresa picked up the notebook. "Over lunch one day, she asked me to sign up with her."

"How long's she been in this country?" Antonio asked.

"Already two years but never bothered to learn more that the basics." Teresa flipped a few pages. "The ***Americano*** she married six months ago wants her to improve her English before they start a family."

"Maybe I'll sign up too." Antonio flipped up the palms of his hands in frustration. "Mina absolutely refuses to give me any more lessons until I . . . you know."

"Sorry, I filled the last spot." Teresa tossed the notebook back onto the end table. "In fact, I went to the first lesson this past Tuesday and made a fool of myself in front of the whole class."

"What'd you do?"

"I made a stupid mistake." Teresa tilted her head and crossed her eyes. "Stood up in front of the whole class and said *I'm ignorant* instead of *I'm an immigrant.*"

"That's not an error." Antonio laughed.

"Thanks a lot," Teresa huffed. "I wanted to surprise Macco. Maybe exchange vows with him in English one day. But the language is full of traps and tricks." She tapped her forehead. "***Si farò uno sbaglio,*** who knows what I might vow by mistake? Instead of *in sickness and in health*, I'll probably pronounce it *in sickness and in wealth.*" Teresa giggled. "Wouldn't I be embarrassed?"

Antonio grinned. "By the way, when do you actually intend to get married?"

"Who's in a hurry?" Teresa stood up. "Remember, Macco and I secretly agreed to make it a trial engagement. And now that Carmela's told me what's involved, I'm petrified that Papà will take a conniption fit when he realizes what a fancy wedding will cost."

Antonio scratched his head. "Why not make it a simple affair?"

"It's out of the question. Macco's sister Giulietta said that Signora Matteo expects me to spare no expense. What's more, Virginia and Natalia want a list of Macco's closest friends and relatives to invite to an engagement party. They'll be in for a surprise if they expect Papà to pay for it."

Antonio nodded his agreement as he looked down at his wristwatch. "Teresa, I thought you were going to church this morning. It's already a quarter past nine."

"Oh, no! I wanted to catch Anna before mass. Now I'll have to wait until it's over."

* * *

Teresa slid into the rear pew as the choir sang the offertory hymn. *I'm tired of this routine. Mass twice a week is too much.* If not for the fact that she wanted to confront Anna to find out why she treated her with such a cold shoulder the previous week, Teresa would have stayed home. *From now on, Sunday mass with Macco will do.*

After communion, Teresa's mind wandered yet again. *I'll wait until Papà approves the engagement party before I ask Macco who he wants to invite. Hmm, if the old goat agrees to it, I'll need to come up with a new dress design.* Her goal was to impress Signora Matteo and all her prospective in-laws. *Speaking of in-laws, where's Anna?* Teresa scanned the pews until she spotted a familiar hat. *There she is. I can't let her get away without some explanation.*

When the priest gave the final benediction, Teresa let out a sigh of relief, exited the pew and stood behind a column, shoulders hunched in anticipation. Upon Anna's approach, Teresa sprung from behind the post and greeted her with a smile, "**Ciao**, Anna. How're you today?"

Anna didn't bother to look at Teresa. "Fine." She scurried through the vestibule and down the stone steps at a fast clip.

Teresa followed Anna and caught up to her a few yards from the church. "Nice dress, Anna. Is it new?" Though Anna failed to respond, Teresa pressed on, "Mind if I join you on your walk home?"

Anna turned up her nose and quickened her pace. "If you insist."

"Anna, is anything wrong?"

"Why do you ask?" Anna turned her chin away from Teresa.

"Well, it is obvious you're angry. Is there something I did to upset you?"

With an abrupt twist, Anna glared at Teresa and flailed her arms. "Only that you flirted with my husband . . . you . . . you . . . **puttana**." She performed an about face and rushed off.

Teresa halted in shock. *What nerve! I didn't flirt and I'm certainly not a harlot.*

Anna twisted her head to the left as she held one hand up to the right side of her mouth and, without slowing her stride, shouted back to Teresa, "And, by the way, ask your fiancé about his illness." Anna faced forward again and marched homeward with her fists clenched.

Bewildered, Teresa gaped at Anna's retreating figure. *What's she talking about, what illness?*

* * *

Damn! This thing's poked me long enough. Iggy pulled the pistol from the waistband of his slacks and shoved it under the front seat of the LaSalle, directly beneath him. He figured that if he hadn't been attacked by then, the person who sent the threat never really planned to carry it out. *Guess I'm the chump who gave some joker a good laugh.* He had grilled just about everyone he knew in the last week trying to determine who the prankster was. *The stinkin' idiot didn't have nerve enough to fess up to it or I woulda' wrung his slimmy neck. Nobody messes with me!* He pulled out of the parking spot in front of the tobacco shop and drove toward the men's club.

While Iggy used both hands to scratch at his unburdened abdomen, steering the swerving car with his left knee alone, he spotted his wife on her way home from church and debated whether or not to give her a ride. *Nah, she looks like she's in one of her moods again. A bitch on the rag's better than a bun in the oven, but why put up with the crab more than I have to.* When Anna waved at him to stop, he pretended not to see her.

Further down the street, Iggy spotted Teresa and pulled the jalopy up alongside her. "**Buon giorno**, Teresa. Need a lift?"

Without halting, Teresa flashed a palm in front of her face. "No, no. Please leave me alone! Haven't you caused enough trouble as it is?" She scooted around the jalopy and, crossing the street, resumed her homeward trek at express speed.

"What's up with her?" Iggy pulled in his chin. "Women! Can't live with 'em and can't screw without 'em."

Chapter Thirty-One

Midmorning on Sunday, September 14th, one month to the day that he borrowed money from Bruno the loan shark, Iggy slouched behind the steering wheel of the LaSalle as he passed a neighborhood gas station. He glanced at the needle on the gas gauge which wavered below the lowest delineation. *Too bad the gas station is closed, or I woulda' filled it up. Yeah, right!* Iggy laughed until he coasted the LaSalle into the Matteos' driveway on fumes alone. He beeped the horn, startling Jake at the side door of the house. "Come here, asshole. I need to talk to you."

Jake let out a forced breath and a few expletives as he slammed the door shut and headed toward the LaSalle. "What ya want, Iggy?"

"Did ja deliver the money to Bruno?"

Jake leaned into the car's opened window. "Yeah, but he wasn't none too happy."

Iggy grimaced. "What'd he say?"

Jake smirked at Iggy's discomfort. "Ya want it word-for-word?"

"Don't be a smartass!" Iggy growled. "Just spit it out."

"Well, after he counted da money, he croaked in dat hoarse Italian a his, 'Tell dat scumbag brother-in-law a yours dat," Jake paraphrased, "if he dunt want two broken legs, he better fork up da rest. I give him tree days tops.' I scrammed outta dere da moment Bruno signaled ta his goons."

Beads of sweat formed on Iggy's forehead. "Aw, I bet he's all talk. You don't think he'd really . . ."

"Ya better not mess wit him, Iggy."

"If I didn't lend you all my cash, I wouldn't be in this fuckin' mess," Iggy complained.

"I know, I know," Jake sputtered in annoyance. "Ya reminded me a zillion times. I donno why ya tink ya got da short end of da stick. Don't ya tink I done enough shit for ya by now?"

"No! You'll do whatever I say till it's all paid back." Iggy shook his fist. "Sides, I think it's high time you start doublin' up on the payments."

"No way! Dat wasn't part a da deal." Once he stood his ground, Jake felt brave enough to add fuel to the fire. "So, tell me, how ya gonna pay Bruno da rest in tree days, Mr. Genius?"

Rubbing his temples as a truck went by, Iggy missed the jibe. "I'll figure somethin' out. Don't worry."

"Why should I worry?" Jake pointed at Iggy then himself. "It's yer ass on da line, not mine." Reconsidering, he frowned. "Ain't it?"

Iggy pulled out the collar of his shirt and rotated his chin. "How many bets did ja book for tomorrow night's game?"

Jake lifted a notepad out of his rear pocket and flipped a few of its pages. "Not so many no more. Lots a yer pigeons switched to some udder bookie."

Iggy bit his lip. "Think Frank will loan me the money?"

"Fat chance," Jake scoffed. "He's still pissed about da bookkeeper." He backed away from the vehicle. "Listen, I gotta go work on da house. I'll be damn lucky if I finish in time for da baby. Maybe if I had me some help. Tink you can lend me a hand dis afternoon?"

"No, sir, no can do," Iggy begged off. "You know I got more pressin' matters to tend to."

As Jake stalked into the house, Iggy tapped the steering wheel. *Maybe I oughta keep my gun handy until I settle with Bruno.* He reached down and fished the pistol out from under the seat, where he had left it weeks ago. *This numbers gig isn't worth half this hassle.* Shoving the gun under the waistband of his pants, he slid his dry tongue between his lips and eyed the gas gage. *Damn, I need a drink!* Desperate for relief, he exited the gasless vehicle and sprinted to the men's club.

* * *

Around 5:15 that afternoon, Iggy swaggered into the vestibule with whiskey heavy on his breath. *Anna's gotten off easy this month. Not once did I bug her for a piece of ass, what with the threat on my life and the pressure of Bruno's payoff. But tonight, no excuses, I'm takin' her on.*

Iggy bumped into the credenza and picked up his previous day's mail then made a sharp turn and almost knocked over Signora Matteo. Head wobbling, he ogled the embroidered bodice of her dress and slurred, "Hey, look at you, Mamma, all decked out in your fancy party clothes." He twirled a finger in the air. "Plannin' to paint the town, or what?"

Signora Matteo sniffed his breath and huffed in frustration. "***Dio, aiutami!*** Whiskey? Why you drink now?" When Iggy shrugged, she told him to hurry up and get ready, "***Sbrigati!*** I no want you be late." She insisted he tell Anna to dress in something discreet, with a modest neckline that covered her breasts, "***Un abito modesto***. She no need show too much. Tell Anna to cover ***il petto***."

Iggy tilted his head. "Dressed for what?"

"You no pay ***attenzione*** to what I say?" Signora Matteo thrust her hand in the air. "Is ***la festa*** for Macbetto and Teresa tonight. ***Non ti ricordi?***"

Iggy scratched his scruffy chin. "Now that you mention it, I do."

"***Subito!***" Signora Matteo ordered. "Go now!"

"Yeah, a party's just what the doctor ordered." Iggy slapped the mail down with such force that one of the envelopes flew off and jammed behind the credenza. Iggy didn't bother to retrieve the envelope but, if he had, he might have recognized the same indistinctive print that had addressed his birthday threat. "Don't worry, Mamma, I'll be ready in a snap."

Iggy tripped up the stairs, barged into their bedroom and startled Anna when he picked her up and spun her around. "Anna get your ass in gear. There's a party tonight!"

Anna clutched him for dear life and, chancing upon the gun stuck in his waistband, pulled it out. When Iggy dropped Anna to her feet, she staggered away with the barrel pointed at his face. "Why's this ***pistola*** in your ***pantaloni***?" She wielded the pistol and, remembering his infidelity, wished she had the know-how and nerve to use it.

"Put that down!" Shocked into sobriety, Iggy flailed his arms. "You crazy? Never point a gun at nobody unless you're set to fire it?" He grabbed the pistol from her hand. "***Capisci?*** Never!"

Anna leaned forward and taunted, "I dare you to teach me to shoot it."

"No! Forget you ever saw it." Iggy buried the weapon in his sock drawer. "Now get ready for the engagement party."

Anna crossed her arms under her bosom. "I've no intention of going with you . . . ***è una festa in onore della tua puttana***," Anna spat, indignant that it was a party in honor of his whore.

His wife's jealousy annoying, Iggy barked, "Move your ass . . . now!" With a sinister look in his eyes, he pointed to one of two closets on the far wall. "Pick out your most modest dress and shove those boobs in tight."

"Tell me, Iago, are her tiny breasts satisfying?"

Iggy flipped up the palm of his hand and thrust it in Anna's face. "Shut up or I'll . . . ."

Anna forced up her chin. "Or you'll what?"

"Never you mind, just get dressed!" Iggy smacked Anna on the rump.

While Iggy ruffled through his wardrobe in the second closet, Anna shimmied into a clingy red dress and, with her lips pressed tight, reached in and hoisted each side of her bosom, exposing more than her usual display of cleavage above its low neckline. *I'll show him modesty!* She wrapped a silk scarf around her neck and tucked it into the front of her bodice. *Let's see who gets his attention tonight!* Anna adjusted the seams of her stockings and slipped into a pair of black stiletto heels.

Iggy ignored Anna's exasperated exhalations while he donned his most dapper outfit, a starched white shirt under a blue sharkskin suit with the collar turned up around his neck. He squeezed into a pair of Italian leather shoes then glanced in the dresser mirror as he fingered his chin, convinced the lighting at the restaurant would be dimmed low enough to camouflage his five o'clock shadow. *Teresa'll never notice.*

Chapter Thirty-Two

As Louie Prima rasped the lyrics of *"Angelina"* from wall-mounted speakers in harmonious waves, an undercurrent of bilingual chatter vibrated the tables. The restaurant, appropriately named **Trattoria di Gusto** since it offered tasteful Italian dining, accommodated the engagement party in cramped coziness.

At one of the six tables, Mack and Teresa settled side-by-side with their parents, Antonio, Mina, Frank and Geneva. Father Romano, the new pastor of St. Christopher's, having been invited to join them at this overcrowded head-table, considerately offered to sit at another less congested table. Scouting the room, he chose the one where an empty chair was available right next to Iggy's voluptuous wife.

Once the short and portly priest departed for his new seat, the remaining eight contentedly adjusted to the additional elbow room. Now able to twist to the side and look Teresa's father directly in the eye, Signora Matteo addressed him, "Signore Camara, Teresa she make beautiful our *famiglia*."

"*Per piacere*, we are practically related." Signore Camara grinned. "Please, call me Arturo."

Mack's mother nodded. "*Sì*, Arturo, if this you like." Then, making the sign of the cross, she asked that, in respect for her dead husband, he continue to use her marital title, "*Pero, in rispetto per Signore Matteo*, you call me Signora. *Va bene?*"

Assuming the more affluent woman thought herself better than him, Signore Camara snapped, "Whatever you prefer, *Signora*."

Not catching the drift of Signore Camara's sarcastic tone, and still dwelling on the memory of her dead spouse, Signora Matteo patted his hand, "Teresa she tell me her mother she die. You miss you wife?"

Spotting his son's table, Signore Camara pulled his hand away and stood up abruptly. "*Scusami*, Tommaso is signaling. Let me go see what my son wants." Signore Camara rushed off to the other table.

Teresa squirmed as Antonio concocted an excuse for his father's rudeness. "Please forgive my father, Signora Matteo. Papà gets emotional at any mention of Mamma."

Frank held up a bottle. "Wine, anyone?" After he poured Geneva and himself a glass, he passed the wine toward Teresa's brother. "What kind of work do you do, Antonio?"

"I'm the storefront manager at Alfonso's Market on Elm St." Antonio gestured toward his date. "Mina's father, an expert butcher, owns the store."

"Antonio may be manager for the time being," Mina grumbled, "but unless something specific happens soon, I've no doubt Daddy will demote him to stock clerk."

Frank coughed into his fist. "I see."

In an attempt to fill the uncomfortable silence that followed, Mack lifted his chin toward one of the loudspeakers. "Anyone know the name of that singer?"

Frank nodded. "It's on the tip of my tongue. It's . . . it's . . ." He held up an emphatic index finger. "It's Frank Sinatra."

Geneva gently slapped his wrist. "Silly man, how can you confuse Louie Prima with the best crooner in the business? Mina, are you a Sinatra fan?"

Mina turned up her nose. "No, I prefer to listen to classic Italian opera."

Signora Matteo smiled and announced which opera was her dead husband's favorite, "Signore Matteo . . . he like *Otello.*" Happy to meet someone who also enjoyed opera, she encouraged Antonio and his friend to visit. "You come my house to listen?"

"*No, grazie.*" Mina flipped a thumb toward Antonio and mocked, "This one here refuses to listen to any opera. He's afraid the sopranos will shatter his *manly* eardrums."

Antonio cringed and whispered into Mina's ear, "Must you be miserable tonight?"

Incensed, Mina bolted up from the chair. "Excuse me! I need to powder my nose." She sped off toward the ladies room.

Teeth gritted, Antonio glared at Mina's back. "My friend doesn't feel well." Then, with an awkward expression directed at his sister, he petitioned her for some distraction.

At a loss, Teresa focused on the table's centerpiece which contained a sprinkling of fall color and was reminded of the autumn festival they celebrated in their youth. "Antonio, do you remember that year we rehearsed together for the feast of *Santa Maria?*"

Not a subject he wished to pursue, Antonio narrowed his eyes at Teresa. "*Sì*, but I'm sure no one here wants to hear about it."

Teresa ignored Antonio's implied warning and relayed the tale with animated hand gestures. "One year, when I was 6 years old and Antonio 8, Mamma insisted that my sister and I dress up in traditional costumes and practice the *tarantella*. Antonio cried and begged for a chance to dance with us. With patience, Mamma wrapped a tablecloth around his waist and put a kerchief on his head. Though we didn't own a camera . . . *no mi posso mai scordare*. No, I'll never forget Antonio, the picture of a little girl with wisps of hair curled against his rosy cheeks. Sweet Antonio . . . I mean Antonia . . . imitated our every move, even our curtsy at the end just as Papà entered the house. Angry that Antonio was acting like a sissy, Papà kicked him so hard that the poor boy wasn't able to sit for a week."

Mack elbowed Antonio and chuckled. "And I thought you were a man's man."

Everyone at the table laughed except Antonio who sat up straighter and smirked. "Want to know what Mamma's pet name for Teresa was?"

"Tell us," Geneva encouraged.

"*La mia scopa secca.*" Antonio lifted a pinky finger and, rotating his wrist for emphasis explained, "Mamma called her 'my skinny broomstick' because Teresa was all skin and bones. That is, until she blew up into a big fat balloon in her teens." Cheeks bloated, he sneered at his sister.

Teresa held up both hands. "*Va bene*, I surrender, Antonio. *Niente più raconti*. No more embarrassing stories."

"*Aspetti!* Wait a moment. It's the Matteos' turn," Frank chimed in.

Geneva grabbed her husband's hand and giggled. "No, Frank, we promised Mack. Remember?"

"Phew!" Mack swiped his forehead with exaggerated drama. "Thanks, Geneva."

"Teresa, has Mack told you about the 'Feast of the Lights'?" asked Geneva. Without waiting for an answer, she turned to Mack, "You will be taking her next week, won't you?"

"Definitely!" Mack took Teresa's hand. "What better time to show off my fiancé to the neighbors." Since Mack so enjoyed this local tradition, he had already described the events of the weeklong festival in honor of the Madonna di Cassandrino in detail to Teresa.

A Sunday morning parade always kick-started the festival. It was a solemn procession led by the pastor of St. Christopher's surrounded by altar boys, followed by men carrying a flower-decorated platform that held the statue of the Blessed Virgin Mary. Behind them little girls attired in First Holy Communion outfits strolled with the church choir singing hymns such as "Ave Maria." Women of the Altar Society dressed in their Sunday finest brought up the rear. But, at night, the holy atmosphere changed into one of secular merriment. Food, jewelry and trinket vendors lined the streets selling Italian wares not so readily available throughout the rest of the year. Most neighbors temporarily gave up old grudges and joined each other in spirited joviality.

Teresa smiled into Mack's eyes, "I'm looking forward to it, Macco."

On the other side of the restaurant, Mina found the restroom and entered it in a huff, smashing into Teresa's sister-in-law, drab as usual in her dowdy gray dress. "Natalia, Antonio drives me crazy! I thought you told me he'd be anxious to marry me if Daddy dangled the business under his nose."

"He hasn't asked you to marry him yet?" When Mina shook her head in the negative, Natalia pried further, "Did you tell him about you-know-what?"

"No, no, of course not." Sorry she'd shared the story of her lost virginity, Mina's cheeks grew as red as radishes.

She clearly remembered the day seven years ago when her father's teenage stock clerk, the flirtatious heartbreaker she adored, enticed her into the back room. Succumbing to his bowed legs and her raging hormones, she did the unthinkable with him. When her father walked in on them, the enraged man fired the boy on the spot and ignored his daughter for weeks. She decided the experience with the young Casanova had been far less than satisfying and not worth the loss of her father's respect or the harm to her reputation. The day after the incident, the disgruntled teenager bragged of his conquest in the boy's locker room, thereby branding her with a scarlet *C* for *cheap*. The word spread throughout the school and the neighborhood. Thereafter, the only males who ever asked her out were those interested in finding out if the rumors about the big-breasted girl were true.

When Natalia had introduced her to Antonio, a handsome man with no knowledge of her past, Mina was determined to marry him. With Natalia's encouragement, she bolstered the nerve to ask for her father's help. Signore DiSalva was more than willing to comply for ever since the stock room incident he regarded his daughter as 'damaged.' In order to move dented cans in his grocery store, he offered his customers the incentive of reasonable markdowns. He justified his proposal to Antonio as a fair incentive to marry his unchaste daughter.

"Why would I tell Antonio about that? Do you think I'm a fool?"

"No, but . . ."

"I certainly don't want him to expect anything for free. He has to marry me first."

"Sometimes you need to trap a man."

"I thought I did." Mina leaned forward. "What else can I do to trap Antonio?"

"Do what his mother did?"

"What do you mean? What'd his mother do?"

"Well, as rumor has it . . ." Natalia paused when another woman entered the restroom. "Remind me and I'll tell you all about it some other time."

Meanwhile, Patricia, Jake, Juliet, Iggy, and Anna gathered around another table with Father Romano. While Juliet listened to an argument between Patricia and Jake over the color of the baby's room, Iggy leaned forward and motioned toward the rotund cleric sitting on the other side of Anna. From behind a hand, he addressed him in English, "Father Romano, some guy told me you were kicked out of Our Lady of Good Shepherd for messin' with the choir director." When the priest's face turned crimson, Iggy let out a hardy laugh. "So it's true. Don't worry, Father. I won't tell a soul. Cross my fuckin' heart." Realizing no one else at the table had paid Iggy any mind, Father Romano let out a sigh of relief.

Iggy poured a glass of wine for the priest. "You know, Father Romano, Anna and I got hitched in Italy." Upon hearing her name, Anna kicked Iggy under the table so he switched to Italian, "We signed papers in front of the mayor of Naples. Can you believe that some holy roller, my sister Patricia over there, keeps insistin' we're not really married in the eyes of the Church."

Father Romano picked up his glass and spoke over its rim. "That *is* the official view of the Roman Catholic Church." He took a sip of the wine.

"Son of a bitch!" Iggy slapped the table and laugh out loud. "So, according to the damn Pope, my kids will be bastards?"

When Father Romano choked on the liquid, Anna patted his back until he was able to catch his breath. Then, with a hint of excitement in her voice, she whispered into his ear, "Are you telling me I'm free to marry someone else?"

The priest tilted forward and eyed Iggy with an indignant twitch, then retreated behind Anna and murmured under his breath, "Well, not exactly." He again swallowed more wine.

Disappointment spread over Anna's face. "What *do* you mean?"

"Simply put, a confession and a Catholic ceremony can rectify the matter. Without the vows of Holy Matrimony, your souls are marred by carnal sin." Worried that Iggy would retaliate with more gossip if he overheard, he drank the rest of his wine.

"Humph." Anna downed a full glass of wine then, gesturing toward Iggy, mumbled, "The dreadful truth, **Padre**, is that I wish I never laid eyes on him."

Oblivious to the sentiments conveyed in the hushed dialogue between his wife and the priest, Iggy tugged Anna's arm. "Hey, give the guy a damn break. He's off duty tonight, no guilty secrets till he stuffs his ass back in the confessional. Here, Father, let me pour you some more wine." He leaned over and started to fill the priest's glass, but stopped short and looked Father Romano directly in the eye. "Hey, one thing you gotta promise me first . . ."

At Iggy's pause, the priest asked nervously, "What's that?"

"That you won't pull none of that holy abracadabra shit on my Chianti here and change it, for Christ sakes. I might act like a goddam cannibal, but I sure don't drink blood." When the priest's mouth dropped at the insolent blasphemy, Iggy roared with delight.

At the other end of the room, Teresa's other two brothers Tommaso and Paulo, Paulo's wife Virginia, and a pair of cousins halted their conversation when Signore Camara tromped over to their table. "**Mannaggia!** Why am I stuck next to Signora Matteo? With one foot in the grave, the snobby hag wants to talk about the dead. Let them all rest in peace!"

Teresa's brother Paulo, his handsome features pink with embarrassment, scolded, "Papà, **comportati bene!** Don't make a scene. Do you want the Matteos to know how uncivilized you are?"

Signore Camara grimaced. "Who's uncivilized?"

Virginia, dressed in sophisticated black, directed a demure smile at Signore Camara and patted his hand. "*Avanti*, go back to the head table for dinner. You can come back later and have dessert and espresso with us."

Signore Camara decided to appease his favorite daughter-in-law. "*Sì*, I will in a minute, *cara mia*." He pivoted toward his eldest son, "Tommaso, can you slip me the money for the banquet now? Signora Matteo doesn't need to know that I can't afford this fancy affair."

As Natalia returned from the rest room and sat down next to her husband, Tommaso scowled, his pudgy face reddening. "You mean you refuse to afford it, don't you?"

Signore Camara pinched Tommaso's chin and responded through clenched teeth, "Let's not be petty, son."

"Natalia," Tommaso shoved his father's hand away, "hand me my wallet."

Natalia fished the billfold out of her handbag and handed it to Tommaso with some reluctance. "*Che farai?* Will you let the cheap miser finagle a handout for the wedding reception too?"

Ignoring the insult, Signore Camara extended his palm toward Tommaso and, when his son forked over a wad of cash, shoved it into the inside breast pocket of his suit jacket. He patted the bulge. "I'll be back for espresso."

At the fifth table, a few close relatives and *paesani* of both families reminisced about their hometowns in Italy. Diagonally across the room, Teresa's co-worker and friend Carmela and her husband, along with two of Mack's buddies and their dates, exchanged small talk at the last table.

Back at Iggy's table, Juliet brooded over her single status and, halfway through a glass of wine, complained to Patricia. "Other than Mamma, I'm the only female here without an escort." She glared at her brother with contempt. "If not for Iggy's interference, I'm sure Devin would've come with me tonight."

Patricia clicked her tongue in indignation. "Stop crying over spilt milk, Juliet, and keep your eye out for an Italian, someone from our own neighborhood."

"What am I supposed to do, latch onto an immigrant like Mack did?"

"Whatever it takes." Flinching, Patricia clutched her stomach. "Quick, give me your hand, Juliet. Feel the baby kick."

Juliet waved off the offer. "No thanks. I'll pass this time."

Across the table, under the influence of the third glass of wine Iggy had poured for her, Anna tousled her hair provocatively. "*Sono così felice! Sì*, I'm thrilled to be here in America and part of this wonderful *famiglia*." She ripped off her scarf, revealing a good six inches of cleavage, and fanned herself with it. "It's soooo warm in here."

His eyes glued to Anna's bosom, Father Romano ran a finger under his clerical collar, too tight to accommodate the lump in his throat. "Yes, isn't it?"

"*Hot* is more like it, Father," Iggy teased. "Anna, shake 'em, but don't break 'em!" In a possessive maneuver, Iggy threw his arm over Anna's shoulder. "Hey, Father Romano, ain't it a damn shame that a horny priest like you ain't allowed to shack up with a broad now and again?"

In an effort to save face, the clergyman sprung up to his full 5 feet 6 inches and announced, "I will now say grace." Unaware that electric static had caused his cassock to cling to his torso, he lifted a hand to his forehead, "*In nomine Patris* . . ." But before he completed the Sign of the Cross, Father Romano noticed that numerous shocked expressions including Signora Matteo's were focused below his waist. Upon realizing he had exposed his weakness for the flesh, he blurted the rest of the prayer in eight seconds flat. His neck as red as the wine he blessed at communion, he sat back down.

Iggy refilled the priest's glass once again. "If I was the Pope, I would've had the whole lot of you castrated."

While the waiters rolled out the salad carts, Tommaso stood and raised his wine goblet high. "Please, family and friends, all join me in a toast." With enthusiasm, he welcomed Mack into the Camara family, "*Macbetto, benvenuto nella nostra famiglia. Saluti!*"

Glasses waved as cheers erupted from the group, "*Saluti!*"

One cousin brandished a fork with bravado then tapped his glass with a jovial sparkle in his eye. Within seconds, others mimicked the good-humored demand which Iggy overstated, "Come on, Mack loosen up! Give Teresa a smooch or I will!"

"You will over my dead body!" Mack planted a peck on Teresa's cheek.

"You call that a kiss!" Iggy jibed.

When Teresa exaggerated a pucker, Mack swallowed hard and dove in for an avid mouth-to-mouth to the crowd's cheer.

As many of the guests were ready to take their first bite of salad, Frank pushed himself up from the table and held up his glass, "*Cent'anni a Teresa e Macco!* One hundred years of good health and happiness!" Relinquishing their forks, the crowd joined in the second toast, "*Cent'anni!*"

The group settled down and dove into each successive course served by the staff of efficient waiters. The salad plates cleared, they ladled spicy minestrone soup, followed by a choice of three kinds of pasta: spaghetti with clam sauce, ***pasta alla Bolognese***, and spaghetti with garlic and oil. Next, they presented the main course: **Saltimbocca alla Romana**, tasty rolls of veal covered by a thin slice of spicy **prosciutto,** a dry-cured ham that the chef had garnished with a sage leaf. Bowls of vegetables offered family style complemented this main dish.

Between the pasta and the veal courses, Iggy jumped up, holding up another full glass of wine. "Hey, everybody, I wanna make a toast." With all eyes riveted on him, Iggy widened his stance and thrust his pelvis forward. "Mack, may you be all the man Teresa deserves." Most of the men howled while the women jeered.

Anna wobbled up and jutted her breasts forward, shimmying them provocatively. "**Sì,** be a man who knows how to please a woman!"

"I'll show you a real man!" Iggy tilted Anna back, muzzled her mouth with his and finished with a loud smack of his lips. Again, the males hooted; the females hissed.

Red-faced, Signora Matteo stomped over to Iggy and, pinching his arm, demanded he stop his nonsense and asked why he was embarrassing the family in public. "**Basta,** Iago! Why you do? **Perché imbarazzi la famiglia in pubblico?"**

Rubbing his arm, Iggy slurred, "Aw, come on, Mamma. It's all in fun."

At another point in the celebration, while Anna cavorted with the priest, Iggy swaggered over and ensnared Teresa in a bear hug. "Welcome to the **famiglia!"**

When he brushed his whiskers against one of her cheeks, Teresa screwed up her nose and averted her face, trying to avoid being pricked by the cactus. "No!" *Anna is jealous enough as it is.*

Mack mustered the nerve to shove Iggy away from Teresa. "Go sit down with your wife, Iggy."

In contrast to Mack's display of backbone, Teresa pondered her own lack of courage. Although Anna had insinuated he might be affected by an illness of some sort, Mack still hadn't mentioned any affliction and she certainly hadn't seen any evidence of one. Debating whether or not to question Mack about it, she remembered her coworker's suggestion that maybe Anna had invented the problem. *Is Carmela right? I don't know, but I'm afraid to ask Macco. He might be insulted if it's not true. I guess I can be patient a little while longer.*

Mack struggled to get Iggy to sit down at his own table. "For one night, can't you behave?"

Once Iggy plopped down onto his seat, he yanked Mack down by his tie and harassed him **sotto voce,** "Bet you've been too chicken to tell Teresa about your disgustin' fits. You don't wanna surprise her with one now, do you? She might hightail it out of your sick-ass life. I'd be more than happy to give her a heads up for you, brother." Iggy snickered into his hand.

"Mind your own business, Iggy." Shoulders slumped and frowning, Mack walked away and headed back toward his fiancé. *Still haven't found the right time to tell Teresa but I can't put it off much longer. I'll come clean tomorrow.*

On the way to the Men's Room, Signore Camara narrowed his eyes and calculated the cost of a full-size wedding. As he approached his grey-haired cousin's table, he stopped and patted the man's shoulder. "**Cugino**, the price of freedom is steep. But, **grazie a Dio**, they all leave the nest sooner or later. The question is *Will I survive the wait?*" Smiling at his cousin's facetious reply, Signore Camara walked on and, entering the bathroom facilities, contemplated that, if Antonio finally decided to marry Mina, her father would be the fool required to pick up the tab. Reaching down to unzip his pants in front of the urinal, his smile broadened.

Signora Matteo, on the other hand, shook her head in dismay at Iggy's wife for she continued to wiggle her bosom blatantly in the clergyman's face. Mack's mother turned to him and moaned that she was mortified by Anna's wanton behavior and shocked by the immoral priest's response to it. "Anna, why she act like **una puttana**? **Sono mortificata!**"

"Don't worry, Mamma," Mack placated. "Most of the guests drank enough wine tonight to forget everything by tomorrow."

Signora Matteo switched the focus to her youngest daughter. "Look Giulietta. Poor girl, she no have man." She insisted that Mack introduce his sister to an eligible bachelor, an educated one like him. "**Uno educato.**"

Glancing at his sister's down-turned pout, Mack spurned his mother's idea, "Juliet doesn't like my friends. She makes fun of them, calls them bookworms."

In between courses, Patricia provided a barrage of unsolicited information to anyone who approached their table. "According to Dr. Spock, it's best to breastfeed babies. We bought a rocker so I can nurse the baby right by the bassinet. We're going to paint it white and the room a soft yellow. Imagine, we'll be the first in the family with a baby *and* our own home. The house *will* be ready by the time the baby's born. Right, Jake?"

"Yeah, oughta be done in 'bout anuder mont or two." Jake picked up a bottle of wine, walked around the table and handed it to Iggy. "Here ya go." He lowered his voice, "Tank God Patricia stopped askin' me where I got da money. I tought she'd never stop buggin' me."

After several polite "someday soon" responses from Frank to interrogations in regards to their timeline to start a family, Geneva released a frustrated sigh into Frank's ear, "I'm tempted to muzzle all these nosey morons."

Frank patted her hand. "Don't let them get to you, Gen."

As for Antonio, he choked on his food when a cousin approached from behind and asked him where he hid Mina's engagement ring. "Please, Alfonso, that's between Mina and me. If I ever give her one, I promise, you'll be the first to know." Mina thumped her foot under the table and glared at Antonio.

At the end of the meal, the waiters carried out large dessert trays and offered the guests their choice of coffee, American-style or espresso. The desserts included traditional Italian pastries: ***cannoli, pastaciotti, tiramisu*** and rum cake. While the guests enjoyed the sweets, Teresa and Mack approached couples and individuals alike, expressing appreciation for their attendance with a handshake and kiss on each cheek.

At the table where Signore Camara had again joined Teresa's brothers and their wives, Mack thanked Teresa's father profusely, "***Grazie per tutto***. Your generosity is most appreciated." Mack patted his stomach. "***Il mangiare era così buono. Delizioso!*** Everything tasted so good that I thought I died and went to heaven."

"Don't die before the wedding. It'll spoil the festivities," Signore Camara chortled.

"Papà, really!" Teresa reprimanded.

Wanting credit, Tommaso started to divulge his monetary contribution to the night's festivities, "Macco, I think you should know that I . . ."

Paulo intentionally cut him off, "Okay, so you ate more than your share, Tommaso. No need to brag." He and Signore Camara laughed heartily.

After they quieted down, Teresa addressed the women and thanked them for their help in making the arrangements for the engagement party, "Virgina and Natalia, ***grazie per il tuo aiuto***. I would've been lost without you." She pointed to one of the centerpieces her sisters-in-law had provided. "***I fiori sono belli***, absolutely beautiful." Teresa lowered her voice. "Too bad I can't preserve them for the wedding. Papà insists flowers are a total waste of money."

At the last table they visited, Mack discussed local politics with a few of the men while Teresa chatted with the women. When the male conversation switched to soccer, Mack drew closer to his best friend, Joe, a studious-looking fellow. Leaning down, he complained, "Iggy's at it again tonight. He's determined to annoy me until the day he dies. I'd like to choke him right about now."

Joe patted Mack's shoulder. "Glad he's your brother, not mine."

Meanwhile, taking advantage of Mack's distraction, Teresa pulled aside her petite co-worker from the factory. "Carmela," she confided, "I'm so annoyed with Anna, the way she's carried on tonight."

Carmela sympathized, "And she's the one that accused you of being a flirt. From what you told me, I think it's all a desperate bid for her husband's attention. With friends like her, who needs enemies?"

Teresa let out a lungful of air. "Can't argue with you there. She leaves a bitter taste in my mouth."

Mack approached from behind and squeezed Teresa's shoulder. "Coffee and dessert?"

"**Dolce**? **Sì,** dessert sounds wonderful?" *After talking about Anna, I need something to sweeten my tongue.* Teresa followed him to their seats where they relaxed with a coffee for Mack and an espresso for Teresa along with a scrumptious **pasticcino** for each of them. Teresa offered Mack a bite of hers and, once she fed it to him, wiped the crumbs from his mouth with her napkin.

Without so much as an "**arrivederci**" to the engaged couple, Patricia and Jake were the first to leave. Shortly afterwards, a few more guests wandered over to the coat-check. Mack noticed the traffic and grasped Teresa's hand. "You must be exhausted from all the excitement. I'll get your jacket."

"**Grazie**. I'm ready to go home." Teresa eyed the glow in Mack's cheeks as he stood up. He looked too healthy to be sick.

"Wait here. I'll be right back." On his way toward the coatroom, Mack repeated his promise to himself. *Tomorrow, I'll definitely tell Teresa sometime tomorrow.*

Zeroing in on Anna across the room, Teresa gripped the table's edge and expelled a hushed groan, "She's such a **bugiarda**." After talking with her friend Carmela, Teresa was now totally convinced Anna concocted the idea of Mack's illness. *The jealous liar wants to punish me for what she calls flirting.* **Beh!** *I didn't flirt, especially not with Iago of all people.*

Teresa refocused on Mack and decided not to approach him on the matter of an illness because he didn't have one. *Macco's as healthy as an ox.*

Chapter Thirty-Three

As Mack handed a ticket to the coat check girl, he glanced over his shoulder and smiled at the guests lined up behind him. Laden with doggie bags, they reminded him of a caravan of ants, eager to depart for their respective anthills.

Teresa's jacket in hand, Mack returned to his fiancé. "Let's go stand by the door. That way we can say goodbye to the guests on their way out."

"*Sì,* whatever you say." Teresa stifled a yawn.

Mack helped her into her jacket and led her toward the exit. A few feet from it, he paused to scan the room and tallied nineteen wine bottles, six at Iggy's table alone. "Hefty bar tab I'm sure. Thank goodness all our guests live no more than a short walk away."

Teresa directed her eyes upward and completed a facetious sign of the cross. "*Dio,* please protect our woozy friends."

"Amen." Mack zeroed in on Iggy and Anna, carousing near the coat check, and murmured an addendum, "Lord, please keep an eye on those two in particular."

Tipsy on his feet, Iggy struggled to help an even drunker Anna into her sweater while she projected her bosom toward any man that passed by, blowing kisses at the youngest ones. "***Buona sera, caro mio. Arrivederci!***"

One of Anna's targets, a cousin of Mack's who was feeling little pain by that time, had difficulty tearing his eyes away from her breasts. Iggy offered the letch a garbled apology, "Sorry, Guido, they're all mine." Once Iggy managed to squeeze his squirming wife into her cardigan, he held her at arm's length. "Relax, missy. Save it for when we get home." As his mother drew near, he released his grip on Anna and adjusted the crotch of his slacks. "I'm too damn big."

Anna snorted a derisive laugh. "If only that were true."

Her face shriveled in annoyance, Signora Matteo stormed past the drunken duo asking God why he punished her this way. "***Perché mi castiga?***" She wrapped her shawl tighter around her shoulders and hurried toward Mack and Teresa.

The rest of the guests gone, Mack offered her his arm. "We'll walk you home, Mamma." Leaving the inebriated pair to fend for themselves, the trio exited the restaurant and turned left toward the Matteo residence.

When they passed Father Romano puffing a cigar outside the restaurant, Signora Matteo wrinkled her nose in disgust. "***Così disgustoso!***" As Mack tugged her homeward, she wondered how many more vices the repulsive little man enjoyed.

Five minutes later, Iggy shoved Anna out the door to the deserted sidewalk in front of the restaurant. "Where'd everybody go?" With a doggy bag containing some of the veal he had so enjoyed clutched in one hand and his opposite arm supporting Anna, Iggy prodded her to the right. "Come on, this way. I know a shortcut to Steward Street. We'll beat 'em all home."

As they shuffled forward along the sidewalk, dark except for the occasional street lamp which cast a limited glow directly below it, a clandestine figure emerged from behind a telephone pole and scrambled after them, keeping a short distance between them. When Anna went limp, almost collapsing to the ground, Iggy halted, compelling the sinister form to dart behind a parked car. Iggy dropped the doggy bag and boosted Anna up and over his shoulder.

Smelling the veal and eager to take advantage of a free meal, the scraggly mutt Iggy had once abused darted out of a nearby alley and, putting further revenge on hold, attacked the bag instead of Iggy. Determined to satisfy his ferocious appetite, the docile-looking creature quickly chomped his adversary's leftovers.

Watching the mongrel benefit from his loss, Iggy kicked clumsily at the dog's rear end, but missed it altogether. "Damn mutt!" Taking his frustration out on his wife, he smacked her derrière. "Don't think you're gonna get outta anythin' by passin' out, little lady." Burdened by Anna's weight and tailed by the satiated dog, Iggy trudged onward, the resolute shadow in measured pursuit.

Once Iggy turned a corner onto Steward Street, he paused next to a metal garbage can, disoriented even though he stood a mere half block from the Matteo residence. "Hey, where the hell are we?" In his drunken state, he was confused by a recent change to the local environment.

Up and down the four-block street, trellises decorated with bright-colored light bulbs lit up the night. Several members of the *Italian-American Men's Club* who were devoted to tradition had installed them that afternoon in preparation for the annual "Feast of the Lights." Though the weeklong festival wasn't due to begin until the following week, the installers had decided to test them that evening for a few hours.

In his struggle to hold onto Anna, by then snoring at full volume, Iggy bumped into the trashcan. Startled rats emerged from the bowels of the canister, scattering in different directions. Iggy and the mutt dodged them as best they could while, taking advantage of a distracted target, the furtive silhouette moved in closer to Iggy.

A foot away from the garbage can, the undetected figure leaped forward and hammered a lead pipe against the back of Iggy's skull. The pipe came down with such force that Iggy lost consciousness on contact. As his body flailed forward, his wife's frame slid to the rear, down along his spine. The shift in weight accelerated Iggy's descent so that his forehead cracked hard against the concrete while, in contrast, Anna's cheek glided softly onto the cushion of her husband's buttocks. The assailant wasted no time in executing a swift getaway but the mutt lingered. Unable to resist this chance for retribution, the dog lifted a leg and urinated on Iggy's feet, then smugly strutted away just as the trellis lights went out.

Fifteen minutes passed before the exhaust and rumble of a diesel truck roused Anna from her stupor. Cold and uncomfortable, she convulsed in a fit of coughing. Once the fumes cleared, she lifted her head and glanced from left to right. "Where am I?" Perplexed, she fingered the lumpy form below her. "What's this?"

Anna pushed herself up higher and jolted when she realized she was resting on her husband's torso. Twisting at the waist, she studied the back of Iggy's head. "What happened, Iago? Why're we on the ground?"

With no response from Iggy, Anna stood up, circled his body and winced at the blood coagulating under his nose and down the side of his head. "Iago!" She nudged his torso, but Iggy didn't move. Subsequent to a closer examination that revealed no sign of life, Anna let out a blood-curdling scream. "*È morto! Aiuto!* Help me, my husband . . . he's dead! *Aiuto!*"

Anna's shrieks roused several neighbors. Astute enough to comprehend the medical emergency, one woman called the telephone operator while her gray-haired husband rushed out in his robe. Holding the still hysterical Anna away from Iggy's lifeless form, he tried to calm her, his Italian consoling in tone. Within minutes, a police car and an ambulance screeched to a halt in front of them.

While the emergency team examined Iggy, a young officer emerged from his vehicle and pushed back the few spectators that had gathered around Iggy's body. He approached the sobbing Anna, her face buried in the chest of her self-appointed guardian. Though this witness was obviously in distress, he nevertheless pointed to the victim and demanded information. "Tell me his name, ma'am. Who did this?"

Not understanding his English, Anna lifted her head and shook it frantically. "*No capisco . . . no capisco. Mio marito è morto . . . è tutto coperto in sangue!*" As the policeman repeated his request for information, Anna sunk into a catatonic state.

The Good Samaritan loosened his hold on Anna and expelled an exasperated breath. "*Sei stupido?* You no can see this woman is in shock?" Anxious to return to the comfort of his apartment, he propelled her into the arms of the policeman. "Take home. She need to rest."

Removing his uniform jacket, the officer draped it over Anna's shoulders and propped her down on a nearby stoop. "First, tell me what she said." He lifted a notepad and pen from his rear pocket.

The older gentleman gestured toward Iggy. "She say husband dead, too much blood."

The policeman jotted down the statement. "Do you know who they are?"

"Sì, Matteo is last name." The man pointed in the direction Iggy and Anna had been headed. "Big white *casa,* end of street. You no can miss."

"Thank you, sir." The officer stuffed the pad back into his pocket and, lifting Anna from the stoop, wrapped his arm around her waist. "I'll take her home, call a doctor for her."

In the meantime, the ambulance attendants attached various tubes to Iggy's still body and lifted him onto a stretcher. Once they tucked blankets around him, they hoisted him into the vehicle and drove away, sirens blaring.

* * *

While Frank and Mack paced the hallway alongside the emergency room of St. Mary's Hospital, Geneva and Juliet huddled around Signora Matteo in the nearby waiting area. Juliet patted her blubbering mother's shoulder. "Mamma, I'll go see what the boys found out." Juliet left her mother in Geneva's care and approached Frank. "Where are Patricia and Jake? Why aren't they here yet?"

"I told them to stay home with Anna." Doctor Piccolo had given Anna a sedative, but Frank was still worried she might awaken in distress. Even though Iggy's wife wasn't blood-related, Frank considered her "family" and, as such, she was just as much his concern as his injured brother. "Somebody has to keep an eye on her."

"Any news about Iggy?" Juliet slipped behind Frank when the door of an examination room swung wide open and two nurses rolled a bed from the room. In it, a man lay unmoving, his head covered in a turban of bandages. Not giving any of them a chance to check if it was Iggy, the nurses quickly wheeled the bed down the hall.

Not even a minute later, a doctor in a blue surgical gown emerged from the room. "Anyone for Mr. Matteo?"

Frank raised his hand. "Over here."

"Who's his next of kin?" the doctor inquired.

Frank rubbed his chin. "His wife I suppose, but she's still in shock. We're Iggy's brothers."

Juliet poked her head out from behind Frank. "I'm his sister." She looked hopefully at the physician. "How's Iggy? Will he be all right?"

"I'm Dr. Rosser, staff neurosurgeon. Please come this way."

Mack stalked after the doctor but, when Juliet tried to follow, Frank grabbed her by the wrist. "Go to Mamma. She needs you right now." With reluctance, Juliet traipsed to the waiting area and Frank, limping behind Mack, entered the room furnished with a couple of chairs and an exam table. All seemed standard in the sterile environment except for a large implement on the counter that resembled the drill Jake had purchased to assist him with house renovations. Resting alongside it was a mound of wet gauze pads, several of them blood-soaked. Assuming the blood was his brother's, Mack eyed it with consternation.

"Gentlemen, please take a seat." The doctor approached a lighted display panel on the wall where three x-ray photos of a human skull hung side-by-side. "Let me explain the medical implications." He pointed to one frame at a time. "Your brother suffered a concussion to the back of his head which caused a severe fracture to his skull evident in this first x-ray. Another impact, perhaps his head's contact with the concrete, further exacerbated his condition with a second fracture visible here over the frontal lobe of his brain. Lastly, the third x-ray shows the spot, right about there, where I drilled through his skull to relieve the pressure of fluid buildup." Both Mack and Frank cringed. "At this point, your brother remains comatose."

Mack spoke up, "How long will he be in a coma?"

"And what shape will he be in when he wakes up?" Frank massaged his leg.

Dr. Rosser stepped away from the screen and slowly approached the brothers, cracking his knuckles on the way. "The answer to both your questions, gentlemen, depends on how long his brain was deprived of oxygen. The damage, whether temporary or permanent, remains to be seen if, and when, your brother wakes from the coma. We'll keep you informed of any changes in his condition."

Mack held out a hand to the neurosurgeon. "Thanks for the candid explanation, doctor." He glanced at Frank. "Now, how do we soften it for the girls?" Preceding Frank, he led the way toward the waiting area.

Under the distress of his brother's condition, Frank gritted his teeth and gripped his hands in a simulated chokehold. "If I ever find out who the hell did this to Iggy, I'll . . ." Even though his brother had always been a thorn in his side, the bad blood between Frank and Iggy seemed inconsequential under the circumstances.

Halfway down the hallway, two men dressed in dark sport coats, followed by a uniformed police officer, accosted Frank and Mack. The senior of the three flashed a badge pinned to the inside pocket of his jacket. "Either of you related to the Matteo victim?"

Halting, Mack nodded and Frank replied, "Brothers . . . Frank and Mack."

"I'm Lieutenant Smathers." The police detective gestured toward the younger man next to him. "My associate Detective Canelli . . ." While Canelli raised a hand in greeting, Smathers tilted his head toward the uniformed rookie behind him. "Officer Clancy you've already met." When he lifted his cap, the brothers solemnly acknowledged the policeman who had escorted Anna home. "We've been assigned to investigate your brother's attack."

Mack's voice cracked, "Who . . . who did this to Iggy?"

"That's what we aim to find out." An awkward moment later, the lieutenant addressed Frank, "Do you both live with the victim?"

Frank lifted his chin. "Yeah."

"How many in the household?"

"Seven others," Frank answered.

"Eight if we include Iggy," Mack corrected.

"Gentlemen, we'll need your family's cooperation during the investigation, but we understand you'll need some time to come to grips with the situation. As a matter of courtesy, we'll delay any further inquiries until tomorrow. Can we stop by your house at 9 a.m.?" The lieutenant glanced at his wristwatch and noted the late hour. "That's not too early, is it?"

Frank shook his head. "No, we'll be ready."

The lieutenant reached into his jacket, pulled out a business card and handed it to Frank. "Here's my contact number. Call if you need to change the time." He then signaled to his men. "Let's meet back at the precinct."

As the two detectives and rookie retreated down the corridor, Frank examined the boldfaced information on the card then grimly passed it to his brother. Mack bit his lip as he reviewed the card that not only identified the precinct the lieutenant represented but also the division: "**HOMICIDE.**" Their expressions somber, the two brothers dragged their feet toward the waiting area.

Chapter Thirty-Four

Although Signora Matteo's swollen eyes remained dry as if her subscription to the local tear bank had expired, she curled in her bed later that same night with a string of rosary beads in her hands and lamented, "Iago, Iago." She lifted her head at a knock on the door. "*Chi è?*"

From the other side of the door, Patricia's voice filtered in, "It's me, Mamma. Can I come in?"

"**Sì**." Signora Matteo flipped over so that her rear faced the door.

Once Patricia entered the room, flooding it with the light from the hallway, she sat at the edge of the bed and placed her hand on Signora Matteo's shoulder. "How're you doing, Mamma?"

Believing her son on his deathbed, Signora Matteo swallowed a sob. "**Che pensi?** You think Iago he will die soon?"

"Don't talk like that, Mamma. Let's keep a positive attitude for Iggy's sake."

Remaining pessimistic, Signora Matteo wailed that she never expected to outlive any of her children.

Patricia stifled a whimper. "No one does, Mamma. But God has his own plan."

"**Sì, è vero**." Signora Matteo sniveled at this truth. "**Primo**, He take Romeo . . . now He will take Iago." She raised her eyes to the ceiling and asked God why He allowed such bad things to happen, "**Perché?**" Though she loved Iggy, she thought about the shameless person he had become and whined to her daughter, "Why, Iago he never talk nice? Why he so . . . so . . ."

"Depraved?" Patricia suggested with a woeful expression.

Humiliated by her son's shortcomings, Signora Matteo buried her face in the palms of her hands and asked what sin she had committed to deserve such punishment. "**Dimmi . . . che peccato?**"

Patricia rubbed her mother's back. "Don't blame yourself, Mamma. It's not your fault. You did your best with him."

Signora Matteo made the sign of the cross. "What Iago do so bad . . . so bad a man try to kill?" Reaching for straws, she hypothesized that perhaps Iago had lashed out at their dreadful new pastor for drooling over Anna. "**Padre** Romano he too no so nice. He make eyes Iago wife? You think Iago he hit **il prete?**"

"Father Romano?" Patricia shook her head at the notion. "You can't actually believe Iggy would get violent with a priest?" She reconsidered, "But, then again, you never know. With Iggy, anything's possible, even the sacrilegious." She stood up and tucked the blanket snug around her mother's form and sighed. "Try to get some sleep, Mamma. We'll talk more in the morning." With her head hung low, Patricia crept from the room and closed the door behind her, leaving Signora Matteo to mourn alone in the dark.

* * *

With shoulders slumped, Patricia entered her bedroom and slipped under the blanket. Cuddled against Jake's chest, she promptly released the flow of tears she'd been suppressing since the police officer escorted Anna home. "Oh, Jake," she blubbered. "Who hurt Iggy?"

"Why ya askin' me?" Jake responded in a defensive tone.

Patricia grasped his arm. "Be honest with me. You were involved in one of his schemes, weren't you?"

"Are ya insinuatin' . . . ?" His guilty expression obscured by the darkness, Jake pushed Patricia away from him.

"Sorry, Jake, my nerves are shot." Patricia rolled over. "Forget I mentioned it."

* * *

Toiletries in hand, Geneva bumped into her youngest sister-in-law halfway down the second floor corridor. "So, Juliet, what do you make of what happened tonight?"

"What do you mean, Geneva?"

"You know. Who attacked Iggy?" Geneva brandished a toothbrush. "Where were you when it happened? I saw you leave the party alone."

Juliet retracted her chin in disbelief. "You aren't implying *I* did it, are you? Even though Iggy ruined my love life, you don't think I'm that evil, do you?"

"Well, no, of course not." Geneva waved off the allegation. "Don't be silly. It wasn't an accusation."

Juliet assumed an ironic posture with one hand perched on her hip and leaned forward, aiming her upturned palm at Geneva. "So, where was *your* husband when it happened? Did Frank leave your side after you came home from the engagement party?"

Geneva recoiled. "Well, he did but only to take out the trash. He was gone less than ten minutes."

"Enough time to walk a half block? With mock contempt, Juliet poked a finger against Geneva's collarbone. "Weren't Iggy and Frank always at each other's throats?"

Geneva smacked Juliet's hand away. "You don't actually believe Frank did it?" After Juliet pursed her lips and shook her head in ridicule of her sister-in-law's gullibility, Geneva whispered, "Isn't it always the quiet one that's guilty in all the murder movies?" She glanced over both shoulders before she elaborated on her own line of suspicion, "If you ask me, Jake's a better suspect. Remember Iggy threatened to expose Jake's dirty laundry to Patricia. Maybe the attack was Jake's attempt to silence Iggy for good."

Juliet let out an exasperated huff. "Do you really think Jake's a vicious mugger?"

Geneva looked down at her feet. "Honestly, no."

"So then who will we blame next, Mamma or my sweet brother Mack?" Juliet placed an index finger on her lower lip. "Hmm, the detectives may suspect any one of us if they find out Iggy was the obnoxious black sheep of the family. Since we're sure none of us attacked Iggy, let's pretend Iggy got along with everyone in the household. Why make the detectives waste time investigating us?"

Geneva stiffened her spine. "We can't out and out lie, can we?"

Juliet rocked on her heels. "No, but we can keep quiet about private matters . . . ones that have nothing to do with why Iggy was attacked."

* * *

Downstairs, Mack entered the dining room where Frank sat in front of a doggie bag stuffing half of a ***cannolo*** into his mouth. "Frank?"

"Yeah, Mack, what is it?" Frank garbled as some of the pastry's ricotta cream ran down his chin.

Mack perched himself on the edge of a chair and faced Frank. "Well, tomorrow, when the detectives ask us questions about Iggy, do we reveal the true man or paint him to be a saint?"

Frank licked his lips then swiped his jaw with his shirtsleeve. "What kind of question is that?"

"God only knows what Iggy might have been involved in. We can't ignore the possibility of . . ." Mack stood up and paced around. "He's family after all."

"I know, but . . ."

"If we're too upfront about him," Mack persisted, "the detectives might dig deeper and end up discovering Iggy was mixed up in something illegal."

"Wouldn't surprise me at all." Frank eyed the other half of the pastry.

Mack wrung his hands. "If they do, what will happen to him when he comes out of the coma?"

"I don't know." Although Iggy was his brother and Frank knew he'd defend him to the bitter end, he refused to admit it to Mack. "I guess he'll get whatever he deserves." Ashamed of his disloyal comment, Frank shoved the last of the ***cannolo*** into his mouth.

* * *

While the rest of the Matteo household verbalized their emotions, suspicions and options, the calming effect of Anna's sedative wore off. Locked in a theater of turbulent nightmares, her body thrashed and her lashes quivered in place. "Iago, you . . . you **bastardo!** You deserved to die!"

* * *

Unaware of Iggy's attack, Teresa awakened in the middle of that same night and pondered whether her father was actually unfaithful to her mother all those years ago. *Or did Mamma dream up Papà's infidelity like Anna did Iago's?* With no definitive answer, Teresa tossed and turned until she finally fell back to sleep.

Chapter Thirty-Five

In his precinct office on Monday, a few hours after the investigators grilled Iggy's immediate family, Lieutenant Tom Smathers tilted his armchair back and propped his feet on top of his desk. He eyed his two subordinates, Detective Tony Canelli, slouched on a seat opposite him, and Officer Shane Clancy, leaning against the far wall. "Well, men, what do you think of this morning's interviews with the Matteos?" Smathers scratched through his salt and pepper mane, unknowingly scattering dandruff on his collar. "Contrary to what I expected, I found them a bit uncooperative."

Canelli blinked his long lashes. "Uncooperative?" He shook his head emphatically, the waves of his jet-black hair shimmering under the flourescent lights. "No. I'd say it's more like they were . . . how you say . . . hesitant." Although still in his twenties, the olive-skinned detective presented the picture of confidence. "Take it from me, Italians are defensive when dealin' with the authorities. It's in the blood. Goes back to our roots in the homeland where the government's padded by the mob."

"Nothing against you Dagos, Canelli, but I agree with Lieutenant Smathers." Avoiding the detective's scowl, Clancy looked down at his polished shoes and, reminded of the grief Canelli had given him in the past, fidgeted with the police cap sandwiched between his freckled hands. "Maybe the Matteos held back information . . . afraid it might sting 'em in the ass if the victim ever recovers." The Irish rookie was unable to resist another ethnic dig. "Fear can make even a Guinea leary."

"What're you, staff psychologist?" Canelli snapped. Even though he was used to the slurs, especially from the older Irish flatfoots, the younger Mick annoyed him nonetheless and made him feel the need to defend his heritage. "To get anywhere in this case, you've gotta understand Italians. Matteo may or may not be a tough fellow, but even Italian thugs are saints in their families' eyes, especially after they've been put out of commission by some sleazy mugger. Remember, blood's thicker than water, especially Italian blood. *"Capisci?"*

"Enough with the violins, Canelli. Though he might be out of it, the victim's not dead yet." Smathers lowered his feet and sat up straight. "Let's go over the Matteos' statements. I'll start with Geneva, the sister-in-law, married to Frank."

Smathers reviewed his notes from a clipboard. "Let me see. I asked her about the Matteo brothers. She told me they were partners in the family business. When I pressured her to tell me if there was friction between Iggy and his partners, she went pale and shook her head. Without my even asking, she supplied an alibi for Frank, claiming he was at home with her at the time of Iggy's attack."

Canelli stood up and paced the room, jiggling the change in his pocket. "The lady's husband seemed kinda edgy too. Broke out in a sweat when I asked how he got along with Iggy. Said they put up with each other. Was like pullin' teeth, gettin' this big mule Frank to say anythin' else. He finally admitted they didn't see eye-to-eye, especially about business, but refused to give me somethin' solid. His tight lips made me wonder if somethin' shady was goin' on behind those bakery doors." He glanced at the window directly to his left and noticed a pigeon landing on its outside ledge. Tucking in its variegated wings, the bird settled down to roost close to the glass.

Smathers signaled to the rookie. "Check for criminal records on the lot of them."

"Don't bother, Clancy. Already sifted through the precinct files, made me a few phone calls." Canelli sauntered back to the chair he vacated moments earlier. "Victim's been picked up for small stuff . . . drunk and disorderly, shop liftin' . . . .shit like that. Never nothin' heavy. The others are clean. But," Canelli brandished an index card, "their father, the late Franco Matteo, *Senior*, he's another story. Had a thick, dusty file. Back in the days of Prohibition, the man was accused of usin' his bakery trucks for bootleggin'. District Attorney never prosecuted him though. Probably bribed some crooked politician to keep his ass out of jail. What do you think, boss?"

"Who knows? But, if he was a lucrative bootlegger, it may explain why the Matteos live in the biggest house in the neighborhood."

Smathers flipped a page on the clipboard. "Jake, the brother-in-law, who talked to him?"

Clancy pulled out a notepad and turned the pages. "My notes are here somewhere. I know I wrote them down."

"Just like a Mick to be such a scatterbrain," Canelli mocked.

Clancy narrowed his eyes. "What'd you say, Canelli?"

"What's a matter?" Canelli asked. "Eat too many potatoes, they clogged your ears?"

"Knock it off, you guys! Back to business."

By that time, Clancy found his notes. "Okay, here goes." He began to read in a clipped fashion. "Discharged from the navy six months ago, Jake married Patricia, the victim's sister. Started in the family business, June of this year. Said he was grateful Frank gave him the job since his wife's pregnant and he's renovating a house for her and the baby." Clancy took a deep breath then looked up at Lieutenant Smathers. "He totally avoided any mention of the victim till I pushed the issue. Then he called him . . ." he looked down at his pad, " . . . quote, *one hell of a guy* and said Iggy made him want to make a better man of himself."

Cannelli snorted. "What normal guy talks like that?" By that time, the pigeon on the ledge was cooing to its own reflection, the sound penetrating the glass. Unable to ignore the monotonous repetitions, Canelli stretched out an arm and rapped on the window. In response, the bird turned its rear to the glass, defecated and, to Canelli's relief, flew away. "I've got a hunch this Jake has somethin' to hide. Did he say where he was at the time of the attack?"

"Claimed he took his wife home from the party and never left her side until I knocked on the door with Iggy's wife," Clancy replied, glaring at Canelli.

Smathers looked up from the clipboard. "Who spoke to the younger sister?"

"Me." Canelli's eyes lit up. "Not a bad looking chick, unattached. Maybe, once we solve this case, I just might ask her out. Juliet," he sighed, "the name's sweet as her face."

Smathers slapped his palm on the desktop. "Don't pull anything like you did in the last three murder investigations, Canelli. No more romancing anyone related to a case." The lieutenant wasn't aware that, although his subordinate would never admit it, Canelli was on a quest for true love. "If you do, your ass'll be on the line. Understand, mister?" Smathers folded his arms across his chest and, with a lift of his chin, urged his undaunted partner, "Proceed, Canelli. Tell us what she said about her brother Iggy."

"Let me see, how'd she put it?" Canelli sneaked a peek at another index card he drew out of his breast pocket. "The pretty lady said he was defensive of Italian tradition and didn't cater to her datin' nobody that wasn't Italian. Can't say I blame the guy. She was my sister, I'd feel the same. Well, anyways, that's about all I got out of her before she asked if my family came from Italy." He turned toward Clancy and whispered behind his hand, "I think she liked my handsome Mediterranean mug."

"Last warning, Canelli, stifle your hormones!" Smathers barked. "*Capisci?*"

"Yeah, yeah." His enthusiasm squashed, Canelli slumped lower in his seat.

"Ask around and find out who Juliet dated . . ." The lieutenant clicked down the top of a pen, one with a novel ballpoint, and pointed it at Canelli. " . . . and find out whether or not there was friction between any of her boyfriends and the victim."

Canelli performed a halfhearted salute. "Gotcha."

Smathers examined the clipboard once more. "Iggy's wife, Anna?"

Straightening his spine, Canelli lifted a finger. "Me again. Phew! What a hot combination, big knockers and a low neckline." He fanned his face.

Impatient, Smather's flicked his hand at the detective. "Go on!"

Canelli crossed a calf over the opposite thigh and leaned forward on it. "The Mrs. speaks only Italian, no English. Good thing my mother taught me the lingo, huh?" He consulted a third index card. "This Anna, she swears she drank no more than two glasses of wine at the engagement party; then she claims she passed out on the way home from Gusto's and, when she came to, found herself on top of her husband's body. The lady said she went berserk cause she thought he was dead. If you ask me, somethin don't add up here."

"I was there," Clancy interrupted, "She seemed really upset before she went into shock."

Canelli ignored Clancy. "Then, out of left field, the lady spouts off that her ex-friend Teresa's a *puttana*, Italian for whore, and claims this Teresa flirted with her husband. What do you think, boss, jealousy? Think Anna's strong enough to knock out her husband?"

"Doubt it," Smathers surmised. "All the same, we'll keep her in mind as a possible suspect. Did you find out who Teresa is?"

Canelli nodded, "Yeah, Anna said she's engaged to Macbetto. He's Iggy's younger brother, nicknamed Mack or Macco. Who talked to him?"

"I did." Smathers flipped another sheet on his clipboard. "Counter to Anna's version, Mack insinuated that Iggy tried to seduce anyone in a skirt. Even his own fiancé wasn't off limits."

"So what do we have?" Canelli ran a hand over his hair, the Brylcreem he used to groom his waves leaving his palm greasy. "Another jealous suspect?" He wiped his hand on his slacks.

"I don't know." Smathers scanned his notes. "Mack did provide an alibi. He said he walked his fiancé to her house after they dropped off his mother and stayed there awhile. Canelli, get hold of Teresa and see if she can pinpoint the exact time Mack left her."

"Will do. Did this Mack say anything else about last night?" Canelli prodded.

"Said he was sorry he didn't insist Iggy and Anna walk home with them since they were both very drunk."

"Has a guilty conscience," Canelli tapped his temple. "You think?"

"You might say that." Smathers skimmed down his notes. "He also implied Iggy's humor wasn't always appreciated by whoever happened to be the brunt of it. 'You have to take him with a grain of salt,' is how he put it."

"Ask me, sounds like Iggy irritated the hell out of Mack," Canelli suggested.

Smathers twirled the ballpoint pen between his thumb and index finger. "Well, he did imply that they just tolerated each other."

"Did he come up with any probable suspects for the muggin'?" Canelli asked.

"Claimed he didn't have any idea who did it." Smathers glanced at the clipboard. "All right, enough about Mack. Who talked to the pregnant sister, Patricia?"

"I did," Clancy stepped forward.

"Well, don't just stand there." Canelli rolled his eyes. "We haven't got all day."

"Hold on." Clancy fumbled with his notepad once more until he found the right page. "Patricia, Jake's wife, said whoever attacked Iggy ought to get the electric chair. After I asked her for a description of her brother, she said . . ." the rookie again referred to his notes. "Her exact words were, 'Iggy's a tough guy. No one dared mess with my brother unless they wanted trouble.' Then, she burst out crying and clammed up on me."

"I'm starting to get a clearer picture of our victim." Smathers stood up behind his desk and rubbed his chin. "So our Iggy's a lady's man, an annoying troublemaker, one who's made a few people jealous and is also a disagreeable business partner. Let's investigate outside the immediate family. Did either of you get your hands on a guest list for the engagement party?" When Canelli held up a sheet of paper, Smathers went on, "Good. Divide it in three and each of us can interview one third of the people on it."

Canelli nodded confirmation as he perused the list. "Looks like all the guests live within five blocks of the Matteos." Using the edge of the desk, he ripped the sheet in three and handed a section to each of the other men. "While we're at it, let's try to size up Iggy's reputation out on the street. Sometimes, you can get a better sense of a person from strangers than from his own family."

"Good idea." Smathers referred back to his clipboard. "Now, did we skip anybody? Oh, yeah, the victim's teary-eyed mother. Between her sobs and her heavy accent, it was hard to make out what she said. But, if I understood her correctly, she was suggesting the priest they invited to the engagement party might've been involved in the attack. The woman insisted Iggy would never put up with the disgusting way the priest drooled over his wife. She was obsessed with the idea that her son must've confronted the priest after the party and he struck back when Iggy wasn't looking. To be on the safe side, Canelli, go ahead and get a statement from this Father Romano. He's the pastor at St. Christopher's, if I'm not mistaken."

"Yeah, sure. I'll put him at the top of my list." Canelli jotted down the name of the priest.

Smathers frowned. "Too bad there was no sign of the weapon at the scene. Fingerprints would've made IDing the assailant a hell of a lot simpler." He approached the office door and opened it. "That's it for today, men. We'll meet here tomorrow, same time, and compare notes."

Canelli stood up and adjusted the waistband of his trousers. "Hey, boss?"

Smathers pursed his lips. "What's up, Canelli, did we forget something?"

"I just wanna make you understand that my people are a special breed. You see, most Italians will back off if somebody tries to get in their face." Canelli waved his arm in the air. "But make them feel special, like they can offer information you can't get nowhere else, and they'll spill their guts out. It's all in the way you talk to an Italian . . . especially if it has anythin' to do with his family. Like I said before, family's everythin' to an Italian."

"Thanks for the heads up, Canelli." Smathers winked at the rookie. "We'll be extra careful with the *Spaghetti Set*. Won't we, Clancy?"

Chapter Thirty-Six

While the detectives analyzed their preliminary interviews in the Matteo case, Antonio carried a basket of apples out the front door of Alfonso's Market. Once he arranged them on the display table, he tightened his bib-apron then grabbed a broom leaning in the doorway. Partway through the task of sweeping the sidewalk, a white-haired gentleman, managing to hold onto his fedora despite a blustery breeze, approached Antonio.

"*Buon giorno*, Signore Ricardo," Antonio greeted. "How are you this morning?"

"*Bene, grazie*." The old man pressed his hat tight to his chest. "I didn't expect to see you here today. I assumed you'd be with your sister."

Antonio pulled in his chin, "With my sister, what for? She's home cleaning house." He returned to his task.

"Well, that's strange." Signore Ricardo leaned forward. "I thought she'd be glued to his side."

Antonio stilled the broom. "Who's side?"

"Her fiancé's, of course," Signore Ricardo replied.

"Why would she be with him? He works the bakery storefront every Saturday." Antonio resumed sweeping. "He's probably busy with customers right now."

"Not after last night, he isn't," Signore Ricardo insisted.

"Last night?" Antonio remembered how exhausted he'd been after putting up with Mina's harassment at the engagement party. Though he planned to go to bed early, Signore Camara didn't give him the chance. Before his father flew the coop to beg his lady friend to reconsider her stance on their rendezvous, the sex-starved rooster ordered Antonio to stay up until Mack departed. He refused to give their nosey neighbors an additional excuse to gossip. Eyes drooping, Antonio had been so grateful when Mack finally said goodbye at 9:00 p.m. "Macco left our house at a decent hour." When a gust of wind blew away the leaves he had swept into a pile, Antonio stewed with annoyance.

"You mean you haven't heard?" Signore Ricardo placed a hand on Antonio's forearm. "I assumed everyone knew."

"Heard what?" Antonio shook off the man's hand. "Stop talking in circles."

"Well, I hate to be the bearer of such bad news but the Matteo boy probably lies in a coma as we speak." Signore Ricardo gestured with his hat at some far off distance.

"What?" Antonio scoffed in skepticism. "He looked fine to me last night. You must be mistaken."

"No, trust me it's true," Signore Ricardo insisted.

"Then tell me what happened to him?"

"Nobody seems to know for sure, but he was definitely taken away by an ambulance."

"You saw it with your own eyes?"

"No."

"So how do you know?"

"My nephew Marco Brunelli told me."

"He was there?"

"No, but he heard all about it from his close friend Gino Lorenzo. You see, Gino lives across the way from a lady named Maria Fagioli, cousin to a Giorgio Ramoli whose house happens to be a half block from the Matteos'." Signore Ricardo shifted from foot to foot. "Now, Giorgio swore to Maria that the Matteo boy was unconscious when they put him into the ambulance. Maria mentioned it to Gino who ran into Marco at the men's club and then my nephew relayed the facts to me." Signore Ricardo folded his arms across his chest and jerked his chin up and down for emphasis. "So there you have it!"

Finally convinced that something dreadful did occur to Mack Matteo, Antonio considered the possible consequences to his sister with consternation. "Thank's for the information, Signore Ricardo, but please excuse me. I need to rush home and tell Teresa." Antonio tossed the broom aside and stormed into the store. With Signore Ricardo in his wake, he pushed through the hoard of shoppers to get to the main counter and accosted Mina who stood behind the register. "I know it's busy, but you'll have to manage on your own. I've got to hurry home."

"You can't," Mina sneered. "Daddy won't allow it."

"Too bad, I'm leaving anyway." Antonio removed his apron and tossed it on the counter. "It's urgent."

"What's so urgent?" Mina griped.

"Ask Signore Ricardo. He'll explain." Antonio bolted toward the door.

* * *

As he entered the house drenched in perspiration, Antonio swiped his forehead and, struggling for breath, shouted into the kitchen, "Teresa, **vieni qui**. Come . . . come here quick!" He turned around and barked up the stairs, "Papà, **scendi subito**. You'll . . . you'll want to hear this too."

While Teresa breezed into the parlor, Signore Camara scooted down the stairs. "***Che cosa è successo?*** What's the matter, Antonio?"

"***Sì***, tell us." Teresa wiped her hand on her apron and approached her brother. "Antonio, you're soaked."

Hunched over, Antonio gasped for air. "I . . . I ran all the way. I thought you'd . . . you'd want to know."

Teresa patted Antonio's shoulder. "Calm down. Take a deep breath then tell me what's so urgent you'd risk a cold."

"It's Macco. He was taken to the hospital," Antonio sputtered.

"No!" Teresa gasped. "When? This morning?"

Antonio wheezed, "***No, ieri sera***. Signore Ricardo said he was unconscious when they carted him off by ambulance last night."

Worried that his devious plan had backfired, Signore Camara grabbed Antonio by the shoulder. "He's still alive isn't he?"

"***Sì***, I think so," Antonio swiped his forehead, "but he's in a coma."

Anna was right after all. Macco does have some illness. Frantic, Teresa headed to the front door. "Tell me, Antonio, what hospital? I want to go to him."

"I don't know." Antonio held a palm face up. "The old man never said which one."

"***Dio Santo!*** I have to find out where they've taken Macco." Still in her apron and without bothering to put on a cover-up, Teresa dashed out of the house into the brisk air and raced down the street in the direction of the Matteo residence.

Signore Camara grabbed Teresa's jacket from a coat rack and shoved it at Antonio, "Go! Follow your sister."

Antonio panted, "***Sì***, just let me catch my breath."

* * *

Desperate, Teresa ran toward the Matteos' house. When she got to Steward Street, the unlit trellises along the road reminded her that Mack had been so looking forward to the "Feast of the Lights." She was heartbroken that her man might not recover in time to enjoy his favorite neighborhood tradition.

Tears streaked down Teresa's cheeks as she rang the Matteos' doorbell and, when no one answered it, she pounded. "Please, won't someone open up?"

Unable to ignore the persistent knocks, Anna cracked open the door and peered out. "Oh, it's you. Leave me alone. I have a headache." When Teresa grabbed hold of the knob, Anna tried to prevent her entrance.

However, Teresa managed to slip her foot between the door and its frame. "Where is he? Please tell me in which hospital," she begged. "I want to be by his side."

Anna clenched her fists. "Have you no shame?"

"Please, Anna, I love him," Teresa implored.

"What? You want to make love to him even in the hospital?" Anna angrily waved an arm at Teresa. "Go ahead! You can't make things any worse now. He should be dead by the end of the day anyway. Go . . . go to St. Mary's Hospital, you ***puttana***!" In another attempt to shut her out, Anna smashed the door hard against Teresa's foot. "***Spero che andate al diavolo!*** May your souls burn together in hell!" When Teresa jerked back her injured limb, Anna slammed the door and bolted it.

Such a hateful woman! Teresa limped down the steps and, unaware of the presence of a concerned bystander, looked to the right and left. *Which way is the hospital?*

From behind the closest fire hydrant, the mutt that had relieved himself on Iggy lifeless body the previous evening watched Teresa. When she began to hobble aimlessly in a circle, the dog took pity on her. Cautiously inching up to the teary-eyed woman, the mutt brushed against her leg and sympathetically whimpered.

Teresa stooped down and gave his scraggly mane a cursory pat. "You poor thing. You look as bad as I feel." She scratched under the dog's chin as she anxiously surveyed the empty street, wondering how she was going get directions to St. Mary's Hospital. "There's no one around to ask." Savoring the rare chance at positive attention, the mongrel licked her face and panted contentedly.

Meanwhile, from a branch above their heads, the cardinal that had observed the dog's previous interactions with humans eyed the duo. Twittering nervously, the bird worried that the brunette might interfere with his plan to pilfer some of the mongrel's fur for its nest.

At the faint sound of Antonio's approaching footsteps, the dog lifted its ears then dashed off, knocking Teresa off balance. As she landed on her butt, Teresa failed to notice the cardinal flapping its wings in hot pursuit of the mutt.

Again covered in perspiration, Antonio eventually reached Teresa. "What're you doing on the ground?"

"The dog . . ." Teresa pointed in the direction the mongrel had disappeared and shrugged. "Don't just stand there. Help me up."

When Teresa grabbed onto Antonio's extended hand, he lifted her to her feet and noticed her limp. "You hurt your foot?"

"Never mind my foot." With her brother's assistance, Teresa squeezed into the wraparound jacket he'd brought along, not bothering to tie its belt. "Antonio, take me to St. Mary's Hospital."

"*Va bene*," Antonio nodded and gestured to the right. "A bus stops at that corner. It'll deliver us right to their door."

Teresa wrung her hands. "How long will it take us to get there?"

Antonio glanced at his wristwatch. "A half hour . . . maybe longer. We should reach the hospital before noon."

"That long?" Teresa whined. "I need to see Macco as soon as possible . . . before he . . . before he passes away."

"What makes you think he'll die anytime soon?" Antonio ushered her forward.

"Anna said he'll be dead by the end of the day."

* * *

At the hospital, Antonio used his limited vocabulary to obtain directions to the ward which housed the Matteo patient. Afterward, he guided his sniveling sister past an elevator posted with an "Out of Service" sign and into the only lift left in commission. He pressed the button marked "11th Floor-Intensive Care Unit."

Behind the closed doors, Teresa bawled into her brother's chest. "I didn't realize how much I loved Macco, not until today."

As the elevator jerked upwards, Antonio patted Teresa's back. "There, there."

Taking no note of the strangers that entered and exited the lift as it stopped several times on the way up to the 11th floor, Teresa mumbled a few desperate prayers for Mack's recovery.

* * *

Since it wasn't yet his turn to visit Iggy's bedside, Mack kept a somber vigil in the Intensive Care Unit's waiting room along with Juliet, Geneva and Frank. Geneva muttered to Juliet, "Jake and Patricia? Why aren't *they* here?"

Juliet whispered back, "Patricia had an appointment with the obstetrician that she *refused* to cancel and Jake's working on their house."

"And Anna, what's her excuse?" Geneva asked with annoyance. "Of all people, his wife should be here."

"A migraine headache, or so she claimed," Juliet supplied.

Worrying about the bakery's closure, unavoidable due to their vigil over Iggy, Frank moaned to Mack, "We're gonna cut it close this quarter."

"How can you think about profits at a time like this?" Mack rebuked.

Frank lowered his head in shame. "Somebody has to."

At one point, Mack licked his dry lips. "It's almost noon. Anyone want something to eat or drink? I'll go down to the cafeteria."

Juliet nodded. "I'll take a cup of coffee."

Frank reached for his wallet, "Sounds good. Get one for each of us and bring up some donuts too. Here's some money."

"I'll take care of it, Frank. You get it next time." Mack headed to the elevator and pressed the "Down" button.

While Mack waited in front of the one lift still in operation, he tapped his foot and watched the dial above its doors indicating the elevator's stop and go progress. He stepped up closer when a bell announced its imminent arrival.

Once the doors sprang open and revealed Teresa huddled close to her brother, Mack's eyes lit up. "Teresa, so glad you're here!"

At the sound of the familiar baritone voice, Teresa raised her head and through a veil of tears focused her eyes on a watery version of Mack. As if accosted by a ghost, her face blanched and she collapsed to the elevator floor in a faint.

Chapter Thirty-Seven

A stern nun dressed in crisp white robes stooped over and examined Teresa's unconscious form as she lay sprawled on the floor of the elevator, her jacket open and her apron exposed. Mother Superior, supervisor of the nursing staff, passed an open bottle of smelling salts beneath Teresa's nostrils.

Once revived, Teresa waved her hands in front of her face. "**Basta, per favore!** No more. **Dio santo,** please leave me alone!"

Affronted by Teresa's lack of respect, the nun haughtily stood up and stepped aside, her old face creased ugly with disdain. "Such dramatics."

Antonio and Mack rushed forward and, each grasping one of Teresa's arms, hauled her up and out of the elevator. At Teresa's baffled expression, Mack explained, "Teresa, you fainted. Sister Josephine was kind enough to help us."

"She'll be fine," Sister Josephine assured in a petulant tone. After Mack thanked her profusely, the nun shuffled back to her station, grumbling under her breath about the weak moral fiber of the young.

Teresa brushed herself off and, tying her jacket, stammered in confusion, "What's going on? When I heard your voice, Macco, I . . . I don't know what I imagined. First, Antonio ran home to tell me you were in a coma. Then Anna insisted you'd be dead by the end of the day." She looked Mack up and down. "Macco, you look just fine to me. If you aren't sick, why are you here in the hospital?"

Mack placed his arm around Teresa's shoulder. "An obvious misunderstanding, Iggy's the patient, not me. Someone mugged him on the way home from the engagement party last night."

Teresa sighed with relief, "Ah, I see." Then, her face reddening in anger, she lashed out at her brother with a vehement whack on the arm. "*Antonio, come hai potuto!* How did you manage to distort the situation?"

This explosive side of his fiancé's personality new to him, Mack retracted his chin in disbelief. "Teresa, calm down." *Never realized she had such a hot temper.*

Teresa buried her face in her hands, mortified that in a matter of minutes she had managed to expose two character flaws: a weak tendency to faint and an ornery disposition. *I'm so embarrassed.*

In retrospect, Antonio recognized that he should have checked out the details of Signore Ricardo's story before telling Teresa. Feeling guilty for putting her through such unnecessary agony, he patted her arm. "Sorry. I only wanted to help."

Teresa thought about it and, realizing that her brother simply had had her best interest at heart, lowered her hands. "Let's forget it ever happened." Teresa glanced at her watch. "Maybe you ought to get back to work, Antonio? Mina must be overwhelmed by now. I'll stay here with Macco."

Antonio turned toward Mack and extended his hand. "*Sì*, I'd better return to the store. Hope your brother gets well soon."

Mack shook his hand. "Thanks, Antonio."

As Antonio departed, Teresa bit down on her bottom lip. She was worried that Mack would think she was self-absorbed too since she hadn't yet shown any concern for Iggy. *I'm such an idiot.* She grasped Mack's arm. "I'm sorry about what happened to Iago. How is he?"

"His vital signs are steady, but he's still in a coma. The doctors don't know when or if he'll recover." Mack grabbed Teresa's hand. "It's my turn to check on him. Come on, let's go see him together."

Teresa hesitated, knowing she had no stomach for such matters. *But it's a chance to prove I'm not so frail.* "Sure, Macco. Let's go. Where is he?"

"This way." With his hand at the small of her back, Mack guided Teresa toward Iggy's intensive care station but halfway there he paused. "Teresa, there's something I've been meaning to tell you."

"**Sì**, Macco, what is it?" Teresa halted and gazed up at Mack with expectation.

"Uh . . ." Mack diverted his eyes and, chewing on the inside of his cheek, fretted over how he was supposed to divulge his epileptic condition to Teresa after she had already fainted over a simple mix-up. *I can't upset Teresa twice in the same day, can I?* He wrestled with his conscience. *But the longer I hold off, the worse it'll be. I have to tell her now.* "Let's sit over here, Teresa." He took her by the hand and led her to an empty waiting area.

"I haven't been totally honest with you," Mack nervously admitted as Teresa took a seat.

"What do you mean?" Teresa frowned.

Mack sat next to her. "About my health."

"What about your health? Are you sick?" Teresa reached for Mack's forehead.

"No." Mack grabbed her wrist and stopped her. "I have this medical problem."

Teresa pulled her hand away. *So there was some truth to what Anna said.* "What kind of problem? Don't tell me you can't have children?" Teresa had envisioned a houseful of **bambini**, a minimum of four.

Mack shook his head. "No, it's nothing like that. It's a medical condition called epilepsy."

"Epilepsy?" Confused by the unfamiliar word, Teresa gathered the fingertips of her right hand, pointed them upwards and flipped her wrist, once for each word of her next question, "What-does-that-mean?"

"It means I have to take medication so I won't convulse in a seizure."

"**Convulsioni?** Like someone possessed by demons?"

"Something like that . . . but the doctor assures me I'll be fine if I take my medication. He said I can live a long, healthy life."

"But what if you do convulse? Will there be permanent damage?"

"Not really, it's just a temporary inconvenience. It takes me a few hours to sleep it off and then I'm as good as new."

"**Ma perché non me l'hai detto?** Why didn't you tell me about this sooner?" Feeling betrayed, Teresa bolted up from the chair and stomped down her foot. "I can't believe you waited this long." She threw her hands up. "This is outrageous!"

"You're right." Mack hung his head. "I'm sorry."

Bending over him, Teresa shouted, "Sorry! Is that all you can say?"

"I didn't think you'd understand?" Mack looked down at his shoes.

"You think I'm stupid?"

Mack shook his head. "No, no, of course not."

"Then what?" Teresa waved a hand in front of his face. "That I'm insensitive?"

"No." When Teresa stepped aside, Mack stood up and paced around the small area. "I didn't tell you in the beginning because I thought you might consider my condition a reason not to get involved with me." He halted and held out a palm. "And then as time went on . . ."

"So you think I'm shallow, do you?"

"No, definitely not. It's just that a woman as beautiful as you are . . . why, you could have any man you want. Why bother with me, a fellow with a health problem?"

Although her heart fluttered at the compliment, Teresa was still upset by his attitude. "What kind of woman do you think I am?"

"A woman too good for me," Mack confessed.

"Macco, what are you saying?"

"That I love you so much and don't want to lose you, but...."

"But what . . . ?" Teresa persisted

"If you want to call off the engagement, I'll understand. You can keep the ring."

"The ring!" Teresa twirled the diamond on her finger. "Who cares about this ring?"

Mack sadly gazed at the woman he thought he'd lost due to his own stupidity and lack of self-confidence.

Teresa lifted her chin. "I'm disappointed that you didn't trust me enough to tell me the truth from the beginning." The forlorn look on Mack's face worked like a balm to soothe Teresa's burning indignation. "But, without you, this ring has no value to me." *I fell apart when I thought he was dying.*

"It doesn't?"

"No, because . . ." The prospect of losing Mack twice in the same day too much to bear, Teresa burst into tears. "Because I love you, Macco."

"You still love me?"

"I love you no matter what . . . problems and all," Teresa whimpered.

"You do?" Relieved, Mack collapsed in a chair.

"**Sì**." Teresa wrapped her arm around his shoulder and kissed his forehead, dampening it with her tears. "I promise to take care of you, *amore mio*."

Ecstatic that Teresa hadn't rejected him because of his epileptic condition, Mack embraced her in a bear hug. "God knows I don't deserve you, Teresa."

Chapter Thirty-Eight

Once Teresa and her brother departed for the hospital, Anna stomped to her bedroom and thrust her hand toward her frustrated image in the dresser mirror. "*Sei così stupida! Sì*, you were an absolute idiot to introduce your husband to the likes of her."

Iago . . . that untrustworthy snake! Remembering what Father Romano had said at the engagement party, that she and Iggy were living in sin because they hadn't been married by a priest, Anna narrowed her eyes. *According to the church, I'm just his **puttana**.* She held up a tight fist. *But in the eyes of the law, I'm still Iago's wife, at least till his heart stops. Then what will I be entitled to . . . his money . . . a share of the business? Humph! We'll see.*

Thank God I'll be free when he's dead. Anna circled the bed and rummaged through her closet. "Let me see. What's suitable to wear to a cheater's wake?" She pulled out a clingy black shift from the back of the closet, one she'd considered leaving behind in Italy. Holding it up, she inspected its plunging neckline, a bitter reminder of Iggy's past lust for her. She'd worn this particular dress to entice Iggy into her bedroom the night her father had caught them bare-naked, sexually entangled on the floor. *This one will do fine.*

Although she never anticipated the possibility that she'd become a widow at such a young age, Anna hoped to save face. Unless Teresa was brazen enough to reveal Iggy's infidelity, she felt sure no one would ever find out that her husband preferred the flat-chested home wrecker over his wife.

At the peal of the front chimes, Anna tensed. *If it's Teresa again, I'll scratch out her eyes.* She shoved the dress back in the closet and stormed down the stairs to the vestibule, her claws extended for battle. Before the fourth ring of the bell, she yanked open the door in a fury. "The nerve of you to . . ." Anna halted in mid-sentence when she caught sight of the attractive detective, her expression softening and her tone melting into a purr, "***Investigatore*** Canelli, it's nice of you to drop by again. Did you already solve my poor husband's murder?"

Anna batted her lashes at the detective. *Iago's not the only one that can cheat.* Despite her husband's critical condition, she refused to forgive him for his supposed infidelity with her only friend, and therefore wanted to punish him. Since her fantasy lover, the mailman, had rejected her advances that very morning, she was determined to prove her sex appeal with someone else.

Anna was sure that the young detective who constantly gawked at her chest would love to be the next man to tango with her under the sheets. A shiver of excitement ran through her body when she thought of the endless possibilities. *Just maybe I'll let him.*

"***Me deve scusare***," he apologized. "I didn't know your husband died."

With the sound of hope in her voice, Anna retorted, "Oh, he's not dead yet. Though there's hardly a chance he'll recover. It's just a matter of time, no?" Through lowered lashes, Anna ogled the detective and expelled a sultry sigh.

Despite Anna's switch in demeanor from one of a wild-eyed cat to that of a wannabe widow, Canelli pursued the reason for his visit. "Signora Matteo, would it be a problem for me to search through your husband's things? I might be able to find some clues to his mugger."

"***Certamente, non c'è problema***. I'm sure a sharp detective like you can uncover *something* of interest. Please come in." Anna retreated further into the vestibule but not far enough for the detective to avoid a collision with her breasts. When Canelli frowned at the narrow path allotted him, Anna backed off, her disappointment evident in her pout. "This way, follow me."

Hypnotized by the exaggerated sway of her hips, Canelli trailed behind her swinging his own buttocks up the stairs, and, at the first landing, cleared his throat. "By the way, Signora Matteo, you familiar with your husband's reputation?"

"No." Anna narrowed her brow. "What reputation?" *Did he have more than one lover?*

"Well, according to my sources, he was runnin' a losin' numbers trade with a stack of angry customers."

"Oh." Anna raised her shoulders and jutted her chin forward. "Who trades numbers? I never heard of such a business."

"It's illegal gamblin'. What's more, he reneged on a payback to a loan shark?"

"Iago went on a fishing expedition? When did he go?" Anna raised both palms up.

"No, no, a loan shark's a man who lends out money at ridiculously high interest rates and demands his payback be on time, or else . . . ." Canelli gritted his teeth and ran the side of a finger across his neck. "*Capisci?*"

Anna shook her head. "Why would Iago do such a stupid thing?"

Canelli shrugged. "Can't say."

After Anna led the detective to the bedroom, she picked up an emery board from the dresser and perched herself on the edge of the bed. With her dress hiked up above her knees, she crossed her legs and swung her foot provocatively. "Let me know if there's anything I can do for you, *Investigatore* Canelli." She began to shape her nails.

Canelli gestured toward the two closets. "Which one's your husband's, Signora Matteo?"

Anna pointed the nail file. "The one on the left." Retracting her hand, she ran the file along the neckline of her dress. "Please, call me Anna?"

Canelli approached Iggy's closet and rifled through each item of clothing and, in due course, reached into the breast pocket of a jacket tucked way in the far corner of the wardrobe, pulling out Iggy's birthday threat. He flashed the sheet of paper toward Anna. "Know who sent your husband this message, Signora Matteo?"

"No." Anna sauntered over to the detective and examined the pasted letters. "I can't read English. "What does it say?"

"Well, it's no invitation to a party." Since Canelli didn't bother to request a search warrant, he was hoping Anna would be amenable to parting with the threat, or any other relevant evidence for that matter. "Mind if I take it?"

"No, go ahead. Take it." Anna returned to the bed and leaned back seductively. *Take me too. I'm all yours if you want..*

Disregarding her suggestive pose, Canelli placed the death threat into an evidence bag and turned his attention to the bureau. "Which side of the dresser does your husband use?"

Anna flipped her wrist toward the drawers on the right of the dresser. "*Quelle alla destra.*" *I'd like to check out the detective's drawers!*

Once Canelli rifled through Iggy's dresser and found nothing out of the ordinary, he flicked a finger at a nightstand on the right of the bed. "This one here your husband's?"

"No, *quello.*" Anna pointed to the one on the left of the bed.

Stooped beside Iggy's nightstand, Canelli opened the top drawer and slid his hand through Iggy's socks until his fingers hit a hard object. He pushed the clothes aside and uncovered the gun Iggy stashed below them on the evening of the engagement party. "Did you know your husband owned a pistol?" About to retrieve it with his pinky by the trigger frame, Canelli noticed the released safety and, careful not to smear any fingerprints, re-secured the gun before he opened it and inspected the full barrel.

"*Sì,* I handled it once." *I'd like to finger **Investigatore** Canelli's pistol!* Anna tiptoed up close behind him and peered over the Canelli's shoulder just as he spun around.

In an awkward attempt to avoid her cleavage, Canelli turned his face to the left. "Your husband always keep his gun loaded?"

Undaunted, Anna whispered seductively into his ear, "*Sì,* his pistol was always loaded, if you know what I mean." She glanced down at his crouch. "Maybe sometime you'll let me handle yours."

The detective grimaced at the implication and scolded, "That's not allowed, **Signora** Matteo," with an emphasis on the word *Signora.* He redirected her attention to the matter at hand. "I wanna take your husband's gun to the police lab. Any objection?"

Anna retreated a few steps. "Take . . . take, matters not to me."

Canelli placed the gun into the evidence bag along with the note, then shuffled through the last two drawers of the nightstand where he found no further items of interest. He straightened up. "I'm done here."

Anna poked out her chest, "Are you sure there's nothing else you want to examine? If there's anything you want to see, I can . . ."

Canelli cut her off, "No, I'll pass, Signora Matteo."

Ingrato! Rejected for the second time that day, Anna spun around, her annoyance at the thankless detective evident in her shrill voice, "Well, in that case, I'll show you to the door."

"Don't bother. I'll let myself out." As if running from a burning building, Canelli scooted past the high-pitched siren and dashed out of the bedroom, down the stairs and out the front door. "Phew! Her husband's not even cold yet and the broad wants to get into my pants."

In his rush to get to his unmarked car, Tony nearly tripped on a pigeon that poked out from behind a garbage can, one of the bins Frank had put out the previous evening. "Scat!" Squawking, the bird flew to the top of the sedan and scratched its claws into the paint of its roof. "Damn pigeon!"

Chapter Thirty-Nine

Two weeks later, while Patricia snored softly next to him, Jake tossed and turned. Eventually falling asleep after a day of kowtowing to his pregnant wife, submitting to her every demand, he found no peace in his dreams either. Though he was finally free of his least favorite brother-in-law by day, Jake was frequently tormented by visions of Iggy in the wee hours of the night.

During one particular nightmare, Jake's eyelids twitched nervously as Iggy emerged from a steamy potbellied kettle wearing nothing but a horned headdress made of bloodstained bandages. Accosting Jake, he grabbed him by the collar, almost choking off his air supply. "Did ja payoff Bruno?"

Barely able to speak, Jake garbled, "Wit what? I ain't got no money?"

"Remember, the shark's your problem now."

When Iggy let go of his shirt, Jake fell to the ground, landing on a heap of smelly fish scales. "Ugh!"

Iggy laughed. "What's the matter? Can't handle the pressure? How about this? Can you handle this?" Snarling, Iggy kicked his brother-in-law in the crotch.

The resulting pain so intense, tears welled in Jake's eyes. "Hey! My balls!" Cupping his hands to protect his scrotum from further attack, Jake feared he'd never father another child.

"What balls? If you had any, you'd tell my damn sister to stop squeezin' the hell outta 'em? Act like a man!"

"What ya expect me ta do?"

"Stand up for yourself once in a while," Iggy shouted down at Jake. "If your dick wasn't as limp as your brain, you'd show her who wears the goddamn pants in the family." Stepping over him, Iggy's forked tail whipped hard against Jake's head and drew a stream of blood from his right temple. At Jake's painful moan, Iggy scoffed, "If Bruno's thugs come gunnin' for the money, you gonna whine to them too, you fuckin' crybaby."

After Iggy slithered back into the black cauldron, Bruno's hatchet men crawled out of it, toting high caliber pistols. Jake cowered behind the potbellied kettle, "I ain't got da money . . . I ain't got da money."

When he parted his fingers and looked through them, the thugs' abdomens swelled while their faces mutated into that of his wife's, their guns into tools. Two Patricia's waddled toward Jake, one opening and closing a large pair of pliers, the other brandishing an adjustable wrench. As they bounced into each other, they multiplied. Eventually, the pregnant bowling-pin forms outnumbered him ten to one and harped in unison, "The house or your balls . . . the house or your balls . . . the house or your balls."

Feeling overwhelmed by the repetitious chanting of ten bitchy pins, he grabbed his crotch and yelled back. "Yer outta luck. I ain't got more den two!" In a defensive measure, he picked up the heavy cauldron with a thumb and two fingers, rolling it along the ground toward the pregnant pins, knocking them all down with the first bowl. "Ooo-wee! I got me a strike!"

When Jake turned over onto Patricia, she woke up and walloped him. "Knock it off, mister! You'll hurt the baby."

* * *

A couple of weeks later, a mid-October breeze blew in through the opened window of the bakery's upstairs office and ruffled the papers on the conference table. Frank eyed Mack sitting across from him and Jake to his right before he confiscated the last donut from a cardboard box. Sticking half of it into his mouth, he garbled, "I guess that's it for today's meetin', unless the two of you have any problems you need to bring up."

Mack, doodling on a scratchpad, looked up. "No, everything's fine from a financial standpoint. Happy to say we're in the black this month."

"Ain't got no problems wit da trucks eder, Frank." Jake rocked his torso. "And since Iggy ain't 'round to pester da drivers when dey come in, dey all show up on time now. All's been runnin' like damn good clockwork."

Frank smacked the tabletop with both of his palms. "Great work, men." Business finished, he relaxed against the back of the chair and folded his hands over the mound of his paunch. "What a relief not havin' Iggy around to start trouble about somethin' or other."

Mack grimaced, "Please, Frank, don't badmouth him while he's laid up."

"Okay, you're right. But you gotta admit it's more peaceful with him still in the hospital." Frank leaned closer toward Jake and patted his shoulder. "You know, we really appreciate how you've picked up the slack."

"Well, tanks for da raise." Jake tapped his breast pocket where his pay envelope formed a bulge. "Came at da right time. I almost got me anuder gig, a mean a side job. Now I don't need ta." Jake stood up and stepped away from the table but, halfway across the room, he hesitated and spun around. "Hey, what's da latest word from dat young detective? Anytin' new? Seems I'm never round when he comes by."

Mack stopped scribbling and focused on Jake. "Detective Canelli stopped by night before last. He told us he found a lead pipe in an alley not far from the crime scene. But he can't be sure it's the actual weapon used on Iggy until the police lab analyzes the blood on it." Mack shifted his gaze toward his brother. "I've got a hunch the detective's sweet on our little sister. Otherwise, I doubt he'd spend so much time on Iggy's case."

Frank sniffed, "Maybe."

"A lead pipe, huh?" Picturing Bruno's thugs, one holding Iggy down, the other smashing the pipe into his skull, Jake clenched his fists. "I hope dey snag da damn hoods dat clobbered Iggy. Den dey can't rub out nobody else."

Mack narrowed his eyes. "What makes you think more than one guy attacked Iggy?"

"Oh, I . . . I dunno." Jake teetered from foot to foot, stalling for an unsuspicious answer. "Since Iggy's such a big guy, I figured, uh . . . maybe . . . uh, dey'd need more den one guy ta take him. Yeah, dat's it."

"Hardly," Mack countered. "He was too drunk to fight anyone off."

"Can't argue wit ya dere." Jake bit his lip then blurted his next question, "Da detective mention anytin' 'bout Iggy's numbers gig?"

Mack eyed his brother-in-law suspiciously. "Why are you asking, Jake?"

Perspiration, blazing bubbles of guilt, beaded on Jake's forehead. "Dere's so many rumors floatin' round, none wort believin' mind ya. I just wondered if da cops were followin' up on 'em."

Frank straightened in his seat. "Canelli said the vice squad pegged Iggy's one runner, but refused to give up his name. Said it was classified since the guy's still under investigation." He squinted distrustfully at his brother-in-law. "Somethin' you're not tellin' us, Jake?"

"No, no," Jake stammered as he swiped his forehead with the back of his hand. "Just curious." He quickly changed the subject, "By da way, how's Iggy doin'? Eder a ya been ta da hospital lately?"

Frank nodded. "Yeah, Geneva insists we go see Iggy every other night even though Mamma sits with him all mornin' and Juliet checks on him after work." Frank paused while he loosened his belt a notch. "He's no better off as far as any of us can tell. He still lays there like a lump on a log, just wastin' away."

"Any news from da doctor?" Jake held his breath for the response. He'd been hoping against hope that Iggy would quietly slip away, that the thorn in his side would spontaneously disintegrate. If Iggy expired, Jake's debt would evaporate since no one else knew about the money Iggy lent him, and he'd be free and clear of his nasty oppressor. His period of indenture to Iggy would end, Patricia none the wiser. Maybe even the nightmares would stop. But Bruno and his goons were another matter. Although they knew he was Iggy's lackey and involved with his numbers operation, he figured they might leave him alone once they found out his wallet was empty, that he had no money they could confiscate.

"Doctor Rosser stopped in last time we were with Iggy." Frank ran his fingers through his hair and, aware that he'd been loosing more and more lately, frowned at the strands that came loose in his fingers. Shaking them off, he continued. "He said there's nothin' else he can do for him." Iggy's vital signs kept getting weaker and, according to the doctor, the longer Iggy remained in a coma, the less chance he had to recover. Since he was taking up needed space in the Intensive Care Unit, the hospital planned to transfer him to another floor by the end of the week.

Jake released a lungful of air. "Dat don't sound none too good."

"No, it sure doesn't." Frank stretched his neck in an effort to get the kinks out. "The way Iggy looks, I doubt you'd even recognize him now. But go see for yourself."

Jake turned his palms up and shrugged. "Who's got da time? Patricia keeps harpin' on me ta get da house done. Ya know how pushy she is."

"And what's Patricia's excuse?" Frank complained. "You'd think she'd wanna check to see if he's still breathin'."

"She's too far long." Jake jutted his abdomen forward and cupped his hands in front of it. "Dint ya notice how big she's gettin' . . . 'n da way she wobbles on dem swollen feet a hers? Not easy ta get round like dat. Anyways, she says dere's too many germs at dat hospital." He retracted his stomach and switched the focus away from his wife, "Hey, what 'bout Anna? How much time she been spendin' wit Iggy?"

Frank pulled in his chin. "Pfff, what're you kiddin'? She cares less than anybody else." He turned toward his brother. "Mack, when's the last time *you* checked on Iggy?"

Shamefaced, Mack looked down at the table and fidgeted with the scratchpad in front of him. "Not in the last week. Teresa gets all squeamish every time I suggest we go to the hospital." He raised his head and thumped his fist on the table. "Even so, I think I'll insist we go see him tonight after dinner."

"Good." Frank smacked his thigh in approval. "Then maybe Geneva won't force me."

Jake made his way toward the door. "Dere's some wood I gotta pick up 'fore I go work on da house. Too bad needer a ya are handy wit a hammer." Jake slipped out of the office with a half-hearted wave.

"Later," Frank called after him then shoved the second half of the donut into his mouth. He wiped his hands on his lap before he stood up and adjusted the crouch of his khakis. "Damn! These pants must've shrunk in the wash."

Mack pointed to the empty box and scolded, "If you didn't eat so many donuts."

"What's it to you?" Frank growled.

"Well, psychologists say people who overeat do it out of guilt. I bet you're feeling bad since you don't miss Iggy in the least. Admit it, Frank."

"Look who's talkin'," Frank shot back. "You don't seem to mind havin' the LaSalle to yourself. Suffer any guilt about that, Mack?"

Mack's shoulders slumped. "Sometimes."

Frank stretched his spine. "Not so much to keep you from hirin' a mechanic. Huh, Mack?"

"Well, I waited long enough for Iggy to fix the car," Mack whined in a defensive tone. "So I invested a bit in its rehab. What's wrong with that?" Mack sneered at Frank. "Hey, sly way to change the subject, Frank. About the donuts, my psychology professor once said . . ."

"Geneva gives me enough shit, so knock off the psychoanalysis."

"Okay, okay." Mack stood up and began to clear the conference table of paperwork as Frank picked at the crumbs in the donut box. "You know, Frank, I finally got around to telling Teresa about my condition. I expected her to be angry with me for not being upfront about it. I could've handled that." He tore off the top sheet of the scratchpad and ripped it into shreds. "But, instead, the girl's started to dote on me like I'm some weak invalid."

"You seem downright irritated, Mack," Frank needled. "Henpecked already?"

"You've got that right. I'm so mad I want to tell her to mind her own damn business, especially when she pesters me to take my medication as if I can't remember on my own. Besides that, she's fusses anytime we try something new, questions whether or not it might cause me to convulse." Mack paced around then stopped directly in front of Frank. "And one night, her father brought it up at the dinner table, insisting I explain what specifically happens during a seizure. I wished she hadn't told him. I felt so defensive."

Frank offered sympathy with a whack on Mack's shoulder, "I can understand that, buddy."

Mack glanced at his watch. "I need to go. There's just enough time to stop next door for a bottle of wine. Signore Camara expects me to bring one every time I go there for dinner. Oh, I better not forget the bread too."

"I gotta get downstairs." Frank hobbled toward the exit. "You know how it is with the bakers. When the rat's away, the mice will play, or somethin' like that. Oh, don't forget to lock up, Mack."

* * *

With a bottle in one hand and a loaf of bread under the opposite arm, Mack dawdled toward the LaSalle parked at the other end of the street. Halfway to the car, he unknowingly passed the tan mutt with the matted white collar that happened to be resting curbside. Unmindful of the dog, Mack continued on his way. *Will Teresa be insulted if I insist she let up on all the fussing? I've seen her temper flare a few times and don't want to be the brunt of it.*

When Mack halted a foot past the dog and stomped a heel hard against the concrete, the startled mongrel stood up and, determined to find out what disturbed the tall young man, sniffed at the cuffs of his pants. Oblivious to his canine companion, Mack punched a fist into the opposite hand and declared out loud, "No matter what, I'll be a man about the situation and tell Teresa to treat me like one." *I'll bring it up on the way back from the hospital tonight.* In reaction to Mack's outburst, the dog barked, catching Mack's undivided attention. Grateful for something to delay facing Teresa, he stooped down and petted the familiar-looking stray. "Hey, look who's here." Mack scratched behind the dog's ears. "What do you think? Will Teresa give me any flack when I tell her to lay off the mothering?"

The love-starved mongrel nosed Mack's hand reassuringly then leaped up and placed a paw on each of Mack's shoulders and licked his face. Mack laughed. "Yeah, I'd like to adopt you too, but Mamma wouldn't be too happy." According to Signora Matteo, all animals belonged outside or in a barn.

Happy to have received a few minutes of positive attention, the friendly mutt jumped down and went on his merry way. Wiping his face dry, Mack called after him, "Hey, Buddy, maybe someday when I get a place of my own, I'll give you a bath . . . and a place to live."

Chapter Forty

The motor purring and the new heater toasting his feet, Mack steered the LaSalle toward St. Mary's Hospital later that evening, oblivious to all but the deserted road ahead. While he casually hummed the 1944 hit tune *Don't Fence Me In,* Teresa wrung her hands in her lap and fidgeted in place as if bugs were crawling up her spine. "Macco, *mi sono preoccupata.* I'm really worried. Are you sure that driving's okay in your condition?"

Mack halted the melody and gripped the steering wheel tighter. "Yes, Teresa, as long as I take my medication."

"What if you collapse in a seizure?" Teresa moaned. "Did you remember to take your pills this afternoon?"

"I did." Mack clenched his jaw so tight that a vein throbbed at his temple.

"Maybe we should've walked," Teresa suggested.

"You want to walk?" Mack slammed his foot on the brake causing Teresa's upper torso to jerk forward.

"Macco, what's the matter?" Teresa extended a hand and placed its palm across Mack's forehead. "Are you sick?"

"*Basta,* enough is enough, Teresa." He pushed her hand away.

With a puzzled expression, Teresa questioned, "Enough what?"

Mack pulled the LaSalle to the curb and parked under a nearby streetlamp which not only lit up the car, but diminished the romantic influence of the full moon overhead.

"The hospital is only another block away. We're almost there now." Teresa lifted her hands, palm up, and shrugged. "Why park here?"

With his jaw taut and both fists clamped tight, Mack leaned his back against the driver's side door and drew in a deep breath. "Teresa, there's something we need to discuss right now. *È importante.*"

Once Teresa noted Mack's features distorted with annoyance, she turned up her nose and stared at the windshield. Then, in what sounded more like a warning than an invitation to continue, she announced, "*Sì,* I'm listening."

Frustrated, Mack took a deep breath before he wearily explained, "Ever since I told you about my health condition, you treat me different. You act as if my epilepsy makes me frail, like a young kid who needs direction. It bothers me to be treated like a sick little boy. I want you to stop. *Capisci?*"

Even though the color rose in her cheeks as she stiffened, Teresa didn't respond. *How dare he!* She gritted her teeth, indignant that Mack harbored such resentment instead of appreciating the extra attention. *I only had his best interest at heart.* Teresa pursed her lips. *Now, I'd like to give him a piece of my mind.*

Despite the dropping temperature in the inert car, perspiration ran down the sides of Mack's face while patches of wetness stained the armpits of his shirt. *Uh-oh.* Afraid he'd unleashed the demons in Teresa, he pulled in his chin and grimaced. *She looks ready to explode.* Turning away from her, he gripped the steering wheel once more and braced himself for a hostile comeback.

Teresa's eyes remained locked in a sneer at the windshield until, unable to hold back any longer, she lashed out with as much contempt as Mack expected. "Macco, I had no idea you felt *this* way. I'm *terribly* sorry I've *annoyed* you." She swiveled toward him and, crossing her arms tight, barked at the side of his face, "You might have told me sooner!"

Mack lowered his head and deflated his lungs, exhaling a raspy mouthful of air. *Something told me she'd overreact.*

Teresa's pulse quickened as she twisted her engagement ring. *Oh, no! Look at him. He's mortified. I'd better check my temper or he'll ask for the diamond back.* She leaned toward Mack and tapped his shoulder. "Macco?"

With no response from Mack, Teresa sucked in her breath before she attempted a timid amends, "**Mi dispiace.** I'm sorry I shouted at you." Teresa placed a finger under Mack's chin, raised his head up and toward her, and then gazed into his eyes. "You're a strong man, Macco. A man I'm proud to call my fiancé." She backed up and flipped her hand in the air. "Maybe it's my protective nature that makes me act like your nursemaid. Both my father and brother seem to enjoy it when they're sick. I actually thought you might too."

"I'm not sick," Mack insisted. "My condition's controlled by medication. Can't you understand?"

"I see. I guess I did go overboard . . . a little." Teresa stared down at her lap. "Do you think you can forgive me?"

After Mack swung around, he clasped both of her hands and shook them, "Someday, I hope to God you'll dote on our babies. I'm sure you'll make an excellent mother." He squeezed her hands tighter. "But I beg you . . . until you deliver my children . . . *please* stop nursing me."

Teresa directed a side-glance at Mack. *He thinks I'll be a good mother? How nice. Who can stay angry with such a wonderful man?* She faced him head on. "Oh, Macco, you'll make a great father too! I'm so lucky you asked me to marry you." She threw herself at Mack and pressed her lips and body against his.

His ego appeased, Mack returned her kiss with a passion that stirred his hormones but, when he detected the evidence in his lap, he pushed himself away with the restraint of a gentleman. *I hope she didn't notice.* "Teresa, let's go. The hospital visiting hours are over at eight."

Although Mack started the engine, he wasn't able to pull away from the streetlamp before Teresa spotted the reason for his discomfort. **Dio santo!** *He must be so embarrassed.* Teresa straightened her skirt. *I'll pretend I didn't notice.* "**Sì, andiamo subito.** Let's hurry before it's too late."

At the hospital parking lot, Teresa waited for Mack to open her door. However, when he raced forward to the hospital's entrance instead, she contemplated the reason. *Does he blame me for what happened? Does he think I was too forward?*

Chapter Forty-One

While Mack chose to suppress his sensual urges out of respect for Teresa, his younger sister struggled with her own hormones. In the back seat of a sedan parked in a remote area across town, Tony Canelli pulled Juliet close and embraced her. Full of romantic expectations, she melted into his arms, their lips and tongues exploring each other's in a frenzy of hot passion.

As Tony leaned back, Juliet fell forward on top of him, their bodies melding into one. "Oh, Tony," Juliet sighed.

Perceiving her breathy reaction as permission to progress, Tony maneuvered his hand up the back of her sweater, his experienced fingers undoing her bra. Lost in the heat of the moment, Juliet didn't notice until he rolled her over and pushed up her sweater. Before Juliet had a chance to object, Tony dove in and ran his tongue across one nipple and tweaked the other.

Overwhelmed by the sensations, Juliet submitted to Tony's magic touch that not only made her nipples quiver but sent waves of pleasure through her lower extremities and areas in between. Lost in a trance of sensual delight, Juliet whimpered, "Ooo . . . ooo."

"Juliet, I love it when you moan." Taking it another step further, Tony kneaded his pelvis against hers, the bulge in his slacks growing firmer. "You drive me crazy, Baby."

"Oh . . . oh, Tony, you take my breath away." Her heart beating faster, Juliet wriggled under him, the friction stoking the sparks into a full-blown blaze. Anxious to move on, Tony slipped a hand up her skirt and tugged at her panties.

Juliet stiffened, her conscience cooling her down. "Stop! What are you doing?" This was the first time she'd let any of her boyfriends get to second base and hadn't realized how fast it might lead to something else.

Tony panted, "Don't . . . don't worry, Darlin'. I'll . . . I'll take it easy." Convinced her objection was due to the fact she was a virgin, he stroked her inner thigh and attempted to soothe her. "It'll only hurt a little."

Grasping that he expected them to go all the way, she tried to push him off. "No! Stop! I can't do this. Not till I'm married." Although her conviction was strong, she worried that he wouldn't be willing to wait for her, that a decent girl wasn't what he really wanted.

Catching his breath, Tony reluctantly retracted his hand. "Jeez, Juliet, I thought you and me were on the same track."

"What track . . . the track to committing a mortal sin or, God forbid . . ." Juliet lowered her voice and anxiously pressed her stomach. " . . . getting pregnant?"

"I'd be careful."

"That's not the point, Tony. I want to walk down the aisle in a white dress."

"Nobody'll know except you and me."

"Is that what you'd want someone to tell your sister?"

Tony expelled a defeated groan. "Course not." He sat up and backed off, allowing Juliet the space she needed to straighten her clothes. "If you were my little sister, I'd beat the livin' crap outta me."

Without refastening her bra, Juliet adjusted her sweater and, still dazed from what nearly happened, muttered, "Don't remind me of what Iggy did to my last boyfriend, the awful way he clobbered him. I had such nightmares." Frowning, Juliet leaned against the seat, recalling how upset she'd been for weeks after the incident.

"Now, the way we sneak around, I can hardly sleep." Juliet faced Tony and grabbed his wrist. "Listen, Tony, it tortures me to keep us a secret."

"It's not easy for me either, Princess," he admitted. "I can't wait to nail the guy that mugged your brother. If I could just wrap up this investigation we'd be free to . . ."

Juliet brandished a frustrated palm face up. "Can't I at least tell Louisa?" She resented that her best friend was able to brag on and on about her boyfriend while she couldn't even hint about her budding relationship with Tony. "I'll burst if I don't tell someone."

"How many times do I hafta explain why we can't let nobody know?"

"Louisa would keep the secret."

Tony let out an exasperated breath. "Listen, Doll. I'll say it one more time. Accordin' to the rules, your way off limits." Tony had been warned time and again by his supervisor Lieutenant Smathers that, by the police department's code of ethics, a detective was forbidden to fraternize with anyone whatsoever involved in an investigation.

"I know. But she's my best friend. She'd never betray me."

"Let me put it another way. My job's on the line. If my boss finds out about the two of us, I'd get canned."

"Oh! Why didn't you say so in the first place?" Finally understanding the severity of the situation, Juliet pressed a hand against her sternum. "You'd risk losing your job just to be with me?"

"Try and stop me." He ran his fingers through her hair. "Besides, if we're careful, Lieutenant Smathers won't ever find out."

"Why do you bother taking such a risk?"

"Cause you're worth it, Sugar." Tony squeezed Juliet's hand. "You're a keeper. No doubt about it."

"Really, Tony?"

"Sure." Tony caressed her face. "You're gorgeous and turn me on like no other chick I ever dated. Besides, we want the same things in life."

"What things?" she asked.

With his thumb pointed upwards, Tony shook his right fist. "For one thing, you want a family, don't you?"

"Yes, a boy and a girl," Juliet declared. He raised two more fingers.

"And a house," Tony reminded her as his ring finger sprung up.

"Yes, go on . . . ." Juliet prodded.

"And we're both Italian." By that time, all five fingers of his one hand were spread open. "You wanna keep up Italian customs and traditions, same as me, right?"

"You know I do, Mister Canelli."

He smacked his lap. "Well then, it's agreed."

"What's agreed?"

He smirked. "That we oughta do somethin' about it."

She jutted her chin forward. "What *are* you saying?"

Tony clasped both of her hands. "That I love you and want us together forever."

"Forever?"

"Yep, no doubt about it. I even bought somethin' to prove I'm serious." He reached over the front seat, opened the glove compartment and retrieved a small box, then plopped back down next to Juliet and presented it to her.

"What's this?" she asked coyly as she fingered the black velvet of the box.

"Go ahead. Open it."

She lifted the lid. "Oh, my God!"

"Will you marry me, Juliet?"

"Tony, I can't believe this is happening. Are you sure?"

"Sure as ever. About time I settled down with a beautiful Italian broad. Come on. Try the ring on for size? You do love me and want to marry me, don't you?"

"Yes, Tony, of course I do. It's just that I didn't expect a proposal so soon."

"Hey, can't let my dream girl slip away, can I?" He grabbed hold of the diamond and slid it onto the ring finger of her left hand. "But, remember, don't never wear it in public until after the investigation is over. Promise?"

"It'll be torture, but I swear I'll keep it a secret." Juliet held the ring up to the moonlight. "It's divine, Tony. I can't wait till we tell my family. Mamma'll be ecstatic."

"You think so?"

"Definitely."

"Why's that?"

Juliet tapped his chest. "Because, once you arrest Iggy's mugger, you'll be a hero in her eyes. What's more, you're a tall handsome Italian with a good-paying job. What more can a mother ask for her daughter?"

He pulled Juliet closer and squeezed her tight. "You know what?"

"What?"

"You're worth every bit of the wait." He rested his chin on the top of her head.

She relaxed against his chest. "Tony, I love you."

"Right back at you, Juliet." A few heartbeats later, he grasped her shoulders and held her at arms length. "Hey, Princess, we almost forgot something important."

Juliet sighed, "What's that?"

"The engagement . . . we gotta seal it." He lifted her chin and dove in for a fiery kiss.

A light flashed in the window and blinded them. "Hey, knock it off you two." The police officer waved his flashlight. "Go on. Get outta here before I take ya down to the station and book ya for messin' around in public."

Tony climbed over the seat and cracked open the front window. "Sorry, officer, we were just leavin'." He started the engine and quickly drove off with his fiancé still in the seat behind him. "Phew! That was too damn close. Thank God that flatfoot didn't recognize me. If Smathers ever got wind of this, I'd be up shit's creek with no paddle."

Embarrassed, Juliet imagined Signora Matteo's reaction if she ever learned what happened that night. "If Mamma ever found out, she'd take a conniption fit and insist I go right to confession."

* * *

That night, a hand between her legs, Juliet groaned in her sleep. The sensual tingle almost too much to bear, she opened her eyes to protest. She screamed when she caught sight of her brother Iggy instead of Tony. "Get off me, you pig!"

"You were beggin' for it." Iggy smirked, the fangs of his incisors exposed. "A slut like you deserves whatever she gets."

"I'm no slut."

"Then tell your boyfriend to keep his pants zipped or I'll rip off his dick." Iggy strutted off, adjusting the crouch of his pants. "Watch your step or I'll tell Mamma to check the greasy fingerprints on your bra?"

Signora Matteo popped out of nowhere shouting how disgraceful their behavior, "*È vergognoso!* She grabbed each of her children by the ear and, praying for their lost souls, dragged them to a conveniently close-by confessional. Depositing them on either side of the priest's booth, she ordered, "No come out till sin is forgiven!"

Juliet bolted up screaming, 'Noooooo!" When she realized it had just been another awful nightmare, she shakily made the sign of the cross and whispered the Act of Contrition, a prayer she reserved for the gravest of mortal sins.

Chapter Forty-Two

While the majority of the Matteos went about their business on November 26th, the day prior to Thanksgiving, Signora Matteo spent the better part of the morning perched on a metal chair, one of two available in Iggy's hospital room. With rosary beads twisted through her fingers, she mumbled prayers in hopes of a miraculous recovery. Nurses and aides every so often interrupted her concentration when they entered the dual-bed room to focus on the sole patient who occupied it.

Except for the occasional quiver of his sunken cheeks, Iggy's features remained impassively pasted on a face that was barely recognizable. Attached to an oxygen tank, he inhaled through tubes inserted in his nostrils and received sustenance from a needle in his arm. The dial on the tank mimicked the slight rise and fall of his chest and the monotonous drip of glucose marked the moments that passed.

At about 11:00 a.m., Patricia waddled into the room, her belly preceding her by a foot. "Mamma?"

Dropping the rosary beads in her lap, Signora Matteo raised her head and glared at the daughter whose visit was long overdue. "***Beh**, now* you come see Iago? You no feel shame?"

"Please, Mamma, let's not argue. I'm here. Aren't I?"

"***Finalmente*** . . . *at last*." Signora Matteo complained.

Patricia ignored the second reproach. "How's Iggy today?"

"Iago, ***povero ragazzo!*** You no can see?" Iggy's mother whined. "Poor boy . . . he no can eat." Her shoulders drooping lower, she griped about what a sin it was that her son was wasting away before her eyes. "***Che peccato!***" Pounding a fist into the opposite hand, Signora Matteo insisted that he needed a bowl of pasta, not sugar from a skinny tube. Speaking more to herself than to Patricia, she continued in a whisper, swearing she would fatten him up once he came home. "***Quando viene a casa*** . . ."

Moved by her mother's drama, Patricia approached her brother's bed, caressed his hand then teetered down onto the empty chair next to Signora Matteo. "Iggy's brain needs time to heal. You have to be patient, Mamma."

"***Che pazienza***?" Signora Matteo retorted as she rocked the gathered fingers of one upturned hand to and fro, indicating her patience had run out. "You want I be strong?"

In an effort to distract her mother, Patricia grasped her hand. "I'll ask Jake to pick up a turkey for our Thanksgiving dinner tomorrow."

Scowling, Signora Matteo pulled away her hand and, extending it in Iggy's direction, asked why she should thank God, "***Perché?*** To say '***grazie a Dio***' for this?"

Before Patricia had a chance to respond, a redhead strolled into the room wearing a badge that identified her as a student nurse. The young woman retrieved the clipboard from the foot of Iggy's bed. "I'm here to check Mr. Matteo's vital signs. It's okay if you stay in the room." As the pale-skinned nurse measured Iggy's pulse rate, his body shuddered a moment then went limp. Knocking the clipboard to the floor, she brandished her stethoscope and, when she pressed its metal disc to

Iggy's chest, blanched even whiter, her freckles emerging like prominent destinations on a roadmap.

Patricia clutched her mother's hand once more. "Miss, is everything okay?"

Without bothering to respond to Patricia's question, the redhead darted out of the room, flapping her arms down the hall as she screamed, "Crisis, Room 666! Crisis, Room 666!" Alarmed, Signora Matteo clutched her rosary beads and scurried to her son's bedside.

Two older nurses responded to the emergency by rolling a metal cart loaded with medical equipment to the entrance of Iggy's room, the smaller of the two women backing in first. "Please leave the room, ladies." Once they parked the cart next to Iggy's bed, the heftier nurse pushed Signora Matteo out of her way and ripped open Iggy's hospital gown before she hoisted a defibrillator from the cart.

A young man dressed in a lab coat with a stethoscope suspended from his neck rushed onto the scene and grabbed the defibrillator from the large nurse's hands while he shouted cryptic technical instructions over his shoulder to the small one.

Signora Matteo searched her daughter's eyes, asking who he was and what he had said. "***Chi è? Che dice?***"

"I think he's the intern on duty, but I don't understand the medical terms." Patricia struggled up from the chair and, grasping Signora Matteo's forearm, maneuvered her toward the door. "Mamma, maybe it's better this way."

"Tell me. How is better?" Without waiting for an answer, Signora Matteo raised her rosary beads to the ceiling and cried out in anguish, "***Dio, per favore***, I beg . . . no take my son." Straining, Patricia pushed her resistant mother from the room into the adjacent hallway.

Despite fifteen minutes of the medical team's intense effort, which included several attempts at defibrillation followed by the insertion of a long needle into his chest cavity, Iggy's vital signs remained stagnant. The heavyset nurse tugged the intern's arm. "It's over. You've done your best, Dr. Paulstein."

With a devastated expression on his face, Dr. Paulstein stood firm. "I can't let one of my patient's die."

"You'll get used to it, Doctor." With a swing of her ample hip, she shoved him aside and raised the sheet over Iggy's face.

Still frazzled, the intern exited Room 666 and approached his patient's relatives, huddled in the hallway a few feet away. Her head bowed in a fervent prayer to St. Jude, the patron saint of hopeless causes, Signora Matteo failed to notice his approach.

Patricia nudged her mother. "Mamma, the doctor's here."

Dr. Paulstein choked on his words, "I'm . . . I'm so sorry."

Signora Matteo lifted her head and, eyeing the intern, asked what he was saying. "*Che stai dicendo?*"

"We weren't able to . . . to revive your son." The intern grasped Signora Matteo's wrist. "We've lost him."

"Nooooooo!" Signora Matteo dropped to her knees and, in a heart-wrenching wail, chastised God for his abandonment, "*Dio, perché mi hai abbandonato?*"

"Mamma, please." While the solemn intern sulked away from Signora Matteo's continued display of grief, Patricia stooped down and attempted to haul her mother up from the floor. "Get up, Mamma, you're making a scene." In a matter of seconds, a puddle materialized between Patricia's feet and spread outward, distracting Signora Matteo from her torment.

"Patrizia, *che cosa è successo*?" Signora Matteo asked what happened.

Patricia released her grip and scrutinized the liquid. "Oh, my God! I think my water's broken." She stepped out of the puddle.

Still on her knees, Signora Matteo swayed back and forth as she assessed her daughter's predicament. "Is too soon, no?"

"I'm not due for another three weeks." Patricia doubled over when a strong contraction overwhelmed her. "Mamma, get the doctor!" During Signora Matteo's scramble to her feet, Patricia whimpered at yet another contraction that walloped her within seconds of the first.

Adrenalin motivated, Signora Matteo stormed off toward the intern who was twenty feet down the corridor at the nurse's station. "*Dottore, il bambino* comes!"

The stocky nurse, having observed the mother and daughter exchange as she wheeled the medical cart out of Iggy's room, made a quick evaluation of the situation. She called to the intern, "Dr. Paulstein, this woman's water's broken. Get back here."

Snapped out of his forlorn stupor, the intern glanced anxiously at Patricia and shouted back to the nurse, "No, get a wheelchair and take her to the maternity ward. Notify them she's on the way!" He was worried he might cause two deaths in one day, possibly three if he counted the baby.

When Patricia expelled a yowl in reaction to a third contraction, the nurse persisted, "There's no time. She's about to deliver. Doctor, get into your scrubs." At the intern's hesitation, the nurse repeated the order in a louder, firmer voice which allowed for no options, "Scrubs, now!" She twisted her neck and directed the slighter nurse behind her, "Prepare Room 667." Abandoning her cart, she guided the hunched-over and hyperventilating mother-to-be toward a room across from where Iggy had expired.

* * *

Inside ten minutes, Patricia lay prone in Room 667 knees bent and legs spread while the now blued-garbed Dr. Paulstein inspected her uterus. "She's ten centimeters dilated; the baby's head has crowned." Upon her next contraction, he instructed his screeching patient, "Push, lady, push."

Since no one bothered to cast her out of the room, Signora Matteo held onto one of Patricia's hands while the stocky nurse slipped behind the drenched mother-to-be and helped her up and forward. Patricia bore down with a loud grunt then inhaled a deep breath. "I can't go on. I'll never make it. Give me something for the pain. Please!"

"It's too late for medication." The petite nurse standing on the opposite side of the bed from Signora Matteo wiped Patricia's forehead dry. "You'll have to do it on your own, honey." Patricia responded with a shriek.

"The head's halfway out. Push again," Dr. Paulstein encouraged.

Several deep groans later, Patricia ejected a slippery ***bambina*** into the intern's open hands. "It's a girl! It's a girl!" he announced with enough enthusiasm to convince any passerby that he had sired the newborn himself.

* * *

Delivery completed and the baby safely deposited in the nursery, an aide dressed in a gray uniform entered Room 667, now empty except for the sleeping mother and the emotionally drained Signora Matteo, slouched in a chair beside her. Basin in hand, the diminutive woman approached the bed. "Ma'am, I think it would be best if you left the room now."

Instead of complying, Signora Matteo stood up and watched the aide begin to roughly sponge down the sleeping patient and asked her to be gentler. "***Per favore, più gentile.*** Patrizia, she is first time mother."

Patricia awakened. "Ow! Take it easy. That hurts."

"Lift your leg please," the woman instructed.

Ignoring the aide's instruction, Patricia peered over the woman's shoulder and searched her mother's eyes. "You're a grandmother now, Mamma."

Signora Matteo forced the aide to the side and feebly asked Patricia how God was able pull the last breath from her son and blow it into the lungs of her first **nipotina**. She puffed into her fist then burst into tears. "Oh, Patrizia, **chi capisce Dio?** He take from me my Iago and give to you **una bella bambina**." Whether her sobs expressed sorrow for the loss of her son or happiness for the birth of her precious granddaughter remained unclear, but Signora Matteo embraced her daughter nonetheless.

Patricia heaved a sigh then wept into her mother's shoulder, "Mamma, I'm so glad you're here."

The aide shook her head at the drama and tapped Signora Matteo's opposite shoulder. "Please, ma'am, you need to leave the room."

Chapter Forty-Three

A few days after Iggy's death, Detective Tony Canelli pulled up to a dilapidated apartment building in a manufacturing town five miles north of Benton. He parked his unmarked sedan and entered the old brownstone, mulling over the facts of the Matteo case. Since Tony had handled most of the preliminary investigation and Lieutenant Smathers was preoccupied with another more high-profile murder, he had assigned the case's wrap-up to his subordinate. Officer Shane Clancy, the Irish rookie Tony always found so annoying, had long ago been reassigned to traffic duty upon Tony's refusal to work with him.

Once Tony had discovered the lead pipe in the alley adjacent to the crime scene and asked the police lab to confirm the blood on it was the victim's, he sent a copy of the fingerprints lifted from it to one of the newest sections of the FBI, its Identification Division. As luck would have it, the person owning those particular fingerprints had a recent petty theft record, and his fingerprints happened to be on file. The fingerprints belonged to Zoltan Hadju, alias Harry Varga, the Hungarian bookkeeper Iggy exploited to embezzle funds from Matteo's Bakery. Using his intuitive sleuthing skills, Tony had narrowed the suspect's whereabouts to the building he was about to enter.

Search warrant in hand, the detective entered the brownstone and climbed the narrow staircase to the third floor. He placed an ear against the door marked 303 and listened. Hearing the shuffle of feet and the clang of metal, possibly pots and pans, he knew someone was home in the apartment. Pulling his gun from his shoulder holster, Tony knocked on the door. When no one answered it, he pounded harder and shouted, "Open up! Police!"

The sound of a window being opened filtered through the door. Assuming the suspect was trying to escape, Tony used his shoulder to smash open the flimsy door and dashed into the studio apartment, rushing to the window where the suspect was attempting to leave via the fire escape. The detective grabbed the puny man's collar and pulled him back into the room. "Goin' somewhere, Harry?"

"Nah, just gettin' some fresh air," Harry replied as three pigeons flew into the open window, one landing on Tony's head.

"Damn birds!" Still gripping Harry's collar, Tony shooed off the pigeon. Once he shouldered his gun, he handcuffed the laughing suspect to a rusty bedpost, and then pulled out a handkerchief. Wiping the wet dung out of his hair, he watched the birds fly out as quickly as they had entered. "Good riddance!" Slamming the window shut behind them, Tony grumbled to himself, "Dumb-ass pigeons . . . let them shit somewhere else."

Furious at the comic interruption, Tony scowled at a still laughing Harry. "You don't got nothin' to laugh about, mister. You're in a heap of trouble."

"What'd I do?"

"Oh, nothin' . . . but commit one brutal-ass murder."

"You ain't got no proof!"

"Just your fingerprints on the weapon, the bloody pipe you tossed into the alley."

Harry sobered at the mention of the pipe. "It was a accident."

"Some accident," Tony replied as he searched around the crowded room.

On an end table, under a large pair of scissors, he found a pile of old magazines. With the threat letter in mind, the one he'd discovered in Iggy's closet, he picked up the magazines and rifled through them. One was missing several cut-out sections. Tony retrieved a folded evidence bag from his pocket, shook it open and inserted the magazine and the scissors. "Premeditation?"

"I don't know what the hell you're talkin' about."

"Oh no? How about a conviction of murder in the first degree, Harry?"

"I wanna lawyer! A free one. I know my goddamn rights."

Tony stuck his face close to his prisoner's. "Don't you worry your little ass none too much, Harry. The state'll give you a hand-out all right." Now that it was his turn, Tony didn't pass up the opportunity to poke fun at the Hungarian's plight. "The judge'll assign you the sharpest public defender around." Tony backed off and smirked. "Yeah, the freshest pigeon in Benton . . . one straight outta law school."

* * *

Meanwhile, back at police headquarters, Jake sat across from a member of the vice squad in a dimly lit interrogation room. After only a ten-minute shakedown, Jake broke down and admitted his involvement in Iggy's defunct numbers operation.

Satisfied with his powers of intimidation, the plain-clothes detective scratched his scruffy beard and looked Jake in the eye. "You're damn lucky, mister."

"Lucky?" Sweat stained the armpits of Jake's flannel shirt, as he wrung a baseball cap in his hands. "How's dat?"

"You have friends in high places." At Juliet's request and without Jake's knowledge, Tony had put in a good word for his fiancé's brother-in-law and had requested leniency. Owing Tony a favor, the head of the vice squad had ordered his subordinate to let Jake off the hook.

"Who might dat be?"

Ignoring the question, the detective stood up. "You're free to go."

"I yam?"

"Yeah, but remember one thing."

"What's dat?"

"I got my eye on you. If you step out of line once more, your ass is mine. Understand?"

As is if he was still in the navy, Jake stood up and stiffly saluted the detective. "Aye-aye, sir."

"Now get outta here before I change my mind."

* * *

While his relieved brother-in-law hurried out of the interrogation room absolved of his criminal connection to Iggy, Frank sat at a table in the bar of the Italian-American Men's Club, troubled over another matter related to his deceased brother. Choking on pungent smoke, he waved his hands in front of his face. "Please, Signore Catorno, I can't hardly breathe."

Bruno Catorno, the loan shark Iggy hadn't repaid in full, took another puff from his cigar. Blowing the smoke in Frank's direction, he addressed him in stern Italian, "**Senti.** I don't think you understand my position. I have a reputation to defend. If I forgive the debt, it'll send out the wrong message." He glanced at his bodyguards.

"But I didn't borrow the money from you."

"**Questo lo so.** But your brother, he did. Since he's dead now, I hold you responsible for double the overdue balance."

"Double! What if I refuse to pay?"

"**Questa linea di condotta** . . . that'd be a very bad decision."

"What the hell do you mean by that?"

"**I miei amici,**" he gestured toward his bodyguards. "My friends don't like it when I'm unhappy. They do strange things to try and appease me."

Frank lifted his chin and tugged at the collar of his shirt. "What kinda things?"

"**Ti dico.** If you think the smoke from my cigar is hard to take, imagine the smoke from a burning building, your bakery for example."

"Is that a threat?"

"No, **paesano**, more like a promise." Bruno signaled to his men and, when the one standing behind him handed him his cane and hat, he stood up. "The money in two days. No later. "**Capisci?**""

Realizing that, even in death, Iggy was still a thorn in his side, Frank scowled. "Yeah, I understand?"

* * *

Late that night, indigestion causing his overstuffed stomach to gurgle and acid to reflux into his esophagus, Frank rolled onto his back, only making his heartburn worse. Despite his discomfort, his mouth eventually went slack and several atrocious snores escaped from it.

Awakened by the discordant clamor, Geneva poked his arm. "Frank turn over or you'll wake up everyone, even the dead."

"Sorry, Gen." As his wife went back to sleep, Frank lay there awake, worrying about where he'd get the money to satisfy Bruno Catorno. The sour taste of apprehension coating his tongue, he eventually fell back to sleep, only to be tortured in his dreams.

In a nightmare that seemed more than real, one of Bruno's collectors pointed a pistol at Frank while the other held his head over the toilet bowl and demanded payback. When Frank said he didn't have the money, the thug dunked his head into the water. "Lemme know when you're ready to pay and I'll letcha up."

A pipe sticking out of his skull, Iggy burst into the bathroom and grabbed the pistol from the gun-toting goon. "Hey, leave my lard-ass brother alone! The whale never did learn to swim." With superhuman strength, he grabbed hold of Bruno's men and knocked their heads together, the sound of their cracking skulls reverberating off the tiled walls.

The thugs slithering to the floor, Frank lifted his head and spit out a mouthful of toilet water. "Damn you, Iggy!"

"Hey, is that what I get for coming back from the dead to save your fat ass?" Iggy grabbed Frank by the collar and shoved his head back into the toilet bowl. "Signal when you're ready to thank me." Frank swallowed more toilet water.

Awakened by the noise, Geneva sprinted into the bathroom and, skirting around the unconscious thugs, picked up a wet washcloth and started to smack Iggy with it. "Leave my husband alone. Leave him alone, you mean, rotten bully!"

"Knock it off." Iggy shoved her away.

As Frank lifted his head out of the bowl, Geneva fell backwards and knocked into Signora Matteo who just then entered with a bowl of steaming spaghetti. The bowl flew into the air then crashed to the tile floor, smashing into smithereens while the spaghetti ricocheted into Frank's face.

Attracted by the aroma of spaghetti sauce, Mack and Juliet entered looking for their dinner, while last to cross the bathroom's threshold was Anna, her larger-than-life-sized breasts as firm as honeydews ripe enough for hand-picking. Iggy's wife shimmied her melons and demanded to know what was going on.

"Darn it, Frank." Geneva bitched as Frank snorted spaghetti out of his nostrils. "I told you you'd wake them all up."

Chapter Forty-Four

On the frigid morning of December 9, two days after Iggy's delayed autopsy and two long weeks after his death, his brothers stood solemnly behind Teresa and the women of their family. The branches of a leafless maple tree, the one centered on the family plot, provided them with a porous canopy of unwanted shade. Gather around them, an antsy crowd of relatives, friends, business associates and neighbors anticipated the priest's long-overdue arrival. At the outer perimeter of the crowd, Antonio and Mina hunched close together, not far from Detective Tony Canelli. A short distance away, the mutt with the matted white collar poked his head out from behind a marble monument and curiously watched the waiting mourners. The dog recognized a few of the people from Steward Street and worried that the burly guy who kicked him might show up.

Camouflaged by a dark veil, Anna shivered in the forefront, a few yards from Iggy's casket and his intended gravesite, in close proximity to those of his father and brother Romi. *I'll sign the papers. Who needs their measly business anyway?* She rubbed her palms together. *I'll return to Naples a free and wealthy woman. I can't wait to be rid of the Matteos.* She folded her arms and pouted. *I thought they'd accept me as part of their family, but they never did. Family?* She paused to consider how her affluence would affect the welcome home she received. *It can't hurt.*

To the rear of Anna, Frank leaned closer to Mack, jutting his chin toward his sister-in-law. "You think Anna will agree to sell us her rights to the bakery?"

Mack hiked up the collar of his coat. "Don't see why not? It's to her advantage. You made the deal too sweet to pass up."

"That's for sure." Frank wrung his hands. "If only the insurance agent had forked over the check." When they originally bought the group policy, the agent had assured them that it would protect the surviving partners in the instance of one of their deaths. When Anna inquired, within a few days of Iggy's passing, if she were entitled to her husband's share of the bakery, Frank quickly made her a buyout offer, assuming the insurance would fund it. But, as he found out, the insurance agent wasn't authorized to issue a check, not until Iggy's murderer was convicted. Frank was still frustrated about the delay. "I'd hate to borrow more money." He'd already used the bakery as collateral for a loan to payoff Bruno Catorno.

"Then you'd better hope Anna is willing to wait." Mack blew warm air into his hands. "Even though Harry's been arrested, the trial may take some time."

"Think a jury will find him guilty?" Frank tightened his fists. "The bastard deserves to be convicted of murder in the first degree."

Mack nodded. "I think the clincher will be the magazine Detective Canelli found in Harry's apartment, the one Harry used in the threat letter." After a brief contemplative pause, Mack looked at Frank. "How ironic . . . one of Iggy's own accomplices killed him."

"Never suspected Harry of all people. I still can't figure out his motive."

"Hmm." Mack twisted his lips to the side. "The way I see it, Iggy probably gave Harry the shaft once we caught onto the accounting scam. Maybe Harry will fess up to the embezzlement during his murder trial."

Frank bit the inside of his cheek. "Awful as Iggy's death was, it saved us the embarrassment of a racketeerin' charge."

Mack checked to ensure Patricia was out of earshot. "And to think, Jake got suckered into Iggy's numbers scheme and actually fell for his blackmail threat."

"Yeah, I pegged Jake for a smarter guy," Frank complained. "He's damn lucky the police let him off the hook." The longer Frank thought about it, the more he seethed at the injustice. "Damn Jake! He got off scot-free, not one lousy consequence!"

"Don't worry, Frank." Mack glanced at his older sister. "Patricia's backlash will be punishment enough. Jake'll never live it down."

Frank exhaled his hot breath in a cloud of mist. "Don't doubt it, not for one stinkin' second."

While the two brothers still kibitzed over the recent turn of events, Jake arrived on the scene and filtered through the mourners. Approaching his wife, he pulled Patricia off to the side. "Who da heck're all deez people?"

Patricia responded with brusque contempt, "Who do you think they are, numskull? At least they showed up *on time* to give their respects."

Jake pulled in his chin. "For who, Iggy?" He shook his head as he looked around. "Dere's no way dis many folks respected Iggy."

Patricia stomped a heel into Jake's foot. "For the family, smart mouth." She perused the crowd then shoved an elbow into her husband's gut. As she saw it, Iggy's brutal death absolved her brother of his wrong doings, but her husband was another matter. He needed to suffer for his sins. "How many people here know that you were involved in Iggy's numbers operation?"

Jake clutched his stomach. "How should I know?"

With a huff, Patricia changed the subject, "I hope the baby's safe with the sitter. She's so fragile."

Jake placed his hand on Patricia's shoulder and, in a submissive voice, made an offer, "If yer dat worried 'bout her, I'll go home and get her. We'll be back 'fore ya know it." Though the renovations to his house weren't quite finished, he had moved his family into it at his wife's insistence.

Patricia glared at Jake's hand then shoved it off her shoulder. "Are you that much of a moron? It's freezing out here." Sensing the engorgement of her lactating breasts, she frowned. "We have to stop home before the luncheon." With the assistance of a few generous neighbors, Geneva and Juliet had prepared a buffet meal to thank the mourners for attending Iggy's funeral. Patricia hoped she'd be able to get home to nurse the baby before her breasts leaked and still arrive at her mother's house in plenty of time to make a grand entrance with her newborn. "I really need to nurse Iaga."

"For Pete's sake, stop callin' her by dat awful name," Jake pleaded. He didn't want a daily reminder of any dead brother-in-law in his home, least of all the one who caused his recent arrest for bookmaking. "I gave in ta baptizin' da baby after yer mudder. But namin' her after Iggy . . . no way!"

With a spiteful indifference to his objection, Patricia lifted her chin. "Who cares what an ex-jailbird thinks." She'd already settled upon the name to christen her baby and didn't care if Jake complained until his face, or his scrotum, turned blue. "I think the name fits her feisty personality just fine."

Jake shuddered at the notion that Iaga's colic might be evidence of Iggy's reincarnation. "God forbid she's anytin' like Iggy." Following a few seconds of hostile silence, he squared his shoulders and tried to win back her approval. "I ever mention dat Frank plans to 'corporate da bakery? Said he'd give me a few a da shares."

"Was that before or after you confessed to the police?"

Jake cowered, his eyes downcast in shame. "Bafore."

"Humph! Frank will probably change his mind now." She moved in closer to him. "But, tell me anyway, what percentage did he promise?"

"Never did say," Jake confessed. Once Patricia spun on her heels and headed back to her original spot, he grudgingly squeezed into the family lineup, his tail tucked between his legs.

A few feet away, Signora Matteo moaned to Juliet that Iggy's funeral had been delayed way too long. "***Troppo tempo ha passato.***" Held up for two weeks due to a large backup at the morgue, the autopsy had been so disfiguring, both private and public viewings had been ruled out.

"An autopsy was the only way to get solid proof to convict the bookkeeper. Tony, I mean Detective Canelli said . . ."

"No make excuse . . . wait is still too long." Signora Matteo whined for she believed that, until a person was buried, his soul floated in an ambivalent state somewhere between heaven and hell, or so she'd heard in one of Father Romano's sermons. "Iago ***sarebbe in limbo.***"

"You think Iggy's in purgatory?"

"**Sì, *Padre*** Romano, he say . . ." Signora Matteo raised her eyes to the heavens and shook her head, " . . . Iago no can go up."

"I thought you lost confidence in Father Romano," Juliet reminded, finding it hard to disagree with her mother's misgivings. That very morning, transferring her anger at her son's untimely death to the clergyman she already disliked, Signora Matteo had ranted and raved when she found out that he was the only priest available to conduct Iggy's gravesite service. "That you didn't trust him anymore."

"*Sì*, I no can deny," Signora Matteo acknowledged, unable to refute her lack of faith in Father Romano. Peering toward the cemetery entrance, she demanded to know where the lecherous priest was. "*Dov'è?*"

"I don't know where he is, Mamma, but I wish he'd get here soon. My toes are frozen." Juliet turned toward Geneva. "Ever since Mack's engagement party, Mamma's dislike for Father Romano has grown." She decided not to admit that she shared her mother's aversion to the crude priest.

"I've noticed." Geneva spewed a mouthful of warm air into her hands. "I'll be glad when this is all over. The strain's taken its toll on Frank." Rubbing her arms, she hoped that her stressed-out husband would lose some of the weight he'd gained and focus on their future.

Tilting forward, Geneva glanced at Signora Matteo to make sure she wasn't listening then crouched down so her mouth was level with Juliet's ear. "Did I tell you about the perfect starter home I found? It's affordable and just down the street from the bakery. We've saved enough for a small down payment. I hope Frank jumps at the chance to buy it. We need a place of our own where we can grow into a family." Geneva looked proudly down at her abdomen, believing it contained the embryo of a baby boy. She hadn't revealed her pregnancy to anyone yet, not even Frank.

"Geneva, now that the police solved Iggy's murder, I'm free to tell you."

Geneva faced her sister-in-law. "Tell me what, Juliet?"

"The good news." Juliet looked off into the distance, daydreaming of her future wedding.

"Now that you've got my attention, don't just stand there. Tell me. What good news?"

Juliet blinked back to the present and lowered her voice to a hushed tone, "Detective Canelli asked me to marry him."

"No!" Too shocked to swallow Juliet's revelation, Geneva wiped the drool from her lips.

Juliet held up a finger. "Shhh, I haven't told Mamma yet."

"You . . . you hardly know the man!"

"For your information, Tony and I have been seeing each other on the sly ever since he started the investigation. We've been engaged for a month already, but I had to keep it a secret. You see, police policy forbids his dating any relative of a crime victim." Juliet continued in an even softer voice, "But, now that the investigation is over, our relationship can come out of the closet. You're the very first person I've told."

Geneva swallowed hard and shook her head. "Another hasty engagement . . . what will your mother say this time?"

"As far as I'm concerned, Mamma ought to be thrilled. He's a second generation Italian, you know." Juliet paused to scheme. "I think I'll suggest she invite Tony to dinner to thank him for solving Iggy's murder. Tony and I can make a surprise announcement at the table. So please don't tell anyone."

Despite her disapproval, Geneva held up her right hand. "I give you my word."

Focusing on her brother's gravesite, Juliet expelled a lengthy sigh. "Sad to say, I never would have met Tony if Iggy hadn't been attacked." She looked up and noticed Father Romano in ceremonial vestments scurrying across the cemetery followed by a young altar boy. The priest's prayer book under his arm, the boy carried a silver vessel, an aspersorium containing holy water, and an aspergillum wand for dispensing it. Overburdened by the sacred trappings, the boy nearly tripped on his oversized cassock. Thankful for their arrival, Juliet shivered. "Finally! I thought my toes might fall off first."

The stubby priest approached Signora Matteo and extended his hand in condolence but, turning up her nose, she looked the other way. Offended by her insolence, he headed grudgingly to Iggy's casket, the altar boy close at his heels. Taking his annoyance out on the boy, Father Romano ripped the prayer book out from under the boys arm, causing the startled youngster to teeter back and land on his butt. Miraculously, none of the holy water spilled out of the aspersorium. While the boy scrambled to his feet, Father Romano brandished the prayer book like a weapon, pointing it toward the deceased's mother.

While the priest incanted a myriad of indecipherable Latin prayers, the women of the family whimpered, but the men remained stoic. Father Romano then floated around the perimeter of Iggy's plot, sprinkling holy water onto coffin and mourners alike. In the process, he splashed Signora Matteo directly in the eye, whether by accident or on purpose only he knew.

Back at the head of the casket, he gave a lengthy sermon in Italian, spouting the merits of Christian behavior in preparation for death and final judgment during which Signora Matteo's soft sobs intensified into a whiny wail.

Once Father Romano performed the final blessing, Frank stepped forward and faced the crowd. "You're all invited to our house for refreshments and a chance to share fff-fond memories of Iggy." Frank almost choked on the word "fond."

* * *

About twenty feet behind most of the retreating mourners, Antonio escorted Mina toward the cemetery's main gate. Halfway there, he stopped and faced her. "I have to tell you something."

"Did you make your decision? Remember Daddy's deadline. You have one more week to take action or you're fired."

"**Sì**, I've decided." Antonio slammed his right fist into the palm of his opposite hand. "I've decided to find another job."

Mina's mouth fell open. "What?" Her disbelief mutating into fury, she pounded his chest, one wallop for each emphatic syllable she shrieked, "You-can't-do-that-to-me!"

Antonio recoiled. "Why not? I can't rush into a commitment that my heart tells me isn't right."

"What about our baby?" Mina screeched.

"What baby?" With a spastic twitch of his head, Antonio scrutinized the immediate area from left to right. "Are you crazy, woman? We only did it one time."

"For your information, I missed my last cycle." She jabbed her fist into Antonio's abdomen. "*You* made me pregnant. What do you say to that? Huh, Antonio?" Mina burst into tears. "You're just like your father!"

His face blanching, Antonio staggered away from Mina and leaned against a monument. "***Mamma mia!*** What does my father have to do with this?"

Mina advanced on Antonio waving an accusatory finger. "When I confided in Natalia, she told me your mother found herself in the same predicament a long time ago. At first, your father denied the baby was his. But, eventually, he did the honorable thing and married her. Are you honorable, Antonio?"

* * *

While Antonio discovered himself at a loss for words, Mack made one last sign of the cross over Iggy's casket before he grabbed Teresa's hand and led her toward the funeral caravan. On the way, he pondered

Iggy's untimely death. *It sure put a damper on our wedding plans.* He stopped in his tracks and guided Teresa to a spot where no one stood within earshot. "I know we agreed to a postponement to give my family time to mourn Iggy's death. But, I have to confess," he cleared his throat, "I'm not sure I can wait much longer to get married."

"What's the hurry? The delay gives me more time to plan the reception.

"Well, I have . . ." Mack searched for the right word. "I have needs."

"What needs?"

"Physical needs."

"Are you not feeling well, Macco?"

"No, no. Do I have to be blunt?"

"I wish you would."

"If you insist." Mack looked around to make sure no one had approached. "The truth is I can't wait much longer to make love to you."

"Oh!" Teresa's face turned beet red as she stammered, "I . . . I don't know what to say." *I would never admit it to Macco, but I have needs too.*

"Can we possibly skip the formal celebration?" Mack placed a hand on Teresa's shoulder. "Maybe we can consider something smaller and simpler, a private wedding . . . close relatives the only guests . . . sometime very soon."

"But your brother just died."

Grasping at straws, Mack said the first thing that came into his mind. "I'm sure Iggy would've approved." When Teresa sniffled in an ineffective attempt to withhold her tears, he pulled her closer. "Don't cry, honey. Iggy wouldn't have wanted you to cry over him."

Teresa swallowed a sob. *What would Macco think if he realized I wasn't crying over his brother, but over spoiled wedding plans?* She nestled close to his chest and blubbered uncontrollably.

Mack stroked her hair. "There, there." He pulled a handkerchief from his pocket and handed it to her. *Who knew Teresa cared that much about Iggy?* He'd always had the impression that his flirtatious brother made her uncomfortable.

As Teresa blew her nose, Mack clenched his jaw and stared toward his brother's casket. *Iggy, you sure gave me a run for my money over the years, tormented the living daylights out of me.* He lifted his eyes to the sky and sighed. *Maybe now you'll be more considerate of the angels.* He refocused his gaze at the ground and, shuddering, bit his lip. *Or should I say the devils.* With a twinge of guilt, Mack squinted toward

Iggy's coffin in the distance and saluted his brother in a final farewell. "Hey, Iggy, wherever you are, ***arrivederci!***"

* * *

Shortly after all the mourners left the cemetery, the gravediggers lowered Iggy's casket into the ground, and then left to retrieve their shovels, leaving Iggy's graveside unattended. Warily approaching the mound of dirt that would eventually cover Iggy, the scraggly mutt lifted his leg to pee on it. The dog's aim off-target, the spray landed in the burial hole instead. When a drenched squirrel jumped out, the frightened mongrel sped off as if the devil himself was on his tail.

* * *

Mack lay in bed later that night with his dead brothers heavy on his mind. Since both had been so young and healthy when they died, he realized how fortunate he was to be alive. He was sure that his brother Romi, a hero who gave up his life for his country, was now sitting comfortably on some fluffy cloud beyond the pearly gates. However, as he had wavered on the subject earlier that day, he wasn't quite sure where Iggy's final destination might be. Picturing Iggy's coffin, Mack drifted off into a frightening nightmare in which he himself became his brother and experienced Iggy's final journey firsthand.

Having watched the so-called mourners grieve over his casket, Iggy, embodied by his brother Mack, guffawed at their numbers. *What a bunch of blubberin' hypocrites!*

He flapped his limbs in an attempt to gain some elevation on his way to what he assumed would be paradise, but the tiny black wings on his shoulders failed to provide the lift necessary. Instead, the bottom of the casket opened and he was vacuumed into a deep, narrow tunnel that led to the cemetery's parking lot. Spitting dirt from his mouth, he spotted his car. Without a chance to take a clean breath of air, he was pulled by an ominous force and inserted into the LaSalle, behind its steering wheel. The jalopy, looking for all intents and purposes like it had the day he and his brother bought it . . . dents, loose springs and all, started up of its own volition and sped to the entrance of another subterranean passageway. At a velocity the car never traveled before, it sped through the black-tiled tunnel and emerged, only to enter a large fiery pit. Metal and leather disintegrating around him, he was left stranded on sizzling coals.

As he hopped from foot to foot, a baritone voice with an Italian accent, as raspy as a toad's, welcomed him, "***Benvenuto***, Iago. Your arrival's long overdue."

The bottom of his feet quickly blistering, he screeched, "Where the hell am I?"

"Exactly!" replied the evil spirit as it grabbed hold of his arm and dragged him to the initiation area where many of his deceased ***paesani***, several of whom he'd swindled out of their ill-gotten gains, welcomed him with open arms. "***Benvenuto! Benvenuto!*** We were wondering how soon you'd get here." They pounced on top of him and beat the livin' crap out of him, until what was left was a limp and ornery soul.

Early the next morning, Mack woke up in a sweat. He quickly glanced into the dresser mirror, thankful he was still alive and kicking, unlike his brother Iggy whose soul was sentenced to eternal damnation.

Chapter Forty-Five

Late the next afternoon, while Teresa diced vegetables at the kitchen table in preparation for supper, tears rolled down her cheeks. After Antonio walked in and witnessed what appeared to be his sister's distress, he sat across from her with a look of concern on his face. Teresa paused in her task, wiped each cheek with the back of her hand and smiled up at her brother. "Hi, Antonio."

"You don't have to hide your tears from me, little sister." Antonio soothed. "For God's sake, tell me what's the matter."

Teresa jeered at him, "***Stupido!*** Antonio, it's the onions. Are you blind?"

Antonio shrugged his shoulders and grinned. "Oh well, you have to give me some credit for effort."

"***Già!***" Teresa waved him off with a lift of the knife.

His concern abated, Antonio retrieved the Italian newspaper from the counter, sat back down and began to read as Teresa recommenced chopping. In short order, tears welled up in his eyes and ran down his cheeks but, even though he blotted at them with a napkin, the flow didn't relent.

Signore Camara strolled into the room and noted his children sniveling. "***Che cosa successo?*** Did someone else die? Is it one of our relatives? Tell me quickly!"

Teresa and Antonio burst into hysterical giggles as their father looked on in puzzlement. Signore Camara threw up his hands in exasperation.

"*Siete pazzi?* Like lunatics, you cry, you laugh." He approached the seated duo and, towering over them, hunched his shoulders and wielded his turned-up palms at them. "What next, temper tantrums?" Antonio choked on a chuckle and aimed a finger at his father whose eyes had reddened and grown watery. When one tear dripped down Signore Camara's cheek, he swiped it away and, disgruntled that he was the bunt of his children's amusement, lashed out, "*Basta!* Cut it out. It's not that funny." He crumpled his lips in a snarl.

Nonetheless, the brother and sister's hilarity continued unabashed. Teresa tittered, "The look on your face, Papà, it's . . . it's priceless."

With a flinch, Signore Camara became aware of the absurdity of the situation and howled from the pit of his belly followed by a series of piggish snorts. His children shrieked even louder. The jovial mayhem went on for several minutes, until Signore Camara screamed, "*Basta!* Stop, my stomach hurts!" Eventually, the laughter died down and Signore Camara turned to the stove to warm up some espresso.

Teresa finished her task and cleared the table. "Papà?" Signore Camara didn't turn around so Teresa frowned at his back. "Papà, do you hear me?"

"*Sì. Sì.* What is it? Spit it out, Teresa," Signore Camara blurted although he still didn't bother to face her.

Teresa clutched her apron. "Well, since his brother died, Macco and I decided we can't get married anytime soon or we'd offend his mother. And, with prices constantly going up, the longer we wait, the more the reception will cost. So, we thought maybe . . ." She choked up and sniffled.

Signore Camara spun around on his heels and scowled at Teresa. "What? *Che dici?* You want me to raise the budget for your wedding? Do you think I'm made of money? Have mercy on me, child!"

"No, no. You don't understand," Teresa blubbered.

"Then what is it? Stop your sniveling and tell me," Signore Camara insisted.

Antonio raised his head from the paper. "Papà, please give her a chance to explain."

Teresa lifted the skirt of her apron and swabbed her tears. "*Abbiamo pensato.* We thought that . . ." Her throat constricted a second time. After her father impatiently prompted her with exaggerated hand gestures, she whined, "We thought that we might get married in a quiet little ceremony in front of our closest relatives . . . no bridal gown, no reception or catered dinner, no fuss whatsoever." She buried her face in her hands and whimpered. "I'll need just a few weeks to sew my wedding outfit."

Signore Camara perked up with a smile. "***Fantastico!*** What a great idea. You and Macco can still be married. Signora Matteo won't be offended. My wallet certainly won't object. And in the end, we get the same results." He cheerfully slapped his hands together, this way and that. "***Basta! Finito!*** Enough said. I approve this plan." Signore Camara pulled out his billfold and retrieved twenty dollars from it. "Here, buy the best material. Of course if there's any change . . ."

When Teresa grabbed the money and dashed from the room bawling, Signore Camara shook his head and flipped up his hand. "***Femmine!*** Who can understand females? Do you Antonio?"

Antonio sighed. "No, not really." He turned a page of the newspaper.

Signore Camara approached the table with a cup of espresso in hand and, peering over Antonio's shoulder at a news article about German war crimes, swigged the steamy liquid. Scalding his tongue in the process, he spewed the muddy liquid down his son's neck. "***Uffa!*** That was downright hot!"

"Papà, please!" Once Antonio mopped himself, he sat up straighter, a serious expression on his face. "Papà?"

Signore Camara took a seat across from his son. "Yes, Antonio. You want to cry again too? Permission granted," he declared facetiously.

Antonio wrung his hands. "***Senti***, Papà."

"What now?"

"I'm really stuck in an awful situation."

"***Che dici?*** What kind of situation?" Signore Camara blew into his cup, took a cautious sip and swirled the liquid in his mouth as he waited for Antonio to go on.

Antonio looked down at the table and divulged his predicament all in one breath, "Mina's pregnant and expects me to marry her before it shows. But I don't earn enough to support three people, not the way Mina's used to living." He raised his head. "What should I do? Ask her to move in with us?"

"Pffffff!" Signore Camara expelled another spray of espresso onto Antonio but this time the explosion had nothing to do with the temperature of the liquid. "Move her in? Here? Son, don't you think that'd be uncomfortable? Where would you . . . ah, um . . . sleep?"

"In Teresa's room?" Antonio dabbed his face dry. "After her wedding of course."

Signore Camara stood up and paced the room. "No, no, that isn't a good idea. You know how I walk around in my underwear." He grasped for another excuse, "And my . . . my digestive winds." He tweaked the tip of his crinkled nose. "Phew! In front of Teresa, that's one thing. She's my daughter. But Mina? No, no, Mina wouldn't be happy here." He halted and held up an index finger. "Maybe her father will let you move into his apartment above the store. You'll be closer to work. Isn't that a better idea?"

"Maybe." Antonio considered the option with consternation.

Signore Camara plopped back down on the chair and chastised, "Son, are you **stupido,** or what? Did you think babies were made in heaven?"

"Well, no, of course not? But I don't know how this could have happened after doing it only one time."

"Let me put it this way," Signore explained in a condescending tone. "A woman's like pasta."

"Pasta?" Antonio asked incredulously.

"**Sì,** when you stir up a hot passionate female with your spatula," Signore Camara explained, "she swells up. You know, like a handful of pasta that doubles in boiling water to make a . . . a bowlful."

Antonio rolled his eyes and looked up at the ceiling. "Don't be ridiculous! I know the facts of life."

Signore Camara pounded the table. "Then why weren't you more careful?"

"I tried to be." Antonio stared his father in the eye. "Tell me, Papà, how would you handle the situation . . . you know, if it was you?"

"What do you mean? I'd never." Signore Camara countered in an apprehensive tone, so different from his usual forceful manner, the one he used when supplying narrow-minded solutions to life's problems.

As though his father's uneasiness was not validation enough, Antonio decided to pursue the subject further. "Natalia told Mina that you and Mamma had to get married for obvious reasons."

As Signore Camara buried his face in his hands, distant memories emerged from the door to his past, the door he usually kept locked. He spurned these bitter relatives of his youth, the ones he seldom visited for the discomfort that their company imparted. Unwilling to endure these unpleasant guests for but a short spell, he shooed them back through the door and bolted it shut, once more forsaking Antonio's mother.

Despite his father's obvious discomfort, Antonio persisted with the prying line of questioning, "It's true. Isn't it?"

Signore Camara stood up in a fury. "How dare you disgrace your mother's memory?" He then marched from the room, abandoning his son and his espresso.

Chapter Forty-Six

"Why do we hafta come here for dinner?" One arm laden with his heavily bundled baby and a diaper bag slung over each shoulder, Jake held the door open for his wife on the evening of Wednesday, December 17th. "I could be workin' on da house."

"Hush up!" Patricia, still burdened by the extra weight she failed to lose after Iaga's delivery, waddled past Jake into the Matteo's vestibule. "We haven't been here in ages." She entered the parlor and pointed towards the couch. "Lay Iaga on the sofa for now. Most likely she'll sleep through dinner." Once Jake complied, she barked another order, "Go find the portable seat in the basement, clean it up and set it up over there for later." Even though Jake wrinkled his nose at Patricia's back he followed her instructions, exiting the parlor seconds before Juliet entered.

With a voice full of concern, Juliet addressed her sister, "Patricia, I'm glad you came early enough. I've been meaning to talk to you about a problem."

"Well, why didn't you call me?" Patricia complained.

Juliet dropped her solemn demeanor and jumped on the chance to brag, "I had every intention but I've been bombarded with so many dinner invitations this past week." When Patricia scrunched her face at the news, Juliet realized her omission. "Oh, sorry, I forgot to tell you. Detective Canelli and I are . . . well, let me put it this way . . . it's become serious between us."

Patricia opened her eyes wider. "Oh really? Have you told Mamma?"

"Not yet." Wondering how her mother would take it when she and Tony announced their engagement later that evening, Juliet massaged the unadorned ring finger of her left hand. "But Tony insisted that he introduce me to all the Canellis. First, we met his parents for dinner at Gusto's Restaurant and then each of his three brothers and two sisters invited us to have supper with their families. His mother's a darling and his father's a riot. Do you believe he already has four nieces and six nephews? Honestly, I don't think I can remember so many new names and faces."

Patricia grimaced in confusion. "And *this* is your problem?"

Juliet's face sobered. "No, no. Mamma's the problem. If you stopped by more often, you'd realize she's still not herself. Actually, she's getting worse as time goes on."

Patricia removed the quilt wrapped around the snoozing baby and unzipped her snowsuit. "Worse?"

"Yes, she's so withdrawn, downright antisocial. She absolutely refused to invite Tony over for a thank you dinner. He deserves at least that for solving Iggy's murder, don't you think? But no, she said she wasn't up to entertaining a stranger. So that's when I decided to invite him over anyway, that I'd even prepare the meal myself if I had to." Since Juliet wasn't that great of a cook, she'd been relieved when Geneva agreed to help with the veal **parmigiana.**

Juliet dug her fists into her hips. "What's more, Mamma's slacked off on her housework. Geneva and I are now stuck doing it all." She pictured her mother's unruly hair and wrinkled clothes. "And she's so unkempt these days."

"Hmm," Patricia frowned at the news. Her mother had always prided herself on her cooking and her appearance. "Do you think she's still mourning Iggy's death?"

"Of course she is, but it's more than that. She wanders around aimlessly when she isn't napping." Juliet held up a hand. "The other night I asked her why."

"What did she say?" Patricia jutted her chin forward in expectation.

"She moaned that she was much too exhausted all the time," Juliet griped. "Then she had the nerve to complain that the house was a mess."

Patricia pursed her lips. "She's sounds depressed."

"Maybe there's something you can say or do to cheer her up. I've tried my best, but I've plum run out of ideas. Her negative attitude is draining."

"I'll talk to her. Where is she?"

"I hear her footsteps on the staircase right now." Juliet turned toward the rear of the house. "I'll go finish up in the kitchen. Please try to bring her to her senses."

Her black dress wrinkled and her hair disheveled, Signora Matteo dragged herself into the parlor as Juliet exited the room. "Ah, Patrizia." She spoke in Italian, since it was too much effort to think of the English words, "**Finalmente,** you find time?"

With lowered eyes, Patricia hesitated to provide an excuse. "Ah-um, Iaga caught a chest cold and, uh, I didn't want to chance pneumonia. Otherwise, honestly, we would have come sooner."

"Oh, I see." Signora Matteo sagged down into an easy chair. "**Perché non mi hai telefonato**? To call on phone is so hard?"

"I tried, Mamma, but no one ever answers your phone."

Signora Matteo hung her head low and stared at her lap. "Geneva, she busy; she clean. Anna, she no care; she shop. Me, I nap."

"All day?" Patricia pulled up a footstool and sat down next to her. "Mamma, Juliet tells me you aren't yourself lately. What's the matter?"

Without lifting her eyes, Signora Matteo murmured, "You care?"

Patricia let out an exasperated breath. "Of course I do. Don't talk like that."

Signora Matteo turned up the palm of one hand. "What is use of living? ***Nesunno*** . . . nobody need me."

"That's not true." Patricia gestured toward the sleeping infant. "If nothing else, Iaga needs a grandmother to dote on her."

"But you move," Signora Matteo whined. "And now Franco buy house, ***una casa distante.*** Who will be next to leave?"

"Mamma, did you expect all of us to live here forever?"

Signora Matteo expelled a raspy lungful of air. "***Nessuno***, no one live forever. You Papà . . . Romeo . . . Iago . . . all gone."

Patricia clutched her mother's arm. "You know that's not what I meant."

"Tell me." Signora Matteo sucked in her chin and pouted. "***Che c'è?*** What here for me?"

"Why, your granddaughter and your children of course!" Patricia reassured. "And what about the Altar Society? They count on your help, don't they?"

Signora Matteo shook her head vehemently. "***Beh!*** They talk too much. I no like listen no more." She didn't want to hear women complaining about their husbands and sons when she missed hers so much. Though some of them may have experienced the same kind of loss, she refused to acknowledge that their pain was anywhere near as traumatic as hers.

"But, Mamma, you always enjoyed their company." When Iaga stirred in her sleep, Patricia tucked a few throw pillows around her. Then, glancing about the unadorned parlor, she decided to redirect the conversation away from the negative. "What about the holidays? Where are all the decorations? Christmas is right around the corner. I'll tell you what, I'll get Jake to buy a tree and set it up for you this weekend. How's that sound?"

Too soon after her son's death to celebrate any holiday, Signora Matteo dismissed the offer with a flip of her hand. "***Niente decorazioni!***"

At a loss for a comeback, Patricia sighed. "Well, from now on you can look forward to my family coming here for dinner at least once a week. And you're welcome to stop by our house anytime during the day to play with Iaga."

"This is no ***problema***?"

"No, of course not. Iaga and I would love it."

"***Veramente?***"

"Yes, Mamma, really."

Signora Matteo gave a reluctant nod. "***Va bene***, I come if I no too tired."

As Jake carted in the baby seat, Patricia patted her mother's hand. "Fine, we'll expect you for dinner tomorrow." Ignoring Jake's disgruntled side glance, Patricia reacted to the sound of footsteps on the staircase by standing up. "The boys are on their way down. Let's go sit at the dining table." She helped her mother out of the chair and guided her into the next room, signaling for Jake to follow.

* * *

Frank stopped at the bottom of the stairs. "I don't understand your rush to get married, Mack. The family's still in mournin'."

"I can't wait a whole year, no way."

"Well, if you insist and, as long as Mamma doesn't object, you can have a small wedding right here in the parlor. No big to-do, you hear, only close family and friends." Not one to pass up an opportunity to eat, Frank added, "If you want, I'll ask Geneva and Juliet to prepare some refreshments."

"Thanks. And, Frank, can you play the wedding march for us?"

Pleased by the request, Frank patted Mack's shoulder. "For you? Sure, why not?"

"Great! As soon as Teresa sets the date, we can finalize arrangements. I'll have to get a priest to agree to perform the ceremony here, someone other than Father Romano." Mack frowned. "You know how Mamma feels about him."

"Don't worry," Frank assured Mack, "Geneva'll take care of it."

"By the way, Frank, how's Geneva? Is she sick?"

Frank hesitated. "Uh, no, why're you askin'?"

"Well, she didn't look so good this morning, kind of green under the gills," Mack whispered behind his hand. "Later on, I heard her throwing up in the bathroom."

"Oh, that." Frank glanced over his shoulder into the empty parlor. "I'll let you in on a secret if you promise not to spill the beans to anybody else."

Mack narrowed his eyes. "What secret?"

Frank expanded his chest and grinned from ear to ear. "Geneva's finally pregnant. She made me swear not to tell anyone yet."

"Really?" Mack seized hold of his brother's right hand and pumped it enthusiastically. "Well, congratulations, brother!"

Frank hoisted an index finger to his lips. "Shhh, lower your voice. Someone'll hear you."

"Sorry, Frank." Mack gestured toward the dining room. "Come on. Let's go eat. I'm starved."

When the doorbell rang, Frank waved Mack onward. "You go ahead. I'll get it." Heavy footed, he limped toward the front door and opened it. "Detective Canelli, it's good to see you again. What brings you here?"

"Juliet invited me for dinner." Tony lifted his chin and adjusted the wide knot of his bold-print necktie. "Didn't she tell you?"

"Oh, yes, it must've slipped my mind." Frank gestured for him to enter. "Come on in, Detective Canelli. I'll get Juliet."

"Please, I'm off duty tonight. Call me Tony."

"Fine with me, Tony it is." Frank faced toward the rear of the house and hollered at the top of his lungs, "Juliet, Detective Canelli is here!"

Within seconds, Juliet pranced into the vestibule. "Tony, you're right on time; we're about to start dinner." She turned to her brother. "Frank, give us a minute."

"Sure." Frank stood there with his arms folded across his chest in a proprietary manner.

"Alone, Frank." Juliet shooed him away. "We'll be right in."

Frank's eyes passed from Juliet to Tony with a glimmer of fraternal wariness. "Okay, but don't take too long. I'm hungry."

Upon Frank's exit from the vestibule, Juliet stood on tiptoe and gave Tony a kiss. "Tony, I can't wait to tell them." She pulled her engagement ring from her skirt pocket and handed it to Tony. "Will you do me the honor, Mr. Canelli?" She held out her hand.

"Try and stop me." He slipped the diamond onto her ring finger before he picked her up and spun her around in a circle. "Hey, you're light as a pigeon."

"Tony, please, you're making me dizzy." Once he dropped her to her feet and she managed to steady herself, Juliet held up the gem to the light. "Maybe this will snap Mamma out of her doldrums. Come on, let's make our announcement."

Arm-in-arm Juliet and Tony entered the dining room where the rest of the extended family, except Anna who remained locked in her room, sat ready to start the meal. Juliet coughed for attention. "Hey, everybody, guess what?" Once all eyes were on her, she held up the diamond. "Tony asked me to marry him!"

As if Juliet had announced an imminent catastrophe, a stampede of turmoil broke loose in the Matteo dining room. With a wretched whine, Signora Matteo bolted upright from the table and scurried into the kitchen while, hand over mouth, Geneva turned a pasty shade of chartreuse and sprinted out the side door. Frank knocked over his chair in his effort to dash after his wife; and, awakened by the racket, the baby let out a colicky screech.

Prompted into action, Patricia rose to her feet. "Excuse us. Iaga needs our attention. Jake, don't just sit there. Come on." After Jake turned up both palms and hunched his shoulders in apology, he marched behind Patricia into the parlor.

Mack, the only one left sitting at the table, lifted his water glass. "I guess congratulations are in order." He stared his future brother-in-law in the eye. "Welcome to the loony bin, Tony."

Juliet burst into tears.

* * *

Meanwhile, upstairs, Anna sifted through her closet and bureau drawers. "***Decisioni, decisioni.***" *I have to decide.* Pausing, she picked up a glass from the bureau, one that sat next to a plate of miniature mozzarella balls, and took a sip of red wine. *Which outfits should I pack in my suitcase?* She only wanted to include her most flattering clothes; the rest she'd store in a trunk for handouts when she got to Italy. She placed the glass down and, with fastidious discretion, arranged her clothes into two separate piles on either side of the bed. She patted the pile on the right which included a sufficient supply of low-cut dresses along with her see-through nighties and a couple of evening gowns with their price tags still attached. *These will go into my suitcase. Who knows who will be on the ship . . . debonair men with loads of money?* She swooned at the mental image of handsome gentlemen vying for her attention. "***Uomini simpatici e ricchi!***" She ran a hand along her bustline. "Rich men appreciate good figures."

After her successful crusade to persuade her reluctant brother-in-law to borrow the buyout money from the bank, she had rushed to a local travel agent, the one who spoke fluent Italian, and planned her return trip to Italy. Although the settlement provided a decent amount for Iggy's widow, it didn't warrant her extravagance in booking first class accommodations on the newest and finest Italian ocean liner, but she felt she deserved no less for enduring her husband's infidelity. The ship was scheduled to depart on December 29th. She'd asked the agent to arrange for her to stay in a high-class hotel the night before sailing.

Anna picked up a ball of the cheese from the plate on the bureau and, devouring it, took another sip of wine. *I still have to put up with the Matteos for two more weeks.* Her face soured at the prospect. "**Non vedo l'ora**. No, I can't wait to be on my way."

Anna reached for the itinerary the agent had provided and reviewed the costly details out loud, "Let me see. First, a taxi will take me to the train station. Then, I'll relax in a private compartment on the way to New York City where a limousine will be waiting to take me to the hotel. The next day it'll take me to the port. There, I'll board the ship bound for Naples. Easy enough." Anna flipped the page. *A duplicate itinerary? Who needs it? I'm sure no one in this family cares about the details of my trip.* She separated the two sheets, and haphazardly discarded the copy. It landed between the bureau and the wall. Not bothering to retrieve it, she verified all her tickets and passport were safely tucked in her purse then sighed contentedly. "Everything is set."

Making room for herself on the bed, she flopped down between the two piles of clothes. *My brother Angelo seemed all too willing to pick me up at the port in Naples. Must have something to do with my promise to make it well worth his while.* She rubbed her right thumb back and forth against the fingers of the same hand. "Money talks." *No doubt all sorts of relatives will pile at my doorstep for a handout now that they know I have some money.* She kicked up her feet and burst into a fit of hysterical laughter. *Let them.* Although she had no intention of giving them any, she thought it would be fun to watch them beg.

Sobering, she pictured herself the night she met Iggy. Exhausted from a day of waiting on drunken sailors and grabby marines, the dark-haired soldier had been aloof in his casual manner towards her, a busty girl with an unremarkable face. At the time, Anna had no clue that Iggy was using his typical MO. His mode of operation was a simple one. Sipping a beer, he'd case a bar to find a female he considered vulnerable, a plain but sexy woman desperate enough to do anything to please him, especially after he insinuated he was fishing for that "special someone" to impress his mother. Thinking she could outsmart the **Americano**, Anna had fallen for his line.

In an attempt to distract herself from the disturbing memory, she stood up and patted her stomach. "**Ho fame**." Starving, she didn't know how much longer she could wait for a real meal.

To amuse herself while she waited, she retrieved one of the evening gowns from the bed and waltzed it around the room. "♪La la, la, la, la♪." *Will I get a chance to dance with the ship's **capitano**?*

Tiring from the effort, Anna tossed the gown onto the bed and reached for another piece of cheese but, instead of a mozzarella ball, picked up something furry. When it began to squirm in her hand, she realized it was a white mouse and, screaming at the top of her lungs, dropped the poor creature to the floor. Startled, but uninjured from the fall, the satiated rodent, a descendent of one of Mack's high school science projects, shook itself off. Then, darting through a hole in the floorboard, the bold mouse retreated to its dank basement home, leaving Anna to wonder if she had ingested any of its droppings.

* * *

That night Anna dreamed of herself in the arms of a man in navy whites. The handsome and debonair captain waltzed her around the dance floor, her flowing gown trailing behind her. The envy of every woman in the room, she tossed her head back and laughed. "If Iago could see me now."

As if prompted by a stage cue, Iggy appeared, donned in the brown uniform he'd worn the first time she laid eyes on him. "Let go of my wife!"

Sneering at the possessive look in his eyes, Anna scoffed, "He was never jealous when he was alive, but now that he's dead . . ."

"Do I look dead to you?" He grabbed her away from the captain and held her tightly by an arm. Though Anna tried to resist him, Iggy ripped the bodice of her gown, her breasts exposed to the shocked audience. "If it wasn't for these boobs, I'd still be a free man."

"*Porco* . . . you dirty lying pig!" As angry tears sprung from her eyes, she smacked him across the face. "If it wasn't for your cheating ways, I'd have been happy in America."

Iggy grabbed her hand before it landed on his cheek a second time. "I knew there was fire in your blood that night I set my lure for you. You fell for it . . . hook, line and sinker. Ha, ha, ha, ha!"

Realizing it was she who'd prevailed in the end, she haughtily pulled back her hand and pushed out her chest. "Who snagged who, Iago?" She laughed louder than he had. "Where's your money now? Huh, Iago?" Breasts still exposed, she approached the captain. "Shall we finish our dance?"

"Go ahead, spite yourself, bitch." Indignant, Iggy adjusted the crotch of his slacks. "Your loss, not mine." He grabbed the closest blonde, shoved her onto the crowded dance floor and, stepping on the girl's toes, faded from Anna's view.

Glad to be rid of her husband once and for all, Anna held tight to her dream man and, as he waltzed her away in the opposite direction, she pressed her cheek against his uniform. "Tell me, captain, how much do you earn in a year?"

While Anna batted her lashes against her pillow, relatives of the little white mouse scampered across her bureau, absconding with the last of the mozzarella balls leftover from the previous evening.

Chapter Forty-Seven

With the red cardinal perched on a branch above him, the scruffy mutt stared at the Matteo residence on the second Saturday of 1948. Baffled by the number of people who had entered the house, he wondered who they all were, and why they smelled so nice. Settling down to wait for a handout from the tall fellow who lived in the house, the dog was distracted by a peck on his tail. Jumping up, the mongrel revolved in full circle in an attempt to capture the annoying bird that had landed to pilfer some fur for his nest. Frightened, the cardinal dug his claws in the matted fur and squawked for dear life.

Meanwhile, inside, with its usual furnishings repositioned tight against the walls, the Matteos' parlor hummed with anticipation. About twenty people, Mack's family and friends on the right opposite Teresa's on the left, chatted as they endured the discomfort of the folding chairs arranged on either side of a makeshift aisle.

Seated at the piano, Geneva turned the pages of sheet music for Frank, who entertained the guests with a few classical selections. In between two pieces, Frank questioned his wife, "I thought you arranged for Father Rossi to perform the ceremony? What happened? Why is Father Romano here?"

Although a few weeks of interacting with her granddaughter had lifted Signora Matteo's spirits, they all knew she still harbored certain unreasonable resentments, especially in regards to Father Romano. To avoid a conflict, Geneva had tried to exclude him when making arrangements for the ceremony. "I did but Father Rossi took sick last night, and Father Battera is on sabbatical. I had to beg Father Romano to take his place at the last minute. He refused until I promised to make an additional donation to his Vatican Pilgrimage Fund." Glancing at the first row where Signora Matteo sat next to Patricia, Geneva winced. "Your mother was so furious when he showed up this morning that she nearly slammed the door in his face. I calmed her down and made her swear not to start any more trouble, but we'll see. She's still utterly convinced the man's an unholy letch."

Forgoing black for the first time since Iggy's death, Signora Matteo adjusted the starched bodice of her navy dress and, glaring at Father Romano, gritted her teeth. "***Guardi***, Patrizia. Look him, ***il impostore. Un lupo*** . . . he is like wolf who wears the clothes of sheep." After the priest slithered back and hid behind the arched trellis rented for the occasion, Signora Matteo thought of another nasty allegory. "***Un serpente***." She ordered Patricia to have Jake watch the snake, to keep him away from the wine. Although Anna had already sailed off for Italy, Signora Matteo was worried the lecherous serpent would prey on some other woman present that day.

Patricia squeezed her mother's arm. "Mamma, please stop. I thought you promised Geneva." Her snoozing baby cuddled in her lap, she glanced to her right and elbowed Jake. "Sit up straight and fix your tie. It's crooked." Distracted when Iaga wriggled in preparation for a squeal, she threw a receiving blanket over her shoulder. Under its cover, she unbuttoned her dress front and shoved one of her nipples into the infant's mouth.

Jake nudged Patricia. "Don't do dat here."

"Oh don't be ridiculous." Patricia waved off her husband's concern. "No one'll notice. Besides, it'll keep Iaga quiet during the ceremony."

Behind Signora Matteo, Juliet snuggled closer to Tony. "I can hardly wait for my own . . . I mean . . . our wedding day. It's a shame Mack insisted they get married right away." Thinking of how she'd feel in Teresa's place, how upset she'd be if she was forced to give up her dream of a full-blown celebration, Juliet sighed, "I'd be absolutely devastated."

"What's wrong with this wedding? Tony countered as he gestured toward the trellis. "They probably saved a bundle."

"Don't be ridiculous." The fingers of her diamond-studded hand pressed against her cheek, Juliet flashed a smile at her fiancé. "I wouldn't dream of such a simple event."

Relieved her mother would be paying for it, Tony wrapped his arm around Juliet's shoulder and grinned. "Whatever makes you happy, Princess."

Across the aisle, parked behind Teresa's two eldest brothers and their wives, Mina twisted the plain gold band on her finger and snarled at Antonio. "Why'd you have to insist on a civil ceremony? Daddy was very disappointed he didn't get a chance to walk me down the aisle."

Hand across his mouth, Antonio parted his fingers. "Did he expect you to wear white in your condition? He should be content I married you at all."

Mina turned up her nose. "And why can't we get our own place?" She folded her arms tight across her belly and lowered her voice. "I'm embarrassed to *you-know-what* in the room right next to Daddy's. He can hear every sound we make."

"You mean every sound *you* make. Don't you, Mina?" Without giving her a chance to respond, Antonio turned away and saluted his father relaxing against the far wall. His greeting, however, went unacknowledged since Signore Camara focused on his future son-in-law as he appeared at the room's threshold.

Donned in a double-breasted charcoal suit with an ivory rosebud secured to its lapel, the groom breezed into the parlor shadowed by his best man whose thick spectacles perched on the edge of his nose. Mack nodded at Teresa's father then looked over his shoulder at his good friend. "You're sure you have the ring, Joe?" Without waiting for an answer, Mack sailed forward on a wave of anticipation, coasting to a stop in front of the trellis. *I can't wait till Teresa's mine.* Joe pushed up his glasses and drifted along in Mack's wake. Another of Mack's friend's stood ready with a camera, searching for photo opportunities.

At 10:59, Frank hit a few random notes on the keyboard to encourage the attendees to settle down and, at a signal from the vestibule, commenced playing *A Mid-Summer Night's Dream: Wedding March* by Mendelssohn. Dressed in a pale lavender frock with a bouquet of violets in hand, Carmela, Teresa's matron of honor, strolled down the aisle in rhythm with the piano. After a dramatic pause in the music, all heads turned toward the foyer in anticipation.

Though Frank pounded the keys once more, Teresa hesitated at the threshold, wondering if anyone would think her less of a bride because she wasn't wearing a traditional gown. *Will they be disappointed?* Despite her reservations, Teresa breezed into the room with the grace of a monarch butterfly and modeled her latest creation, a tailored suit fashioned in white cashmere with lapels and cuffs trimmed in ivory satin. Flowing from a crown of baby's breath, a short veil covered Teresa's face while a denser section cascaded down the length of her French braid. Clutching a bouquet of rosebuds identical to the one in Mack's lapel, the anxious bride glided closer toward the aisle, a roomful of appreciative eyes riveted on her.

A grinning Signore Camara offered Teresa his arm and, forgetting all about their tedious rehearsals, led her toward the trellis, his quick and arrhythmic stride reflecting his eagerness to once again enjoy a love-life free of his children's interference. Teresa did the best she could to keep up with him. *Did we practice for nothing?* Coming to an abrupt halt at the end of the aisle, Signore Camara lifted her veil and, tickling her cheeks with his waxed mustache, planted an exuberant send-off kiss on each side of her face. He then bowed away, allowing Mack to take his place at Teresa's side.

Dazzled by Teresa's coy smile, Mack whispered, "Teresa, you look absolutely beautiful." Hearts pounding, they faced Father Romano.

Under the canopy of the trellis, Father Romano consulted his prayer book and canted a few prayers in Latin before he initiated the wedding ceremony in earnest, intermingling both English and Italian so that all might comprehend. "We are gathered here today to unite this man, Macbetto Matteo," he nodded at Mack and gestured toward Teresa, "and this woman, Teresa Camara, in holy matrimony." Father Romano lifted his chin and scanned the group with a stern expression. "If anyone here knows a just reason why they should not be united today in holy matrimony, speak now or forever hold your peace." Although Signore Camara appeared apprehensive, no one spoke up. "Very well, Macbetto and Teresa, it's time to exchange your marriage vows."

The bride and groom turned toward each other and, with a tight grip on Teresa's hands, Mack gazed into her eyes repeating the priest's words in Italian, "I, Macbetto, take you Teresa, to be my lawful wife, to have and to hold, from this day forward, for better or for worse, for richer or for poorer, in sickness and in health, to love and to cherish all the days of my life."

When it came time for Teresa to do the same, the priest began in Italian. However Teresa interrupted him, "I wish-ah to speak-ah in *Inglesi*." Struggling in a halting but, nonetheless understandable form of mutilated English, she mimicked Father Romano and recited her vow. Mack rewarded Teresa with a smile while several attendees applauded her effort.

After they exchanged rings and, at Father Romano's directive "You may now . . . uh . . . kiss the bride," Teresa and Mack engaged in a rather long passionate kiss to the applause of the spectators and the excitement of the clergyman.

Father Romano quickly hunched forward and successfully hid the evidence of his lust to all but Signora Matteo. As he concluded the ceremony with a quick nuptial blessing, Iaga burped disproportionately loud for such a tiny infant and, to Father Romano's relief, Signora Matteo's accusative eyes shifted toward the baby. Unfazed by the attention Iaga elicited, Patricia continued to pat her back until she ejected another loud belch.

The bride and groom took the distraction in stride and giggled along with the rest. When Frank keyed the *Ode to Joy* by Beethoven with all its fanfare, Teresa and Mack faced their families and ran down the center aisle hand-in-hand, to the vestibule and up the staircase. Everyone traipsed behind the newlyweds and halted at the foot of the steps, except for Father Romano who sneaked out the front door, determined to find some physical relief.

Teresa spun around at the top of the staircase and aimed her bouquet at the loudest and most enthusiastic target, Juliet. After her sister-in-law caught the bouquet and flaunted it along with her diamond-studded hand, Teresa recaptured the crowd's attention by hiking her skirt way above her knees and snapping the blue garter against her thigh. Oblivious to the blanching of her mother-in-law's face, Teresa enticed Mack in a breathy challenge, "***Per favore***, Macco, don't be shy." The men hooted.

"My pleasure, Signora Matteo!" Inspired by his wife's theatrics, Mack jumped at the chance to roll the garter brazenly down Teresa's leg as she expelled a provocative sigh. Once he slipped it off, he stood up and perused the male guests. "Anyone need a garter?" He twirled the lacy band in the air.

"Over here!" Tony blew a shrill whistle through his pinky and index fingers.

"Make room! I believe the man's desperate." Laughing, Mack tossed the garter out into the crowd and everyone stepped back, except Tony who shot up and caught the garter between his teeth to the cheers of the spectators.

Garter in hand, Tony enticed Juliet closer with repeated curls of his index finger. "Come here, ***bella mia***." After Tony knelt down on one knee, Juliet posed cross-legged on his opposite thigh and he proceeded to slip the garter seductively up her leg. The men encouraged him and the women hissed.

When she caught sight of her mother's disapproving eye, Juliet stopped Tony halfway up her thigh and giggled. "That's far enough, mister."

"Ah-hum," Frank cleared his throat, diverting the group's attention. "Please join us in the dining room for the scrumptious feast Mamma and the girls prepared."

Signora Matteo let out a sigh of relief and waved the guests into the dining room. "***Sì, sì, venite a mangiare!*** Much good food to eat."

While all nibbled on the Italian delicacies, the newlyweds made their rounds of the guests and before long Mack convinced Teresa to retreat to their bedroom. "Let's go change for our honeymoon. I want to take off right after we cut the cake." Mack grabbed Teresa's hand and they escaped to the privacy of their own quarters.

Behind the closed door, Mack snatched Teresa by the waist. "Will my wife give me another kiss?"

"Only if you insist, *marito mio*." Teresa extended on the tips of her toes and tilted her chin upwards as Mack leaned downward and pressed his lips against hers.

Mack and Teresa melded together with guiltless delight until Frank banged on the door. "Come on, you two! Everyone's anxious for some cake."

Chapter Forty-Eight

"Jeez, Teresa, what kind of aim is that?" Mack chuckled good-naturedly as he wiped the cake from his cheek. "Here, let me show you how it's done." He scooped up a finger-full of butter cream from the wedding cake and smeared it onto Teresa's chin, right below her lips. "Oops, I missed!"

Teresa licked off most of the frosting and dabbed the rest away with a napkin. "Oh well, maybe we'll be less clumsy in the bedroom." Everyone in the dining room hooted except for Signora Matteo whose jaw dropped at the innuendo and Signore Camara whose mustache camouflaged his grin.

Ignoring his mother's reaction, Mack grabbed hold of Teresa by the waist. "*Cara mia*, let's hurry up and leave. We want plenty of time to practice tonight." Again, the dining room vibrated with laughter.

"So what's there to stop us, *amore mio*? *Andiamo*, let's go!" Hand-in-hand, Teresa and Mack zipped from the room and raced up the stairs to retrieve their suitcases.

As most of the guests lined up for a slice of cake, Tony and Jake slipped out the side door and approached Mack's LaSalle armed with the trappings of tradition: a bar of soap, a ribbon bouquet, a few strands of string, and six tin cans. While Jake secured the ribbon to the hood ornament, Tony etched the soapy message "Just Married" across the rear windshield before he scribbled "Honeymooners Onboard" on the driver's side and "Newlyweds" on the passenger side. His chalky inscriptions completed, Tony supervised the remainder of Jake's operation. "Be careful with that jackknife. I don't like the sight of blood."

"Some homicide detective!" Once Jake punched two holes through each can with one of the knife's tools, he looped the strips of string through the punctures and tied them to the back bumper. Finished, he walked around the car and inspected their efforts. "Hope Mack makes out better den me after da honeymoon's over. A crabby bitch came out of Patricia's shell da instant we got home from ours. Now, wit Iaga for an excuse, I can't get nowhere near da woman."

"Aw, come on. Can't be that bad," Tony taunted.

"Dat's da half a it. If ya knew da rest, ya'd never get married.

"Pffff," Tony brushed off the warning. "If you wanna know my theory on women . . ." Before Tony was able to divulge the gist of his premise, the side door to the house sprung open.

Mack and Teresa stumbled out burdened with two small valises each. "Will you look at my car, Teresa?" Mack whined facetiously. "Can't imagine who'd mess it up with all that graffiti." He winked at Jake and Tony.

Within seconds, an entourage of well-wishers exited the house and showered the newlyweds with rice and farewells. "***Buon viaggio! Buon viaggio!***" Attracted by the commotion, the scraggly mutt, Mack's psuedo-pet, squatted inconspicuously next to the LaSalle and the dog's pesky bird-friend, the cardinal, pecked at the rice.

Meanwhile, caught up in the frenzy of excitement, Frank smacked Mack on the rump, "Don't do anythin' I wouldn't do, brother."

Mack lowered his suitcases to the ground and, in a takeoff of Groucho Marx, raised and lowered his eyebrows several times as he flicked an imaginary cigar. "What wouldn't you do? Maybe we'll try it." A handful of well-wishers roared while a couple of them booed his attempt at the impersonation.

After Mack loaded the suitcases into the trunk, he held the passenger side door open for Teresa and gestured toward the seat. "Are you ready to depart, Signora Matteo?"

Index finger extended, Teresa aimed an arm to the right. "**Sì**, onward to Niagra and the Falls."

Mack pivoted her torso in the opposite direction. "It's this way, **cara mia**."

Teresa laughed, "All roads lead to Rome."

Again in Groucho mode, Mack took a puff of his invisible cigar. "For an extra quarter, I can offer a side-trip to Rome, New York."

"No, no. Deliver me straight to the Falls," Teresa ordered.

"Your wish is my command." Mack performed a deep bow; and, once Teresa slipped onto the seat, he shut the door and scrambled to the other side of the car.

With a broad smile, Teresa waved out the open window. "**Ciao, tutti**. We'll see you in one week."

With an exuberant bark, the mutt wished Teresa and Mack a safe and enjoyable honeymoon; but after they pulled away, the dog leaned his chin on his paws, sulking at their absence. Taking pity on the mongrel, Juliet went back into the house to retrieve some leftover scraps from the wedding feast. But, by the time she returned, the hungry dog had been shooed away by Signora Matteo; and, satiated, the bird had flown off.

* * *

When the last of the guests departed and the women retreated to the kitchen, Tony offered to help Frank and Jake stack the folding chairs and return the furniture to its rightful place in the parlor. That completed, they carted the metal chairs down to the basement. Despite the ruckus, Iaga napped peacefully in one corner of the dining room, pillows arranged protectively around her quilted blanket.

Their task finished, Frank uncorked a bottle he pulled from a wine rack in the cellar and offered it to the other two as a reward for their efforts. "Drink up men, you deserve it." While they passed the wine around, the cellar mice remained discretely hidden, except for one brave fellow that lapped at a spill. Catching sight of the white rodent, the same one that Anna had weeks before mistaken for a mozzarella ball, Frank picked up a broom and chased the feisty creature around the basement until it disappeared behind a stack of boxes. Huffing, he leaned against the stack. "I . . . I'll have to set out a few traps."

"Why bother, Frank?" Tony laughed. "The exercise will do you good."

"Fff-funny, Tony." Frank caught his breath. "Very funny." As he wiped the sweat from his forehead, he noticed that his brother-in-law was also smirking at his expense. "You've got somethin' to add, Jake?"

"Not me, Frank, not me."

* * *

In the meantime, the women busied themselves in the kitchen with clean-up duty. Having stored enough leftovers for three large meals, they formed an efficient production line along the kitchen counter. Signora Matteo meticulously washed the dishes and flatware, Geneva and Juliet dried them and Patricia returned them to their rightful place in the cupboards.

When the phone rang, Signora Matteo halted, tilting an ear toward the parlor, but Patricia kept right at the task. "Don't stop, Mamma. One of the boys will answer it."

*   *   *

Frank struggled up the cellar stairs, took a deep breath and picked up the telephone receiver on the fourth ring. "Hello, Matteo residence, Frank here." He paused to listen before he replied in Italian, "No, we haven't heard from your sister since she left over a week ago. Why're you askin'? Is somethin' wrong?"

Frank frowned at the answer. "I'll see what I can do. How can I reach you? Hold on. Let me get a pen." He scrambled for a pen and scratch pad from the secretary and jotted down a long list of numbers. "I'll call you as soon as I figure out where she went." He dropped the receiver onto its cradle and trudged toward the kitchen, his eyes full of trepidation. Having come up from the basement, Tony and Jake caught the tail end of the conversation and, curious, followed Frank to the kitchen.

Upon her husband's entrance, Geneva scrutinized his solemn expression. "Frank, what is it? Who phoned?"

"Anna's brother Angelo called from the port in Naples. The connection was full of static, but his concern was clear enough."

Juliet accosted her brother. "Concern about what, Frank?"

"Angelo shocked the hell outta me when he asked me if Anna was still here. According to him, she never got off the boat in Naples." Frank explained that, when Anna's brother inquired, the ship's steward assured him that all the boarded passengers had already debarked. Swiping his forehead, he continued, "I told him she left here over a week ago, but I guess she never made it to the boat." Though Angelo refused to admit the real reason to Frank, that his family had been counting on Anna to boost their financial circumstances, he had expressed his parents' bitter disappointment when she didn't show up. "They're worried about her. Angelo begged me to find out where she is." Frank huffed, "I said I'd try my best. He gave me this phone number where I can reach him." He held up the scratch paper.

Geneva pounded her right fist into her opposite palm and sputtered, "We . . . we never should've let her leave on her own. Why didn't we drive her to the pier ourselves?" She wiped the drool from her chin. "What were we thinking?"

Juliet untied her apron. "She insisted she'd rather go by train."

Tony stepped forward. "Signora Matteo, did you hear from Anna?"

Signora Matteo and Patricia exchanged nervous glances before Patricia whispered into her mother's ear. The older woman wrung her hands and shook her head in response.

"Come on, don't hold back," Tony pressured the two. "Either of you have a clue where Anna is?"

As Jake drew near to his wife, Patricia shrugged off his attempt to wrap a comforting arm around her. "Tell him, Mamma." She nudged her mother's arm. "Some of your worst nightmares have come true."

Signora Matteo turned her head away. "No, **non posso**. If I do, it *will* happen."

Despite her mother's resolve to keep it a secret, Patricia decided to reveal the dark premonition Signora Matteo received in her sleep. "The night before Anna's departure, Mamma dreamed of a woman dancing around a blazing fire. Although she didn't see the woman's face, Mamma's positive she was dressed in orange. Tony, I'm sure you're aware that, according to Italian legend, the color orange is an omen of death."

"I know, I know. But, please, let's not get carried away." Tony spread his arms outward. "There's probably a logical explanation. Maybe somethin' caused Anna to miss the ship and she hopped another boat. No doubt she's dancin' with the ship's captain right about now."

Juliet approached Tony and inserted her hand in the crook of his elbow. "Tony's probably right."

"I'll investigate if you want me to," Tony offered.

Frank nodded. "Thanks, good to have a cop around when you really need one."

Feeling guilty for the grudge she'd held against Anna for not sharing the household chores, Geneva shuddered. "We're to blame if anything bad's happened to her."

Frank extended an arm around Geneva's shoulder. "Let's not jump to conclusions before Tony finds out where she is."

As Signora Matteo whimpered anxiously into her fist, Geneva buried her face into the folds of Frank's shirt. "I know you're right, honey, but . . ."

* * *

While the Matteos on Steward Street speculated on Anna's whereabouts, a shoeless Signore Camara climbed the stairs to the second story of his Chambers Street home. Entering his bedroom, the one he no longer shared with his son, he removed his suit and shirt and hung them in his armoire. The garters still fastened to his argyle socks and his arms gesticulating in wild abandon, he slid across the hardwood floor and belted a few lyrics of **Mala Femmena,** a Neapolitan ballad about unrequited love:

♫ *Femmena,*
Tu si na malafemmena
Chist'uocchie 'e fatto chiagnere.
Lacreme e 'nfamità. ♫

♫ *Femmena,*
Si tu peggio 'e na vipera,
M'e 'ntussecata l'anema,
Nun pozzo cchiù campà. ♫

His voice hoarsening from the effort, Signore Camara halted. "Not bad for a Sicilian." He glanced at his wristwatch. "I'd better freshen up a bit." On the way to the bathroom, he tucked his tank top into the waistband of his jockey underwear, snagging the wristband in the process. He disentangled it as he entered the bathroom.

Once he brushed his teeth, he reached for the Listerine, gulped a mouthful and gargled for a few seconds before he spit it out and seized a container of talcum powder, applying a liberal dose to each armpit. **"Bene, sono pronto.** I'm ready for some passion." He returned to his bedroom and, the moment he extended his arm toward a silk robe hanging from the hook on the back of the door, the doorbell chimed. **"Finalmente!** Finally, she's here."

Rushing down the stairs, he slipped into the robe without bothering to tie it, then, eyes closed and lips puckered, opened the front door. When the kiss he expected didn't occur, he opened his eyes to investigate why.

"Papà, we love you! But, really, it's winter." Antonio snickered. "You'll catch your death of cold answering the door like that."

Mina peeked around Antonio and jolted at the sight of her father-in-law in such a state of undress. "How disgusting!" Her features twisted with repulsion, Mina hid behind Antonio. "It's freezing out here, but I refuse to go inside until your father makes himself decent."

Signore Camara stammered, "I . . . I didn't imagine *you* would show up. Why're you here?" He clumsily tied his robe as he moved away from the door toward the stairway.

His father's underwear safely out of sight, Antonio guided Mina into the house, explaining that they were there to retrieve the few relics of his childhood that he'd brought along with him from Italy. "I want to show them to Mina." Teresa had told him where she'd stored them, upstairs in the hallway closet.

"Well, go ahead and get them and be on your way!" Signore Camara ordered, blocking the staircase. "***Subito!***"

Trying to pass Signore Camara to get to the steps, Antonio seesawed back and forth with his father, until his old man finally lost his patience. He grabbed hold of his son's arms and spun Antonio closer to the stairs. "I said hurry up!"

Looking back at his father, Antonio tilted his head and jutted his chin forward mischievously. "Why're you in such a hurry for us to leave, Papà? Expecting someone, are you?"

"No, no. I'm just eager to take a nap. The wedding exhausted me." Signore Camara embellished a yawn with a wide stretch of his arms. "Please hurry up."

"A nap you say," Antonio smirked. "Tell me, Papà, how often do you nap?"

"What business is it of yours?" Signore Camara waved him on. "Go on. Get your things. Quickly!"

"***Va bene***, I'll only be a minute." Antonio raced up the stairs.

Huffing with impatience, Mina hung her head and studied the knots in the hardwood floor as she waited with Signore Camara.

"So, Mina, how's married life? Is it all you expected?"

Distracted by a spider that crawled along the floor, Mina didn't bother to look up at her father-in-law. "Things are fine I suppose but we'll be much better off if we get a place of our own. Privacy is hard to come by in my father's apartment."

"***Capisco***. Believe me. I know exactly what you mean." Signore Camara checked his wristwatch before he shouted up the stairs, "Antonio, what're you doing? What's taking so long?" When the spider reached Signore Camara, it crawled up his leg. Unfazed by the eight-legged creature, he nonchalantly brushed it off and stomped on it with his stocking foot, then kicked it across the floor toward Mina. As she backed away, cringing in disgust, Signore Camara wondered who would dust away all the spider webs now that Teresa was gone. He doubted his lover was up to the task.

Antonio's strained voice reverberated down the stairs, "They're in a box at the bottom of this pile." The sound of cardboard crashing made both Mina and Signore Camara jump. "I'll be right down as soon as I . . ." Antonio trailed off as he gathered the fallen items.

Within a few minutes, Antonio trotted down the stairs with the box in hand. When he reached Mina, he lifted its lid and pulled out a pair of tiny cloth slippers. "Look, Mina, my first pair of shoes. Maybe our baby can wear them."

Mina gritted her teeth and averted her eyes in humiliation. "What baby? What are you talking about?"

Since Antonio continued to admire the slippers oblivious to her discomfort, she stomped down her foot. "Antonio, put those back in the box and let's go home. Now!"

As Mina bolted toward the door, Signore Camara sneered, hand-over-mouth. "Yes, Antonio, listen to your wife. Take her home before she exposes her fangs."

Trying to restore his dignity, Antonio chased after Mina and grabbed hold of her wrist. "Button your coat," he ordered and, on second thought, added, "and your lips." He opened the door and pushed her out.

Mina shrieked at Antonio, "How dare you treat me like that! Wait till we get home!"

Signore Camara winced as he shut the door behind them. Then, with a dismissive twist of his hand, he criticized his foolhardy son, "**Stupido**! He picks a woman just like his mother. Nag! Nag! Nag!"

Chapter Forty-Nine

As Mack directed the LaSalle north on the interstate, Teresa peered out the window at the unfamiliar highway. "Do you know the way to Niagara Falls?"

Mack placed a hand on the road map that sat on the basket between them. "I found a route through Pennsylvania into New York State. Lockport is the closest town to the Falls. It should be an easy six hour drive."

"So, Macco, where're we going to stay once we get there?"

"A place called Honeymoon Haven."

"Did someone recommend it?"

"No, not really. It's one of five resorts I found in the back of an old travel magazine," Mack explained. "Since Niagara Falls is a top spot for honeymooners, I didn't want to take a chance. I booked the first one with a room available."

Leery of his selection method, Teresa pressed her lips together. "Hmm."

"The advertisement claims it's a quaint lodge close to the Falls. Quaint is good, right?"

Teresa turned her head away and murmured under her breath, "We'll find out, won't we?" *I assumed he'd take me to the best hotel available. It's our honeymoon after all.*

"Something wrong, Teresa?"

Teresa shook her head and waved a hand in the air. "No, not really. It's just that I expected you to use a more reliable source."

"More reliable? What's more reliable than a travel magazine?"

"Seasoned travelers," Teresa suggested, "or an experienced travel agent."

"Remember you're the one who insisted *I* make the arrangements, Teresa."

"*Certo!* What did you expect?" Teresa bristled with annoyance. *It was his idea to move up the wedding, not mine.* With less than a month to sew both her wedding suit and Carmela's bridesmaid dress, she'd had no free time in the last few weeks, barely a chance to breathe, what with her job and all the housework her father still demanded of her. *Does he think I'm a machine, for heavens sake?* "I didn't have the time, not even one spare second."

"Okay, then don't complain about the arrangements." Mack gripped the steering wheel tighter. *Didn't think she'd care where we stayed as long as we were together?*

Teresa turned up her nose. "Who's complaining?"

Mack let out an exasperated sigh. "Why don't you relax and enjoy the scenery?"

"I'll do that." Teresa belligerently crossed her arms and stared out the window.

Further along the highway, they approached the barbed-wire fencing of a dairy farm and, in her scrutiny of a brown bovine cordoned off in its own coral, Teresa forgot all about their squabble. "Look at that huge cow over there! *Mamma mia!* Her udder is so big it looks like its ready to explode."

"Teresa, that's a bull, not a cow. And that's not an udder."

"Oh." Teresa covered her mouth and giggled.

The further north Mack headed, the lower the temperature dropped. After they entered Pennsylvania, dark clouds threatened bad weather. "You cold, Teresa?"

Teresa rubbed her arms. "A little."

"If I turn up the heat, I might nod off. But there's an afghan and a pillow under the seat in case you need them."

Teresa reached over the basket and patted his thigh. "*Grazie*, thoughtful of you. By the way, what's in this basket, Macco?"

"Mamma packed us a thermos of coffee and some snacks. Help yourself."

Between sips of coffee and the cookies she shared with Mack, Teresa practiced her English skills. To start off, she described the highway, "Dee road-ah . . . it-ah eez long-oh and-ah black-oh." Later, in a bilingual muddle, she commented on the elevation of the Pocono Mountains in the distance, "Deez hill-lay . . . dey **grande** like-ah dee **montagne** in **Italia**."

At one point during Teresa's concerted effort to sharpen her English, Mack pressed his lips together and suppressed a chuckle. *Don't want to offend her.*

As the sun began to set four hours into their trip, Mack realized Teresa hadn't uttered a word in some time; so he glanced in her direction and found her leaning on the locked door, the pillow tucked under her head and the afghan wrapped tight around her legs. Her mouth hung open and drool dripped down the side of her jaw. *She must've been exhausted.* Mack yawned and stretched his spine. *Wish I could take a nap too.*

Noticing the almost empty gas gage, Mack stopped at the very next service station available; and, while the tank filled up and Teresa used the bathroom facilities, he went over his route with the attendant. "Yep, dat's the right way, but why ya goin' so far north dis time a year?"

"Isn't it obvious?" Mack pointed to Tony's scrawl on the rear windshield. "We're on our honeymoon."

"Ya might wanna forget about goin' ta da Falls," the attendant advised as Teresa slipped back into the car and again snuggled against the pillow. "Dey's callin' for heavy snow up dere."

Mack sighed wistfully, picturing a bearskin mat in front of a cozy fireplace. "All the more romantic."

The man pursed his lips and shook his head. "Newlyweds."

As the attendant retreated to the warmth of the garage, Mack shrugged. *No big deal, no more than an hour's drive left.* His mind playing tricks on him, he looked through the cars window and saw Teresa lying naked on a furry rug, her arms extended toward him. The intoxicating vision caused blood to rush to his groin, the crotch of his pants getting tighter by the second. *I can hardly wait.* When another car pulled up to the next pump, he turned his back to it, his apparition fading and his slacks loosening their grip.

Mack reentered the car and gobbled the last of the cookies before he downed the remainder of the lukewarm coffee. Teresa stirred when Mack turned the key in the ignition, but slid back into blissful oblivion as he maneuvered the LaSalle onto the highway.

A few miles down the road, snowflakes flurried from the sky and began to accumulate on the windshield, persuading Mack to switch on the wipers. The further north he drove, the narrower the roads and the icier the snow. Visibility worsened after the sun set and navigation became so difficult that the muscles in Mack's neck knotted and his eyes bulged from the effort of staring at the snow-covered pavement. At one point, the tires encountered a patch of ice and Mack barely managed to keep the car out of a ditch.

When Teresa roused from her sleep, she witnessed the cottony-white roadway in the beam of the headlights. "Oh, Macco, the snow is absolutely beautiful. *È meraviglioso!*" She stretched her arms wide and yawned. "Tomorrow, you can build me a snowman, no?" Adjusting the blanket, she cuddled the pillow and dozed off once more.

She wouldn't feel that ecstatic if she had to drive under these awful conditions. Mack snarled and squeezed the steering wheel so tight that his knuckles turned white from lack of circulation. *I'll build her a snowman all right.*

At 8:30 p.m., after navigating the treacherous roads for at least another two and a half hours, Mack squinted at a neon sign that flickered in the distance: **HONEYMOON HAVEN**. To Mack's chagrin, the closer he drove toward the so-called *resort*, the more obvious it became that the place was no *haven* since the first thing to catch his eye upon entry into its driveway was a caravan of corroded snow removal equipment. Besides the fact that the tourist trap's parking lot resembled a junkyard, the recent snowfall emphasized one of its obvious structural defects, namely the sagging roof of its main building. Likewise, the shabby cabins that surrounded this focal point in a semicircle failed to make a positive impression. One of the cottages seemed to have mislaid its front door while another had lost its chimney.

Mack pounded the dashboard. *Don't care if it's a dump. I refuse to look for somewhere else to stay, not is this storm.* He eyeballed Teresa and cringed with apprehension. *How'll she react to this hellhole?* Mack swallowed the lump in his throat and tapped Teresa's shoulder. "*Svegliati, amore mio.* Wake up, darling."

Teresa lifted a stiff neck from the pillow and looked out the window at the dismal surroundings. "*Dove siamo?* Tell me, where in God's name are we? How much longer before we get to the resort? I need to unwind in a hot bath."

"We *are* here." Mack gestured toward the sign. "This is it."

"*Stai scherzando?* Please tell me you're joking." Teresa sat up straighter. "Stop the nonsense and tell me how much longer until we get there."

"I'm not joking and we're not going anywhere else tonight. Come on! We need to check in." Mack got out of the car and trudged through the snow to the passenger side and opened the door. "This way, the office is over here."

"***No, non vado là dentro!*** I refuse to enter that shabby shack." She crossed her arms in front of her. "It doesn't look fit for rats! Let's find somewhere else to stay."

His annoyance rekindled, Mack stomped down his booted foot. "No, I'm not driving anymore tonight! It's not safe. Unless you want to freeze out here alone in the dark, you'd better follow me." Mack lifted his collar and, with his head bent against the blustery storm, took a few steps toward the office.

The wind howled and the car door almost slammed shut on Teresa's foot. "***Aspetta!*** Wait for me." Shoving with all her might, she opened the door wide enough to exit the vehicle. "I'm coming!" Mack stopped in his tracks and, without turning around, offered her his arm.

Teresa exited the LaSalle and sank into a drift. "***Mamma mia!*** I didn't realize how much it snowed. Sorry I gave you such a hard time." She caught up to Mack and grabbed his arm. "You're smart not to drive anymore tonight."

Mack guided her to the office door which posted a sun-bleached sign apologizing for the condition of the facility during renovations, along with a notice of its hours of operation: *9:00 a.m. to 8:00 p.m.* Mack nonetheless turned the knob. A gust of wind sprung the door wide open, banging it against the inside wall. Surprised that no one responded to the noise, Mack ushered Teresa into the building and secured the door behind them.

Inside, a dim lamp illuminated a rustic reception area that one accustomed to primitive conditions might consider charming. Along with the handiwork of a skilled taxidermist which included the heads of both a growling mountain lion and a rather tame-looking moose, the room contained a group of six pine tables with mismatched chairs arranged in front of a stone hearth, its fading embers still exuding some warmth. On the far wall, a registry counter supported a bell and a sign discouraging its use, "Ring me if you dare." Behind the counter, muslin panels draped from ceiling to floor.

"Maybe this place is not so bad," Mack professed with restrained optimism. "I'll ring for the manager." While Teresa warmed her hands by the fireplace, Mack approached the counter and tapped the bell gently. But, since no one responded in a reasonable amount of time, he smacked it harder two more times.

Eventually, a disheveled and yawning male dressed in a plaid flannel robe emerged from behind the drapes. "Didn't ya read the sign? The office closes at eight."

"We got delayed by the storm," Mack explained. "I made reservations. The name's Matteo."

"Well, in that case, lemme see here." The manager squinted down at the registry, blank except for one name. "Matteo you say? Matteo? Matteo? Why, here ya are. We cleaned cabin No. 6 for ya. That's the second cabin from the office on the left. Please sign here." He pointed to a spot on the registry. "Payment's due in advance; $35 for the week."

Against his better judgment, Mack signed the registry. Then, pulling out his wallet, he reluctantly handed the manager five ones and six five dollar bills. In exchange, the fellow furnished Mack with a key and a smile. "Nearest restaurant's eight miles down the road. If ya like, ya can eat here." He pointed to the tables by the fireplace. "Meals're served at 8 a.m., noon and 6 p.m." He yawned once more. "See ya around. Good night." The man retreated behind the curtain.

Mack spun around and, with a pathetic look on his face, held the key up to Teresa. "We're in cabin No. 6." He motioned toward the exit.

As Mack reached for the door knob, the manager poked his head out between the drapery panels. "By the way, firewood's behind the cabin, matches'er on the hearth. Get a blaze goin' as soon as ya can. The furnace can't keep up with the temperatures this time of year. Good to see young folk willin' to rough it. Well, have fun. Oh yeah, keep the water drippin' in the sink and the tub, or the pipes'll freeze up on ya." His guests forewarned, the man again disappeared behind the curtain and left the couple to their own devices.

* * *

After Mack single-handedly carted their four suitcases into the 10' x 10' cabin, Teresa unpacked them by the light of a dim lamp, shoving most of their clothes into the drawers of a dresser. Once she caught sight of her trembling reflection in its mirror, she retreated from it and rammed into the four-poster bed. *Ahi! That hurt.* Glad that Mack was too busy checking out the bathroom to witness her clumsiness, she rubbed her shin. *I'm a nervous wreck. Will I know what to do when the time comes to . . .*

Mack returned to her side. "Teresa, you're shivering. I'll go get some firewood." He again scrambled into the blizzard and returned with an armload of logs and twigs. After he dumped the wood onto the hearth, he ignited the kindling and arranged a few logs around it so that, in no time at all, the cabin, decorated in shades of muted rust and gold, began to warm up.

Mack slipped out of his boots and tossed his coat onto a cowhide chair then flopped down beside Teresa, his wife cowering at the edge of the mattress next to a bag of toiletries and her lacy lingerie. Stretching his arms high and wide, he let out a deep yawn as he exchanged glances with a grizzly, its head hanging from a plaque above the fireplace. As he lowered his arms, Mack draped one nonchalantly across Teresa's shoulder. "It's kind of romantic in here now. Isn't it, **amore mio**?"

Teresa twisted her hands together. "If you say so." *Maybe I can stall him until tomorrow.* "You're tired, Macco. No?"

"A little." Mack snuggled closer to Teresa. *I may be exhausted but I've waited too long for . . . .*

Teresa jumped up from the bed and snatched up the bag of toiletries along with the lingerie. "Feel free to go to sleep while I freshen up in the bathroom."

Mack pulled in his chin and shook his head in the negative. *Yeah right, sleep is my top priority.* "No, I'll just relax here till you're ready."

"I need a bath." Teresa's shaky hand rattled the bathroom's doorknob. "It'll take me awhile."

Mack patted the bed. "I'll wait right here, **cara mia**." *I hope she's not having second thoughts.*

Teresa ran a hand down her braid. "**Va bene**, but I have to wash my hair too. Don't wait for me to go to . . ."

"I'm not going anywhere, darling." Mack eyes twinkled under flagging lids. Once Teresa's knees began to knock, he attempted to soothe away her jitters, "Don't be nervous, sweetheart."

"I'm not nervous." Teresa clamped her knees together and blushed. "I have to go to the toilet." *I sound like a three-year-old.*

"Go ahead," Mack encouraged. "Take whatever time you need. I'll change out here."

Teresa's eyes darted around the room for another tactic to further delay the inevitable until she caught sight of the grizzly. "What if there's a wild animal in there?"

"Remember, I already checked it out. No animals." He held up his hand, palms forward. "Honest."

"**Va bene**, I'll be out soon," Teresa entered the bathroom, the fixtures old but much cleaner than she expected, and locked the door behind her.

After a long soak, she stepped out of the water shivering; and, as she toweled off, Mack knocked on the bathroom door. "How much longer will you be?"

"Are you trying to rush me?" Teresa responded in an anxious tone.

"No, no. Take your time, sweetheart."

He's such a patient man. Teresa set aside the towel and applied body lotion from head to toe then brushed her hair until it was practically dry. Afterwards, she spritzed perfume into the air and stepped into the spray, coating herself with its fragrance. Finished primping, she slipped into the ivory negligee and panties before she unlocked the door. *I guess I'm as ready as I'll ever be.*

As she turned the knob and cracked open the door, a raspy snarl accosted her ears, causing her to stop short of opening the door any wider. When a more feral growl resonated from the other room, she slammed the door shut and leaned against it. **Mamma mia***! It can't really be a bear, can it?* Teresa cringed at a third and more prolonged gnarl that penetrated the door. *It sounds ferocious, but I can't stay in here forever. And what if Macco's hurt?*

Teresa scanned the bathroom for a potential weapon and, spotting a plunger in the corner under the sink, confiscated it. Wielding it like a sword, she kicked open the door. "Leave my husband alone!"

However, when she entered the room, she encountered no bear, nor any other beast for that matter, only the tame creature sprawled flat on his back, a man passed out from sheer exhaustion, her husband. Plunger still raised, she approached the bed and leaned over his body, taking advantage of the opportunity to scrutinize the physical attributes of the man she married.

Undressed down to his jockey shorts and his wristwatch, his legs dangling over the side of the bed and his arms splayed out, Mack lay there vulnerable to her inspection. Averting her eyes from the mound of his crotch, she noticed his lean body was covered by a layer of fine hair, thicker where it encircled his nipples and caressed his armpits. *So I married one bear of a man.* Suddenly, Mack's lips parted, allowing another atrocious snort to emerge between them.

Startled, her arms came crashing down, the plunger barely missing Mack's head. Catching sight of her assault pose in the dresser's mirror, she imagined the newspaper headlines, *Virgin warrior assaults bear in the Pocono Mountains!* Bursting out in hysterical giggles, she tossed the plunger aside and flopped down on the bed, her legs and arms flailing as unrestrained as her laughter.

Once Teresa recovered from her convulsive laughter, she frowned at the limp posture of her still snoring husband and clicked her tongue in disapproval. *Macco's spine will ache if he sleeps in that position much longer. I'll straighten him out.* With a considerable amount of struggle, she lifted his legs up and over the bed so that his torso was left twisted at an awkward angle. **Ah beh***, I tried my best.*

Reaching over Mack's body to retrieve the opposite end of the blanket, Teresa caught sight of the dial on his wristwatch. "**Mamma mia***, midnight already!*" *No wonder the poor boy fell asleep.* As Teresa draped the cover over him, Mack expelled his loudest snort yet, directly into her face.

"*Uffa!*" Hands cupped over her ears, she headed into the bathroom and, when she exited with a wad of toilet paper stuck in each ear, she approached the bed to test the tissue's effectiveness. "*Dio santo!* I can still hear him."

Hands on her hips, Teresa ejected a forced breath and sulked. "*Ahimè, such an exciting honeymoon.*" Wide awake with nothing but time on her hands, she added another log to the fire then dragged the cowhide chair closer to its warmth and sank into the chair's cushion. For lack of anything better to do, she focused on the grizzly. "Signore Bear, how would you like to hear a story?" Since the grizzly didn't object, Teresa began with a prelude, "Actually, it's more like a comedy of errors." She flipped a hand toward Mack. "At the end of my tale, you'll understand how I wound up snowbound in a desolate cabin with this prince who serenades me as he sleeps."

Teresa reached behind her for Mack's coat and, draping it over her shoulders, once again addressed the bear. "How, you might ask, is it possible for a stupid immigrant like me *to trap*, excuse the expression, an educated prince?" She paused to contemplate the answer. "Maybe if I backtrack to the very beginning, you'll understand the obstacles I faced.

"Well, let me see. It all started . . ." With a painstaking thoroughness, Teresa revisited the events of the last six months but, in the middle of a lethargic rendition of their wedding vows, nodded off at 3:00 a.m. with the words "I do" drifting from her lips.

Chapter Fifty

Four and a half hours later, a bit of sunshine filtered through ominous clouds and, reflecting off the snow, bounced into the cabin's lone window. Awakened by the glare, Mack rolled over, finding himself precariously close to the edge of the bed. *Is it morning already?* Realizing where he was, he bolted upright and, stretching his stiff body, scanned the cabin for Teresa. She was curled up on the cowhide chair by the cold fireplace, his coat on the floor next to it. *I don't believe it! Our wedding night and we didn't even sleep together.* The last thing he recalled from the previous evening was knocking on the bathroom door.

Some man I am! The way he perceived the situation, instead of making love to his bride, he had passed out cold and hogged the bed, forcing the poor girl to sleep on the chair. His expression fraught with humiliation, Mack pushed the blanket aside.

Approaching Teresa, he rubbed his arms, his warm breath escaping in a cloud of mist. Since no once had stoked the fire since Teresa had fallen asleep, it had burned out. *It's downright frigid in here.* On cue, his wife shivered, her hardened nipples visible through the lace of her nightie. The sight of them stirred Mack into a state of heightened arousal, the bulge of his eyes not nearly as pronounced as the one in his jockey shorts.

With a dream inspired sigh, Teresa combed the fingers of one hand through her hair, exposing the toilet paper she'd stuck in her ears. It caught Mack's attention. *Earplugs?* As a flush crept up his neck, his underwear deflated. *Was I snoring?* He backed away from her. *How embarrassing!*

When Teresa's teeth began to rattle, Mack decided to move her to the bed where he could make her comfortably warmer. With little effort, he lifted his comatose bride and carried her to the mattress. But, before he set her down, Teresa's jaw went slack and several gravelly breaths escaped her open mouth. *Listen to her. I'm not the only one who saws logs.* Finding humor in their shared imperfection, Mack's embarrassment abated. *I may just have to stuff my own ears.*

After he secured Teresa under the blanket and ignited a fresh fire, Mack grabbed hold of his shaving kit and retreated into the chilly bathroom. After a quick shave and hot shower, he returned buck naked to the bed, his bride still sleeping exactly as he'd left her, the blanket tucked under her chin. *I hoped she'd be awake by now.* With disappointment etched in his face, he redirected his attention to his growling stomach. Mack picked up his wristwatch. *Seven-fifty? That's more than fifteen hours since we've eaten anything.* Remembering that the motel manager's said food was available as early as eight a.m., he threw on some clothes and shoved his feet into his boots. *I'll get us some breakfast.*

Mack tossed a few more logs onto the fire, bundled up and, despite the urgency of his mission, stopped outside the cabin's window to construct a simple snowman, unadorned except for the dismal face he designed out of twigs. The snowman's sad expression reflected Mack's disappointment in his so far unfulfilled honeymoon expectations. Admiring his creation, he rubbed his frozen hands together, his tongue salivating for food, his body needing some warmth. *Hot coffee . . . mmm.*

* * *

Bearing a tray of tasty nourishment and strong caffeine, Mack returned to the cabin and approached the bed. "***Amore mio***, wake up . . . breakfast time!"

Inhaling the aroma of coffee and maple syrup, Teresa sprung up and pulled the tissue out of her ears. "Breakfast did you say, my love?" Her hunger outweighing her curiosity over how she ended up in the bed, Teresa reached for the tray. "Let's eat. I'm starved."

"Whoa! Hold your horses." Mack pulled the tray away. "There's something I want you to see first."

Teresa frowned. "Please, I'm hungry."

"It'll only take a second, dear." Mack put down the tray and dragged Teresa to the window. "I made something for you." He rubbed the condensation from a pane. "Look."

"How sweet! You built me a snowman." Teresa squinted for a better view of its face. "Tell me. Why's he so gloomy-looking?"

"Funny you should ask," Mack replied, a sparkle of amusement in his eyes. "Just before he died of boredom, the poor stiff confided he didn't get a chance to make love to his bride."

Teresa giggled. "Oh really, and why's that may I ask?"

"Well, you see," he chuckled. "On the night of their wedding, she made him wait out there, cold and alone," Mack feigned a shiver, "while she scrubbed herself raw in a steamy bath." With exaggerated feminine mannerisms, he impersonated a woman scouring herself. "By the time she was ready to warm up to him, he'd passed out and froze solid."

Teresa laughed. "I'll tell you what, if you let me eat first, I promise to snuggle in bed with you for the rest of the day."

"Sounds good to me. Let's dig in, Teresa."

They settled in bed on opposite sides of the tray and, with an enthusiasm sparked by hollow bellies, feasted on pancakes, eggs, home fries and coffee. His stomach satiated, Mack disposed of the tray and tossed two more logs onto the fire before he held his arms out to Teresa, ready to appease another one of his appetites.

Teresa stood up, "I have to go to the bathroom."

Mack blocked her path. "Promise me you won't take forever."

Teresa held up her right hand and covered her heart with her left. "***Prometto***."

"In that case, be my guest." Mack let her pass.

The instant Teresa closed the door behind her, Mack stripped off his clothes, slid between the sheets and propped his head against a pillow, his hands clasped behind his neck. When Teresa reentered the room, a section of the sheet above Mack's hips rose higher, forming a lust-inspired teepee. Teresa slowly averted her eyes, but her breath and heartbeat quickened.

Mack promptly extended his arms and, in husky Italian, beckoned Teresa closer, "**Vene qui, bella.**" He lifted the edge of the blanket and patted the mattress in invitation. "I can't wait another moment to hold you in my arms."

Teresa slipped under the blanket next to Mack. As he wrapped around her, his bare chest warm against her, a pleasant sensation settled in the pit of Teresa's stomach.

Mack pushed her hair aside, kissed her neck and, with a tremble in his voice, whispered, "I love you, Teresa."

Tingles ran up and down Teresa's spine. "Oh, Macco, I love you too." She pressed her lips against his; and, to her delight, Mack parted them to experience the taste and texture of her tongue.

Following a slew of kisses, Mack came up for air. "Teresa, you take my breath away." Throbbing with anticipation, but positive that a virgin should be treated with kid gloves, he repressed his urge to cut to the chase. *I'll take it nice and easy.* Convinced that slow was the way to go, he wandered from her mouth and placed tender kisses on her cheeks, her eyelids and nuzzled her ear before he sighed into it, "Can I touch your beautiful body?"

Quivering in his arms, Teresa nodded. "I'm yours, Macco." However, after he pressed himself hard against her thigh, Teresa tensed up. *What am I supposed to do with it?*

Although his hormones were still raging and the pressure to please his wife weighed heavy on his mind, Mack remained outwardly composed. "Please relax, **cara mia**." Closing her eyes, Teresa tried to comply with his request.

His experience limited, Mack nonetheless proceeded to incite Teresa's nerve endings with the finesse of a practiced lover. He ran his hand down the inside of one of her arms followed by his lips in a procession of moist pecks. When he shifted his concentration from her one arm to her other, Mack inadvertently grazed one of her taunt nipples. Never having tolerated intimacy from any of her Italian boyfriends, Teresa gasped at the arousal the incidental brush generated.

Using the tips of his fingers, Mack caressed Teresa along the sides of her abdomen, down the outside of her legs and then up the insides until he came to the hem of her nightgown. He slid it up a bit and glanced at her face for a reaction. Her blissful expression prompted Mack to raise the gown further yet, above her waist. Inhaling sharply, he gawked at the lace panties that covered his ultimate destination, but didn't stop there. Instead, he hoisted the gown further up her body. Eyes still closed, Teresa raised her arms above her head providing all the consent Mack needed to remove it completely. While Mack's virility tested his willpower, Teresa sizzled, her small breasts aching for attention.

"Teresa, your body's exquisite. Do you mind if I touch more of it?"

Teresa bit her lip and nodded, acknowledging that she didn't mind in the least.

Leaning over Teresa's torso, Mack fondled her breasts and kissed one nipple and then the other, running his tongue over them until Teresa's breath escaped in short gasps and Mack's excitement grew painfully taut. Consumed by the titillation, Teresa clamped his face tight against her chest, cutting off Mack's air supply.

Mack choked out a protest, "Teresa, please, I can't breathe."

"Sorry, Macco." Once she released her grip on his head, Mack resumed his efforts to gratify her. While Teresa melted again under the spell of his lips, Mack nonchalantly glided his one hand down past her stomach and rested it above her triangle. Lost in the moment of elevated arousal, Teresa tilted her pelvis.

Taking it as a sign she was ready for more, Mack slipped his hand down further. His assumption correct, Teresa lifted up her hips even higher and allowed Mack to remove the last obstacle between them, her panties.

Naked and aroused beyond her wildest dreams, Teresa reached out to Mack in return with kisses and caresses. When her fingers landed upon the evidence of his vitality, she pulled her hand away; but Mack brazenly guided it back. With a hesitance that heightened the drama, she surrendered to her sense of fair play. *Hmm, hard yet warm and smooth.* On second thought, she shuddered at its girth. *How will it fit into me?*

Savoring his own euphoria, Mack moved in closer and stoked the embers of her desire, gently kneading, provoking a steamy hot spring of passion. Qualms forgotten, Teresa writhed beside him, his touch inciting a persistent throb, the pressure building in her untapped cavern until, to her astonishment, she unexpectedly climaxed in a geyser of exhilaration. "Oh, Macco, I never imagined!" She reeled him in for a fervent kiss.

With his wife gasping for breath, and he anxious for his own fulfillment, Mack proceeded with the consideration a virgin deserved, but Teresa stiffened at the intimate approach. "Will it hurt?"

Mack placed a hand under her chin and raised it up. "I'll be gentle."

When he searched her eyes for permission, Teresa nodded. "I trust you."

With tenderness motivated by affection, Mack crossed her fertile threshold ever so slowly, softly whispering, "Teresa, I'll love you forever." Although she cried out when the sheath of her innocence snapped, Teresa didn't resist his advance. Encouraged, Mack plunged deeper into the narrow cavern; but, when Teresa whimpered again, he hesitated. "Teresa, I love you."

"I know." Though tears filled her eyes, Teresa reassured him, "Please, go ahead, *amore mio*. I'll be fine."

Mack took Teresa at her word and, before she had a chance to reconsider, he began to thrust with wild abandon until, to her surprise, the raw friction rekindled the embers of her libido. His rhythm contagious, she danced with him in a grinding salsa of passion, panting to the staccato rhythm of their heartbeats.

With a loud moan and a jolt of his torso, Mack reached the point of no return while Teresa, climaxing a second time, trembled euphorically beneath him. Too weak to hold himself up any longer, he collapsed on top of her.

Teresa embraced him tighter. "*Ti amo*, Macco. I love you with all my heart. You're my prince . . . my lover . . . my husband."

Totally exhausted, both physically and emotionally, they rolled to the side. Her head on his shoulder, Teresa drifted peacefully to sleep in Mack's arms.

Chapter Fifty-One

As the newlyweds enjoyed a mid-week dinner at the Matteo residence a few weeks later, Signora Matteo's animated Italian captured their attention. "*Vi dico*, I no like *stupida* Signora Castagna. Woman is like bad itch and she stubborn like mule. *C'e da ridere*." Signora Matteo shook her finger in the air. "Today, she fight with Signore Frutta . . . *fino che* . . . till poor man lower price to almost nothing." Signora Matteo choked on a chuckle. "Is own fault, ha-ha, she walk home with, ha-ha, bad bananas, rotten like her." She picked up her fork and dove into her pasta with renewed gusto.

Teresa grinned and whispered into Mack's ear, "I didn't think your mother had a sense of humor." Mack shrugged noncommittally.

On the opposite side of the table, Patricia turned to Juliet. "I'm glad Mamma's in such better spirits these days."

"Yes, ever since they transferred Father Romano to another parish," Juliet giggled behind her hand.

Patricia sat up straighter. "What's so funny, Juliet?"

"Didn't you hear the rumor?"

"What rumor?" Patricia demanded.

"They transferred him to hush up his affair with the, tee-hee," Juliet tittered, "with the rectory housekeeper."

"You shouldn't spread nasty rumors, Juliet."

"Ah come on, Patricia, can't you picture dumpy Father Romano trying to bed skinny Mrs. Albero?"

Patricia gasped. "That's sacrilegious!"

Juliet stifled her giggles. "Ever since Mamma stopped obsessing over 'evil **Padre** Romano,' she's been in much better spirits, spending more time at church and working with the altar society again. Her newest passion is bingo. And, thank God, she's finally taken an interest in our wedding plans." Juliet glanced at Tony busy conversing with Jake. "Yesterday, she agreed to visit the florist and . . ."

"That's all well and good, Juliet," Patricia curtly interjected, "but you ought to see how Mamma plays with the baby. She stops by everyday on her way home from church." Despite Juliet's frown of annoyance at being so rudely cut off, Patricia prattled on. "No one calms Iaga's colic better than Mamma. You can't imagine the funny faces and Italian nonsense rhymes she recites to the baby. It's wonderful the way Iaga quiets right down whenever Mamma . . . ."

Frank interrupted Patricia's monologue with a tap on the table. "Listen, everybody. Geneva and I plan to move in two days. We wanna invite you all to an open house Sunday after next."

Signora Matteo pouted, "You leave so soon, Franco?"

"Yes, Mamma." Frank gestured toward Jake and Tony. "Thanks to these two men and a coat of fresh paint, we're all set to go."

"If you'd like, I can give you a sneak peak, Mamma," Geneva pacified. "How about lunch next Saturday?"

Anxious to check out where her son would be living and make suggestions on how to arrange the old furniture Geneva had confiscated from the basement, Signora Matteo nodded. "**Sì**, I like see house."

After Geneva invited the other females at the table to join them for the preview, Frank refocused his attention on his meatballs as his mother and Patricia proceeded to give Geneva advice on homemaking.

Meanwhile, Juliet addressed Mack, "Where've you been hiding? Tony and I want to hear all about Niagara Falls."

"I've been running around like a chicken without a head. In between doing income tax returns for all the neighbors, I've had to drive Teresa to just about every furniture store in the area," Mack lamented. "She's determined to find a sturdy bed at a rock-bottom price."

"Can you blame me?" Teresa held a hand to the side of her mouth and whispered to Juliet, "I think your mother had an ulterior motive when she gave us that rickety old bed from the basement. It squeaks worse than a hoarse mouse dangling from the teeth of a hungry cat." Teresa sighed, picturing the ship's stowaway she'd no badly wanted. She still resented the fact that her father and Signora Matteo both had refused her the privilege of pet ownership. Maybe once they had a home of their own, she'd convince Mack to get one.

Juliet laughed. "I wouldn't put it past Mamma." She redirected her attention to Mack. "Did you enjoy the Falls? Tony and I are considering going there for our honeymoon. I hear it's breathtaking."

"Well," Mack responded with a smug look on his face, "it certainly took my breath away. Incredible. Don't you agree, Teresa?"

"*Si, fantastico!*" Teresa flashed a provocative smile at Mack. "Let's go there again, Macco, sometime soon."

"A sight for sore eyes, huh?" Tony chimed in as he wrapped his arm around Juliet's shoulder. "That settles it. Honeymoon solved."

"Tell us more about it, Teresa. Anything worth seeing besides the waterfalls?" Juliet encouraged as Signora Matteo went into the kitchen to retrieve their dessert.

Teresa paused to consider, then broke out in unconstrained giggles, attracting the attention of everyone still at the table. Staring at her, they waited expectantly for her to reveal what was so funny. Teresa eventually caught her breath. "How you say in *Inglesi*? Dee ceiling, dee ceiling over dee bed-ah." She finished in Italian, "It was *stupendo*. Flat on my back, I memorized every single crack." Eyes twinkling, she smiled seductively at Mack.

As they all gaped at Teresa with open mouths, Mack's face turned crimson. "Let me explain!" He went on to tell them about how they had arrived in a blizzard and, when the snow didn't let up for days, they weren't able to get the car out from under the snow until it was time to leave. He gazed into Teresa's eyes. "We never got around to sightseeing." He squeezed her thigh. "But a fellow would be crazy for complaining. My wife managed to keep me quite entertained." Despite her previous audacity, Teresa concealed a blush behind her hands.

Returning to the dining room, Signora Matteo came to Teresa's rescue. "*Deserto!*" She held up a three-layer cake and smiled at Tony. "Giulietta, she bake for you."

"The cake's to celebrate Tony's promotion to Detective First Class," Juliet boasted.

"Oh, it's just a routine promotion," Tony protested. "Nothin' to get excited about."

Juliet waved off his modesty. "Don't be silly, Tony. You're the best homicide detective at the precinct."

"There're only two of us," Tony confessed to the others, "me and Lieutenant Smathers. He's the one with all the experience. Ask me, he's the sharpest investigator in the county."

Juliet turned up her nose. "Well, I beg to differ. Which one of you solved Iggy's murder?" Unmindful of Signora Matteo's flinch, Juliet swelled with pride.

Tony clicked his tongue. "You know it was me, sweetheart."

Juliet turned a palm up and out. "There you go. Ask anyone in this house. You're the finest detective as far as we're concerned." After Tony conceded with a grin, Juliet stood up. "Geneva, please help me bring in the coffee cups."

* * *

Once the strong aroma of coffee accosted Teresa's nostrils, her stomach flip-flopped several times, her dinner rising toward her esophagus. Hand-over-mouth, she bolted up and rushed from the room. Inquisitive eyes followed Teresa and then landed on Mack.

With both palms extended upwards, Mack lifted his shoulders. "What?" When their visual third degree didn't let up, he added. "She must be coming down with the flu."

Lips pursed, Signora Matteo glanced at Geneva then shared a shrewd expression with Patricia, two fingers flashing in her lap, one for each of her daughter-in laws. Though her mother-in-law and sister-in-law obviously suspected two pregnancies in the family, Geneva ignored their silent exchange, refusing to admit to hers.

In the meantime Juliet sliced the cake and gloated over the men's enthusiastic response to it. "There's enough cake here if anyone wants a second slice."

Frank's hand shot up. "I'll have another piece." Salivating while Juliet took her time to slice it for him, he ignored Geneva's glare.

* * *

As the women cleared the table, the men shuffled noisily into the parlor and in so doing awakened Iaga. Attempting to quiet her colicky screech, Jake picked up the infant and bounced her in rhythm to a nursery rhyme, "Jack 'n Jill . . ." However, when Iaga's yowls didn't let up, he carried her to the vestibule. As Tony and Frank settled side-by-side on the sofa, Mack headed toward the staircase. "I'd better check on Teresa."

Frank sat up straighter. "Mamma's busy in the kitchen. Quick, fill me in, Tony. Did ja find Anna?"

"Not yet," Tony acknowledged under the cover of Iaga's shrieks.

"What's the hold up?" Frank wrung his hands. "I'm getting' a lotta pressure from her brother."

"Hey, gimme a break. Since we finished paintin' *your* house, I've spent most of my free time tryin' to find her. Investigations take a lotta time, Frank."

"How long?" Frank whined. "Anna's been missin' over a month already. When you gonna have somethin' concrete?"

"Soon," Tony pacified. "I filed the Missin' Persons Report and checked all the hospitals for any unidentified patients fittin' her description."

"Yeah, over three weeks ago. It's already February fourth." Frank stomped down his foot in frustration. "Anna's brother called again last week and threatened me. He swore he'd involve the consulate and register a complaint against us if he doesn't get some answers soon. The Matteo family doesn't need anymore bad publicity."

"Well, accordin' to my own *unofficial* investigation," Tony hesitated to go on.

"What? Out with it," Frank urged.

"Okay, okay." Tony leaned forward and lowered his voice, "I searched Anna's room and found a carbon of her travel plans stickin' out from behind her dresser." He pulled out a wrinkled sheet of paper from his pants pocket, unfolded it and waved it in front of Frank's face. "Retraced her steps workin' backwards from the ship."

"So, what'd ja find out?" Frank flipped up his hand impatiently.

Tony refolded the sheet and returned it to his pocket. "First called the fleet's main office, asked them to check the ship's roster to see if she ever boarded. Turns out, she never did."

"We already knew that."

"Had to confirm it." Tony insisted. "That done, I phoned the limo service. They claimed that, even though the limo driver was waitin' for her at Penn Station, she didn't get off the scheduled train. I called the hotel in New York and the manager said she never showed up for her room neither."

Frank expressed his disbelief, "She didn't take the limo or register at the hotel?"

"Exactly."

"So how do we find out if she ever left Benton or not?" Frank asked impatiently.

"I'm gettin' to that. The next thing I did was contact the train depot. Accordin' to them, there wasn't no cancellation. It's possible she took the train to Penn Station and didn't spot the limo driver, or she got off at the wrong stop. I got no way to confirm either. Another possibility is that she never made it to the train station."

"We gettin' anywhere?" Frank complained.

Tony exhaled an exasperated breath. "Since there wasn't no taxi service listed for Anna's ride to the train station, I called every single one of the taxi companies in Benton. In case you don't know, Frank, there's five of 'em. Asked their dispatchers to confirm a pickup at this address on the date she left."

"Why didn't you contact the travel agent?"

"I did," Tony grudgingly declared, "but her answerin' service told me she was on a month-long vacation."

"All right, get to the point," Frank huffed.

Tony gritted his teeth in irritation and wielded a hand in front of Frank's face. "Let me finish!" He took a deep breath and composed himself before he continued with the chronicle of his investigation, "Finally on Monday, Tim's Taxi Service called back and verified the pickup; so I asked if they kept a record of the drop-off." He held up his index finger. "That's where it gets tricky."

Narrowing his eyes, Frank scratched his jaw. "What do you mean *tricky*?"

Tony revealed the cab's fate with a dramatic smack of his hands in front of Frank's face. "The taxi collided with a bus," he flashed his hands up and out, "and went up in flames." Tony backed up a step and hung his head. "Sorry to say, there weren't no survivors in the cab. It got burnt to a crisp."

Frank cringed. "Before or after the driver dropped off Anna?"

"It's not that simple, Frank. I contacted the dick in charge of the accident investigation, a Detective O'Malley from Precinct 9. Said his men scrutinized the evidence and there were definitely two bodies in the cab. But, since the taxi spun around so many damn times, nobody's sure if it was on its way *to* or *from* the train depot. You see, Frank," Tony explained, "there's a chance the driver picked up some other passenger after he dropped off Anna, without botherin' to call the dispatcher."

"Damn!" Frank pounded the arm of the sofa. "Now, how do we find out if Anna was the passenger who died in that cab?"

"Got that covered." Tony shifted from foot to foot. "Cause of the fire, they had no papers to I.D. the passenger. Without a lead, they shelved the investigation."

"Didn't they check the Missing Person Reports?" Frank asked incredulously.

Tony lifted his chin. "I would've if the case had been one of mine."

"Yeah, but it wasn't," Frank reminded him. "Did ja tell them you thought it might be Anna?"

Tony tightened his fists. "Yeah, Frank, I did. But the only chance for positive I.D. is through dental records."

Frank eyes lit up. "I'll get Anna's!"

"Stop second guessin' me, Frank," Tony seethed. "Already gave the coroner's office the name of Anna's dentist, and they court-ordered her records. Medical Examiner's gonna compare them to the victim's teeth."

Frank winced before he bellyached, "How much longer will that take? And when will we know if it's really her?"

"Detective O'Malley said he'll send me a copy of the report by tomorrow, day's end the latest. Whether or not it's Anna on that coroner's slab, I'll call you with the results."

"I don't wanna sound ungrateful," Frank griped, "but seems to me you coulda saved yourself a lot of time and effort if you'd started your investigation with the Benton taxi companies in the first place."

"Well, sure, hindsight's 20/20," Tony defended.

At the tail end of the conversation, Juliet walked into the room and inserted her arm into the crook of Tony's elbow, "Isn't my fiancé something, Frank?"

"Yeah, great," Frank grunted, and, on second thought, added reluctantly, "Thanks, Tony." He turned to Juliet, "Now, if Tony actually found Anna, it'll be my job to tell her brother and Mamma? I'm afraid Mamma will get upset all over again."

Juliet buried her face in Tony's chest. "Poor Iggy and Anna, both so young. Such a dangerous world."

As Jake reentered with Iaga now whimpering in his arms, Tony enclosed Juliet in a bear hug. "Don't worry, angel. I'm here to protect you."

Frank approached Jake and grumbled behind his hand. "Humph, hope Tony protects better than he investigates."

Chapter Fifty-Two

At the end of a religious service a week later, the new pastor of St. Christopher's bowed his head. "Let's take a moment once more and remember Iago Matteo and all the faithfully departed."

In exchange for a small donation to the Roman Catholic Church, anyone wishing to dedicate a service to a particular soul was able to request a "mass card." Traditionally, mass cards were often presented to a grieving individual or family, usually at a funeral or wake, as an expression of sympathy. A specific date for the service was posted on the card so that the family might attend the mass if they so desired. The Matteos had received numerous mass cards on the day of Iggy's burial, each with a different date.

Since that day's mass was the first in the series of religious services in memory of Iggy's passing, Signora Matteo had insisted the whole family be present. At Juliet's request, Tony Canelli was among the worshippers.

Stooped over the cushioned kneeler, Signora Matteo whimpered, "***Dio, benedici Iago e Romeo.*** Please bless my two dead son."

Patricia wrapped an arm around her mother's shoulder and consoled her throughout the priest's final blessing, "***In nomine Patris, et Filii, et Spiritus Sancti. Amen.*** Go in peace with the knowledge and comfort that Iago has been reunited with our Lord and Savior."

Remembering his awful nightmare about Iggy's introduction to hell, Mack bowed his head and said the Act of Contrition that began *Oh my God, I am heartily sorry...* He hoped both God and Iggy would forgive him for generating such a pessimistic dream. Seeing his distress, Teresa patted his shoulder.

Meanwhile feeling no less guilty, Frank salivated in anticipation of a hearty breakfast. In keeping with Catholic convention which forbade food or drink after midnight if one planned to receive communion the next morning, he had skipped his usual omelet. His stomach grumbled in harmony with the closing hymn.

After the priest made his way to the sacristy, most of the family exited the church, leaving Patricia to escort Signora Matteo out. "Let's go, Mamma."

Contemplating aloud whether or not Iggy was brazen enough to harass God's angels, Signora Matteo refused to budge. "***Che pensi?***"

"I don't think it's allowed in heaven, Mamma."

Signora Matteo wrung her hands, thinking of Iggy's horrible behavior. "***Non ho mai capito.*** No, I no know why Iago was no so nice."

Patricia patted her arm. "Why worry about it now?"

Signora Matteo wiped a tear from her cheek. "***Prego per lui***. I pray he be nice *in cielo* . . . to stay in heaven he must be good."

"I'm sure he will." Patricia tugged her mother's arm. "Come on. I need to get home. If Iaga wakes up hungry, she'll drive Jake crazy until I get there to nurse her."

* * *

Outside, at the top of the church steps, Tony approached Frank. "How weird . . . like a funeral without a casket."

"It wasn't my idea we all come. Mamma threatened me if I didn't. Ah-ah," Frank turned his head to the side and sneezed away from Tony, "ah-choo."

Tony recoiled. "God bless you. Comin' down with a cold?"

"Maybe." Frank pulled out a handkerchief.

Although, Juliet had told him that most of the Matteos had come to terms with Anna's plight, Tony was curious about Frank's personal take on the situation. "So tell me, Frank. How did your mom react to findin' out about Anna?"

"Oh brother! At first Mamma was relieved that her dream didn't come true. But then . . ."

"What?" Tony encouraged.

"She ranted and raved about Iggy's bad choices, Anna being the worst."

"Can't say that I blame her." As far as Tony was concerned, any woman had a right to be upset with such a daughter-in-law, one who flirted with the first man that gave her the least bit of attention, especially so soon after her son's death.

Frank clenched his fists. "Anna wasn't the best wife, but didn't deserve to end up alone in a big city." He rehashed some of the particulars of Anna's fate with Tony.

* * *

In route to the Big Apple, Anna had met a well-dressed man in the dining compartment of the train and, feeling alone and bored, she flirted with him. Fingering her bodice, she sighed, "***Mio marito***, Iago . . . he died and left me all alone." Noticing the fine clothes and jewelry she wore, the con artist who spoke fluent Italian decided the busty widow was good prey. So, pretending he was a rich tycoon who fell in love with her at first sight, he promised her the good life. Believing he was sincere, Anna fell for his line. But, without her notice, he grabbed hold of her purse and, pretending to go to the men's room, jumped off at the very next scheduled stop, Newark, New Jersey.

Waiting impatiently for his return from the bathroom, she fantasized a life of passionate luxury with the handsome man. However, when he didn't come back, she realized she'd been duped, and not knowing any English, panicked. The man had not only stolen her handbag, but all the documents it contained: her passport, her itinerary, and her tickets for the cruise back to Italy. She cursed the day she came to America. "**Mannaggia all'America**!"

Distraught over what to do, she went to the ladies room and sat on the toilet, replaying the scenario with the scam artist over and over again in her head, trying to lay the blame on anyone other than herself. First, she decided it was Iggy's fault for withholding the love and attention she'd deserved. Then she switched tactics and decided the Matteos were culpable for not insisting that they escort her to the boat. Eventually, she held her parents liable because they hadn't taught her to steer clear of handsome strangers, Iggy included. Eventually, she decided it didn't matter who was responsible, she was still broke and alone and too embarrassed to return to Benton.

While lost in this monologue of blame, she missed her stop at Penn Station. Not knowing what to do, Anna paced back and forth from one train car to the next until the train's final stop in Boston, Massachusetts. *What do I do now?* Since she had no choice but to get off the train, she returned to the private compartment to retrieve her luggage. It wasn't there. A porter had taken it to the "Lost and Found" when a new passenger had boarded to take her seat. She approached the train conductor with her problem, but he didn't understand Italian or her pantomime effort. Unable to find someone to translate, Anna gave up and got off the train without her luggage. *All Americans are stupid!*

Unencumbered by any suitcase and with no identification papers, she wandered the city and eventually found herself in the north end of town, in Boston's Little Italy. Realizing she was in dire straights, she decided she needed some wine to help her calm down. She entered the first tavern she came upon and drank several glasses, not knowing how she would pay for them.

As luck would have it, the tavern's owner was also a Neapolitan immigrant who sat down next to her and engaged her in conversation about their hometown. Enjoying the company of this tipsy and flirtatious **paesana**, the old man waived the cost of the wine and offered the voluptuous Italian a job and a place to stay. Desperate but too proud to call the Matteos or her brother collect, Anna agreed to work as his barmaid, serving mainly an older Italian clientele. "So kind of you, Signore." She intended to keep the position, and live in the studio apartment above the bar, only until she could come up with a plan to return home to Naples or find a new man to marry her. *I can only take working so long.*

One day towards the middle of the second month, a familiar-looking gentleman entered the tavern. *I remember him.* He was an old friend of the Matteo family, one she'd met casually through Iggy. The man just happened to be visiting his relatives in Boston. Though she tried to avoid him, he spotted her and recognized her, but, before he had a chance to approach her, she scurried to the Ladies Room. By the time she came out, he was gone. ***Grazie a Dio!*** *Thank God he didn't see me.*

Contrary to Anna's belief, the man not only noticed her, but mentioned it to Frank Matteo the very next time he ran into him, the day after he returned to Benton. "Franco, I saw your sister-in-law Anna in Boston, working at a bar down the street from my cousin's house. I thought you told me she was going back to Italy."

Shocked at the revelation, Frank immediately asked for the name of the bar. With Tony Canelli's help, he found the address and phone number of the tavern. After calling the owner to confirm Anna's employment, he asked to speak to her. Tired of working for a living, Anna tearfully confessed all that had happened to her and begged Frank to help her return to Italy. "***Voglio andare a casa.*** I want to go home to Naples. I hate America!"

With Frank promising to navigate, Mack agreed to drive the LaSalle to Boston to pick up Anna, intending to bring her back to Benton until new arrangements could be made for her repatriation to Italy. On the way back, Anna was at first grateful and solicitous to the two men. Flirting and chatty, she pretended it was a pleasant outing, that is, until Frank start questioning her about the details of how she lost the money.

"You're just like Iago. You think you can badger me. I didn't put up with it from him and I won't from you!" Folding her arms tight under her bosom, she remained close-mouth for the rest of the way to Benton.

When Frank contacted Anna's brother with the news, he expected him to be ecstatic. Instead, Angelo was annoyed as hell that his sister had lost all of her money and refused to send her the funds she needed to get home. Therefore, the Matteos were again stuck footing the bill. But, since they'd already given her more money than Frank thought she deserved, he refused to pay the high fare of an ocean liner and looked for another option. At a suggestion from Teresa, who knew that passengers could receive reduced fares in exchange for work, he arranged a job for Anna aboard the same freighter that had transported Teresa and her brother to America.

Anna baulked at the idea, "**Dio Cristo!** You want me to do what?" But, like it or not, Anna was forced to work her way across the Atlantic waiting tables in the ship's cafeteria and scrubbing toilets in the communal bathrooms.

Having known no other home, the tabby that was confiscated from Teresa's suitcase by the custom officials had returned to the freighter and again resumed his position as ship mascot. Anytime this cat tried to get the big-breasted lady to feed him some leftover table scraps, Anna kicked the tabby away with her heel. "**Leviti dai da sotto** . . . get out from under my aching feet!"

Anna didn't want to return to Italy penniless. Therefore, she devised a plan that worked extremely well, considering it didn't involve much effort on her part. During her free time away from the galley and the bathrooms, she'd walk outside the portals of the Italian sailor's quarters singing seductively, "♫Money for a peak . . . double for a touch♫." Whenever a sex-starved sailor came out to see who the siren was, she would loosen her bra and lean forward, "To see more is worth at least two dimes, no? But to touch is a quarter each." During the two-week voyage, she earned enough quarters to cover some groceries and the first month's rent for a waterfront apartment in Naples.

* * *

Frank shook his head at the irony of his sister-in-law's fate. The part of it that bother him the most was that some train-hopping shyster had absconded with all her cash, the very money Frank borrowed at a high interest rate to buy back Iggy's share of the bakery. The first time Anna had told Frank she was returning to Italy with the settlement money, he had offered to transfer it to a bank in Naples via Western Union. But Anna had refused; she insisted on taking the cash in hand. Now some swindler was enjoying the fruit of his backbreaking labor. "What a waste of our hard-earned money!"

"What'd you say?"

"Ah, nothin'."

"How'd her brother take the news," Tony asked.

"Not the way I expected. That's for sure," Frank complained. "Some brother! He refused to help."

"Damn cheapskate," Tony commiserated. "Thank God my family's nothin' like that. They'd jump over barrels to help me, or anybody related by blood or marriage."

Although he paid most of Anna's fare, Frank looked guiltily at his feet, "Yeah, us too."

Halfway down the stairs, Tony asked, "Goin' to work now, Frank?"

"Nah, Mamma insisted I close the bakery for the day, in honor of Iggy." Frank headed down the steps and griped to himself, "That damn token of respect's gonna wipe out this week's profits."

Meanwhile, at the bottom of the church stairs, Geneva drew near Juliet, "Why didn't I feel sad for Iggy?"

Juliet shrugged. "I guess for the same reason I daydreamed about my wedding during the service. I hate to speak ill of the dead, but, even though Iggy was my brother, he was no joy to live with."

"You may be right but I still feel guilty." Geneva jolted the moment the baby kicked her for the first time. "Oh, my!"

"What's the matter?" Juliet grabbed Geneva's arm. "Are you okay? You're not going to faint again are you?" Unlike her mother and sister, Juliet had no clue that Geneva was pregnant.

"No, no, I'm fine." Geneva patted her stomach. "A little indigestion is all." She looked up the church stairs at her approaching husband and smiled. "Excuse me. There's something I want to share with Frank."

Further down the sidewalk, Mack guided Teresa toward the LaSalle. "Iggy was so disrespectful to Anna. Don't know how many times I tried to get him to treat her better, but he always brushed me off. Now look what happened to her."

"*Sì*, your brother was terribly inconsiderate of her. "***Grazie a Dio***, you're nothing like him." Teresa squeezed Mack's arm. *But Anna . . . it seems she got what she deserved.*

Mack looked down at Teresa. "You feeling all right? You still look a bit pale. It's about time you were checked out by a doctor. You've put it off long enough."

"No, I don't like doctors." She stood back while Mack opened the car door.

"Really, Teresa, I insist."

Before Teresa had a chance to get into the car, the scroungy mutt with the matted fur collar raced up to the LaSalle and jumped inside. In a moment of excited mayhem, he leaped back and forth between the front and back seat. Mack tried to grab hold of the dog. "Whoa, Buddy. Take it easy."

Teresa laughed, "Can we keep him, Macco? He's so cute."

The dog calmed down enough for Mack to wrap his arms around him. "Not as long as we're living with Mamma. I'll drop him off at the animal shelter."

"No!" Teresa got into the car and petted the dog. "If you do, we'll never see him again."

"You're right." As Mack ruffled the dog's fur, he failed to notice the involuntary jerk of his left hand, an indication that a petite mal seizure may have occurred, a strong warning sign that his seizure medicine might not be strong enough anymore. "Let's stop on the way home and get him some food."

Chapter Fifty-Three

Later, after feeding the mutt and letting him loose in the park, Mack and Teresa returned home and retreated to their bedroom. As Mack rifled through his closet, Teresa slipped into a cardigan, her face wrinkled with apprehension. *I suppose Macco's right about seeing a doctor. My symptoms don't seem to be letting up.* Teresa buttoned the sweater. "Macco?"

"Yeah?" Without bothering to turn around, Mack sniffed the air. "Do you smell something, Teresa?"

Teresa inhaled sharply through her nostrils. "No, nothing unusual."

"It's like . . . it's like . . ." Mack started to pace around the room, his eyes unfocused in a trance. He smacked his lips together several times.

"Macco, what're you doing?" Staring at her husband in disbelief, she tugged at his arm. "Macco, it's me Teresa. What's happening to you? How can I help?"

Mack continued the bizarre behavior until suddenly he froze in place, his spine rigid. Within seconds, his head jerked back as if an invisible force pulled him by the hair; and he collapsed onto the bed, arms and legs flailing. When Mack's face contorted, his tongue protruding at an unsightly angle, Teresa covered her eyes and turned away. "**Dio santo**, my husband's possessed by *il diavolo!*"

Once she peeked through her shaking fingers, Teresa noticed the bluish tone of his skin and panicked. "You can't die now. I need you!"

Not even three heartbeats later, Signora Matteo knocked at their bedroom door. "Macbetto . . . Teresa, you eat?"

Teresa jerked open the door and cried out, *"Aiuto!* Macco needs help!"

Signora Matteo pushed Teresa out of her way, rushed to Mack's bedside and, after she made sure there was little chance of him falling off the bed, made the sign of the cross over him.

Ter___ ___outed, *"Per favore* do something. Don't just stand there!"

"___ ___iente da fare." Signora Matteo shook her head and he'___ ___, palms up, saying there was nothing either of them ___ept make sure he didn't hurt himself. Over the ___ ___the hard way that it was best to leave her son ___ as he was on a safe, flat surface. Any effort ___tect his tongue might cause additional ___y. *"Dobbiamo aspettare*. We must ___s so Signora Matteo pulled her close and ___ _ene*. It will stop soon. No you worry."

___atteo's prediction, Mack's seizure ended within ___ ___e began to return to its normal color, although he rei___ ___se. "Teresa, *aiutami*. Help me to clean my son."

T___ ___they removed Mack's soiled clothes and changed the sheets. ___en Signora Matteo brought in a wash basin and started to give Mack a sponge bath, Teresa took the washrag from her hand. "I'll do it."

Signora Matteo nodded, *"Va bene,"* and left Teresa to tend to her husband.

* * *

In fifteen minutes, Signora Matteo returned to take away the basin. *"Vieni di sotto con me*. Come, you need eat."

"No. I'm not hungry. *Preferisco stare qui*. I prefer to stay by Macco's side till he wakes up."

"As you like, *fai come ti pare*." Signora Matteo headed toward the door, but before exiting the room, she bent down to pick up one of Mack's discarded socks. She turned around once more and started to say something to Teresa. Her mouth open, she paused and watched her daughter-in-law, touched by Teresa's devotion to her son.

Teresa knelt on the floor beside the bed and caressed Mack's hand. "Macco, I'm here for you, as I vowed before God, in sickness and in health." She made the sign of the cross and looked up at the ceiling. "Mamma, is this *Dio*'s way of testing me? If so, have I passed his test?"

Overhearing Teresa's prayer, Signora Matteo was impressed by
the way she still spoke to her dead mother. She herself used to pray
to her deceased husband when faced with an overwhelming problem;
but, exiting the room, she realized how long it had been since she'd last
communicated with the lost love of her life.

Once Signora Matteo closed the door behind her, Teresa slipped
under the blanket next to Mack and, with her head on his shoulder,
cried herself to sleep.

* * *

That night Signora Matteo had trouble falling asleep, concerned
about Mack's seizure and once again worrying over Iggy's status in
heaven. Eventually she fell into a fitful sleep.

"Hey, Mamma!" Iggy shouted down from a dark cloud with a red
glow surrounding it. "There's nothin' for you to lose sleep over. I'm
having a ball up here."

"Iago, you no miss my spaghetti and lasagna?"

"Nah, they serve steak up here. Even on Friday nights. Yeah, these
angels sure know how to treat a guy. It's better then a high-priced
whorehouse . . . backrubs . . . the works. All damn free! All I gotta do
is ask."

"Iago, *che vergognia*!" Signora Matteo cried out in indignation.
"You no know is trick?" She lectured him on the likelihood that he would
be sent to hell if he kept taking advantage of the angels. "To be good one
time too hard for you?"

"Good? Who wants to be good? That's no fun. I'd rather go to hell in
a handcart. By the way, since Papà's busy with a couple of pretty angels,
he asked me to say 'hi' for him." When the Archangel Michael suddenly
appeared before him, he called down one last time to his mother. See ya
later, Mamma. Mike here says he's sending me to one hell of a party!"

Signora Matteo bolted up in a panic. "Noooooo!"

Chapter Fifty-Four

A few days later on Saturday afternoon, Geneva welcomed Signora
Matteo and her sisters-in-law into her new home. Once she provided
the ladies with a tour of the house, she prepared lunch while they
conversed over the half-wall that separated the galley kitchen from the
narrow parlor. Juliet ran her hand over the worn arm of the couch and
gazed down at the scuffed hardwood. "Your home is, uh, lovely."

With Iaga snuggled against her breast, Patricia wrinkled her nose at the windows. "It has potential, but it desperately needs something to dress it up right now, maybe some window treatments would help."

"I know the pull-down shades are an eyesore," Geneva moaned, "but I can't afford to buy expensive drapes right now. There's no room in our budget. That's why we settled for Mamma's second-hand furniture."

Teresa decided to throw in her two cents. "Geneva, did you consider valances to dress up the windows. They wouldn't cost as much as drapes." She noted the muted shades of green and plum in the area rug under her feet. "You can pull the colors from this **tappeto**."

"Oh, I already thought of that." Geneva sighed. "But, since I can't sew a stitch to save my life, I decided to leave the windows bare for now."

"If you buy **la stoffa**, maybe an inexpensive cotton, I'll design and sew the valances for you," Teresa volunteered. "I'll use my sister-in-law's sewing machine for the project." Teresa hoped it wasn't an abuse of Virginia's generosity.

"You'd do that for me?" Geneva asked in disbelief. "Why, that's wonderful, Teresa." She counted on her fingers. "Altogether there are ten windows in the house. I'll let you know as soon as I find some decent fabric on sale."

Teresa looked down at the floor and tried not to grimace for she had only meant to volunteer to create a unique valance for each of the two living room windows, not all the windows in the whole house. *Oh well, I certainly can manage the time. Macco's still busy preparing income tax returns.*

From the throne of a wing chair, Signora Matteo once again looked approvingly at her new daughter-in-law. Reeling in strident Italian, she invited Teresa to use her sewing machine, ***"Usa la mia macchina da cucire."*** She glared reproachfully at her daughters. "Patrizia and Giulietta, they never use. **Infatti**, if you want machine, is yours." She told her to ask Mack to take the machine in for servicing since it hadn't been used in years.

Thrilled with the offer, Teresa leaped up, clapping her hands beneath her chin. "***Grazie***, such a generous offer, Signora Matteo!"

"Is time you call me Mamma, no?"

"**Sì**, of course, Signora Matteo . . . I mean Mamma." A rosy glow of anticipation blossoming on her face, Teresa smiled. *I'm one step closer to starting my own business.*

"Lunch is ready." Platter in hand, Geneva approached a rectangular table opposite the sofa and, centering the dish on it, proceeded to slide the table set for five away from the wall, the dishes rattling in protest. "Please take a seat in our dining area, ladies." Complying, Patricia and Signora Matteo parked their wide cabooses on the roomier side of the table while Juliet and Teresa squeezed their smaller frames into the space against the wall, leaving the place setting at the head of the table for Geneva.

Patricia juggled Iaga on her lap and scoffed at the baby grand that dominated the other half of the parlor. "That monstrosity takes up too much of your room. It feels cramped in here."

Geneva sneered at Patricia and then addressed her mother-in-law. "Mamma, Frank and I are grateful you insisted he take the piano with him. I think he'd be lost without it."

Signora Matteo smiled. "Tell Franco I come to hear music each Sunday."

Assuming her mother-in-law would expect a full-course dinner after each recital, Geneva picked up the serving plate and quickly changed the subject. "I hope you like my new recipe for chicken **cacciatore**."

As Geneva dished out the chicken braised in a tomato base, Signora Matteo's smile faded for she was insulted that Geneva used a recipe other than hers. "You no like my **ricetta**?" Forking a morsel into her mouth, she garbled, "This **pollo,** it need more garlic."

After a taste from her own plate, Teresa kissed the gathered fingertips of her right hand. "**Fantastico!** Will you give us your recipe, Geneva?"

"Yes, please." Juliet chimed in. "I'll add it to the collection I've started."

Patricia noted the frown on Signora Matteo's face. "I'll pass. Jake absolutely loves Mamma's recipe."

* * *

Over dessert and coffee, Juliet dominated the conversation with a rundown of her lavish wedding plans. "I've picked out several bridesmaids gowns as possibilities." She made quick eye contact with Geneva and Teresa then focused on Patricia. "They're all rather loose fitting styles; so none of you should have a problem." Juliet coughed. "But there's still some time, that is, if anyone wants to lose some weight."

Appalled at Juliet's nerve, Patricia turned up her nose and, in a caustic tone, retaliated, "Mamma, don't you think there ought to be a limit to the amount a person splurges on a wedding? I didn't spend a fraction of what Juliet intends to." Patricia dove into a heated debate with her mother over her sister's excessiveness versus her own frugality. Reluctantly, Geneva mediated.

Refusing to defend her extravagance, Juliet escaped to the sofa. Teresa followed and seized the opportunity to engage the bride-to-be in a private conversation, "Juliet, do you like the dresses I wear?"

Juliet scrutinized Teresa's outfit. "Why, of course? They're stylish yet different."

Teresa patted the bodice of her dress. "***Ho cucito tutti.*** Not only did I sew them, I designed them as well?"

"Yes, you've mentioned that before," Juliet acknowledged.

Teresa enthusiastically expanded on the topic, "I also intended to design and sew a wedding gown for myself. But, when Iago . . ." She glanced to make sure Signora Matteo wasn't paying them any mind. "I thought a formal gown might be in bad taste so soon after a death in the *famiglia*." Teresa sighed. "My dress was going to be ***magnifico***."

"I'm sure it was, Teresa." Juliet pressed her lips together. "Hmm, if only there was some way I could afford an original." She shook her head. "No, it's definitely out of the question. You see, my gown is the only thing Mamma insists I pay for myself."

"***Il mio motivo***, the reason I mention it," Teresa hesitated.

"Yes, go on," Juliet encouraged.

"Well, I thought maybe I could sew a wedding gift for you." She fingered the folds of her skirt. "If you'd like, I can design and sew a marvelous bridal gown, one that'll accent your great figure." Before Juliet had a chance to respond, Teresa added, "I promise I won't be offended if you say no."

Smiling, Juliet bounced up off the sofa cushion. "Why, Teresa, I'd be a fool not to take advantage of such a generous offer." She paused to consider the ramifications. "Of course, I'll buy the fabric but," Juliet's cheer evaporated, "with the wedding less than five months away, how will you design and sew my gown in your spare time? Remember, you promised Geneva window treatments. How can you handle both projects at the same time?"

Bored with Patricia's arguments and eavesdropping on the younger women's conversation, Geneva offered a solution, "Teresa can always put mine on hold."

Patricia turned away from her mother. "Put what on hold?"

Pointing to the front windows, Geneva explained, "My valances. I can wait a few more months until Teresa finishes a wedding gown for Juliet."

While Juliet gave Geneva an appreciative glance, Teresa sat up straighter. "Since Geneva's not in a hurry, I'm sure I can squeeze in a custom-fitting bridesmaid gown for each of us."

Juliet rejected the idea, "No, no. We'll order the bridesmaid dresses from the bridal shop like I originally planned. I want you to concentrate *all* your efforts on *my* gown."

"*Va bene*," Teresa acquiesced. "If that's what you prefer, Juliet."

For the third time in four days, Signora Matteo nodded her approval at Teresa, then, in a generously good mood, redirected her attention toward Juliet. "I will pay for fabric."

Juliet rushed over to Signora Matteo and hugged her. "Oh, Mamma, *grazie!*" Now my gown won't cost me a penny. I'll add the money to our kitty instead. Tony will be thrilled."

"What kitty?" Signora Matteo huffed. "No cat in my house."

"No, no you don't understand." Juliet backed away from her mother. "Our kitty is what we call our savings account, the one we opened to save for a down payment on our own house."

"*Perché?*" Signora Matteo pouted. "You no like live in mine?"

"Not really," Juliet admitted, thinking of Mack and Teresa's rickety old bedframe that Signora Matteo would now pawn off on her. "There's no privacy. The walls are too thin. Ask Teresa?"

Signora Matteo stared at Teresa. "Is there a *problema*?"

"No, no, not anymore." Teresa reddened as she sat back down at the table. "Not since Macco bought us a new bed."

Signora Matteo folded her arms tight under her bosom. "*Beh!* Why look free horse in mouth?"

If it's so free, why do we have to pay room and board? Teresa zeroed in on her coffee cup for a distraction and lifted it to her lips but, when its aroma accosted her nostrils, she began to gag. Hand over mouth, she pushed herself away from the table and ran up the stairs. Geneva followed right behind her and guided her to the bathroom. While Teresa leaned over the toilet and released her lunch, Geneva stood outside the room and expressed her sympathy through the door, "If you need any help . . ."

After Teresa's stomach settled down, she rinsed her mouth and dried it off with some toilet paper, then opened the door. "I'm sorry. Don't know why coffee makes me nauseous nowadays. I think I'll switch to tea."

Without delay, Geneva confronted Teresa with a list of riveting questions, "Do you ever wake up feeling queasy in the morning? Are you more tired than usual? Are you late with your menstrual cycle? Do you feel like peeing every two minutes?"

"*Sì*, how did you know?" Teresa pulled in her chin. "Did Macco tell you? He thinks I've caught some kind of influenza, but I haven't had a fever."

"No. Mack hasn't said a word. I don't even think he suspects."

"Suspects? Suspects what?" Teresa wrinkled her brow. "What do you mean?"

"I had the same symptoms. They just recently eased up." Geneva let out a forced breath. "What a relief!"

"What caused them?" Teresa asked apprehensively.

"A condition called," Geneva paused to look over her shoulder and finished in a whisper, "pregnancy." She stifled a laugh behind her hand. "I'm pregnant and I think you are too."

"No! *È impossibile!*" Teresa backed up a step. "I've only been married for a month." Since her mother had died before having a chance to share the facts of life with her youngest daughter and Teresa's older sister Nina had never bothered to provide the information, Teresa had learned what little she knew from her peers. Caught at a disadvantage, Teresa questioned Geneva. "It can't happen that easily, can it?" *If so, Papà would have had a houseful of **bambini** by now.*

Believing Teresa didn't completely understand the science of conception, Geneva decided she ought to fill her in. "Well, for some people, like me for example, it takes way too long. For others, maybe someone like you, it might have happened the first time you . . ." Uncomfortable discussing such intimate matters, Geneva had difficulty swallowing. As Teresa waited expectantly for her to finish, her sister-in-law wiped the saliva from her lips. "Well, sometimes conception can occur the first time a couple sleeps together . . . you know . . . as man and wife. Didn't anyone ever sit you down and tell you how it all works?"

Embarrassed by her ignorance, Teresa fibbed, "Of course, but . . ."

Relieved that she was off the hook, Geneva relaxed. "You should be happy. I'm sure Mack will be."

Teresa shrugged her shoulders. "*Non lo so.* We never actually discussed when we'd start our family." Teresa bit her lip and focused on the floor. "He might be annoyed about it. He's not been himself lately."

"What do you mean?" Geneva pried.

"Maybe I shouldn't share such private *informazione.*"

"You can confide in me. I won't tell anyone."

"*Va bene*, you're family after all." Teresa looked down at her feet and wrung her hands. "It's just that, since Macco convulsed two times this past week, he's been moody and quiet. Maybe it's something I said or did. I don't know."

"Oh, I see." Geneva pursed her lips.

"I think I'll wait until he's in a better mood," Teresa shifted from foot-to-foot, "to tell him, that is."

"First, you'd better make sure you *are* pregnant," Geneva advised. "Make an appointment with the doctor."

Teresa grimaced. "Is that really necessary? I don't like doctors."

"It's the only way to be certain. I'll go with you if you want."

Teresa lifted her chin. "***Grazie***, I'd appreciate that."

"Now that that's settled, let's go downstairs." As Iaga's wail floated up the staircase, Geneva swallowed hard. "I need to make an announcement that some people may consider long overdue."

Chapter Fifty-Five

After finishing her assigned household chores the following Saturday morning, Teresa rested in bed, the recent blood test and pelvic exam fresh in her mind. She blushed at the recollection for it had been the ultimate in humiliation. "***Cosí imbarazzante!***" *And to think, a poor rabbit had to die in the end.* Picturing a nest of orphaned bunnies, her mouth drooped sadly. Tears welled in her eyes as she vacillated between sympathy for these motherless creatures and trepidation for the task that lay ahead of her.

Rubbing her eyes, Teresa stood up then walked over to the window and looked out at the tree directly in front of it. On a sturdy branch, she spotted a nest, an intricate one that some bird had begun to build in anticipation of the spring to come. Though disappointed that the bird was nowhere to be seen, she blinked several times in order to scrutinize the nest's construction. The twigs and branches seemed to be interwoven with what appeared to be dingy white fur. Teresa wrinkled her nose. *Now where would a bird get fur for its nest?*

Suddenly, she heard the disgruntled bark of her favorite stray dog, the one Mack always referred to as "Buddy." She looked down in time to see a cardinal diving down at the mutt and attacking his matted fur collar. Upon the bird's return to the tree with both beak and claws white with fur, Teresa smiled half-heartedly. *Poor Buddy.*

Eventually bored with the industrious bird's task, Teresa's thoughts returned to her current problem. Wringing her hands, she sat down on the edge of the mattress and worried about what might happen when she told Mack about her pregnancy. *Will the shock provoke another seizure?* Shuddering at the possibility, she raised her eyes to the ceiling and made the sign of the cross. "***Dio***, I leave it in your hands." Despite her resolve to let God handle the situation, Teresa nibbled nervously at her fingernails.

Once she whittled them down to the quick, she smacked her lap. "This is ridiculous." She knew she needed to find something to occupy her mind until Mack came home. *If not I'll go absolutely stir crazy.*

Teresa glanced at the corner of the room where Signora Matteo's sewing machine sat, oiled and ready for action. But ignoring it, she focused instead on the sketchpad resting on top of it. Until recently, all her designs had been etched in her mind, no pencil required. But since her first client insisted on prior approval, she had promised to commit her ideas to paper. Deciding to lose herself in its pages, she retrieved the pad and glanced at her most recent designs. *These are my best yet, but I'll draw even more sketches to appease Juliet. It's her gown after all.* Redirecting her negative energy, she tackled the project with such intense concentration that she forgot to stop for lunch.

* * *

While Teresa feverishly sketched away the hours, Mack suffered the minutes that dragged by for him in the storefront of Matteo's Bakery. At one point toward the end of the day, he leaned his elbow against the cash register and cupped his chin in the palm of his hand. *Ever since that last epileptic attack, I haven't been able to look Teresa in the eye, let alone be intimate with her. She must really be annoyed with me.*

What brought on those seizures last week? Mack tugged at his ear. *Was it the strain of trying to make an extra buck?* He'd spent hours on end preparing tax returns for just about every Italian in the neighborhood. *Who knows?* Though his doctor had again boosted the dosage of his medication, restoring his healthy equilibrium, Mack's confidence had suffered a blow that pills couldn't cure. Deciding it was necessary to do something about it, he banged his fist onto the counter. *I need to make up to Teresa.*

To that end, Mack purchased a dozen red roses and a box of chocolate truffles on his way home. Parking the LaSalle in the driveway, Mack dashed into the house armed with the gifts and the determination to set things straight. *Maybe if I tell her how much I've saved toward a down payment on a house, Teresa will forget how bad I've behaved.*

Once Mack entered the foyer, he ascended the stairs mulling over what words might convince Teresa to forgive him for his recent sullenness. Half way up, he paused. *The heck with it! I'll just wing it.* He ran the rest of the way up to their bedroom.

Meanwhile, with the sketch pad put aside, Teresa slipped into a red lace bra and panties then stood before the mirror, tilting her pelvis forward. *These ought to grab his attention.* With one hand behind her neck and the other propped on her hip, she checked her profile. *It will be a relief to tell him tonight. Should I get it over with before dinner?* She glanced down at her stomach which audibly gurgled.

At that moment, Mack threw open the door and slammed it shut behind him. "Teresa!"

"*Sì*, Macco, I'm here."

Mack froze at the sight of Teresa's suggestive pose, shivers running up and down his spine, his blood surging. "I wanted to tell you how much I love you, Teresa." He held out the roses and chocolates to her. "These are for you."

On the tips of her bare toes, Teresa stepped forward across the cold hardwood floor, her hips swaying with the effort, and accepted the gifts from her husband. Though her mouth watered for the chocolates, she sniffed the roses and focused her eyes on Mack's. "*Grazie*, so sweet of you." Using the term of endearment she usually reserved for lovemaking, Teresa held up the box of chocolates, "*Amore mio*, feed them to me now. I'm hungry for them, and for you."

When she dropped the roses and candies onto the bed and held out her arms to him, Mack pulled her close. In between their passionate kisses, she eyed the truffles.

Mack whispered into her ear, "Teresa, your skin is softer than rose petals and your lips are sweeter than chocolate. I've missed your touch and your taste."

"I was here, *caro*." Teresa ran a finger up his arm. "You only had to reach out for me."

"Please, Teresa, can we make love right now, before dinner?"

"You don't need to beg. I'm ready for you if," she reached down and stroked him, "you're ready for me."

"Oh, Teresa," Mack groaned and guiding her onto the bed, he helped her out of her undergarments.

The chocolates forgotten, Teresa raised her hips and moaned, "Macco, *portami in cielo*."

Mack didn't need any further prodding to jump at the chance to transport Teresa where she wanted to go, *to the heights of heaven.* Fumbling, he managed to strip off his own clothes and then mounted his wife. Their bodies melding as one, the couple danced to a passionate rhythm, one that encouraged their mutual satisfaction.

Once they caught their breaths, Mack stretched out an arm, his hand landing on a truffle that had fallen out of the box. As he placed the chocolate into Teresa's eager mouth, he whispered, "Maybe, if we practice more often, we can make a baby."

Her teeth pasted creamy brown, Teresa propped herself up on an elbow and garbled, "It's funny that you should mention a baby."

Chapter Fifty-Six

On a crisp afternoon in late September, multihued leaves fluttered to the ground, abandoning their green brothers, the ones that stubbornly clung to their branches. It was a day perfect for washing cars, hanging storm windows or wrapping a fig tree in insulation to protect it from the bitter cold ahead. However, instead of using the well-suited Saturday for outside chores, countless neighbors packed into the rear pews of St. Christopher's, behind the family and friends of the bride and groom, and waited for the ceremony to begin.

In the church's vestibule, the tension was palpable. As Juliet clutched the handgrip of her calla lily bouquet, she paced around, the tight set of her jaw obscured by a layered veil. In contrast to her furrowed brow, her ivory gown smoothly hugged her curves, the low scoop of its silky bodice exposing a bit of cleavage. Scalloped lace both caressed her wrists and trimmed the gown's hem, while her train hung only long enough to cover her rounded derrière, adding the allusion of height to an otherwise petite frame. The picture of a stunning but apprehensive bride, Juliet waited for her brother's return.

Sporting a snug tux and cummerbund, Frank eventually limped through the vestibule's side entrance and, before the door closed behind him, his youngest sister lifted her veil and confronted him. "What's the holdup, Frank? Did you find out where Father Paterno is?"

"Yes, calm down. He's tied up with a funeral, but his secretary swore he'd be here any minute. The organist will signal us when he arrives." Frank tugged at his cummerbund then stretched his neck in an attempt to avoid the bowtie digging into his double chin. "Boy, it's hot in here." He yanked off his jacket and slung it over his shoulder.

"What are you doing?" Juliet reprimanded. "Put that back on!" As Frank grudgingly slipped back into his jacket, his sister grimaced at her two attendants who bided their time a few feet away from them. "Will you look at my bridesmaids, Frank?" she moaned into her bouquet. "Who do you think will get more attention today, me or them?"

"You of course," Frank appeased as he peered over his shoulder at his wife, their overdue baby weighing her down.

Geneva gripped her lower spine and arched it forward so that her gown, a parachute dipped in Pepto Bismol, rose a foot above the marble floor. "Ugh, my back is killing me."

"*Povera ragazza,*" Teresa commiserated. "If it's any consolation, there's an elbow digging into my ribs." Teresa adjusted the pink sash that wrapped tight under her bosom and massaged the barrel of a belly protruding beneath it.

At a volume loud enough for her bridesmaids to overhear, Juliet lamented, "Frank, look at them. How awful!" Juliet had never expected that Geneva would still be pregnant or that Teresa could swell into Moby Dick so quickly.

"Hey, it's not my fault my baby refuses to show face," Geneva defended.

Teresa flicked her hand in the air with indignation. "*Che pensi?* Do you think I'm having this baby to spite you?" When Juliet stepped back, Teresa gripped the skirt of her bridesmaid gown and accosted her. "If you agreed to have me sew our gowns in the first place, I could have hidden our bellies better than this." Instead," she looked down and grimaced with disgust, "instead, you ordered these awful sacks that arrived way too late to be altered."

"How were you supposed to sew another three gowns?" Juliet countered. "It took forever to finish mine."

"*Dio santo!*" Teresa retaliated. "That's only because you drove me crazy by insisting I raise the scoop of the bodice, five times at least, before you accepted my original design in the end."

For lack of an appropriate rebuttal, Juliet turned away from Teresa and griped to Frank, "I planned for three attendants, not two hot air balloons." Juliet had rejected the idea of her friends as bridesmaids because she thought their figures might divert attention from her, the bride.

"Come on, girls, let's fight nice," Frank pleaded.

Ignoring her husband, Geneva taunted the bride, "At least we didn't drop out of the wedding party like your sister."

Juliet jerked up a hand. "If only I kept my mouth shut." She regretted telling Patricia to borrow one of her mother's girdles. Insulted, Patricia had refused further participation in the wedding. "She couldn't have looked any worse than the two of you."

"*Grazie,*" Teresa shot back a sarcastic thank you.

"I'm sorry," Juliet whined. "It's just that I'm so nervous."

"*Va bene*, apology accepted." Teresa patted Juliet's shoulder and kicked up a foot. "As long as I don't fall flat on my face in these tight heels, I'll survive the embarrassment."

"Imagine, Juliet," Geneva spewed as she raised her nose in the air, "compared to the two of us, you'll look like a fairytale princess in that *mah-vah-lous* gown. All the women will be absolutely green with envy."

Afraid Geneva was criticizing her work, Teresa fretted. "Don't you like my design, Geneva? I tried to highlight Juliet's best feature, her bosom." Teresa fiddled with the silk trim on Juliet's bodice and then ran her hand down the bridal train. "And I did my best to play down her rear end."

Juliet flicked Teresa's hand away. "Please, stop. I'm frazzled enough without worrying about my boobs . . . or my butt."

"Girls, girls, settle down." Frank stepped between Juliet and her bridesmaids and wrapped an arm around his wife. "Gen, you sure you can walk down the aisle alone?"

"I'll be fine," Geneva sulked. "I just can't wait to deliver this baby."

* * *

In the sanctuary, tucked behind and to the right of the main altar, the perspiring groom agonized alongside his boss and best man Lieutenant Tom Smathers. "Where is that damn priest, Smathers?"

"Take it easy, Canelli." Smathers examined the face of his wristwatch. "I'm sure he'll be here any minute."

Tony pulled a handkerchief from the inside pocket of his ivory tailcoat and swiped his forehead. "Can't wait to get this over with!" He returned the damp hanky to his pocket. "Hope I don't mess up the weddin' vows. Juliet expects the ceremony to be downright perfect."

The lieutenant smirked. "Is this the same man who holds his cool under fire? Look at you. You're as nervous as a defendant on the witness stand, a guilty one at that." He pulled a flask out of his jacket. "Here take a sip of this. It'll calm you down."

* * *

Distinguished as an usher by his tuxedo, Mack unrolled the white carpet down the center of the aisle toward the altar, fretting along the way. *Hope Teresa doesn't trip on this fabric. She's been so klutzy lately, even in bed.*

Since his pregnant wife had been more passionate than ever in her last trimester, Mack was worried she might hurt the baby, especially during their awkward lovemaking. He had begged her to take it easy, but Teresa always brushed off his concern.

Last night . . . Blushing at the recollection, he let go of the carpet's edge and genuflected before the flower-studded altar. Mack made a quick right and anchored himself at his assigned post for the ceremony, in front of the first pew where his mother sat beside Patricia and Jake.

* * *

A corsage of orchids pinned to her maroon mother-of-the-bride dress, Signora Matteo adjusted the angle of her hat. "***Patrizia, sembro stupida in questo cappello?***"

"No, Mamma, you don't look stupid. Your hat looks lovely on you," Patricia assured her.

Signora Matteo folded her hands in her lap. Sighing, she complained that once Juliet left, she'd be all alone in her big house, "***Senza Giulietta, sarò da sola nella mia casa grande.***"

"Mack and Teresa will still be there." Patricia reminded her mother.

"No, Macbetto want to buy house." Mack had told her that he planned to purchase the house two doors past the one Juliet and Tony had bought.

Patricia pulled in her chin. "I didn't know he was in the market for one."

"***Sì***," Signora Matteo pouted.

"Well," Patricia hemmed, "we'll all be within walking distance."

Signora Matteo shrugged. "***Forse.***"

Patricia jutted her chin forward. "What do you mean, *maybe*?"

"Maybe I sell," Signora Matteo proposed.

"Sell what?" Patricia asked in confusion.

"***La mia casa.***" Signora Matteo brushed a piece of lint off her dress.

"How can you sell your house, Mamma? It's where we all grew up . . . so many memories."

Signora Matteo complained about the house having too many rooms. "***Troppe stanze!*** Who clean, you?"

"No, of course not." Patricia lowered her eyes. "How can I, what with Iaga and my own house to keep?"

"***Va bene***, it is settled," Signora Matteo retorted. "I will sell house."

"Where do you plan to live, Mamma?"

"In house of my . . ." Signora Matteo trailed off when Patricia turned away from her.

Distracted by Jake who ogled one of Juliet's curvaceous friends, Patricia poked him in the ribs. "Knock it off, mister."

Jake turned up a palm. "Knock what off?"

"Stop starring at Maria Russo," Patricia demanded. "You're embarrassing me."

Jake pinched Patricia's midriff. "Why stare at dat girl when yer sittin' right next ta me, sweetheart?"

"Humph!" Patricia slapped Jake's hand away. "It wouldn't hurt you to lose a few pounds either." Patricia turned away from him. "I'll start us on a diet, tomorrow for sure."

* * *

Several aisles behind Signora Matteo and to the right of Mina and Antonio, Signore Camara twiddled his thumbs and muttered under his breath, "Conchetta insists we tie the knot after all these years."

"Conchetta?" Having never heard his father call his lover by name, Antonio leaned in closer. "Who's she?"

"She's my very close friend," Signore Camara divulged. "Hmm, maybe it's not such a bad idea. It might work in my favor." He decided it would be nice to have a live-in cook and housemaid once again. "*Perché no?* Besides, Conchetta demands a ring or she refuses to continue our . . ."

His curiosity peaked, Antonio prodded, "Continue your what?" But, before his father was able to answer, Mina cleared her throat in a disgruntled manner. Antonio glanced to his left and, noticing the scowl on his wife's fattened face, whispered to his father. "*Non ci posso credere*. I can't believe Mina's angry with me again."

"What'd you do to irritate her this time?" Signore Camara smirked.

"Oh, probably something I said about all the weight she's gained," Antonio admitted.

Signore Camara stifled a laugh. "Learn to think before you speak, my son."

"*Sì*," Antonio agreed. "I can't wait for her to deliver the twins."
"Twins?" Signora Camara snickered into his fist. "Two bowls of pasta, one with meatballs and one without?"

Wise to his father's attempt at humor, Antonio pictured the miniscule family jewels of an infant boy as he squirmed in one pasta bowl and a peanut of a girl nestled sound asleep in a second. "Don't care if they're boys or girls as long as they're healthy." He folded his arms and pouted. "But once they're born, I hope Mina let's me back into her bed."

"*Her* bed?" Signore Camara pulled in his chin in disbelief. "**Sei maritato.** Don't you sleep together as husband and wife?"

"Not for months. She insists that I sleep on the sofa until she delivers. You know, I never expected . . ." Startled by the organist's abrupt tap on the keys and the sudden appearance of the gangly priest at the altar, Antonio hushed up and, along with everyone else, turned toward the vestibule.

As the wedding march resounded, Teresa waddled toward the altar, her eyes focused on her feet. *Please, God, don't let me slip.* Panting, Geneva followed ten paces behind Teresa and, midpoint down the aisle, an insensitive soul giggled at the unsightly duo, inciting a wave of chuckles throughout the church. Mercifully, the priest's loud cough discouraged the crowd and the laughter dwindled before the bridesmaids arrived at the front of the church.

After a dramatic pause in the music, all the spectators again turned toward the vestibule in anticipation of the bride's appearance. When the organist resumed, Juliet warily approached the entry, a strained smile fixed on her face. As rehearsed, Frank offered her his arm and, with his limp diminished by the music's slow pace, escorted Juliet toward the altar and her apprehensive groom. When Juliet caught sight of her man, the tension in her face melted. She directed a radiant smile at Tony; and, in return, he beamed his adoration back at her.

Cameras flashed and whispers filtered throughout the church, "How beautiful!" "What a lovely bride!" "Look at that gown!" "It's so different!" "Isn't that neckline a bit low?" "Where'd she buy that dress?"

* * *

At the end of the traditional wedding ceremony, Father Paterno proclaimed in a jovial voice, "You may now kiss the bride!" However, before Juliet and Tony were given a chance to embrace, a high-pitched squeal from the front of the church and a grunt somewhere further back in the pews diverted them from their objective. All heads, including those of the bride and groom, rotated in search of the persons responsible for the disturbance.

Exposing one offender, Frank rushed to Geneva's side and escorted his stooped and whimpering wife towards the exit. Meanwhile, Antonio anxiously ushered a hunched and groaning Mina from their pew. The coincidence of two women evidently in the throes of labor astounded the crowd; and, unable to ignore the women's tortured breaths, all eyes followed them out of the church.

Oblivious to the cause of the commotion, the organist in the choir loft commenced the exit march, directing the crowd's attention back to the bride and groom. Motivated by their expectant eyes, Tony pulled Juliet into his arms and engaged her in an ardent kiss. Then, smiling broadly, the lovebirds soared hand-in-hand down the aisle, through the vestibule and into the autumn breeze, startling a flock of hovering pigeons, ones anxious for some celebratory rice.

Chapter Fifty-Seven

EPILOGUE

Although the building on Chambers Street looked no different architecturally than the other row homes that flanked it on either side, a canopy above the entrance flaunted the name of the business which occupied its interior:

L'UNICO
UNIQUE GOWNS & DRESSES
Custom Alterations

A placard hung from its lavender entryway which declared the establishment "CLOSED ON SUNDAYS." Nevertheless, behind its glass door on this particular Sunday in 1954, Teresa Matteo hunched over a sketchpad while her longtime friend Carmela Compagna lifted a gown from a dress rack.

Teresa laid down her pencil and looked up from the pad. "Do you believe we've come this far, Carmela, that our hard work has finally paid off?"

"It was inevitable," Carmela declared as she inspected the gown's hem. "Your designs are incredible. *Sono stupendi!*"

"I'll admit they're better than average. But, without you, I might still be dreaming of success." Teresa approached her friend and partner. "Did I ever thank you for your support?"

Carmela looked up at the ceiling and shook her head with facetious annoyance. "Countless times, countless times."

"And for your terrific business sense?" Teresa wrapped an arm around Carmela's shoulder.

With a click of her tongue, Carmela nudged Teresa away. "What did I do that deserves this flattery?"

Teresa let out a forced breath. "*Per piacere*, please take credit where credit is due, Carmela. Not only did our sales double since you suggested we hire two more seamstresses, the alterations side of the business, again your idea, absolutely exploded."

"*Va bene*." Carmela shrugged. "For that, I'll take some credit." Carmela hung up the gown.

"And to think, this business all started from one simple wedding gown." Teresa had never expected to receive any design requests as a direct result of gifting Juliet a bridal gown, let alone four the very afternoon of Juliet's wedding reception.

Teresa glanced up at Carmela. "You were the only one at the factory, that hot and stuffy hellhole, who showed any confidence in me when I handed in my resignation." Teresa tossed the pad aside. "I might have reconsidered if you didn't agree to be my partner."

"*Beh!* Who didn't need an excuse to quit?" Carmela placed her hand on her hip and pursed her lips. "I wonder how many of those factory workers would laugh at you now."

"They did poke fun at me, didn't they?" Teresa reminisced. "At any female with ambition. Such shortsighted skeptics. They'd be thrilled to walk in our shoes today, even if forced to wear them on the wrong feet."

"*Certo,* of course." Carmela laughed and glanced around at the premises they had purchased from Teresa's father. "I never did understand why your father sold us his house, and at such a rock-bottom price."

"Since it's apparent he won't be coming back, I guess it's okay to tell you. Papà was dying to get away from his nagging mistr . . . I mean wife. It's funny. Now that he's gone, I kind of miss the old grouch."

After marrying his mistress, Signore Camara realized that he was no better off than he had been with Teresa's irritating mother. So, bent on being rid of his second wife, he decided to sell the house and leave America. Shortly after the closing on the property, Teresa's father abandoned Conchetta and hopped the first freighter available back to Italy.

If Signore Camara hadn't lowered the price on his house so much, Teresa and Carmela might not have been able to afford the building that now housed their business. It had been impossible to convince the bank manager to lend two young women the start-up money for a dress shop until Mack finally agreed to put up their house for collateral.

Remembering, Carmela let out a sigh of appreciation for Mack's help. "If it wasn't for Macco . . ."

Reading her friend's mind, Teresa crossed her hands over her heart and laughed sarcastically. "*Sì*, our hero, he saved the day!"

"All that paperwork . . ."

"He rescued us from an ocean of red tape. Ha, ha! But he drowned himself in gallons of lavender." She pictured Mack covered from head to toe in splatters of paint. Though intent on proving his capability with a paintbrush or any tool for that matter, Mack's effort had been disastrous. On the other hand, Carmela's husband had performed miracles with the place. There was nothing he couldn't do with a hammer and a saw.

"Thank goodness one of our husbands is handy," Carmela bragged.

"I know, I know. Don't rub it in," Teresa whined facetiously. "I can't thank him enough for all his help with the shop. Tonight, when you make love, be sure to give him two extra kisses, one on each cheek. Tell him they're from me, your friend with a fumbling husband," Teresa joked.

"Give Macco some credit," Carmela good-naturedly chided. "He always finds time for your children."

"That he does, that he does," Teresa agreed. "Why, just yesterday, he took Benito and Emilia to my brother's house for the twins' birthday party." Mack had agreed to accompany them, leaving his wife free to work without their children running underfoot. Although Saturday was one of their busiest days in the shop, Mack returned home more exhausted than Teresa. Mina had told her husband to dress up as a clown for their sons' party, but Antonio imposed on Mack to wear the costume instead. "You should have seen him. Macco came home still wearing the rubber nose and red wig."

"Mina probably napped through the whole thing?" Carmela chuckled.

Teresa shook her head. "Antonio . . . Antonio, the fool is at that woman's beck and call. I don't know how he puts up with her." Teresa still couldn't understand how Antonio had allowed Mina to trap him into a loveless marriage. Never having learned of her father's true reason for marrying or abandoning her own mother, Teresa felt no sympathy toward Mina. "He never should have married that woman. There's nothing but bitterness between them."

"But Mina was pregnant."

"Or so she pretended," Teresa huffed. Although her brother still believed otherwise, Teresa had recently cornered Mina into a confession that she had faked her pre-marital pregnancy. Luckily for Mina, Antonio had impregnated her soon after their elopement. Teresa had never had the heart to tell Antonio the truth.

Teresa made an adjustment to her design. "Speaking of pregnancy, did I tell you that my sister-in-law Giulietta is expecting again." It was

Juliet's fourth pregnancy in six years. "If the woman's not dealing with morning sickness, she's in labor at St. Mary's Hospital." Carmela's wince went unnoticed as Teresa laughed into her hands. "And she's the one who, ha, ha, swore she'd wait to start a family. Tony needs to keep his, ha, ha, pistol strapped in his leather holster. All those boys to feed!" Fortunately for his family, Tony had been promoted again and now earned more than enough to support six people.

Wondering if Teresa would next be telling her that she was pregnant again, Carmela moaned. Before she was able to wipe the scowl from her face, Teresa noticed it and realized she'd been insensitive to her friend who desperately wanted a child. She walked over to Carmela, and wrapping her arms around her, apologized, "I'm sorry. I should have known better."

"Don't worry. It's a natural part of life. I shouldn't be so sensitive about it." Carmela quickly changed the subject. "Did your mother-in-law come home?" Signora Matteo had gone on an extended trip to Italy to visit a hoard of relatives she hadn't seen in years.

"Oh, yes, she's home," Teresa complained.

"You don't sound happy about it." Carmela lifted an eyebrow. "What happened?"

"She's at it again . . . playing favorites. It's so unfair."

"Unfair?"

"*Sì*, she's always too busy trying to amuse Iaga. Never has time to give my two a little attention."

"You know you don't have any right to complain, Teresa." Carmela knew full well that, to the rest of the Matteo family's relief, Patricia and Jake had been the only ones who agreed to take in Signora Matteo after she sold her house. That is, after Patricia twisted Jake's arm and he cowered under the pressure. "Don't you think Patrizia deserves the help."

"Hmm." Teresa reconsidered the situation, again appreciating the fact that she didn't have to put up with the day-to-day presence of a serious food critic and interfering busybody. Furthermore, if Signora Matteo lived in their house, they would have had no room for her own relatives when they immigrated. "You're right as usual. I'll have to thank Patrizia again next time I see her."

"I ran into her at the fish market last week. My, my, she's gained a ton of weight." Carmela puffed out her cheeks.

"*Sì*, she overeats to calm her nerves. But who can blame her for being so stressed out?" Teresa knew that Jake was hardly ever around to lend a positive influence on his daughter. Patricia was usually left to her own devices when it came to controlling their unruly child. If Patricia complained, Jake used the excuse of being overworked, for he had his hands full. Ever since a second branch of the Matteo Bakery had been opened, he was managing a much larger fleet of trucks. Thankful the brat wasn't hers, Teresa bit her lip. "With a daughter like Iaga, anyone would be a wreck."

"Both Patricia and Signora Matteo spoil the little monster." Teresa shook her head at the travesty. "When Iaga throws a tantrum, they give her whatever she wants." Unable to drop the subject, Teresa rambled on, "*Ti dico*, that little girl is such a terror. And such a conniver!"

Teresa believed none of Iaga's cousins stood a chance when they played with her. The Christmas before last, Iaga convinced Benito to give her all his gifts. Shoving her water pistol into his groin, she threatened, "Give 'em ta me or I'll shoot off your tinkler." Until Teresa had stepped in to rectify the situation, her son was forced to beg Iaga to play with his own toys. Another time, angry with one of Juliet's toddlers, Iaga sat on his head, practically suffocating him. "I'll fart on you if ya don't hand over the stinkin' fire truck."

On one Halloween, dressed in a Satan's costume, Iaga had persuaded all her cousins to put their candy into one bag. "Tee-hee! Say 'hell' five times and I'll shoot a piece back ta ya." Her cousins had to stand on one side of the room while she used her sling shot to fling the candy into their mouths. Unfortunately, no parent noticed until one of the children was hit in the eye and began to wail.

But the worst instance of Iaga's shenanigans that Teresa could remember happened on the previous Easter Sunday. Her impudent niece had insisted on wearing her cowgirl getup instead of the yellow pinafore Teresa sewed for her, a crinoline that matched the one Teresa designed for her own daughter. After dinner at Frank and Geneva's house, Iaga confiscated their son's rocking horse and road it wildly. "Giddy-yup! Poopy express comin' through. Outta my way!" Then, jumping off, she accosted little Emilia with her toy pistol. Punching her in the face with it, she gave her a bloody nose. Patricia was unable to deny her daughter's aggression, for Mack had caught the action with his home movie camera, his latest passion. Dropping the camera, he reprimanded Iaga and carried Emilia to the kitchen for a towel and some ice.

Not only that, Iaga had Signora Matteo wrapped around her little finger when it came to breaking rules. For example, Iaga refused to eat fish or pasta with marinara sauce on Fridays. "Smelly fish! Stinky sauce! Gimme meat! Gimme meat!" To shut her up, her grandmother would slip her a small piece of beef when Patricia wasn't looking.

Teresa gripped a fist in frustration. "Macco says Iaga's the image of his brother Iago. Who can disagree? You might think that, after chasing that little devil around, Patricia would be as thin a rail, but no such luck."

"Maybe Geneva can tell her how to lose the weight." It was no secret that, without his mother constantly adding extra food to his plate, Geneva had finally motivated Frank to shed his excess pounds and keep them off.

"Are you kidding? They aren't even speaking."

"Why's that?"

"Geneva tried to give Patricia advice on how to control Iaga."

"I should have such problems," Carmela whined and then again changed the subject as she filtered through a second rack of clothes. "Did they pick the spot for the new bakery?"

Eager to move to the suburbs and send their son to a private school, one that would cultivate his musical talent so that he might be able to attend Juilliard one day, Geneva had convinced Frank and his partners to open the third store. With the extra profits of a third bakery, the possibilities for her son were endless.

"*Sì*, near the new food market on Hudson Street," Teresa acknowledged. Mack had voted for that location because it was near his new accounting office.

"How will Macco juggle all those numbers with three bakeries now?" Even though he still owned thirty percent of the bakery chain and would oversee its accounting functions, Mack preferred to devote his attention to attracting new corporate customers. Now that he was a CPA, he planned to transition his business into a larger public accounting firm.

"He's hired a competent bookkeeper." Mack had thoroughly investigated the new bookkeeper's background. He wanted no repeats of the past embezzlement disaster.

"I see." Carmela looked down at her lap and frowned. "Excuse me. I need to go to the bathroom."

* * *

Upon Carmela's return with a sullen face, Teresa questioned her. "What's wrong?"

"Oh, I hoped I was pregnant, but no such luck." Tears gathered in Carmela's eyes. "I guess it wasn't meant to be."

Again Teresa approached her friend, this time she stroked her hair soothingly. "Does Michael still harp about it, Carmela?"

"No. The last time we babysat your angels, Michael spun in circles chasing them from room to room. Afterward, he actually thanked God out loud for my infertility problems, and then laughed when I smacked him. Can you imagine? Remember how sensitive he used to be about not having children. But now, he accepts our lot." Carmela gazed out the window. "Me? I'm not so sure."

Just then, the bell on the front door jingled and in rushed a miniature version of Mack with a small paper bag in hand. "Hi, *Zia* Mela! Mamma, look what I got!"

"Let me see, Benito?" Teresa peered into the bag of candy. As she fussed over its contents, Mack entered the shop.

His one hand grasped that of a toddler's, a little girl favoring Teresa, while his other held onto a leash. Tugging at the end of it, a frisky dog, one with a shiny tan coat and a fluffy white fur collar, barked an exuberant greeting, then managed to pull away from Mack. Running through the dress racks, he almost knocked one over. Letting go of his daughter, Mack chased the dog around the room until finally catching him. "Jeez, Buddy, settle down. I know you're excited about it, but please calm down."

Laughing, Teresa stretched out her arms to the two-year-old and, hugging her, asked, "Emilia, do you know why our doggy is so excited?"

The little girl nodded. "Puppies."

"Puppies?" Teresa looked at Mack and questioned him, "Whose puppies?"

As Buddy licked his face, Mack tied his leash to the doorknob. "Stay." He then turned to Teresa. "Do you remember the last time Buddy went missing for a few hours? Well, it seems he snuck into Signora Castagna's backyard. Now, Signora Castagna is complaining she's pregnant." Mack chuckled. "Her poodle that is, not Signora Castagna."

"So, Buddy is going to be a Papà. Starting his own family, is he?" Teresa laughed

"Can we keep one?" Benito cried out. "Please, Mamma, please."

"Puppy! Puppy!" Emilia chimed in.

"We'll see . . . we'll see," Teresa pacified.

Mack quickly changed the subject, "Are you ready to go yet, Teresa? If not, I'll take Buddy and the kids to the park."

"We can all go together. I'm finished for today. Once we visit the duck pond, we can go home and eat some delicious *manicotti*." She new the crepe-like pasta sleeves stuffed with mozzarella and ricotta cheese were Mack's favorite.

Mack folded his arms in front of his chest. "Uh-oh."

"Is there a problem, Macco?"

"You tell me, Teresa," Mack griped. "Every time you go to the trouble of making **manicotti**, you manage to drop a bomb on me afterwards. So, tell me, does this mean another one of your relatives is coming to live with us?"

Teresa cringed. "Well, now that you mention it, my cousin Salvatore is coming to America. He's due to arrive in a month. Can he stay with us? It'll only be a temporary visit."

"How temporary do you mean, six months to a year?" Mack smacked the side of his head with a palm. "How many cousins are left in that tribe of yours?"

"Too many to count. But don't worry. Salvatore won't send for the rest of his family until he finds a job and gets his own place."

"In that case," Mack conceded. "I guess we can manage with *one* extra person. But I get priority use of the bathroom. Understood?"

"Of course, Macco, of course. But if we buy your mother's old house like I suggested, we can add an extra bathroom and we'd have plenty of room no matter how many of my relatives show up." Before Mack could answer, Teresa picked up Emilia, grabbed her purse and turned to her partner. "Carmela, you'll be sure to lock up. Won't you?"

"Sure, go on. Enjoy your family," Carmela encouraged with a forced cheer.

"*Ciao!* See you tomorrow." Teresa waved and, skirting Buddy, ushered Benito through the exit.

Mulling over the purchase of his old Steward Street home with a more positive attitude, Mack watched his family leave. They needed more room, not only for visiting relatives, but for the additional children they wanted. As the dog barked after them, Mack called out. "I'll come out in a second, Teresa."

"*Va bene*, we'll be in the car." Teresa scrambled down the front stoop as the door slammed behind her.

"Where's the ledger, Carmela. I'll take it with me and go over the numbers at home."

"Right there by the register. I appreciate your help, Macco."

"No problem." Mack retrieved the ledger and headed for Buddy and the door. "Thanks for being a good friend to my wife, Carmela." After he untied the leash, he opened the door. "Don't forget to say hi to Mike for me."

"I will," Carmela replied with a forlorn expression.

When Mack noticed the look of despair on Carmela's face, he hesitated to leave. "Is everything all right?"

"Fine, fine." Carmela shooed Mack and his canine father-to-be out the door. "***La tua famiglia**, go to them, Macco. Your family waits for you." Carmela locked the door behind them and leaned against it. "I wish I had a family waiting for me." She glanced up at the ceiling and made the sign of the cross. "Someday, maybe if **Dio** wills it." She let out a wistful sigh. "***Famiglia**....family . . . isn't that what life's all about?"

About the Author

The author grew up in an Italian section of Trenton, New Jersey, called "The Burg." To the background music of her mother's native tongue, she danced around old world customs and traditions practiced by the local immigrants who lived there. Her favorite annual tradition, the "Feast of the Lights," a weeklong festival in honor of the Madonna di Cassandrino, was celebrated in the streets just outside her doorstep.

With the Americanization of her first name and then her marriage to Carl Boyd, Jr., Rosa Maria Maisto became Rose Marie Boyd. However, a few old friends and many relatives still prefer to use her Italian name.

A graduate of Trenton State College and the proud mother of her successful children Jessica and Justin, she relocated to Prescott, Arizona, with her husband ten years ago. As she basked under the Southwest sun, the writing bug decided to bite her. Since then, she's been expressing her creativity through poetry and novels.

An avid reader, she enjoys critiquing a bestseller or an old classic with the women in her monthly book group. The author also loves a competitive game of tennis and volunteers for both an adult literacy program and a women's domestic violence shelter.

You can follow her poetry blog at http://rosemboyd.blogspot.com/.

CPSIA information can be obtained at www.ICGtesting.com
262852BV00001B/5/P